"GUILTY! GUILTY . . .

"Guilty," he repeated, stopping before Jude. She looked up into an archetypal madman's face. Her fingers gripped her chair, as, suddenly, the restaurant seemed full of madmen whispering, gaping with red, open mouths, pointing cruel fingers at this calm stranger who waited like an island of sanity, offering sanctuary. Then Jude shook her head violently, and the vision receded.

"What do you want?" she asked.

"Just to see," he replied. "Oh, not you. What you will be."

"Do you read the future then?"

"Not before. Sometimes now."

"Well, ah . . . what do you see?"

Before he could answer, a hand fell gently on his shoulder. "James," said a quiet voice, "come along, leave the lady alone." And, to Jude, the newcomer explained, "You must understand, miss . . . he was with the Kramer Expedition. The only survivor."

An expeditionary! He's been Out There! What was it like, she wanted to ask. *What's Out There that could make you like this? What will it do to me?*

A RUMOR OF ANGELS

Science Fiction from SIGNET

A RUMOR OF OF ANGELS

by
M. Bradley Kellogg

A SIGNET BOOK
NEW AMERICAN LIBRARY
TIMES MIRROR

SIGNET TRADEMARK REG. U.S. PAT. OFF. AND FOREIGN COUNTRIES
REGISTERED TRADEMARK—MARCA REGISTRADA
HECHO EN CHICAGO, U.S.A.

SIGNET, SIGNET CLASSICS, MENTOR, PLUME, MERIDIAN and NAL BOOKS
are published by The New American Library, Inc.,
1633 Broadway, New York, New York 10019

First Printing, June, 1983

1 2 3 4 5 6 7 8 9

PRINTED IN THE UNITED STATES OF AMERICA

In loving memory of
Hal R. Kellogg
and Jarvis, his son

The author is grateful for the support and guidance of Antonia D. Bryan and Barbara L. Newman, and to Sarah Jane Freymann, who took the chance.

CHAPTER 1

". . . and in those golden, dew-kissed mornings, I open unbelieving eyes and swear that I am still dreaming. But if this alien paradise, this Arkoi, if it were my mind's creation, I would have surely fallen prey to a more heroic imagining. Titans would walk the paradise of my soul, but here, divinity hangs about the land casually, like a favorite shirt on the bedpost. It is a divinity accessible even to the most hardened rationalists among us. We pursue our daily scientific duties like sleepwalkers, each lost in his own wonderings. We travel each day enraptured, full of awe from walking among the blessed . . ."

"Crap," muttered the prisoner, lifting the yellowed page to expose an attached photograph. It was a landscape, a broad stretch of grassy plain, mountains behind, without a sign of human habitation. The colors were faded and the edges of the photo crumbled as she fingered them. The mountains interested her briefly, and the utter emptiness, so unfamiliar. She squinted for signs of retouching, then let the top page fall back in place. She blinked and yawned, and because it was in front of her, read the passage again. It was handwritten on a lined sheet torn from an old-style spring-bound notebook. Pale, crabbed letters were strung together in an awkwardly leisured scrawl, as if the writer were half asleep, or drugged.

Drugged. She remembered the wrinkled apple she had purloined three days ago from the communal mess, before she'd been thrown into solitary. Fruit was one of the few things the warders found too troublesome to add the tranquilizer to. She reached beneath the bare mattress and pulled it out. It was mealy and slightly flattened where she had rolled on it, but as she bit into it slowly, even its bitterness was ambrosia, because she knew it was free of the drug. She intended to make it last, the whole night if she could, at least for that period that she had

9

decided was probably night. She would allow herself one bite an hour, as best as she could estimate. Such games dulled hunger's ache.

She placed the apple, with a single bite removed, where the pillow would be if there had been one, and stared at the pile of papers in her lap. She was unable to work up anything so passionate as hatred, but she surely resented them. They were taking up too much room. Sitting cross-legged on the sleeping shelf, she could touch opposite walls of the cell. There was the shelf, room to stand at the water spigot or the waste hole, a door so faceless even its locks didn't show, and four sweating metal walls. She swallowed saliva flavored with apple, and admitted that the real reason she resented the papers was that they were requiring her to think. With deliberate malice, she flicked them one by one onto the damp cell floor. Then, shielding her eyes from the ceiling's fluorescent glare, she lay back and wondered what time it really was.

Mountains. Wilderness. Arkoi. The prisoner tried to blank her mind and could not. Arkoi intruded, Arkoi in dusty photos, old maps, the flowery prose of an old journal, the hard weight of mineral reports and surveys. Three days ago, she'd known no more about Arkoi than any schoolchild knew, few facts, mostly rumor, though the name carried a connotation she had learned somewhat later than school, in those secret corners of the city where her emerging politics had led her. There Arkoi was a symbol of oppression: the rich man's escape, a playground for the privileged scientific community, a fantasy forever out of reach of ninety percent of the population. In actuality, it *was* a fantasy come true, that often dreamed-of impossibility, a parallel world. It was Terra's sister a dimension or so removed, discovered thirty years earlier, quite by accident. That she remembered. It had happened the year she was born. But she'd known that she would never go to Arkoi, unless a client sent her, and her clients were never the kind who could afford that. So, as a self-kindness, she had cultivated her ignorance. Now, she knew more about it than she ever cared to know, and still it all added up to mysteries and will-o'-the-wisps.

"Why me?" she growled. The warden herself had delivered the bulging armloads of photos and documents, thrusting them at her like a weapon, with orders to commit it all to memory. *All of it?* The prisoner gave the mirthless ghost of a laugh. If this was some new kind of psychological torture the warders were testing, she was ready to vouch for its efficacy: Isolate a prisoner without warning or explanation from the security of a daily routine,

10

force-feed a lot of irrelevant information, then leave the poor fool alone to wonder what's the point or even if there is one, all the while waiting for the ax to fall.

Of course, the worst of it was the photographs. Not so much looking at them as touching them, especially the newer ones. The pain, as the glossy paper slicked through her fingers, was nearly physical. This caught her off guard. She had thought that wound closed, but knew now that she had merely denied it for the six years of being separated from her cameras.

Six years in this place . . . six and what? Four months, maybe? So deny it some more. Got a lot of years to go.

She flopped over on her stomach and tried to breathe as little of the hot stale air as possible.

Should have known better tonight. Should have eaten that old protein mash. That's always good for a heavy dose of trank. Why fight it?

A muffled clanging sounded outside in the corridor, approaching, slowing. Two vicious clicks at the door announced the loosing of the locks. The prisoner sat up. *What? Now? At this hour?* The metal door slammed aside in its tracks. Two security robots flanked the opening, armed with prods and stunners. A single-celled transport awaited the prisoner's entry.

She rose grudgingly from the mattress, refusing to look concerned. The left-hand robot blocked her way. It pointed a plastic joint at the littered floor.

"Bring it all," it ordered.

She gathered the papers slowly, knowing it was foolish, because you could not irritate a robot. But you could run over your allotted time, and soon the shock sticks were raised threateningly. She clutched the disordered pile to her chest, rose, and slouched into the transport. The closing door brought total darkness and a moment of panic.

She had once been lured by darkness, easily fond of mystery. Had that been what had encouraged her to carry her camera like a banner into the night streets, to the forbidden places? She could no longer recall that original reckless impulse. Darkness was no longer her lover. In the Wards, warrens of perpetual light, darkness meant punishment or, worse, a systems breakdown that could leave the cells without light or fresh air for hours.

The transport lurched squealing down the corridor, its rusty wheels fighting the rails. The interior smelled of urine and the fear of past occupants. The prisoner wondered what her own fear smelled like. She tried to count turns in the corridor, to fill the waiting, though you could never know where you were in the

Wards, up, down, day, night, with no point of reference but yourself.

After a black and sweating eternity, the transport jarred to a halt. The door clanged open, sticking halfway. The prisoner had to squeeze her way out. She faced another door, chipped gray paint, unlabeled. The right-hand robot punched its ID code into the lock. The door shuddered and inched open regretfully. *The doors in this place have lost the habit of opening*, the prisoner noted. The other robot grabbed her arm and shoved her brusquely inside.

She looked around a low-ceilinged cubicle, a cell converted into a temporary office. The sleeping shelf was massed with papers. The four walls lined with photographs called up a painful memory of her own tiny studio. In the middle was a battered metal desk, too large for the room. Behind mounds of file folders and computer printout sat a muscular, balding man in WorldFed army fatigues. A single straight-backed chair waited opposite him. The only sound was his wet, congested breathing and the steady hum of the portable computer terminal at his side.

He looked up from his reading. His appraisal was brief and authoritative. He glanced quickly back at the file he'd been studying.

"Rowe. 338171 TE? That you?" He seemed mildly incredulous. Like the desk, his voice was too big for the room.

"That's me." She did not take the waiting chair.

The army man had big features, a wide mouth full of square teeth lined up like a tile wall. He shrugged. "Well, says here you're the youngest. Hope you're healthier than you look. If I'd taken a look at you first . . ." He snapped the folder shut. "First name?"

Does it matter? "Judith . . . Jude," she supplied listlessly.

The big man dabbed at his upper lip with a sodden handkerchief. "Okay, Jude. I'm Julio Ramos. I'll be briefing you. You've read through the material?"

Jude nodded, faintly sullen. *Army. Not the police.* Her mind fumbled. He had mentioned no rank. *Briefing me?*

Ramos mopped his lip again and blew his nose wetly. "Always this hot in this place? What'd you think?"

"Think?" she repeated dully, as if it were the most extraordinary question. She sank down in the hard chair. The big man's energy was like an assault.

"Clennan'll have his hands full getting you in shape," Ramos complained, impatient. The prisoner lowered her blank gaze to

12

the heap of papers in her lap as he looked her over more carefully.

"City-born and -bred, eh?" he commented.

Her skin was indoor-sallow, long years indoors, more than a mere six in the Wards. Her hair was a clipped brown fringe around a fine-boned face devoid of expression. Standing at the door, she had looked tallish and scrawny. Hunched in the chair, she looked merely scrawny, a poor specimen. "The living dead," Ramos intoned as if she weren't there. "What'd they expect if they give me *this* to work with?" He repeated himself with patient sarcasm. "What did you think of your complimentary reading matter?"

Her shoulders moved somewhere beneath her shapeless prison coverall. Her voice sounded scratchy, unused. "Does it matter what I think?"

Ramos regarded her darkly, his thumbnail tapping intricate staccatos of irritation on the steel edging of the desk. "Oh, yes, Rowe. Contrary to current Ward policy, it does matter, for your sake and mine. You're not being tranked anymore, so I advise you to start having an opinion." He coughed lengthily as he fished among the folders with manicured hands, tanned sunlamp brown. He pulled one over in front of him. "Now. '91. The Discovery. You know about that, so we won't bother to review it. Just keep in mind that Arkoi's still unique. Since you've been inside, there have been dozens of attempts to duplicate the original accident, none even vaguely successful. We'd be happy with a dozen Arkois to colonize, but for now, we've got to do with one. At any rate, our present concern starts with the Langdon expedition . . . ah, here. Duncan Langdon . . . blah, blah . . . April, 1997: first expedition into the mountains after initial exploration of the discovery sight .... blah, blah, blah . . . Is this all familiar? Here we go. Langdon's journal. Your material included a few pages of it."

He slapped a weathered notebook on the desktop and flipped through it. A page ripped loudly, and he pulled back as if burned, then proceeded more gingerly. The prisoner wet her lips. The notebook's fragility was somehow touching. *Maybe they want it copied. Some clerical work to reward my placid behavior over the years? But how would that involve the army?*

Ramos read from the journal. "Eleventh day out. This is the last entry: 'The clouds smile at us this morning. The crystal city glimmers in the distance . . .' " He grunted nastily. "Didn't get far, this one. Off the deep end. All this divinity nonsense." He grunted again, searching his handkerchief for a dry corner. As he turned, a gleam on his collar caught the prisoner's eye: the brushed-steel I of WorldFed Intelligence. Again, no rank insignia.

Ho. Wait. So much for that fantasy. Intelligence wouldn't be doling out clerical work to a political prisoner.

The big man attacked a second bulging file. "Later expeditions, all fatal, except for the loonies . . . the establishment of the Terran colony at the discovery site . . . you've memorized all this, of course? Ah. Yes. Kramer's notes from the last expedition before the frontier was closed." His sigh said he was glad to be back on steadier ground. "These notes are much more exact. Less inclined toward, shall we say, personal observation."

Jude arched a thin eyebrow but remained silent. An Intelligence chief should appreciate the value of reading between the lines. *What makes me so sure he's a chief? If objective fact is his only concern, he'd take lousy pictures.*

Ramos read to himself but commented out loud. His voice boomed in the tiny room. "Good old Kramer. I knew this guy. Kept his head. Coherent all the way." He shoved the handkerchief into a pocket and began tossing tattered documents around the desk with building energy. "Readable maps, good mineral reports, minute details concerning terrain and flora, etc., etc., and then, poof! He breaks off right in the middle of a weather report!" He slapped the emptied plastic folder against one balled fist. "Right in the goddam middle!"

He rose and paced along the wall behind the desk, jabbing an accusing finger at photo after photo. "Langdon, Elias, Kiyama, and Roth. Kramer!" he declaimed. "And the others. Seventeen years of money and equipment down the drain, the best of a generation of scientists, all dead or in the loony bin! All with one thing in common. It runs through all these journals and notes and studies: a consuming need to carry on about how beautiful it is out there in those mountains, how it's a paradise . . . Langdon actually calls it Shangri-la!" Ramos halted and leaned over the desk. The prisoner sank against the hard back of her chair. The jabbing finger now aimed at her. "What kind of paradise leaves you dead or crazy? You tell me that. And if it is such a paradise, how come it looks so piss-poor in the pictures? Look at this trash!"

Jude looked, half expecting a blow if she did not. The photos again. She attempted objectivity, as he seemed to be asking her professional opinion. Mentally, she divided them by subject. There were the wide-angle plains shots, noteworthy for their lack of buildings but otherwise bland, even where an attempt to compose the frame was evident. The mountain vistas also stared

14

back unimpressively. *That's wrong. Mountains! How can mountains look so dull?* While Ramos fidgeted, she studied one shot in detail, squinting, tilting her head. She could find nothing technically wrong with the photograph. It was simply . . . boring.

Something off about the color, too. Doesn't look real.

"And these?" Ramos directed her attention farther down the wall.

Ah yes, the cloud studies. Row after row of them, with the self-consciousness of inferior portraiture. Details of cloud formations floating in blue skies too oddly clear to be Terran skies. There was a certain spark in the contrast of pure blue and white, but the most arresting aspect was their sheer numbers.

Ramos fixed the wall with a dogged eye. "What the hell did they *see* up there?"

Jude recalled her young photographer's drug-art phase, the obsessing on a single subject or detail while aesthetic distance went out the window. The process was always more stimulating than the result. *But, come on, they can't have all been doing drugs . . . several different photographers on several different expeditions.*

" 'The clouds smile at us,' " Ramos quoted dismissingly. "What bullshit. Move on to these."

Where the wall turned, a border of space surrounded a huge photo of the Kramer party: ten women, nine men, in mountain gear, smiling stiffly into the camera. Below, a ragged strip of paper mounted on a card. Jude thought she recognized Kramer's neat print recording date, location, camera information, names of party. Only in the end had Kramer failed in his compulsive recording. Stapled to the bottom of the card was a page from his journal. Ramos tore it off and read it aloud. It was a description of the landscape, in which even the dispassionate Kramer waxed poetic, attempting to paint with his scientist's vocabulary a resounding vision of a wilderness Eden such as remained nowhere on Terra.

The big man took a breath. "Well?" he demanded.

Jude blinked. Her instincts were aroused, but she was cautious. *What does he want from me? Fact? Opinion?* "The photos . . ." she ventured.

"Yes, yes?"

"They're kind of . . . lifeless. They look like cheap studio work."

"Right. And?"

"Ah . . ." She backed off. "Technical problems?"

"You don't believe that." Ramos leaned over her. "They had

the best equipment available, and what kind of self-respecting pro blames his equipment?''

"I was avoiding the obvious," she replied carefully. *Just give me a clue.* . . . The Kramer expedition had gone out about the time she was arrested, so if there had been gossip about this problem along the photographers' network, she would have missed it.

"No, no, no," Ramos pursued impatiently. "All these guys took plenty of good pictures before they ever went to Arkoi!"

Jude wished he would move farther away and wondered if he would know a good picture if he saw one. "You can't very well blame the subject, can you?"

"Ah-ha!" It was as if she had stumbled upon the hidden treasure. He actually smiled, and his smile, feral and greedy, was like a glimpse through a curtained window. He whirled to the opposite wall and ripped off one photo, then another, thrusting them onto her lap. "Take a look at these."

She had not seen these photos before. The top one was a shot of a towheaded child, or what seemed to be a child, pale and bedraggled, with the face of an old man. The other showed a group of equally downtrodden figures, apparently just standing around. Typed labels, added later by some army research department, read simply: "Native population."

These are the natives? Jude postponed her disappointment and studied the photos more carefully, searching out some element of the exotic. She found none.

Ramos grabbed the group shot from her hand and turned it over, reading aloud, with the voice of one more accustomed to speechifying than interpretive reading. " 'We camped by their lovely village that night, and spoke with them long into the summer darkness, with hands and pictures in the dirt, with whatever means we could find to communicate. They have a miraculous gift for language. The golden ones seemed most beautiful to me, perhaps because, if I were to picture God's angels, they would look just like this.' " He grimaced and tossed the photo down on the desk. "Langdon again."

God's angels? The phrase stopped her. She fingered the photo of the towheaded child. Obviously the religious type, this Langdon. Rare these days. Obviously crazy. Though she did not share Ramos' distaste, she understood it. You could hardly trust the word of a fanatic. Yet beneath the florid literary style, there was something compelling in the very excesses of Langdon's enthusiasm, rather like reading a fairy tale. It wasn't reality, but it kept you turning the pages. Jude tried to understand Langdon, to be him for a moment, to assume that out there in Arkoi's mountains, he had seen something that had moved him profoundly, something that his camera had been unable to capture. Something real or unreal, in the landscape, in the Natives, those drab little aliens, something his own language had better expressed, that was being lost in translation to film. *What?* She felt the first warning signals. *I'm getting too interested in all this.* Very little was safe in the Wards, but caring was surely fatal. Ramos must not know that her carefully cultivated passivity was vulnerable. She leaned back stiffly in her chair and distanced the entire subject.

"Why don't you just bring back a Native for questioning?"

He snorted, disgusted. "You don't think that's been tried? We got a lot of wild tales and hocus-pocus. Good for nothing."

She rubbed the greasy arm of the chair noncommitally. "The journals don't seem to describe them as good for nothing."

The feral smile came out again. "Well, good, Rowe. I'm glad to see the tranks haven't dulled your brain completely." He dug out his handkerchief once more, then perched his bulk on the edge of his chair, looming over the desk as his thick elbows crushed mounds of paper. "Now," he began in a lowered voice, although they were alone in the room, "think about this. There's a guy in an office somewhere who's been studying this material real carefully for me. He's trying to match what the journals say with the present-day facts about the Natives living in the Terran colony. Now, those Natives claim to be the entire population of Arkoi, but this guy is convinced that the journals can't be talking about the same Natives. He thinks there must be others."

"Others?" She felt a slight prickle. She was suspicious of the greed in his eyes. *This is getting very weird. . . .*

"Others." His jowled face was eager, almost conspiratorial. He tapped the Langdon file with a ringed pinky. "These angel ones. I think they're out there, where we haven't been able to get to yet. There's gossip like that, you know, in the colony, only the tourists make them supernatural, call them 'the Dark Powers,' the usual nonsense. But if there are others, and if we could find them . . ." He paused, then sat back, as if regretting his own enthusiasm. The change in him was like a cold front blowing in. He retrieved Jude's dossier from under the scattered mess on the desk and mused over it silently for a while.

"You know," he commented finally, "Breaking into a WorldFed accounting office . . . a stupid thing to wreck a promising career on. It *was* promising, am I right? What the hell good did you think that was going to do?"

If you think it was so stupid, why the hell do you want to know? She knew she could not remember anyway. Oh, intellectually it still made sense. She had been photographing so-called classified information, government information that should be public information, especially in regard to government spending, when that spending seems to be promoting suspiciously personal benefits in certain quarters. But the anger, the outrage, that pure flame of righteous indignation that had compelled her late one night into a locked office: that had died in the Wards in order that something of her could survive.

"With an eighty percent tax rate, people have a right to know how their money's being spent," she attempted weakly, out of respect for her anger's memory.

"Eighty-seven, now," Ramos replied with tolerant malice. "You've been out of action, remember? Hell, that's what the Petition Courts are for, Rowe. You want information, file for it."

"The Petition Courts, sure. If you don't mind waiting ten years."

Ramos shrugged. A man who has prospered in the military is unperturbed by bureaucracy. "Fifteen billion people out there at last count. What do you expect, instant service?" He pushed the dossier aside. "At any rate, about these so-called angels. We're sending out another expedition, a different kind of expedition. We need more and better pictures taken by someone who knows what to expect. We want to know who's lying and why."

Expedition? Jude pursed her lips grimly. The ax she was waiting for had just fallen. Hopelessness emboldened her to sarcasm. "Well, that's one way to empty the jails."

Ramos found this hugely amusing. "Don't take it so hard, Rowe. You could be the very one to make it back alive."

"Yeah. A real honor." She felt cold, even in the stifling heat. She had overlooked that the hunter would have many quarries and one of them would be her. She watched the hunter watch her, and savor the fear that she could not hide from him.

"You've got a real treat in store, Rowe. The Arkoi colony has become quite the tourist resort since you've been inside. Hotels, water sports, gambling, and lots weirder things besides that I can't mention in mixed company. You'll be in training there a month or so before you go out. Believe me, it's the nicest place you've seen in a long while."

"See Naples and die," she quipped bitterly.

"What?"

"Nothing."

18

"Or, you can stay in the Wards for the rest of your life."

"Would have done anyway."

"Think positive, Rowe. Fresh air, sunshine. A fantastic opportunity."

Finally, she looked him straight in the eye. "Why the sales pitch?"

He shrugged again. "It would be easier if we had your cooperation."

"I see." She laid her fingers in a frame around the photo still waiting in her lap. The Native child, if it was a child. She thought it looked out at her sadly. She pictured her dingy cell, remembered the long years of hard gray days, the harassment, the deadening despair, the sleep suffocated by drugs. Whatever Arkoi held in store, could it be any worse than a lifetime in the Wards?

Ramos was impatient enough to lecture. "If there were a window in this place, Rowe, I'd shove your nose out it so you'd recall what it's like to watch a world choking itself to death. Now, just next door is a brand-new world, clean air, open land, raw materials enough to revitalize our industry. We're going to win that world, with or without your help, so do you want to come along for the ride or not? There are a few other photographers in the Wards."

Don't know . . . can't think. She hadn't expected to be faced with a choice. "What time is it?"

"What?"

"Time. You know."

Ramos' fingers drummed. "It's four o'clock in the goddam morning, Rowe, long past my bedtime." He pulled a neat plastic envelope from an inside pocket. "Here's a shower pass, new-clothes requisition, walking papers, ID. Your very own robot waits outside to run you through the steps. The airbus leaves for the Transport Corridor at six-thirty. If you're with us, Rowe, you'd better hustle."

In the short run, it was easier just to do what he said. The long run she had lost all sense of in the Wards. "I'm just supposed to go out there and take pictures?"

"That's it."

There had to be a catch, besides the big one. "What if I do come back in one piece?"

His eyes narrowed, as if assessing a risk. "You bring us back what we want, you're a free woman."

Free. *Free?* Still she resisted. "Do I get my choice of equipment?"

He had left the most tempting bait for last. "You name it."

Silence. Just the purring of the computer terminal. Then: "I guess I'd better get going."

Ramos nodded, supremely satisfied with his own cleverness. "I guess you'd better."

CHAPTER 2

Twelve prisoners in gray coveralls sat glumly in the first-class waiting lounge of the Transport Terminal, surrounded by luxury and security robots. Tall bony men and big-framed women with puzzled anger in their eyes, waiting like cattle in a market, all strangers to Jude, who drew apart from them, trying to adjust to the sudden unfamiliarity of her surroundings.

The airbus that had delivered them to the terminal had, in typical Ward style, no windows. A fancy chrome clock high on the lounge wall told her it was 6:20 A.M. on the Terran side of the corridor, and 7:20 P.M. on the Arkoi side. She knew the corridor was somewhere along the equator, but could not see outside. The first-class lounge was buried deep inside the gaudy package of steel and glass that housed the one precious point of connection between the parallel worlds. Jude still longed for a glimpse of the true light of day.

She stood by a transparent wall that overlooked the vast main floor of the terminal. First class was cool and hushed, raised behind its protective glass. Beyond, among the arching girders, a sour haze of grease and smoke drifted through garlands of plastic vines hung with grapes and limp paper flowers. A huge picture sign announced in lurid color: ESCAPE TO ARKOI! GO TERRATRANSIT!

When Jude had entered prison, construction of the big terminal had just begun. She and her colleagues in the underground had protested at the groundbreaking, calling the new building a boondoggle for the state building contractors. Who, they asked, but a handful of adventurers and mad scientists will want to vacation in an alien world?

Boy, were we out of touch. . . .

The floor below was jammed with people. Without regard for order or efficiency, the tourist-class crowd milled and pushed, arms waving, mouths open wide. The glass wall vibrated gently beneath Jude's hand, and she knew the noise down there must be deafening.

Watching, she recalled her only childhood crime. (She had come late to being a lawbreaker.) Her crèche had acquired an ant terrarium when she was five years old. For reasons she understood only later, she had found it intolerable to stare in at the thousands of mindless busy creatures running about trapped in their claustrophobic corridors. Late one night, she lugged it with enormous effort into the nursery recreation hall, and emptied it into the sandpile. Just like those spilled ants, she thought now, looking down at the mob of tourists. Rushing in circles, swarming over each other in foggy desperation, dreaming of escape.

Escape. Now that the word had the ring of a commercial to it, she found the irony unbearable. For her, escape would be temporary at best. She was not putting much stock in Ramos' promises, even if she did come back alive. And sane. She moved away from the window wall and sat. The unaccustomed plush softness of the couch was an invitation to relax, but she could not. Her new coverall scratched, the stolid security robots lurked about the walls, the camera case she carried, chosen by herself, seemed much heavier than it had six years ago, and she had finally realized that she was being packed off to an alien world where people went mad in the mountains. *An alien world*. Jude shook her head in wonder.

Her hand strayed to the hard plastic of the camera case. It was good-quality. She found comfort in its hardness and in the thought of the fine machinery nestled inside. The supply officer had nearly refused her the outdated models she had selected. Ramos had ordered the best, Ramos would have his head, Ramos this, Ramos that. But these are the cameras I'm used to, she had replied. When he pouted, she had tried to make him understand. *My hands know them*.

Suddenly there were buzzers sounding, soft but insistent. The robots sprang to work, hustling the prisoners roughly up the loading ramp. Waiting in line along the glass wall, Jude noticed a freshly erected partition at one end of the tourist floor. From her elevated vantage, she could see over it to where workers bustled around with huge crates of vegetables on forklifts. She recalled Ward gossip about food riots at the Transport Terminal and felt a murmur of indignation. There would be no more riots now that this innocent-looking barrier concealed from the tourists'

21

eyes the luxuriant masses of fresh vegetables that streamed from the fields of Arkoi straight into the kitchens of the rich.

A security robot barked her into motion. At the top of the ramp was a small white room set about with couches. The carpet was thick and soft. The robots lined up in phalanx formation on the ramp until the door slid shut, sealing the prisoners inside.

In the cramped white room, the other prisoners regarded each other dully, without hope or fear, anticipating only a more oblique form of execution than the Wards provided. Jude had learned that fear as a consistent state ceases to be frightening, and one either commits brave outrageous acts or lies passive in fear's hand. She had also learned that the Wards were not the place for brave, outrageous acts.

An electronic purr broke the silence.

"Citizens, please take your seats. Transport will begin in ten seconds."

A warning bell sounded, and the coughing hum of giant engines. The prisoners jostled for seats.

"Transport in five seconds." A muffled buzzer rang. Jude instinctively shut her eyes, though transport was supposed to be painless and instantaneous.

Four . . . three . . . *where are we going?* . . . two . . . one . . .

In the white room, the lights dimmed. Jude looked up and in the pit of her stomach felt a sickening kick. Then silence, absolute. An instant of hanging, out of time, out of space . . . the smell of . . . flowers? Dizziness. Wrenching vertigo. A deep humming in the ears, and then, in front of them, the wall disappeared.

Light flooded the room, blinding them with warmth and color. Jude stumbled out of her chair to squint out at a sky of perfect story-book blue, ablaze with cotton-candy clouds and a sun brighter than she had ever seen. A path in a green lawn stretched invitingly away down a gentle hill to vanish behind a leafy hedge. Faint music floated in the air, tuneless and sweet, weaving sensual melodies with scents of unseen blossoms and wet grass.

Jude stood dazed at the opening as the other prisoners exclaimed, jostled, pushed by her, and spilled out onto the lawn. She felt unbalanced, simultaneously elated and troubled. She looked, tried to see more clearly. Her back prickled and she thought of a dog's hackles rising.

But I see nothing to be afraid of . . . ahh!

She caught her breath as a jarring flash of déjà vu enveloped

22

her and vanished, will-o'-the-wisp, as she grasped to understand it.

What is it, this undeniable sense of coming . . . home?

Then there were human voices bawling orders and the spell was broken. Jude steadied herself with a hand against the rough stone that framed the opening. The music and the sweetness were gone. She sniffed, already nostalgic, and smelled only hot, dry air and the arid tang of pine. A quite ordinary gravel path ran away through trim hedges. The heat was like lead weights on her shoulders. Nothing stirred but the red-faced guards striding toward her. No birds. Not even an insect humming in the bushes.

At the very least there should be birds. Jude stumbled dazedly as someone grabbed her arm. *A vacation paradise should make certain to have a few around for local color.* This seemed only reasonable. She searched the sky. Surely, in the midst of her confusion by the door, she had sensed a coolness, had heard a bird, faintly, like the music, a high wild bird cry in the distance?

The guards lined them up in pairs and marched them down the path through a stone gateway covered with vines. A tendril brushed Jude's cheek, and she started, flinched against her partner, then recovered with an embarrassed apology. They filed through the gate into a dusty monorail station packed with arriving tourists. The bolder ones ceased their milling and shouting to stare as the guards shouldered their charges through the crowd. Jude heard the words "penal expedition" whispered up and down the platform. She pulled her concentration inside herself until her back hunched, and waited, sweating in the hot sun, to board the monorail. Motion drew her attention to a line of taxicars collecting passengers. Excitement flickered in her briefly. *Will there be Native drivers?* But only bored Terran faces met her gaze as she struggled onto the train.

CHAPTER 3

The monorail whooshed through a leafy tunnel in the treetops. The roof was a transparent bubble, and the interior was green with the premature twilight of the forest, broken by strobic flashes of sun. The guards retired to the head of the car to play five-handed poker, and slowly, the prisoners overcame their astonishment at the miles of forest whipping by outside, loosened up enough to talk fitfully among themselves, feeling each other out. Jude curled herself into a window seat, her eyes riveted by the trees, her ears tuned to the fear welling through the conversational tones.

"When we come back crazy, you know what they'll do?"

"*If* we come back."

"They'll leave us to run around in the streets, they will."

"If we come back," repeated a scar-faced woman. "Most of those guys they never found at all."

"Bodies."

"They don't call them the Mad Mountains for nothing."

"Yeah."

"Whaddaya mean, run around in the streets?"

"The loonies. Come on, you've heard that. The ones that crawl back out of the mountains with brains like mush, they let them roam the streets here to scare the tourists."

"What the hell for? Aren't the tourists' own lives enough to be scared of, in the cities?"

"It's good for business," said a dry voice. "Fear is a highly salable commodity if carefully controlled."

Jude glanced over to locate that speaker. He was a small bearded man, prim manner, educated tones. Another political prisoner, no doubt, of the academic persuasion.

"The travel brochures play up the sun-and-fun aspect," he continued pedantically. "All the fresh air and greenery. But the truth is, the Arkoi colony is just as crowded as it is back home."

Murmurs of dissent greeted this statement.

"No, really," he insisted, warming to his lecture. "You've

got a city in a basin, surrounded by enormous mountains that nobody seems to be able to cross, and people pouring in every day by the thousands. Land's built up near to the limit, or eaten up in big tracts owned by the rich. I tell you, people don't come here for space, they come to get scared. It's exotic. It's a little excitement to break up the boredom of their lives.''

"No space? What do you call all these trees?''

"A year or two,'' said the academician with a grim wave of his hand, ''this'll all be bungalows.''

"Why not send the tourists into the mountains, if they're so eager for excitement?''

"*Armchair* excitement, not the real thing. Nobody'll go out there willingly anymore.''

Pregnant silence settled for a while. Jude returned her attention to the remarkably endless forest. *What else is out there besides trees?* Beyond those trees, somewhere, must be the terrible mountains that they called the Mad Mountains, where the tourists said the Dark Powers held sway. But she had also read that the Natives referred to the mountains as the Guardians. Now there was grist for Ramos' mill: guardians of what? Could mountains alone drive people mad?

Haltingly, a woman broke the silence. "I've heard some other stories, though.''

The prisoners glanced at one another as if she had opened forbidden doors. They knew which stories she meant.

"Yeah, and I suppose you believe them. We're going out to find King Solomon's Mines, right?''

The prisoners shifted uncomfortably. Jude understood their ill ease. Nobody likes to expose his fantasies for others to tread over.

"More tourist hype,'' commented the academician sourly.

The woman was insistent. "Then why's WorldFed always squelching those stories if there's nothing to them?''

"First they make them up, then they pretend to squelch them. Adds credibility. What would build a tourist trade more quickly than rumors of mermaids and floating cities? Doesn't everyone like to think that Eldorado is out there waiting just for them, if only they had the guts to go out and find it?''

Jude curled more tightly into her corner. She had her own store of these illicit tales in dusty exile at the back of her brain. *Which is where they will stay.* They were too seductive, too achingly beautiful. How could a civilized imagination play such tricks on the heart? *Easily, unless you keep a tight rein on it.*

"Crap,'' she muttered to herself defensively.

Suddenly, sunlight flooded the car. The train slowed and someone let out a low, unbelieving whistle.

They had reached a ragged gap in the trees, a clearing, still and overgrown. In the center towered a ruined metal structure. The Terrans gazed at the alien thing in awe.

It was huge, thirty or forty meters tall, a once-building, that was not rotting or broken down but worn smooth, without parts falling away, as if only the wind and rain of centuries were capable of undoing the builders' intention that this monument should stand forever. Contours once drawn sharp and spare had softened, melted out of focus, until shape no longer communicated function. Yellow vines flowered up and down its length with fringed blossoms lying soft and bright against the polished metal. Grass waved solemnly on flattened ledges where dirt had gathered high above the ground. There was no sign of rust.

Jude blinked. Her eyes were not seeing it clearly. There was an echo, as with transparencies overlaid and held up to the light. One layer stood solid and serene in the clearing. The other behind it wavered and swelled. Ghostly spires rose. The tangling vines coalesced into a web of hieroglyphs climbing cold, ageless walls. She thought it unrelenting, magnificent.

"That ain't no Terran building," whispered someone.

"Those scroungy little Natives built that?"

Jude shivered. Uncontrollably, her body cringed before an irrational fear, as if the tower itself radiated ancient terror as palpable as an electric shock. She wrenched her eyes away and grappled for her camera, refusing to let her imagination run away with her for the second time in a single hour. It was a withdrawal hallucination, tranquilizer DTs, something easily explained. Her fingers fumbled with the snaps on the case and the smooth sides of the new equipment. She tore at the plastic wrapping of a film cartridge, could not break the seal. Oh, for the tranquilizer to calm this tremor in the hands, to lower the curtain of numbness again.

The monorail picked up speed. Jude wrenched the packet open and shoved the cartridge into the camera. But the tower was disappearing behind the trees as the train slid from the clearing. With the camera lying useless in her lap and passages from Langdon's journal raising bright phantoms in her head, she watched until it vanished completely, its menace evaporating in the green-golden air.

Trees and trees. An age of trees. Looming pine and mossy-trunked hardwoods. Hidden thickets of broad-leafed jade and olive, tipped with the apple green of new growth. The cool flash of spruce and hemlock, and then, abruptly, the forest ended and there were the mountains.

Straight up they rose from the valley floor, like a mammoth wall across a world, blotting out the horizon with a sawtoothed joining of darkness and light. Jude gasped and forgot her camera completely.

The Guardians! The valley cowered in their shadow. Puffy fair-weather clouds misted their knees. Above, a tortured rampart of bright sheer cliffs and black crevasses. Higher still, a crown of frozen silver gleamed like armor. From the topmost ridges, the winds blew up a veil of snow to drift off like smoke into the hard blue sky.

The other prisoners stirred.

"Oh, brother," breathed the scar-faced woman. Then she chuckled dismally.

The Guardians, Jude repeated to herself. *The Mad Mountains*.

The monorail sped across the valley floor and banked in a gentle curve to reveal a distant gleam ahead, silver against the dark mountain wall. On the edge of a vast lake, a city squatted, stacked along the shore in broad rectangles of flamingo, peach, and lemon yellow, spreading inland to the foothills in low-lying domes and irregular contours. As the monorail approached the lake, it glided above a wide boulevard that cut through a wedding cake of vacation bungalows. Miniature castles, pink confections of mosaic and transparent plastic, fat crenellated turrets dressed with banners that hung like limp dishrags in the hot still air. Overgrown gingerbread houses that sat like open jewel boxes, windows inlaid with rainbowed glitter. Jude decided she could do a great piece of photojournalism on the subject of vulgarity. *Probably not what Ramos has in mind*.

An odd gaiety spread through the car, relief tinged with hysteria.

"Look at that! Freeways! Good old hard-top roads. Takes me back."

"Man, you must be older than you look."

"They'd have aircars here if they could make them work."

"I used to have one that worked just fine."

"Not here. Up above a hundred feet, the instruments go bananas. You think we're walking into the mountains for our health?"

And the monorail swept into the business district. Jude waited patiently for something alien to appear, but it looked more and more like a Terran fantasy park. Tiny trees threw dry shadows on the red-and-white pavements from branches manicured into

27

fantastical shapes: a great fish leaping, a dragon, a mermaid with snaking tail. Shops spilled cheap merchandise out among the crowds thronging the sunbaked streets. Shoppers drooped beneath café awnings. They clutched their cold drinks like lifelines, glancing up wearily as the monorail sped past.

Now the tall colored prisms by the shore rose up rapidly to meet them. Jude caught a glimpse of sand and green water, then the nearest wall swallowed them up, out of the sun into a cavernous dark interior. The monorail glided to a stop.

"Hotel Celestial Sea," a loudspeaker intoned. The doors to their car did not open.

The prisoners sat back through a blur of hotels, flickering in and out of the brilliant day into lobbies they were too sun-blinded to see. Finally, the guards roused themselves and packed up their cards. At the final stop, the chill of air-conditioning invaded the car. The prisoners were herded out onto thick carpet masquerading as grass.

"Hotel Amazon," said the speaker.

The Hotel Amazon was still being furnished. Workers bustled about carrying sofas and tools. The lobby was huge. It seemed to have no proper boundaries such as a room should have. The ceiling was shadowed, the walls were suspended panels of translucent smoky green. A clutter of scaffolding surrounded a vast chandelier that dripped mosslike from the upper reaches. Somewhere in the gloom, water gurgled. Jude eyed it all dubiously, as they were packed into elevators and taken to the fortieth floor, where they picked their way through ladders and drop cloths to a long green hallway free of workmen. The guards unlocked the first two doors and split up the group, six to a room. Jude was left standing alone with a guard at her elbow. He hauled her down the long corridor to a room at the end, shoved her inside, and locked the door.

CHAPTER 4

The room was a jungle-green box, with a full window wall of smoky plastic. The bedspread made the bed look as if it were hiding under a pile of leaves. If Jude had been in a laughing mood, that bed could have kept giggles coming for hours. But it was a bed. A real one with springs and a pillow. She sat down on it heavily, thankful it was not a prison bunk.

So. Here we are. Here I am. Alone. Why do I get the isolation treatment? She rubbed a tired shoulder and sighed, unable to think clearly. She got up and wandered about the room. It was stuffy and still partially unfurnished, though the bathroom seemed in working order. Anticipating her first warm bath in six years, she found herself at the window, gazing abstractedly at dusk falling over the valley. *Well, sunset. It's been a long time.* Far below, the quiet lake reflected the last light of the day. The sun sank in amber behind the dark mountain wall, melting freeways and buildings together into a shadowed abstract where lamps began to wink on like infant stars. Over the city, gulls flew wheeling and crying toward the hills.

Jude smiled dreamily. *Birds! At last!* She squinted to make them out more clearly. One flew nearer, with an echoing cry that shrilled joyously through her.

Oh! Look!

The gull was furred, had tiny paws like a cat, curled beneath its breast. *A native creature, an alien!* Its cry was the sound she had heard earlier, back at the corridor.

She stood transfixed, long after the creatures had soared off into darkness. A quiet rhythm of dying light led her gaze across the landscape to rest here and there without focus. Ebb and flow and wait and flow again . . . words half-formed . . . whispered thoughts and images murmured in her brain, rising and falling like the play of light across the flank of a sleeping animal. She breathed with it, let its rhythm become her own. Then, as some barely perceptible restraint deep within her began to slip, she

29

panicked and backed away into the darkened room, to break the siren rhythm before it swallowed her completely.

"I will not be crazy!" she choked aloud. And thought then that it was not her fault, that if it was not trank withdrawal, then there was something irrational in the very air of Arkoi. Aircraft that wouldn't fly, mountains that would not be crossed, and this . . . overwhelming sense of . . . *yes, that's it, presence.* Presence . . . everywhere.

A sharp knock spun her around. She shrank against the wall, shaken and alert. The door opened and a man walked into the darkened room.

"You decent?" he called out. "Turn a light on, for Christ's sake."

CHAPTER 5

The intruder touched a panel by the door. A balmy glow lit the room. He made a quick but thorough survey and shut the door behind him.

Jude waited. No doubt he would explain himself. A man who lets himself into a locked room has specific reason to be there. But instead he looked her over brazenly, favoring her with a sloppy, calculating grin. His impeccably cut shirt was rumpled and zippered open at the throat to frame a muscled chest. Glossy brown hair fell in a conveniently dashing slash across a sun-flushed, handsome face.

"Better than your pictures," he commented finally.

Her mouth tightened. "Pictures of me, or pictures I took?"

His grin broadened approvingly. "That's the spirit. Maybe Ramos did okay with you." He moved in on her, circling. "I'm Bill Clennan. We'll be working together, but first, I'm taking you to dinner. How long will it take you to get dressed?"

Jude blinked. Things seemed to be happening too fast. "Dressed? This is all I have."

"Check out the closets. You think I want to be seen with a lady in prison duds? May be the latest fashion in the Wards, but . . ."

Already, she disliked him. Big, confident, overbearing. Obviously used to trading on his clownish good looks. Obviously expecting her to be charmed by his offhand manner. *No way*, she assured herself. *I know those jailer's eyes*.

"I don't recall any mention of partying in this deal," she said quietly.

"Consider it a surprise fringe benefit." He took her arm and urged her across the thick carpet to a closet. He threw open the double doors. A riot of color and sparkle greeted them. Clennan fingered a backless peach evening dress. "How 'bout this one?"

"I'd go into shock if I put that on." She pretended to search for something she preferred. "What about the others—do they get in on this deal too?"

"Others?" It was as if the word meant something different to him. "Oh, the others from the Wards." Again the grin, lazy and smug. "You won't be seeing much of them, no. They're cannon fodder. You're the talent. Or so Ramos tells me."

"He didn't seem so impressed."

"Handled you himself. That's an honor, from the chief."

Called that one at least. "And you?"

"Local head, newly appointed." He gave a mocking bow. "Some great assignment, eh? Here in vacationland? Little Billy Clennan's playing in the big leagues at last." His enthusiasm was disgusting. "Welcome to the team," he beamed.

"I always hated baseball." Jude chose a dressy jumpsuit, the best she could do. At least it was merely brown. While she fled to the bathroom to change, Clennan lay back on the leaf-pile bed, whistling.

The taxicar driver was jovial. His fat sweaty arm oozed over the back of the seat as he turned to shout above the traffic noise, simultaneously snaking a wicked line between vehicles and pedestrians.

"Yep, this ole town's gettin' rougher every year. Yep, the more folks pilin' in lookin' for thrills, the harder it gets to keep 'em in line. Used to be a nice quiet burg, nothing but millionaires and science fellows, heavy tippers, y'know? Then the mines opened and the factories, and all the tourists, and well . . ." He lifted a stunner from the seat beside him and shrugged eloquently. "Just like home."

The setting of the sun had hardly diminished the heat. The cab called itself air-conditioned in bright letters on its side, complete with yellow exclamation points, but inside the passengers sweltered. Through the sealed window, Jude searched the crowded

31

streets. It still looked like Terra, only gaudier, especially now that the darkness concealed the clear lake and the looming bulk of the Guardians. She did not want to talk to Clennan, but finally, she had to ask.

"Where are the Natives everybody keeps talking about?"

The driver overheard. "You won't find 'em in this part of town," he supplied with a smirk. "Gotta try the Quarter. You see someone running around in an orange tunic, that'll be them."

"The orange is day regulation for the Natives," Clennan explained. "By colonial law. After curfew, I guess they can wear what they like."

"Do they always stay in the, ah . . . the Quarter?" Jude pursued.

The driver's smirk became a leer. "Some of the smart ones get out during the day to work in the shops and the farms in the hills, but it's after curfew now. The Colonial Authority puts 'em under wraps at night to keep the tourists happy. Scared of 'em, you know? They want 'em where they can go look at 'em for a lark in nice safe daylight, not sitting next to 'em at dinner."

The cab drew to a stop where the crowds were heaviest, the lights brightest. They got out, and Clennan guided her firmly through the mob. Jude saw police everywhere, but the general hot night hysteria was friendly enough. Total strangers clapped each other on the back and offered drinks, dinner. Talk was boisterous, laughter shrill. Ahead, under a vast mural of neon, a tooth-shaped cleft opened into blackness that pulsated with music and the sounds of eating and drinking. Inside, a complex of cavernlike rooms dripped with stalactites and fish net, strewn with sequined starfish and pink seashells. The floor was checkered red and white. The air was smoky and close. Diners jostled each other cheerfully at tables knocked together out of rough planking. Real wood was no luxury on Arkoi, Jude noted.

At a table wedged into a small crevice, Clennan flashed his smile and signaled the waiter for more wine.

"You don't look like a criminal," he said.

Jude did not smile back. "What does a criminal look like?"

Clennan rested his chin on one hand, aiming the smile into her eyes. "I take it back. You look like a criminal . . . one who's spent, what is it, six years in the hole?" He cocked his head. "What does that fuzz hair look like when it's grown out?"

"I always wore it short."

"To go with your temper, no doubt." He reached to refill her salad plate. "All you need is a good meal or two, or ten. So what'd you think of the old Jewel?"

32

Jude looked blank.

"Ramos. The Colonel." Clennan spoke through a mouthful of cucumber. "Julio. I thought everyone in the Wards knew about big bad Julie."

"Not me."

"Taught me everything I know." Clennan nodded.

"That so." *Is that supposed to make me feel better or worse?*

"Yup. He's the best and baddest."

Worse.

Across the cavern, a band of mirrored mannequins sawed at their instruments as if playing the tinny Muzak. Jude sipped at her wine gingerly, toyed with her food. "I'm not exactly used to all this plenty," she mumbled.

"Get used to it. Your man here's highly skilled at stretching an expense account." He touched her wrist, a casual gesture of camaraderie. "That salad's fresh, you know. I mean, grown here in the colony, out in the open, in the dirt. No hydroponics here."

Avoiding his hand, she studied the tomato quarter impaled on her fork. "Thought it tasted funny."

"Yeah, the Natives are natural farmers, it seems." He sat back with a proprietary wave. "That's one of the few things we've been able to get them doing right. Someday, Arkoi'll be Terra's greengrocer." He sounded as if he were repeating somebody else's words. "Goodbye soy mash, so long syn-protein. Feel like a new man on what I've been eating since I came here, though there's still no meat 'cept what we ship in. Natives don't understand about raising animals for food. They're vegetarians, I think. But we'll get that going, too, when we clear enough room."

Jude finished chewing the tomato and swallowed it. The taste was earthy and sensuous. She found it distracting. "With twelve billion on the verge of starvation all the time, the sooner the better."

Clennan's smile quirked. "Ah, yes, I forgot. You're one of those. Well, power to the people," he mocked. Then experimented with sincerity: "Hey, we're on the same side, babe, where food's concerned. Lots of tourists come here just to eat, meat or no meat."

One thing he'd said had caught her interest. "The Natives don't keep any animals at all?"

"Well, there's the occasional donkey to carry things around. And they did take to the dairy stock we brought in, but it hasn't meant much yet. They don't understand large-scale operations,

33

where you can feed enough people to make the effort worthwhile." Clennan mopped his plate deftly with a huge hunk of bread, soaking up the last dregs of dressing before the waiter stole his salad out from under him and brought the main course, a crisp broiled fish. "Fish is great here, since we stocked the lake."

"What happened to the fish already in residence?"

"Didn't you know?" His grin was eager. "There weren't any."

"Oh."

He looked disappointed. "Doesn't that seem strange to you?"

"Well, there aren't all that many left at home, either."

Clennan twirled his fork in the air. "Think, woman! This is a clean world. Underpopulated. There's no normal excuse for the lack of wildlife." He leaned forward, as if about to reveal a state secret. "You seen any insects since you've been here? Where's our old pal the cockroach?"

"Well, I've only been here . . ."

"Or a bird, maybe?" Jude nodded, but he held up a forefinger. "No, you haven't. You think you have—we all do, because we assume they'll be here. But they're not, take my word for it. No birds. No bugs. Not even rats. Only a handful of humanoid vegetarians, our friendly Natives. A genuine biological puzzle."

Jude sat silent for a moment, picking bones out of her fish. Had she imagined the gull-beasts? Down to the last bizarre detail? Cat paws and downy fur? The shiny razored beak? The boundary between reality and fantasy weakened by the hour. She swallowed. *Better not mention the gulls to this guy Clennan. Not right now.*

"I'm surprised I hadn't heard this before, about the fish and all," she ventured casually.

Clennan slumped gracefully in his chair, diddling with his wineglass. He held the misted glass up to the light and squinted. "There are certain things about this world that are guaranteed to give the tourists the creeps—I mean the real stay-away primal creeps, not the adolescent kind they come here for—and this is one of them. It doesn't get aired in public too often, and if you don't talk about it, these city dwellers don't notice it."

Jude pushed away her plate with a cold smile. "Yeah, well, the tourists can always leave the primal creeps behind and go home. What about me, Intelligence man? Isn't it about time you let me in on what you have in mind?"

But Clennan, without moving, was suddenly alert, looking over her shoulder. The restaurant had grown quiet. A woman at the next table nudged her husband and stared. Jude turned around.

A stoop-shouldered man stood near the entrance, alone. With great concentration, he was squaring his feet off on a red floor tile.

"Guilty," he said out loud to his feet. "Guilty," he said to those seated near him. Nervous titters leaked from the surrounding diners. The man shook his head sadly, then focused his gaze on Jude as surely as if she had called out to him.

"Guilty," he repeated, and took a step toward her. Silence followed him across the room, leaving a wake of whispers and jittery laughter. Jude turned back to Clennan and found him watching her impassively. The silence enveloped their table, and Jude forced herself to look up at the man, who stood a few feet away. He stared at her intently, without menace. He was tall and bony, like a wire armature draped in dusty rags. His face was a devastated landscape, slack-muscled, ragged with worry and remorse. His skin was fishbelly pale, like her own, as if untouched by Arkoi's burning sun. It was an archetypal madman's face, framed with ashen hair worn long and tied behind the neck with a piece of twine. Looking closer, Jude saw the clothes were not really rags, just old, but clean and meticulously patched. His faded high-collared jacket had once been part of a uniform.

Not knowing what else to do, Jude met his stare. *He holds him with his glittering eye*, she thought self-consciously. But this madman's eyes did not glitter. They absorbed. They were a light, luminous gray, with fine arching brows, unsettling in their calm yet passionate sensibility. She blinked. *The Wedding-Guest stood still, and listens like a three years' child: The Mariner hath his will*. Her fingers gripped her chair. Perception was sliding, warping. The bland Muzak grew raucous. Lights and colors brightened, shadows sharpened. The room was full of madmen, whispering, gaping with red open mouths, pointing cruel fingers at the calm stranger who waited like an island of sanity, offering sanctuary.

Sanctuary. Me!

Jude shook her head violently. The vision receded.

The madman drew out a chair and sat down facing her, folding his hands deliberately in front of him. Without moving his chair, Clennan seemed to shrink away from the table. The madman ignored him. Sadly, gently, he smiled.

Jude's throat was dry. "What do you want?"

"Just to see," he replied, as if it were obvious.

"To see what?"

When he spoke again, she had to lean forward to catch his words. She had forgotten Clennan's existence.

35

The madman's smile was whimsical. He opened his gray eyes very wide. "Oh, it's not you. It's what you will be."

Jude considered this blankly. How does one converse in riddles? "Do you read the future, then?"

"Not before. Sometimes, now." It was shy, diffident, but he made it seem perfectly reasonable. Or at least reasoned.

"Well, ah . . . what do you see?" It was impossible not to ask.

He seemed about to answer when a hand fell gently on his shoulder. "James," said a quiet voice, unmistakably apprehensive. "Come along. Leave the lady alone."

The passionate gray eyes still held her. Obscurely, she knew something was being demanded of her. Impulsively, she reached out a hand. Across the table, Clennan stifled an urge to grab her hand away before it could touch the madman's arm.

"Wait," she begged. "I want to know . . . I mean . . ." She withdrew her hand. "We were just talking." Her impulsive behavior confused, embarrassed her. She couldn't look at the man whose large hand rested with such familiarity on the madman's bony shoulder. The madman continued to smile at her with his sane eyes, then sighed with the finality of a purpose accomplished.

The other man shuffled nervously. "You must understand, miss . . . he was with the Kramer expedition. The only survivor."

Clennan was nodding to himself. He had seen the loonies before. Jude's sympathy for the madman gained new dimensions. *An expeditionary! He's been Out There!* What was it like, she wanted to ask, but looking at him, could not. *What is Out There that could make you like this? What will it do to me?*

"I understand," she said quietly, though she did not, for to say that this creature was insane and let it go at that was not enough of an explanation. She glanced up at the newcomer dubiously. She guessed he was in his mid-fifties. Not a big man. Only his broad hand had made her think that. He was oddly dressed, in an old-fashioned buttoned shirt and brown pants that bagged with age on a taut, nervous body, trim but frail. He stood his ground, but his flitting blue eyes were uneasy, the measure in his voice an obvious lie. Jude could feel his discomfort as keenly as her own. Only the madman James, lapsed into contemplative sadness, seemed relaxed. She saw now that he was not much older than herself.

The room had become noisy with relief. Jude held out her hand. "Goodbye, James. I hope I'll see you again."

"Oh, you will," he replied. The hand on his shoulder tightened.

"Now how do you know that?" she whispered. Their heads drew close, secret sharers, but James only smiled.

"He's fond of riddles, miss," the older man put in, beginning to urge the madman out of his seat. "He'll keep you going for hours, but I must get him out of here. The crowds are hard on his nerves." He got James to his feet, then nodded awkwardly. "Sorry for the disturbance," Jude received a last sidelong smile from James as his companion ushered him out.

"Question there is, which one's the real loony," remarked Clennan, returned from his silence.

"The older guy? You know him?" Jude murmured as if waking from a dream.

"Of him. That's Mitchell Verde, one of the local vocal eccentrics. Ex-conservationist from back home, still beating the same old drum here in Arkoi. Says we're upsetting the ecology, already, mind you, one stinking little city, says we ought to all pack up and go home or learn to live like the Natives."

"How do they live?" Jude felt she knew but didn't know, as if someone had just given her a hint.

"Who knows? Like any primitive folks, I guess. No machines, no comforts. Verde's nuts. This place is a long way from terminal pollution." Clennan brushed crumbs into his hand and dropped them into an unused ashtray. "He does take care of the crazies, though. Another personal crusade of his. Now . . . you wanted to talk business."

"Yeah. Business." Jude regarded him critically for a moment. "You know, there's no real point wasting all this charm on me, Clennan. I'm not forgetting that I'm here under duress."

He looked taken aback. Then he pushed his hair out of his eyes boyishly and chuckled. "No, I don't suppose you are. But I was doing all right there for a while, eh?" His grin was unashamed.

Jude said nothing.

"Well. Ramos told you that you'd be going out with a penal expedition, right?"

She nodded glumly.

"That expedition is a cover for your operation, which is being kept secret. You won't be going out with them."

"Secret? Why?"

The glass band tinkled out its Muzak behind them. Clennan had put his charm aside and chose his words carefully now. "Because it's a very special operation. We've found you a very special guide. A Native. We've never had a Native guide before." Casually, he refilled her wineglass. "And you'll be going out with him alone."

37

"Now, wait a minute." Jude felt the butterflies begin, deep in her stomach. The soft flap-flap of fear. "Just me and one alien?" she demanded incredulously.

"That's the story."

"An expedition of two? Against the Guardians?" If she had allowed herself an inkling of hope, Clennan's announcement stopped it dead. She snorted cynically and shot him a look of murderous dejection. "Not giving me much of a chance, are you?"

CHAPTER 6

In a quieter part of town, a mismatched pair straggled down an ill-lit street. The smaller urged the other along with patient insistence, while the tall one regaled him with a stream of soft patter, illustrated with many sudden gestures. His pale hair, loosed from its tie, floated about his thin shoulders like mist. Water ran in the gutters and between the cobblestones. The streetlights were weak pools in the darkness.

They approached a massive steel gate in a wall that cut one part of the city off from the rest. A blue-uniformed guard stepped out of a brightly lit booth that bore the label "Native Quarter. Authorized personnel only after 9:00 P.M."

"ID, mister!" the guard barked, loosing the safety on his stunner. "Oh, it's you, Verde. Taking that one home for the night?" He waved aside the plastic card the little man had reflexively pulled from his pocket.

"Strayed a bit far tonight," Verde explained.

"Poor devil. What'd they do without you, eh?"

Verde shrugged. "Been quiet tonight, Mike?"

"Mostly, though there's a big convention in town, and a bunch of guys came hollering around a while ago wanting to see the 'alien weirdos.' Same old stuff. We're putting on extra men tomorrow, just in case. Sometimes I think this wall protects the Natives from us, rather than the other way around."

"Of course it does," the madman giggled.

"Sure, kid, sure. And you loonies are just lucky the Natives don't mind your being locked up with them at night." The guard laughed, then tapped out the release code on his console. The big gate slid open noisily. "Hey, Verde, you spend much more time in there and the tourists will start taking you for crazy."

"Most of them already do."

The guard laughed again and waved them through.

Inside the wall, no streetlights shone. The houses were small, their windows black and silent. Here the madman led the way, quietly, surely, through the night.

CHAPTER 7

There were no more leisurely dinners for a while. At 7:00 the next morning, Jude's training began. Clennan drove her mercilessly, a cruelly cheerful taskmaster who insisted on pointing out how far she was from the shape she needed to be in to even think of surviving in the wilderness. Early to bed, even earlier to rise. Painful, sweating hours in a stifling gym, not the spotless air-conditioned gyms of the Intelligence Complex, which Clennan rejected as not "secure" enough, but a falling-down sweatbox near the Native Quarter. There she endured endless briefing sessions on survival technique, self-defense, first aid, local botany, repair and handling of all her equipment, geology, meteorology, swimming, and finally a wide variety of mountain-climbing techniques. Soon she wondered why she didn't just break out screaming and run off into the mountains of her own accord. Perhaps Clennan had just that in mind, that by the time he had finished with her, she'd look forward to going Out There, just to be rid of him and his insistent schooling.

All the while, he kept her away from her cameras. Her fingers itched for them, but Clennan pointed out that photography was the one skill she already possessed, and there'd be plenty of time Out There to take pictures. *Just one more reason*, she thought, *to look forward to departure*.

"I still don't understand why this Native is only willing to take one person into the mountains," she complained one night as they sat in a pool of lamplight, working through another fat stack of scientific data. "I'd think the chances for success would be better the more people there were."

"The Native says different. He wants to keep the operation small and quiet: one person, no radio, doesn't want the other Natives to know about it. He's some sort of renegade, brought up by a Terran or something. Seems his own guys have been a bit rough on him."

The shadows were assuming threatening shapes in the darker corners of the old gym. "And how come no weapons? Karate can only get me so far."

"Especially yours." At her look, Clennan rolled his eyes. "It's a joke, kid. Next we'll work on your sense of humor. . . . Look, the weapons thing was another of his conditions. We had to play it his way, or he wouldn't take the job."

"How do you know you can trust him?"

Clennan grinned evilly. "How do I know I can trust you? Besides, I don't have to trust him. You do."

"Thanks." The table rocked as she shoved back her stool. She crossed the room to stare out at the neon-jangled city. It was raining. Steam rose from the pavement through red, then green, then amber until it dissipated into darkness. Jude did not like knowing she was afraid. "It's all a big game for you, isn't it, Clennan?"

"You might say that. What's to take seriously? You live, you die. Might as well have fun doing it."

"You're not at risk here."

"I have been. I tell you, be a little more of a gamesman, babe. It'll do you good."

She had a sudden temptation to smash the window. *You are a bloody robot bastard, Clennan!* But she caught his reflection in the dust-streaked glass, watching her with a semblance of compassion. Or was it merely pity?

"So he's agreed to take me over the mountains?"

"Into. We made no mention of over, or that we suspect he's hiding an entire population out there. He thinks you're putting together one of those fancy picture books. Just play it by ear and get as far as you can."

Jude wiped her damp palms on her coverall. She left smudges of darker grime against the gray. "Have you, uh, met this person?" She moved back to the work table in weary resignation.

"Nope. Alien Division deals with him. I keep clear of the Natives mostly."

"So I noticed." She tossed her head, taking aim at where she hoped his ego lay. "I don't understand how you guys run things.

40

You stay in Arkoi, Ramos stays on Terra, you don't communicate with him, you don't talk to anyone here. Seems so inefficient. I mean, who's *really* in charge? How does the right hand know . . ."

His ego was annoyingly intact. "Don't worry your head about that. Old Julie'd be here by the next transport if he thought things weren't going just right."

"How would he know?"

"Gut instinct, even across dimensions." Clennan shifted. "Besides, I'd tell him."

She tried not to whine. "Well, couldn't we at least have a look at the Quarter, kind of a dry run? I've been scouring these files for two weeks and still I know nothing about the Natives. When do I get to meet this guy?"

"Soon, soon." Her expression brought him vast amusement. "Hey, girl, he doesn't wear two heads or screw with his feet, if that's what you're worried about. You've seen the pictures. They look pretty much like us."

"But you keep away from them."

Clennan shifted, for once ill at ease. "Well, I never know what to say to them. I mean, you can't just hand them a string of beads and smile, for Christ's sake."

Jude was dissatisfied. "I can't understand why everyone pretends that these creatures aren't important. Think of what we could learn from them! They live in this crazy world!"

Clennan put up a defensive hand. "We've tried all that, dammit. These folks are basic medieval. They're better off by themselves in the Quarter, weaving their baskets and giving the tourists something tame to point at. What could they tell us about aircraft that don't fly? They don't even use electricity. Take my advice, crusader. Just do your job. Don't get involved. Landed you in the Wards last time, eh?" His wink was a genial warning.

"What makes you think the others Out There, if there *are* others Out There, will be any different?"

"With luck, they won't be. When we move in, the less resistance the better."

In the fifth week, an appointment was set to meet the alien guide. Jude was to find him in, of all places, the main reading room of the notoriously unvisited Museum of Cultural Anthropology. The museum was near the Quarter, thus presumably convenient for a Native to get to without undue harassment in the streets, but Jude suspected someone of a heavy taste for irony in the choice of meeting place. Clennan? It didn't seem likely,

41

somehow, irony being hardly his strong point. The Native himself? Jude tried to envision one of those stubby peasants in the photo files possessing a flair for grim humor. It didn't compute.

In the early morning, Clennan escorted her to the museum, watched her climb the already sun-baked steps, and settled in to wait in a shadowed doorway. The alien had demanded that she meet him alone.

Inside the museum, it was cool and shaded. Jude padded down long silent halls lined with half-empty cases. The anthropologists had little to show for their thirty years of study. She lingered in the hallways, postponing her meeting a little longer, hoping to glean a few more morsels of information to make this creature she was about to confront somewhat less mysterious. She listened to tape loops until she could no longer abide their patronizing tone. She read hand-lettered labels, dusty beneath the glass. She scrutinized artifacts: wooden spoons and hoes and crude garments of cracked leather, some lovely pottery and thick handblown glass. But for the lack of weapons, the normal trappings of a primitive society. She thought it bizarre that there were so few of them, less than a few thousand living in the Colony, yet with a racial diversity that anthropologists could not explain within so small a community. They theorized a past plague or cataclysmic natural disaster that had wiped out the population, but could find no reference to it in native memory or legend. Jude understood why someone had come up with the idea of Others, out of sheer desperation. For instance, who had built the ruined tower that had terrified her from the monorail?

Further down the hall, life-sized models of the three racial types rested dully in their glass cases: the blond and stolid peasant, inclined to farm work; the tallish, ruddy-skinned craftsman; the third, the least human, whom the anthropologists had christened fishfolk. The hands and feet were delicately webbed, the limbs shone silver, tarnished here by a layer of dust. Jude rather hoped her Native would be one of those. The mannequin's full round eye seemed to regard her kindly.

When at last she faced the door of the reading room, she stopped to take a deep breath. Not at all fortified, she slid open the big door.

It was a long high-ceilinged room, lined with tape racks and small sections of real books. Microfilm readers and video monitors were scattered among the tables and couches. At the far end of the room, a tall figure stood alone before a wall of windows. Beyond him, in blue-and-white splendor, rose the Guardians. As she entered, he turned crisply but did not come toward her.

"Ms. Rowe? I am Ra'an tel-Yron."

What she had expected she would never recall afterward, so struck was she by his appearance. Nothing had prepared her for a creature of such extraordinary beauty. He was not handsome, though his features, lean and regular, could pass for Terran in a dim light. The full effect defied so ordinary a description. His skin was russet, his long thick hair so black it was like an absence of light. He had high cheekbones, white teeth, a face of startling color contrasts and keen intelligence. His long-fingered hands hung stilled at his sides. His carriage was erect, almost military. Oddly, he was dressed in Terran clothing, black shirt and pants, without ornament. He was unarmed, as the Colonial Authority did not allow natives to possess weapons. The alien was beautiful, yes, but closer study revealed a tension about him that eroded his beauty, that lent a disturbing severity to his expression, angularity to his stance.

Primitive? Medieval? Jude stared at him.

"Is there something wrong?" he demanded coldly.

She glanced away, chagrined. "No . . . ah . . . no. It's just that . . . you're not exactly what I'd been led to expect. I don't mean to be rude."

"Of course not," he replied.

Either she had to stare, or not look at him at all. She chose the latter. "Well, Please sit down, ah, Ra'an . . . is that what I should call you?"

He came toward her but did not sit. "Ra'an is my given name, as you would say. There are no other forms of address among the Koi—'tel-Yron' conveys birthplace and . . . other things that need not concern you."

Jude dragged a heavy chair up to a big round table. *There must have been a diplomat or two in the Wards,* she grumbled inwardly, *better suited to this job. Where do I start? I should have written my questions down, but that'd make a book.* "The sooner I start learning about your . . . the Koi, did you call them? . . . the better."

His sculptured chin lifted icily. He hates me, she decided. I'm a total stranger and already he hates me.

"Linguistic subtleties, Ms. Rowe. To appreciate them would require a more extensive command of the language than I gather is yours at present." His eyes surveyed her briefly through a veil of dark lashes. "I hesitate to place an . . . employer in that most difficult position of having to say that one understands what one does not."

Jude pursed her lips, momentarily stymied. *He's an alien,* she warned herself. *You have never met an alien before. Don't immediately assume that he's being obnoxious. This behavior could be the height of Koi hospitality, unlikely as that may seem.* She pretended to adjust her chair closer to the table. Whatever his intent, his command of Terran was certainly complete. A sort of rolling slur of the hard consonants was the only trace of an accent. It gave his speech a soft, cornerless quality totally at odds with his precise wording and officious manner.

"Is your language difficult?" she asked finally, wondering if normal conversation would ever be possible with this creature.

"For Terrans, it seems. Few ever learn."

"Well, I shall do my best."

"Do not feel obligated, Ms. Rowe. One language between us should prove sufficient."

Sarcasm. No doubt this time. "Perhaps you could find time to instruct me?" The Wards had taught her bottomless patience. She would use it to defuse him.

"There is no need."

"But I want to learn."

"Why?"

I'm not really sure. "Is it so odd to learn a language for its own sake?"

The alien looked straight at her for the first time. His eyes were the color of purple velvet. "Frankly, yes. For a Terran, it is odd."

Jude felt dwarfed by the high curved back of her chair. "Tell you what. I'll toss away my preconceptions about you, if you will do the same. We'll start over again with clean slates."

He smiled faintly, looking down at her. "Whatever you wish."

He's baiting me, she decided. *That's it. There's some hostile game being played out here, I've walked into the middle of it with no rulebook, and I'm losing already.* She backtracked in hopes of regaining her advantage.

"How did you come to speak *my* language so well?"

He shrugged, barely restraining his contempt. "Language comes easily to the Koi. We have four of our own, and are perhaps more used to being polylingual than you who have only one."

"Regional languages are still spoken in many parts of Terra," she retorted, piqued. "A universal tongue is imperative in a mobile, centralized society." Then she thought, *Wait a minute. Since when did I become a defender of the faith?*

"We have no universal, as all four are known to all Koi."

"Then why have four at all?"

"Language is more than a practical necessity to a people who

44

are . . ." He stopped himself, then added merely. "It's an art form. You'd have to learn them all to understand."

"You were going to tell me how you learned Terran," she pursued. If she was going to be swept up in this game of linguistic one-upmanship, she might as well squeeze some information out of it.

He made an awkward gesture of dismissal. "When I was younger, there was a man, a Terran, with whom I became acquainted." ~

He obviously intended this to close the topic, but she smiled, trying out a little casual cheer, Bill Clennan style. It felt like an oversized garment, graceless. "Well, I'm glad to hear that there've been some Terrans who've taken an interest in your people. This museum is a disgrace." Too late, she realized how patronizing she sounded.

"He did not regard us as a subject for academic study, Ms. Rowe!" The alien had not raised his voice, but there was anger in the room, humming like the static electricity before a storm. Suddenly, he was menacing.

"I didn't mean it that way," she said quickly. "Look, I'm sorry. I don't seem to know how not to offend you."

But he was mistrustful of her apology. The intense violet eyes watched her as if scanning for subtext. Then he turned and went to stand at the window again, his back straightening. It was as if a door had closed in her face. When he spoke again, his tone was stiffly businesslike. "Have you ever done any mountain climbing, Ms. Rowe?"

"Er . . . no." She attempted a laugh. "Not much chance for that anymore on Terra."

"Ah, yes. You've torn most of them down, haven't you? Well, even if there were, the Guardians are not ordinary mountains, you understand."

She laughed again, nervously. "Is there such a thing as an ordinary mountain?"

"What makes you think you will fare better than all the others who have attempted them?"

Actually, I don't think anything of the kind. But she made an effort at nonchalance. "Sounds like you're trying to scare me off."

"No. I am trying to discover why you want to go."

I don't! "To take pictures. Didn't they tell you? I'm a photographer."

A sharp movement of his head negated her explanation. "You are afraid of the mountains, are you not?"

45

She was losing ground. "Well, who wouldn't be, with their history?"

"You were afraid when you walked into this room," he accused, stalking her. "Not knowing what kind of monster you might find. You are afraid of me now. Why are you forcing yourself to go out there?"

The aura of scarcely restrained power about him threatened to overwhelm her. She rubbed the table with her hand, finding strength in its wooden solidity. "I guess there are a few things they didn't tell you." She paused, collecting herself. "Do you know what the Wards are?"

His brows arched. "You?"

She nodded. *He certainly knows a lot about Terrans.*

"What did you do?" For the first time, there was interest in his voice.

"Does it matter?"

"Yes."

"Why?"

Instead of answering he laughed, a short ironic bark. Then he asked, "Did you know, by the way, that you will be the first to attempt the Guardians with a 'Native' guide?"

"So they tell me." She noted that he spat out the word "Native" as if it were something vile.

"Has it occurred to you to wonder about that?"

She blinked. *Who's conducting this interview?* "It occurs to me that you are probably no typical, ah, Native."

"Ah. Perceptive. Not in the way you might think, but I'm sure the other 'Natives' would agree with you." His long regal fingers clenched tight over his thumbs.

She couldn't play this hateful game any longer. "It's an ugly word," she said in a low voice.

"Yes, it is, isn't it." There was a silence as the alien paced around irritably, glowering at her. Then he stopped, and a moment of decision-making passed over his face. "Well, I'll take you."

"Thank you," she said, bewildered, not having realized this was in question. If she had considered having any respect for Clennan's Alien Division, it was gone now. They obviously had no idea what they had on their hands in this extraordinary creature. He was rude and scary, totally unpredictable, and one hell of a lot more than medieval. Winning him over was not going to be easy, but she must, if she was going to face the Guardians with only him for protection.

"Have you seen any of the photos taken by the early expeditions?" she asked finally.

"Some." He had put on his chill formality again.

"Do they look right to you? I mean, does it seem to you that they"—*that phrase again*—"lose something in translation?"

"That depends on what you expect the original to have been."

Well, that's rather evasive. She approached him from another angle. "Do you find the photos interesting?"

"Not particularly."

"Any idea why?"

"I am not familiar with the workings of the instrument. We have no such things here."

That's odd, she thought, *for one so sophisticated and well versed in Terran ways.* But it went along with Clennan's claim that the Koi had no interest in technology. "Perhaps I'll teach you," she offered brightly. "I'll trade you your language for my camera, what do you say?"

"I am not sure you would find it an even trade."

"I'll risk that." She smiled at him, which seemed to unnerve him, for he turned away, his beautiful face as hard as a stone wall.

"If there is nothing more you require at present . . ."

Surprised, she leaned forward. "I have a thousand questions, but I suppose they can wait."

He nodded abruptly. "Good." With that, he turned on his heel and headed for the door.

"We'll talk again soon," she called weakly as the massive door slid shut behind him. Then she collapsed back into her chair. The aged plastic seat creaked as she swung her leg back and forth, exhausted. *Next time, I'll bring a camera and take some pictures of him, and see how they come out. If he'll let me.*

They've no idea what they've got here, she repeated to herself. *And dammit, neither do I.* But as she contemplated the mysteries he presented, an inkling of hope began to work its way through the deep layers of acceptance and inaction the Wards had laid down in her mind. What if . . .? What if the alien could take her over the mountains? Who was to say she had to come back?

CHAPTER 8

The great steel gate to the Native Quarter stood open in the still tropical heat of the late afternoon. Two guards slouched in the shade of the wall, one fanned himself lazily with his hat.

A brightly dressed tourist family walked tentatively up the street and stopped by the gate. The children waited wide-eyed while the parents peered inside at the old shop-lined market square where Native handicrafts were sold. The husband mopped his face with a striped handkerchief. Other tourists bustled up and down, in and out of stores, meeting friends, laughing through armloads of purchases, ignoring or avoiding the occasional lone figures wearing the regulation orange tunic. One passed the gate carrying a covered basket, and the tourist father touched his wife's arm and pointed. The children stared.

The guards nudged each other. The shorter shook his head and produced a coin, balancing it in his palm.

The tourist woman looked longingly at a stall hung with woven rugs. She gave her husband's hand a reassuring pat, and in they went. Each held a child firmly by the hand.

The second guard chuckled and caught the coin as his partner flipped it to him with a shrug.

"Takes 'em longer to decide every day," the loser grumbled. "Most haven't been taking their kids in lately."

The coin changed hands several times that day. It was a silly game, but it passed the time.

Across the market square, Mitchell Verde sweltered in his tiny office, trying to generate enough patience to finish the day's mail. The street door, a marvel of hand-hewn planks, was propped open with a filing cabinet in hopes of luring a stray breeze inside. The white stucco walls sweated, and Verde muttered to himself as he ripped open envelopes and added to the weeks-old piles of litter crowding his ancient desk.

At the rear of the office, a lanky adolescent in an undershirt worked a hand-cranked mimeograph machine.

"You would insist on an office in the Quarter, Verde," the boy grouched as the machine squealed and jammed. His short, straw-colored hair stuck out like porcupine quills. "I mean, anywhere else you could have air conditioning and a computer to do your printing. Some technology makes sense, you know."

"You can leave anytime you want, Lacey."

"Oh yeah?" He extracted a mangled sheet of paper from the bowels of the machine. "And who'd get these flyers out for you?"

"I would. Somehow." Verde's sigh was pained as he wrenched his concentration back to the mail. "What a waste of trees," he said, crumpling an official-looking letter.

"Now even you gotta admit that it'd be easier if they could establish a telecommunications link through the Transport Corridor."

"Too easy. Terra's close enough as it is. I'll deal with the paper, thanks. It's the content I was complaining about."

It was mostly bureaucratic, today and every day. The Terra-based Veterans of Exploration was a management-heavy charity intended to provide food and shelter for the returned expeditionaries, referred to in tourist parlance as the loonies. Verde was its on-site representative, office manager, and general caretaker. Its executives often vacationed in Arkoi, charging their expenses to official business on the strength of five-minute flying visits to the front step of Verde's office in the Quarter. But for that, his meager salary, and the stupefying amount of printed matter they generated, Verde would doubt their existence.

"Now here's something we all need." Verde waved a bound booklet above his head. "The collected minutes of the year's board meetings, or 'The Use of *Robert's Rules of Order* as an Offensive Weapon.'"

"File it." Lacey grinned, wiping ink on his pantleg. "You're in a great mood today, Mitch."

Verde flipped the booklet at the wastebasket with a flourish. "Done." The basket was full. The booklet slid to the floor. "Wrong side of the bed . . . I don't know . . . the air doesn't smell right today. Did I do trash yesterday or the day before?"

"My turn," the boy replied. "Soon as I finish these flyers. Whaddaya mean, the air doesn't smell right?"

"Tension, you know? How you can smell tension?"

"So what else is new?"

"More than usual, I mean."

Lacey gave the machine a final whining crank. "You want me

to deliver these? Maybe I can get Hrin to run them around to the hotels later.''

"Hrin's at Stahl House today," Verde answered abstractedly.

"Mitch, for God's sake!" Lacey stalked over to the desk and scribbled on a handy sheet of paper: "This place is probably bugged six ways from Sunday."

With exaggerated patience, Verde wrote: "I know, but they wouldn't know Stahl House if they fell over it. It's a Koi name." Then he muttered aloud, "Intelligence is the biggest misnomer ever perpetrated."

Lacey grabbed the paper and shredded it carefully.

"Aren't you going to eat it?" Verde asked caustically.

A tall shadow sidled in at the doorway.

"Well, if it isn't our star boarder." Lacey grumped his way back to the mimeo corner. He began stacking and folding with an irritable burst of energy.

Verde greeted the madman with a smile. "Where've you been all day, James?"

The madman shrugged like an errant child. "Around." He settled himself on the red-tiled floor beside the wastebasket and began to study the discarded mail.

Verde returned the shrug, his habitual frown returning as he pulled a magazine from its wrapper. "The *Green Monthly* is here. Maybe it's in this issue."

Lacey snorted from a distance. "Like it was supposed to be the last three months? Nobody's going to print that article."

"Maybe I should have softened it a little, as Lute suggested," the little man mused. "I don't really want some editor hauled up before the censors on my account."

"Don't worry. Neither do the editors. For a smart man, Mitch . . ." The boy shook his head with an old man's cynicism. "You know what the Terran definition of conservation is? Moving to Arkoi at the earliest possible moment. You and your endless articles are an embarrassment, Mitch. The last thing your so-called colleagues want to hear is that it's their duty to the cause to stay away."

"It's the only way to keep Arkoi from becoming another Terra," Verde defended automatically.

"No," commented the madman, as if to the booklet he was reading.

Lacey rolled his eyes. "I know that, and you know that, but try and explain it to them! *You're* here, aren't you?"

"I have a job here! . . . speaking of which, oh, Lord, look at this." Between two fingers, he held up a single typed sheet, with seal and letterhead, very official.

"More hate mail from the happy tourists?"

"Not this time." Verde stood and began to pace like an angry terrier. "I am reminded by His Nibs Mr. C. Williams Brustein of the Colonial Authority that my employment here concerns the Veterans of Exploration only and does not include—get this— 'fraternizing with the Native population.' Can you believe it?"

Lacey made a rude noise. "Good thing he hasn't taken a look at some of the office staff."

"That son of a bitch," Verde fumed, crushing the letter vengefully.

Suddenly the madman let out an inarticulate yell. Lacey held up his hand, listening. Muffled shouts and running footsteps were followed by the crash of breaking glass. Verde was on the street instantly. Next door, the window of the Café Montserrat lay in shards on the cobblestones. Three panes remained intact, clinging to the frame. Verde groaned as he scanned the now empty square. The café's proprietor ventured out cautiously and joined him to mourn over the broken glass and mullions. He carried a weighted soda can in one hand and a scrap of paper in the other.

"This was tied to it." He handed the note to Verde. His smile was a wan light of resignation on his ebony face. "Perhaps they were too young to appreciate the irony."

The note read: "Nigger lover!"

Verde stared at it. "Feels as if I just walked into a time warp."

The black man chuckled sadly. "Haven't heard *that* word in a long time."

"Dirty words never die." Verde spat. "They just find themselves new meanings."

The madman sat on the doorstep with his head buried in his arms. Lacey emerged to kick at the shattered glass. "Damn tourist punks."

"Lousy aim," Verde commented. "Missed my office by a mile."

The proprietor sighed, wiping his hands on his spotless apron. "No, I think they got what they were after. Ten years of serving Koi and Terran under one roof, and suddenly Montserrat's on the shit list. My tourist business is way down, and . . . well." He stopped with a weary shrug.

Verde eyed the black man with apprehension. "Hate mail, Damon?"

51

"Some. Recently."

Lacey did a sudden angry dance around the broken glass, a clenched fist in the air. "Got to get them out, out, *out!*"

"Out," echoed the madman from the doorstep.

"Let's just keep it calm, Lacey," cautioned Verde, with an eye on the seated madman.

"Guess I'll go find a broom," said Damon without moving. He stooped to pick up a shard. "Lute poured this glass himself."

The madman rose, a brilliant smile flooding his face. "Meron," he said.

The other three turned to face the empty square. Verde shoved the crumpled hate note into his pocket. A slight figure rounded a corner across the square and hailed them in a musical voice.

"He always knows when she's coming," Damon marveled softly.

"Yes," said Verde with a touch of what might have been envy.

The madman went to her like a happy dog, and she wrapped her tiny arms around his waist in greeting. She could have been a Terran child of ten or twelve, light agile body, angelic face with blond hair as bright as a halo. She was wearing the short coverall common to Terran children. The orange Native tunic was hidden in the Terran satchel on her shoulder.

She regarded the broken window solemnly. "It was not an accident?"

"No," Verde answered tightly.

She took Verde's hand, then went to Damon and laid her shining head against the black man's big arm. "We're sorry, Damon."

Her presence seemed to energize him. "Hell, little one, nothing a little carpentry won't fix." He rubbed his hands together, bent to kiss the top of her head, and disappeared briskly inside.

"Bad things have twins," said Meron, turning back to Verde.

"Oh? What now?"

"It is hard to understand. I was near the museum this morning, and I saw Ra'an go in, where he never goes. I waited and soon comes the new man from Terran Intelligence, with a woman. She goes inside, and then later, Ra'an comes out and sneaks back to the Quarter. Then she comes out and she and the Intelligence man leave."

"Could be nothing," said Verde uneasily. "Coincidence."

"He *sneaked* home," repeated Meron indignantly. "The Koi keep their secrets but they do not sneak."

"Spy tactics," put in Lacey. 'Your classic clandestine meeting."

"But what about? Ra'an meeting in secret with a Terran? Ra'an hates Terrans."

"We did think so," murmured Meron, her face clouding at the possibilities her imagination suggested.

Verde's unconscious pacing began again. "Meron, isn't there anyone who can get through to Ra'an? Even a little?"

The little Koi lowered her eyes. "He closed himself off to us a long time ago."

"Ra'an," repeated the madman, now down on his haunches reading the broken glass as if the shards were a thousand crystal balls. "Ra'an is my brother."

Verde glanced at him, frowning. "You know, I saw Clennan a while ago, in a restaurant. He did have a woman with him, and it was the damnedest thing. James was wandering off the beaten path, and zeroed in on her like a homing device. He was acting very oddly, as if he had some big secret."

"James sees many things," offered Meron enigmatically.

"So you keep telling me. It's just that he's been a little odder of late than usual, even for him." Verde shoved his hands into his pockets as if to keep them from untoward nervous gestures. "I spoke to that woman briefly, as I was pulling James out of there. She's not exactly your prototypical Intelligence op, if that's what she is. She looked as if she hadn't eaten in months." His hands came out of his pockets and began to tug at his gray scrawl of hair. "What do we do?"

"We watch. What else is there to do?"

"There must be something," Verde fretted. "If he tells them about the Wall, we're done for."

Lacey made a noise, then shut his mouth abruptly, kicking again at the glass shards. He did not see the look the madman threw him, a lightning strike of ferocious anger that vanished as quickly as it came.

Verde paced. The hate note weighed heavily in his pocket. "Meron, we've got an ex-Intelligence man in our own camp. He and Lacey can keep an eye on goings-on outside the Quarter. I don't like the idea of you running around alone out there anymore. It's not safe."

Meron laughed, a soft gurgle like a running stream. "Mitchell, you worry too much. The tourists are easily fooled. Without the orange, they do not suspect. Today a man came up and asked, 'Do you know where your mommy is, little boy?' " She smiled up at Verde luminously. "Sometimes I think you forget yourself that this is not really a ten-year-old!" Then she went to the

53

madman and took his hand. "James will eat his supper with me tonight."

Verde waved them off and stood pensively chewing his lip. Finally he turned to Lacey. "Close up the office, will you? I'm going to talk to Lute."

Lacey lounged with his back against the whitewashed café wall, his eyes lidded. "We ought to be doing a lot more than talking and watching, Mitch."

"Such as?"

"Such as a little return action. You know, guerrilla-style."

Verde faced the boy irritably. "Where do you think we are, some twentieth-century jungle? Our worry right now is Ra'an."

"Mitch, we could *scare* the tourists away. The Colonial Authority has already put the tool in our hands by encouraging the Dark Powers bullshit."

"Just what did you have in mind?"

Lacey's tone was elaborately casual. "A taste of what the 'Dark Powers' can do—a few jinxed com networks, blackouts here and there, water-supply problems. Kid's stuff, really."

"You can say that again." Verde found himself beginning to sweat. "We'd all be hauled in for heavy questioning, and the Lord knows we won't keep our secrets then. It's not worth risking for a few guerrilla games. The service robots would have it all repaired within minutes and we'd be in cold storage for life . . . or worse."

"They'd have to catch us first."

"How many wardbirds have said that? Look, kid, it's *no*, you hear me? Absolutely no."

The boy glared at him sullenly, rubbing a foot along the worn paving stones. "You're always playing God, Verde. You think you're the only one who knows what's best to do!" Then he tossed his head. "Okay. Forget it. Forget I even said it." He turned away abruptly and stalked toward the office. "I'll close up. See you tomorrow."

Verde, hoping he had heard the last of guerrilla games, hurried off to confer with Lute.

CHAPTER 9

———— •—◆—• ————

Jude awoke from a restless dream of seagulls. Mingling in her ears with their wheeling cries was music, drifting and alien, the trill of white mornings and clear lavender evenings spiced with salt air. She lay still, groping for the words she had been singing a moment before waking. She had never had so vivid a dream before.

Then Clennan was on the phone with her wake-up call. Six o'clock. Jude moaned. He'd had her up late the night before, drilling her in metals prospecting, pushing, pushing, to the limits of her endurance. *Does he actually hope I'll find gold Out There?* His debauched choirboy face materialized in her head, and she smiled sourly. He was disgusting. He even made her eat properly. Often she hated him, but she was dependent on him, and occasionally his boisterous humor could distract her.

And with the Guardians looming each morning out her hotel window, she needed distraction.

That afternoon, in the steamy gym, Jude stood panting, laughing a triumphant laugh. *That felt good!*

Bill Clennan groaned from the floor in comic exaggeration. "Okay, okay, so you're finally getting yourself into shape. Second time won't be so easy. I'll be ready for you."

"You ought to be glad I'm a quick learner."

"I ought to be glad I'm a good teacher," he retorted, pulling himself to his feet and hitching up his sweatpants. "Remember that familiarity with your opponent's body is an advantage you won't often have." His brown eyes smiled suggestively, then sobered. "Always study him carefully, even in the last few seconds before an attack."

As he took a long swig from the water jug, she studied her trainer. A muscular body fighting a tendency toward pudginess. *He'll be a portly old man, if he lives that long. Intelligence men seldom do.* She guessed him to be a man of strong appetites who prided himself on controlling them, to whom exercise was part

55

of the job, not the luxury it was for most people. Jude guessed he could survive well enough out in the wilds, at least against the natural adversaries of weather and terrain. As for the other adversaries, whatever they were Out There, who knew? Only the returned madmen, and they weren't telling. It didn't bear thinking about.

"Do the Koi practice any martial arts?" she asked to distract herself.

"Don't know. Why? You afraid your pal the alien might attack you?"

"No, I was just . . ."

Bill wagged a finger. "All the more reason to get busy and apply yourself."

"I can't figure out whether it's me he dislikes or Terrans in general. He's not very . . . pleasant, you know."

"Too bad. He's all we got."

"Are you sure he's in this for the money?" She didn't add how unlikely that seemed now that she had met the alien in question.

"You and I could live happily ever after on what he's getting for this caper." Clennan grinned slyly. "Maybe I should go instead. Be nice, just you and me out there in Nature's wonderland."

Jude eyed him with mild suspicion. He stared back, handsome, flushed, still grinning. "Well, how 'bout it?"

She drew a cautious breath. The room smelled of bodies and stale sweat. "Bill, you promised there'd be none of this."

"And I haven't forced it, have I? Hell, it would have been easy enough." He threw up his hands. "I just can't help thinking it's a stupid waste, you going home to an empty bed every night."

"It's not empty. I'm there." *Me and my dreams . . .*

The dreams. Since they had begun, sleeping alone had new drawbacks. Sleeping alone she was used to, but the dreams . . . They were not exactly unpleasant—unsettling, rather. Definitely creepy. Not your usual nightmares of knives or suffocation or falling. These dreams were like a psychic invasion, either too primal for her to grasp, or too alien.

Clennan pitched his voice soothingly. "Babe, no threat implied. Just to let you know I'm available."

"Of course you're available. I'm just not interested."

He had not expected an abrupt refusal. "Why the hell not? You got something better going at the moment? All that time in

56

the women's ward stacked up against a good-looking guy like me? I'd think you'd be grateful for the offer."

"Gods, Clennan," she yelled, "did Ramos promise you that as part of the deal? Don't you people own enough of me as it is?" She dropped her voice, fingers clamped around her thumbs. *I must not shout.* Between anger and fear was a thin dividing line. Shouting could lead to hysteria. Fleetingly she wished for the familiar security of the Wards and their tranquilizers. She leaned back against the grimy wall, pulling at the sweatsuit that clung so damply to her. "Look, I don't blame you for wanting to have a good time on the job, but it's just another job to you. To me, it's my life you and your boss Ramos are throwing around so casually here!"

"And how much was your life worth in the Wards?" But he sighed, and wet a towel from the water jug, passing it to her with his best paternal air. "Girl, it's part of my job to keep you up and swinging. Where do you think you'd be if I let you mope around drowning in self-pity?" He brushed her cheek with a finger. "No tears now. You gotta have faith. You'll be ready for anything when I get through with you."

Ready for madness? "Yeah, sure."

He shrugged, apologetic but firm. "As for this other matter, it's strictly personal, believe it or not. But it might be a healthy distraction, you know what I mean?"

Jude pulled away and paced down the length of the wall. "Bill, what I need is a clearer idea of what's Out There!"

"Honey, I've given you all we've got."

"Well, then." She collected herself. "I guess it's time for me to face Ra'an again."

The alien shook his dark head in answer to her queries.

"But you're supposed to be my guide!" Jude's voice echoed shrilly among the dusty tape racks of the reading room.

"Indeed I am. But I do not make a habit of leading tourist safaris into the Guardians."

"All right." Jude exhaled loudly, gathering the shreds of her self-possession. She shouldn't throw at the alien the backlash of her frustration with Clennan. "So. How far into the mountains *have* you been?"

"That would mean nothing to you unless you had been there to recognize the landmarks."

"Well, what's it like out there? As far as you've been?"

"Trees, mountains. The mountains are very beautiful, as

57

you can see from here." He gestured out the grime-specked windows toward the Guardians, towering serene in the late ruddy light.

Jude felt her Wards-learned patience evaporating. "Ra'an, there must be something more than mountains there. What happened to all those expeditions?"

The alien stood tall in his black Terran clothing and smiled faintly at her. "Ms. Rowe, the unseen lands, the impassable mountain ranges, will always conjure phantoms in a mind that fears to journey into them."

The anger that Clennan had kindled flared up unbidden. She slammed her palm down on the table. "Curse your infernal deviousness! Can't you give me a straight answer? One? You are so bloody evasive and superior! The least you could do is meet me halfway!"

The alien said nothing as she glared at him in wild frustration. He sat stiffly, his mouth tight with resentment, seeming to mull something over in his mind. His violet eyes pinned her to her chair until her tantrum faded into mute rage. The silence grew like distance between them. Finally, he spoke, his voice strange and slow, his eyes still watching her.

"Do not make the mistake of dealing with this world in terms of your own. Remember that it is you who are the alien here. Here an unknown is no mere absence of information, but an infinite possibility."

Jude's anger found its voice again. "That's just what I mean! More doubletalk! It's all you—"

"Listen to me!" the alien hissed, rising suddenly. Jude cringed in agonized surprise as the shock force of his fury struck. Anger as tangible as heat tore through her brain like a vengeful beast. She held her head as if it would burst and moaned in terror.

And the beast in her brain vanished. When she could move again, she raised her head and found her confusion mirrored in the alien's eyes, together with an anguish so profound that a sob convulsed her throat.

"What . . . how . . .?" It was all she could manage.

He turned away, gripping the edge of the table as if it were a lifeline. For a long time neither moved, while a branch ticked at the window like an old clock.

"I think," he said at last, in a toneless whisper, "that I have given you a straighter answer than I intended."

"I don't understand."

"Nor do I . . . you . . ." He gave her a wary, opaque look,

moving away from the table, away from her. Just as he seemed about to speak again, he shook his head and left the room. His footsteps rang hollowly down the corridor.

The only thing Jude understood was that he was running away.

CHAPTER 10

The sun was high, the whitewash blindingly new. The steep-walled courtyard was a maze of light and shadow in Verde's eyes as he paced along its concentric pathways. Bright flowers nodded as he brushed by them. At one end of the court, an ancient gnarled tree shaded an oblong of grass. Glass wind chimes hung throughout its spreading branches, silent in the weighted air. A gentle tinkling sounded under the tree, in Luteverindorin's hands, as the old Koi glassmaker tied the knots that strung together a new chime.

Verde circled, frowning. The harsh sun picked out a ghost of freckles across the bridge of his nose. In concentration, Verde looked boyish, despite the gray scrawl of hair and the deep-cut worry lines, like an earnest adolescent who has recently discovered the problems of the world. His long arms with their too-big hands swung at his side as he paced.

"Ra'an's met with this woman again, and now he's given us the slip." He halted in midstep, debating over which of the narrow paved walks he should pace around next. "I just can't get a handle on it, Lute."

Luteverindorin nodded from the shade. "If he wishes to help the Terrans, he has merely to tell them what he knows, yet I don't think . . ."

"No, if he'd done that, Stahl House would be overrun with police. Unless they're holding off for some reason, which I can't imagine. But Ra'an . . . what possible stake could he have in dealing with Terrans?"

The old Koi laid down his glass and string and turned a liquid eye toward the center of the little garden. The madman James sat on the tiled edge of a shallow wading pool, with his bare feet in

59

the water. He was feeding breadcrusts to five enormous gull-like creatures. Huge white water lilies floated on the green water. The gull-beasts waded among them restlessly, picking crumbs from the madman's palms with furred forepaws. "The past?" Lute suggested soberly. "The memory of Daniel?"

Verde stooped under the tree and crooked his arms over a low-slung branch. "I suppose that's possible, though with one as insufferable as Ra'an, it's hard to believe he might have feelings, too."

Lute laid one webbed hand upon the other with practiced calm. "Perhaps your psychologists could explain it. Experts at hidden motivations, are they not? We have not known the need for such a science before, but now our old methods fail us. Ra'an is closed. We cannot read him."

"Ummm. Well, neither can I, if that's any consolation." Verde resumed his pacing, moving back into the sun. "Damn. Damn!" he breathed as he passed the pool. The madman favored him with a brief disapproving glance before returning his concentration to the gulls.

Lute raised a silvered palm. "Please. Sit down, friend. This garden is intended for contemplation, not exercise."

Shamed, Verde retreated to the shade. He hunched down on a rock by the old Koi's knee.

"There is actually a more serious problem at hand," began Lute gravely. He held up a polished icicle of glass for Verde's inspection. "The Wall is losing power."

Verde made a small sound of dismay.

"We've known about it for a while, but didn't believe that the loss could increase so rapidly. It's the accelerating tourist population. Every day, it's more of a struggle to maintain the Wall against such force."

Verde fisted, unfisted his hand. "But there's that penal expedition going into the Guardians . . ."

"I know." The glassmaker traced the pattern of leafshade on his thigh. "I know."

Verde put his head in his hands. The garden's verdant tranquility only made him more desperate. "Ah, Lute, it's going bad so suddenly . . . Damon's window, the hate mail, young Lacey and his crazy guerrilla ideas, Ra'an with whatever he's up to . . . and now the Wall. We kept the balance for so long, so long." He worked his temples with the heels of his hands. "The colony's grown too big for us to handle."

"Despair does not become you, friend," chided Lute as if to a favorite student.

Along the entire frail length of his body, Verde winced. "By isolating the colony, we've created a pressure cooker in this valley. The more Terrans, the higher the pressure, with no place to let off the steam except over the mountains. You should be out there in the streets, Lute, to feel it, to see these people for yourself. The temperature is rising."

"I would only make them more hysterical," said the glassmaker, turning his gossamer-laced fingers in the dappling light.

Verde gazed up into the narrow purple leaves feathering the overhanging branch. "Twenty years ago when I finally woke up to the fact that it was too late to save Terra, I ran here to save Arkoi. Thought it would be better here, more possible. And it was, for a while." His shoulders drooped as memories lit his mind like fireflies. A fragile boy who buried his face in the sun-warm grasses on a windy hill, trying to become part of the earth. A young man whose tears blinded him from the sight of a giant redwood bowing to the saw.

"It still is," said Lute. "And though the Koi do not war as the Terrans do, you will have powerful allies when the time comes to . . . how would you put it? . . . raise the standard."

Verde chewed a knuckle. "I'm a lousy politician," he admitted morosely. "I've spent my life in politics, and still I stand on the hills yelling, and expect people to see the light. What, out of the goodness of their hearts? If you're going to be a prophet of doom these days, you need the voice of a nightingale and a new vocabulary. The old one's been debased. Conservation is a dirty word."

In silence, they watched the madman dust crumbs from his faded uniform with meticulous care. The gull-beasts paddled among the lilies, preening and murmuring. Fine white wool floated on the water.

"Lacey says I have a messiah complex," Verde remarked.

Lute dug his bare webbed toes into the close-cropped grass. "Messiah means 'savior,' does it not?"

"I'm afraid it does."

"Have I told you of the Diamo?" The glassmaker's expression was ambiguous. The madman cocked his head like a listening mongrel, then pulled his legs out of the pool and crawled around the flowers, across the paving stones and grass, to curl up at Luteverindorin's feet.

"I've heard Hrin talking about them." Verde scratched his jaw. He was never sure how much of Koi mysticism he was ready to accept. "They claim to be able to read the future or something?"

"They are an ancient sect," Lute continued. "Undergoing a certain revival of late, perhaps because they foretell an event that offers hope to those of us in the Quarter. They promise a gathering of saviors at a time not very long from now. Perhaps you will be one of them." Lute seemed to find this pleasantly amusing and smiled at Verde to share the joke. The madman stretched his legs and giggled secretly, as if such a thought were charming but inconceivable.

Verde laughed, though he was left mystified. The old Koi's humor was often beyond him. He pulled up a fat blade of grass to chew on. "The Koi could use a savior."

Lute's hairless brow raised. "One savior? No, that is dangerous. A group of saviors, working together, yes."

"Now, Lute. Leaders are sometime a necessary galvanizing force."

The madman muttered softly.

"To lead means to assert oneself over others," the glassmaker replied. A ripple that might have been a frown passed across his face. Above his head, the wind chimes whispered in the still air. "Such behavior is not balanced. Our past is darkened with such leaders, as is yours."

"But there's a difference between a leader and a dictator," Verde argued. It disturbed him to see the Koi so suddenly serious over a philosophical issue, when the real and pending crisis of the Wall seemed barely to touch his serenity.

"It is a difference that exists only in battle. When peace and the victory are won, what leader will willingly step down to give back the power he has taken for himself?"

I've lived my whole life trying to be a leader, Verde thought. Can this be wrong? "Good leaders inspire, organize, urge the best from us, sometimes better than we know we have to give."

"The benevolent dictator?" Now the old Koi was stern. "This is a uniquely Terran concept. Don't you see the illogic of it? Power is shared or it is not. There is no middle ground."

Verde lowered his head. "But you are a leader, Lute."

"No." The glassmaker's hands shook with denial. "I am oldest. I am experienced. I give the benefit of that experience when asked for it. I am, in this special circumstance of the Quarter, sometimes a focal point. I am not a leader."

"The whole Quarter looks to you. I look to you."

"Please, Mitchell. I fear the black past rising again each time I hear Hrin preach of the Diamo and their saviors."

Verde had no heart to push him further. "Lute, Lute. You were laughing at them a moment ago."

The Koi's silvered face softened. He rubbed the silken fringe of hair at his temples. "I am getting old," he said. "The past haunts me of late, and you reminded me. Forgive me."

The madman started. "Ah!" he cried. The gull-beasts had taken wing.

"There goes the *second*-best-kept secret in the Quarter," Verde commented admiringly as the gulls soared up into the azure sky.

Lute's porpoise eyes sparkled once again. "The shanevoralin are very clever. Somehow they are never here when the colonial inspectors arrive."

Verde relaxed momentarily, leaning against the gnarled tree trunk with a sigh of release. "I don't know, Lute. You tell me it isn't magic, but sometimes I wonder. It can be a hundred and fifteen out there in the godforsaken streets, but it's always cool under your tree."

The old Koi smiled, mysterious, satisfied, benign. "That is to encourage your visits, my friend."

At his feet, the madman chuckled.

CHAPTER 11

At six o'clock, Bill Clennan wiped his face and said, "Honey, you look beat. Let's take the night off. What do you say to a little R&R?"

"Mostly the former, I hope," Jude returned wanly.

"What, no dancing? No big night on the town? I know a guy who throws big scare parties every night of the week: the special attraction, a black mass to the Dark Powers!" He chortled fiendishly. "Live it up! It may be your last chance!"

"Very funny, Bill. Ha ha."

"Then how 'bout a nice quiet dinner and early to bed?"

"Better, much better."

"I'm thinking of moving here permanently. What do you think?" Bill tossed the remark out lightly while studying his antipasto.

Jude glanced around the terrace. It was crammed with diners and overlooked the lake. "You mean, train here in the restaurant?"

"You *are* tired. No, really. I mean stay here in the colony."

Her mouth was full of spiced chowder. "What will Papa Ramos think of that?"

"In three months here, I've nosed into enough to earn my keep. It's a chance for me to be in on the ground floor of a big operation."

"I thought I was a big operation."

"I mean the opening up of the planet."

"Oh. That."

Her sarcasm was too private, or Clennan was too lost in his own speculations. "It's no palace I'd be leaving at home, you know, not on what I make. I've got a room to myself and my own bath, but still . . . So headquarters said they might be able to swing me a rental in one of those new places they're building farther along the lake. Two rooms, maybe three. And . . ."

He pointed to the clusters of bright excursion launches bobbing along the pier. "I saw some little boats for sale the other day." He caught her look. "Come on, now. You have to admit, there is something about the place."

"About Arkoi?" *Oh yes. That certain something in the air. The gentle madness that stalks through your dreams, that makes you see birds that don't exist.* But she nodded unenthusiastically as they watched a massive powerboat move out onto the lake, laying down a rainbowed oil slick in its wake.

"Well, they're nice, boats," Clennan prodded, demanding more than her indifference. His defensive tone disconcerted her.

"What's the matter, Bill? The gulls getting to you, too?"

"The gulls?"

"Never mind." She pretended to change the subject. "Do you ever wonder if there's anything to all those rumors?"

"The Dark Powers ones? There are so many around here."

"The ones about the gardens of Eden and all, beyond the mountains?" Saying it out loud, she felt foolish.

"Come on, you're a smart girl. You don't believe in angels anymore." He chuckled knowingly. "That's just Terratransit's publicity department working overtime."

"Ummh. Yeah." Jude returned to her chowder. But in her mind's eye, she saw the gull-beasts, winging wild and free toward the mountains.

That night, her dream was more vivid than ever before. She was in a small café, unfamiliar to her, but somehow she knew it

64

was in the colony. It was low-ceilinged and quiet, lit by hanging lanterns and fat yellow candles. A mild black man served her a mug of herb tea. Music floated out of one corner, where a tanned young man played a thick wooden flute. Occasionally someone would glance toward her, smiling, and nod approvingly. "Listen," they would say, "do you hear?"

Sitting next to her was the madman James. He whispered to her, an endless stream of whispering of which she did not understand a word.

Then a woman began to sing softly. The song began without words, the woman humming to herself as she would while going about some other chore. It was a melancholy tune, full of sighs and resignation and loneliness, a sense of exile. In her dream, Jude closed her eyes and listened. The words came in a language she did not recognize, but emotion made them articulate. The singer sang of sadness and yearning, bringing tears with the pull of a note born deep in her throat and soaring up into a high, clear sob. Through the tears behind Jude's eyelids, images swam in a mist, swirling with the rhythm of the song. As the singer moved into a long crescendo, the mists cleared to reveal a long shoreline that sparkled like a wet jewel. From white bony cliffs hung a crystalline honeycomb of translucent structures, frozen in a tumble down to the waves. Silvery figures leaped in the green water, and it was their singing that laughed and crooned while high above, the gull-beasts swooped an accompaniment in the wind. It was a vision of such heartbreaking purity that Jude woke herself sobbing.

She lay awake for a long time, unable to shake a longing to be there, singing under that sea-washed sky. In the morning, she tried to recall the song, and could not.

CHAPTER 12

———◆•◆━━◆━◆———

"The least you could have done is give me some warning!"

In the driver's seat, Clennan watched the road and offered no excuse.

"Smug bastard. Two lousy months and I'm supposed to be

superwoman. What about all that gear I spent weeks training with? I won't last very long out there with nothing but a pack full of cameras!''

"You've been dying to get your hands on those cameras. Quit griping. I sent your gear in a logging truck. For anyone who's watching, this is a little day trip to the country."

Jude turned away to mope out the window, only privately admitting relief at being in action at last. The camera pack snuggled at her side. She rubbed at the plastic seat cover, sharply conscious of its indestructible man-made blandness. Civilization. She was leaving it behind.

The freeway was a corridor of heat. It looped upward through the pastel suburbs choked with squat tiny houses as identical as mushrooms, set on dirt-and-gravel lawns. Row after row, boxes on a grid, they brought a lesson home to Jude's urban mind: More space is not automatically better if the landscape is ignored. Terra's megalopoli created their own landscape; there was nothing left of the original. But on Arkoi, with wilderness mountains all around, new homes should look a little less like a host of alien devices parked temporarily on a hillside. *Are these Bill's dream houses?* she wondered.

Farther along, Clennan urged the reluctant car past a convoy of heavy open trucks groaning up a steep grade. Slouched in morose groups in the back of the trucks were the other prisoners she had traveled to Arkoi with. They clung to their seats without speaking, packs and boxes piled high around them.

Clennan glanced over at her sharply as she craned her neck for a better look. "Be a good girl, now," he warned and then smiled to make a joke of it.

"Where are they going?"

"Somewhere where you're not, with full press coverage and lots of noise. Hey, be happy. You're the lucky one."

Lucky? To die alone instead of in company? Her camera pack nudged against her as they jarred over a bump, and she chided herself for her pessimism. *The other possibility is freedom, after all* . . .

Passing the suburbs, they entered the industrial zone that ringed the colony. Factories and power plants, dumps and gravel pits were strewn about with little thought to containing their spread. The sky was obscured by colored pipe networks and smoke plumes, and the noise of machinery was deafening. Clennan slid the windows shut. Jude's eyes narrowed in dismay. *I could be back on Terra, looking at all this.* But it was worse, for beyond the maze of cranes and steam and trusswork rose the blue wall of the Guardians, a reminder of the beauty that was being destroyed.

Clennan was driving very fast. They left the factories behind and were soon in the midst of new construction, vast scars cut into the green to make way for developments and private enclaves. Farther on were the larger estates, fenced and heavily guarded. As they moved up into the first stand of tall trees, the estates grew bigger and the walls higher and more forbidding. Three hours later, they were deep in the foothill forests, solid ranks of pine trunks on either side and the hot bright road curving endlessly in front of them. Clennan was making no conversation. His tanned face was set in a tight smirk, his eyes on the road. Jude unbuckled her camera pack and limbered up with a few experimental shots of moving scenery.

Finally, Clennan gave a satisfied grunt. Ahead was a break in the trees and a cluster of small buildings on one side of a grim electrified barrier that vanished into the trees in either direction.

"The border," he explained unnecessarily.

They pulled up to the gate, sweltering in the open sun. The three guards lowered their stunners and waved aside the papers Clennan held out to them. Jokes and grins were exchanged. One peered across at Jude and raised a suggestive brow.

"Day trip, eh, Bill?" He nodded to his companions. "And I gotta spend my time with this riffraff."

Clennan laughed. Jude stared straight ahead until he jogged her elbow proudly and pointed ahead. "There's a manned gate at the four points of the compass. Otherwise it's all computerized. Even a leaf blown across this fence will register on the monitors."

"That must be very inconvenient," Jude replied dryly. "All those leaves . . ."

"Necessary."

"They used to threaten us like that in the Wards. 'No point in this complex is more than four seconds from an armed robot.' "

"Foolproof security system," he gloated.

Gloating, he was at his most annoying. "Yeah, but you know something, Clennan? It's got to be pretty puny compared to whatever's Out There. Five million free Terrans imprisoned by a wall of mountains? Now *that's* foolproof." Her smile was bleak and ironic.

Clennan put the car in gear. The guards opened the gates and waved them through. "My boys," said Clennan and threw them a final rakish grin. He drove until they were out of sight of the border, then pulled over to the side in a small clearing, where a roughly paved logging road led off into the forest. He did not stop the engine.

"This is it, kid. Out you go."

"You're just going to leave me here?"

He nodded and favored her with his most innocent smile. "Your boy will be along in a while."

She regarded him a moment, then finally shook her head. "Bill, I must compliment you on your cold-blooded dedication to your job. I'm sure you'll go far."

The grin weakened, then shut down completely. He laid one arm across the seatback, fingers touching her shoulder. "Look, kid, there is one thing I can do for you, off the record." He leaned forward, and from under the seat, produced a small bundle. He slid it across the seat toward her. "Couldn't let you have this before 'cause it's against the flight plan, but Ramos'll never be any the wiser, and I'll feel better knowing you have it."

Jude unfolded the wrappings. Nestled in an old shirtsleeve lay a battered service stunner. The sight of it sent a surge of hope and guilt through her. She fingered its pitted surface thoughtfully. "Charged?"

"Full." The hand on the wheel tapped a nervous rhythm.

She grasped the handle. The whole gun fit neatly into her palm. It was warm and felt like security. Momentarily, she considered turning it on Clennan. *I could steal the car, leave* him *stranded in the wilderness.* But no, Bill Clennan would never hand over a loaded weapon without some contingency plan. Besides, the gesture touched her. He had actually risked himself to do her a favor, a minor risk for him, true, but Out There, a stunner could be her lifesaver.

"Make sure your Native boy doesn't see it until you need it," he advised. "Remember, he said no weapons."

"What if he finds it?" she asked rhetorically, and in asking, realized that it was the alien's disapproval she feared as much as his anger. *What will he think of me?*

Clennan shrugged. "Don't let him find it."

Jude gazed down at the little weapon. A gouge in the handle smiled up at her. She could not refuse it. She put the stunner away in her camera pack. "Thanks."

"Sure." He reached across her and opened the door. Jude shouldered the pack and climbed out into the sun. Clennan whipped the car around, and with a mock salute, sped back down the road.

Jude stood motionless in the dust. The clearing was deserted.

She felt a momentary rush of elation, so intoxicating that it dissipated for a time even her urbanite agoraphobia. Such freedom, to stand on an empty road in the middle of a wilderness! She stretched her arms and smiled benignly at the blistering sun. "It's fantastic out here!" she shouted.

But the empty silence soon closed in on her. She feared and wished for the alien's appearance. She walked the circuit of the clearing, peering into the trees. While she remained in the sunlight, the green forest depths drew her. As soon as she ventured into their shade, chills crept through her and drove her back into the sun. Finally, she chose a large rock out in the open and sat down to wait.

Before long, she was sweating and thirsty. Her trail clothes were too heavy for such heat, the boots still stiff and new. Clennan had left her no water, and she hadn't eaten since their very early breakfast, now six hours ago. The hot sun made her sleepy, enough to dull her reflexes. She didn't hear the alien enter the clearing until he spoke from a few paces behind her.

"In this sun, Ms. Rowe, it is advisable to wear a hat."

Jude spun around. "Where have you *been?*"

He looked twice his weight in heavy overalls. He shrugged stiffly and brushed bark and sawdust from his arms. "You must know that 'Natives' are not allowed past the border except on guarded work details. My pass described me as a logger, so I came with the trucks." Then he turned and whistled sharply, one high note. From out of the trees trotted three shaggy mules, loaded with packs. They made straight for Jude and nosed at her curiously. Despite being unused to nuzzlings from large animals, she sat still and allowed each a gingerly pat.

"Did they come with the trucks?"

"Ms. Rowe, *nothing* gets through that border without a pass." He started across the clearing toward the logging road, the mules following behind in a line. The last one waited for Jude to precede it, its ears cocked at her expectantly until she got the idea and walked ahead. She would have sworn its clear golden eyes held a glint of amusement.

The alien set a slow pace up the winding road into the mountains. All the hot afternoon long, climbing and climbing, they saw nothing but trees, tall evergreens, thick-trunked and straight, spaced so regularly that Jude contemplated the possibility that they had been planted, all at the same time. She gave that up when her mind boggled at the hugeness of such a task. It was not at all what she had expected a wilderness forest to be: no picturesque forest cottage, no deer crashing off into the thickets. *But then, this is Arkoi. I should expect these endless swaying groves to be devoid of animal life.* Her camera banged uselessly at her side as anticlimax drained away all initial excitement. There was nothing to distract her from the heat, now becoming unbearable, or her thirst. When the paved road gave out and turned to a swirl of dust beneath the mules' feet, she began to cough convulsively. Her new boots slipped on the scattered pebbles. The alien watched her covertly for a while as he continued his uphill plodding. When it finally seemed to her that she would choke, he dropped back with a canteen in his hand. He allowed her one hasty gulp. She scowled at him as if she would tear the canteen from his grip, then subsided as he scowled back. Petty aggression was a prison reflex, out of place here in the wilderness, where she was at a stranger's mercy. They faced each other silently. Jude felt her sweat running rivulets through the dust on her cheeks. She brushed a wisp of hair back, aching with sudden loneliness, standing in the road with this pitiless alien. His face was hard under the shadow of his brimmed hat. She brushed at her hair again, a totem gesture to ward off the fear that was rising inside her. She wished for the stunner, out of reach in her pack.

"Do we have to be so careful with the water?" she asked, trying not to sound querulous.

He stared as if trying to read secrets in her, but to her surprise, handed back the canteen. "We must be careful with everything if we wish to survive," he lectured distantly.

She gave the canteen back and did not ask for it again until it was offered.

When the sunlight grew long and amber, and the gloom behind the tree trunks deepened into darkness, Jude wondered how long the alien intended to keep going without a break. As if in a trance, he trudged along, hour after hour, with unbroken pace. She thought of how Clennan had worked her mercilessly, and how she had complained. Now she offered him a silent vote of thanks for whipping her into shape from the physical wreck she had deteriorated to in the Wards.

Ahead, the alien slowed, alert. Jude heard a distant whine of power saws.

"Logging camp?" she asked.

He nodded. "This far up into the woods, they're usually fully automated. We should be able to get by unnoticed."

They proceeded cautiously upward into a devastation of clear-cutting. Under the glare of huge portable lights that made noontime out of the late gloom, logging machines moved ponderously about their destructive business. Acres of cut logs waited in stacks by the roadside. Ra'an used them as cover, skirting swiftly around the camp. The road ended at the camp. On the far side, Ra'an plunged several paces into the forest, then stopped to look back. The saw whine sharpened, there was a deep cracking, and a giant tree crashed to the ground.

"The robots don't mind being up here by themselves," he remarked, "and they can do six of those big trees in an hour, limbed and stripped."

Jude found his tone obscure. "Somehow I had gotten the idea that you don't approve of all this technology."

"Ah, but you are wrong, Ms. Rowe. It is not the fault of the technology that it is so often misused. In this case, those robots are doing a boring and dangerous job very efficiently." He pointed out a humanoid form whirring briskly among the huge machines. "That supervisor will never go to sleep in the shade or get drunk on the job. The Terrans who created him are ravaging our forests, but he himself is an admirable creation, don't you think?"

Jude grimaced in distaste. "Have you ever known a robot that could take a joke? Or make a decision based on compassion rather than the letter of the law?"

"That is the fault of their programmers," he replied smugly.

"Sorry. After six years of Ward security robots, anything that close to human without actually being human gives me the creeps."

Ra'an raised a dark eyebrow, then turned away. They walked through the trees in silence for a moment. Then he added flatly, "Myself, for example."

Jude laughed, taken aback. "That's absurd. You're human."

"No, I am not. Do not make that mistake. It may surprise you to learn that the Koi have a word which roughly translates as 'human,' but it is used to differentiate not between Koi and what you would call animal, but between Koi and Terran."

"But . . ."

"A critical distinction, Ms. Rowe. The Koi are unique to themselves, not some lesser offshoot of your human race. Arkoi is a parallel world in another universe, not a minor planet in yours." His voice took up a lecturing cadence. "But the Terrans cannot bear to have their homocentric egos threatened by the possibility of equal nonhuman intelligence."

"Ra'an, I would be mad to doubt your intelligence."

"So you rationalize me away into some safely *human* category?

71

The tourists are more honest with themselves. They regard the Koi as animals, and fear them as they fear anything strange.''

Jude stopped and planted her feet. ''Look, I admit I find you strange . . . *alien*, all right? But I'm willing to assume that's because I don't know you. Believe me, there are a lot of Terrans I find pretty strange, too. If you consider yourself something other than human, fine, I accept that. It doesn't mean we can't figure out a way to get along. I wish you would at least give credit to my good intentions.''

The alien looked bored. ''The road to hell . . . is that not the saying?''

The long hot climb had sapped the patience that nurtured those good intentions. ''Of course, there's always the possibility,'' she said slowly, ''that the problem is not that you're an alien and I'm a racist, but that you are just plain disagreeable.''

He regarded her icily. ''A neat way of avoiding the dilemma altogether. Dismiss me as an individual, alien or human.''

''I don't see that you're giving me much choice. Why?''

He would not answer. He stalked on ahead, threading a slim path through the underbrush, and leaving her to puzzle out his contrariness on her own. His tightly controlled manner did not successfully conceal his deep reserves of anger and pain. Jude had had a hint already of the dangers of provoking him in that tangible aura that his anger had generated. There at least was one thing about him that was unhuman, yet . . .

As she struggled after him, through the thickening forest, she gave some thought to her definition of the word ''human.''

CHAPTER 13

Late into dusk, the alien halted at last, his choice of a camp-site governed more by the failing light than by comfortable terrain. The forest offered no friendly clearings. All signs of a path had disappeared hours ago, swallowed up by a blanket of pine needles. Jude collapsed with her back against a tree and shut her eyes to ward off the nausea of exhaustion. With the ceasing of the steady crunch of their footfalls, it was still as a void beneath the trees, as unreal as a dream, thick with the pungency of sap and heat-soaked earth. A silent rain of needles fell on her hands, her lap, her hair. Her courage balked at the idea of sleeping in the open with nothing to shut out the utter blackness of a night without electric lights. She made a private plea to the sun not to set.

The alien set to work unloading the mules. The equipment he unpacked was devastatingly primitive: two sleeping bags, two metal cups, a pot, some aluminum utensils, a single tiny lantern, more or less what Clennan had outlined as the barest necessities for survival. Somehow it had never occurred to Jude that the alien would bring only the bare necessities.

He cleared a small circle in the pine needles and built a fire. Jude roused herself and wandered over hazily.

"You know, there are camp stoves available that weigh almost nothing at all," she offered ingenuously as he balanced the pot on the pile of crackling twigs.

"Yes. I'm saving it for when we run out of wood." He went on with his cooking.

Run out of wood? She eyed the forest around them as if such a thing were inconceivable, then pursed her lips musingly. A month or so back, on Terra, having any wood at all would have been equally inconceivable. Only rich people had real wood. Now that it surrounded her in excess, she wondered, *Is it possible to value a thing before it becomes scarce?*

Later, she huddled among the needles, arms wrapped tightly around her knees. She watched the tiny fire fade into coals and contemplated her insignificance at the feet of the forest giants. The darkness closed around her like a velvet blindfold. She slipped the stunner out of her pack and into her shirt. She would carry it there from now on. The alien lay in his sleeping bag a few yards away, yet as she struggled alone with her fear, it might have been miles, for he had no comfort to offer her. His presence was negative, as giving as polished steel, reflecting only the difference between them.

The days led them relentlessly upward, through the sun-drenched forests, now choked with undergrowth that slowed their progress. Jude took a picture now and then, more dutifully than with enthusiasm. There were still no signs of other life. She longed for the wonders of Kramer's and Langdon's journals, regardless of the dangers they might bring. She was bored with trees, constantly tired, hungry and hot, too tired even to complain.

On the fourth afternoon, as they approached the higher reaches of the foothills, she found a spot where the mountain granite poked through the ground cover in worn ledges carpeted with moss. She spent two film cartridges trying to capture what it was that moved her so in the sharp contrast of hard and soft, her tears all the while misting the viewfinder.

There was little conversation to fill those long days, even if she had possessed the energy for it. Ra'an and his mules seemed tireless, while Jude waged subtle war with her body, driving it through the painful transition from classroom to the field. She was winning, gradually, but at times she feared the worst, that she couldn't go on, that she would be left alone to die of exposure. The ground she must sleep on was harder than cement; the trail rations, which the alien insisted on preparing himself, were barely palatable. And he, a cheerless companion, offered no information and less sympathy, often refusing to answer what seemed to her the most innocent questions.

Once she asked about the absence of animal life in the colony and the surrounding mountains. His reply was curt.

"They cannot live up here any more than Terrans can."

"But the mules . . ."

"They're different."

"Different?"

"Smarter."

She wasn't sure if he meant smarter than other animals or smarter than Terrans, but she let it drop to avoid another racial argument. But there was one thought she did venture.

"What about the gull-beasts?"

She had his attention so fast it startled her. He made her describe what she had seen and when, but when she had finished, all he said was, "Try not to let your imagination run wild, Ms. Rowe. Not up here."

Somehow, she knew this was not a dismissal, but a specific warning.

The eighth night out, they camped in the last hour of light in a high rocky clearing. Above the trees, the Guardians loomed in frigid splendor, as high as ever for all the upward miles so arduously traveled.

Exhausted, starved but avoiding the meager excuse for a supper she would have to force herself to eat, Jude did her camp duties. She fed the mules, which for their own reasons would not eat the local grasses. She laid out the sleeping bags in the least rocky spot she could find, and watched Ra'an construct his little fire. It fascinated her, the meticulous precision with which he

74

laid twig upon twig, each just slightly larger than the one before, the kindling placed just so. It was his ritual each evening, as if in honor of the arcane art of woodsmanship. The ritual accomplished, he hunched over his tin pot with concentration pulled up like a wall around him. The long dark hair, the russet skin, his trail boots with their wide soft laces wound around his legs, his easy crouch by the open fire . . . for all his claims of alienness, he reminded her of every photo or painting she had ever seen of the ancient Terran people called Indians. Here among the trees and pine needles he was centuries away from the sophisticated creature she had met in the colony, and she understood how people like Bill Clennan could consider these "Natives" primitive. Ra'an was both, primitive and urbane, but not in an even mixture. It was as if two natures lived an uneasy coexistence within one body, one or the other seizing complete control as the occasion required. *Perhaps this is natural and proper for a Koi.* But Jude didn't think it too homocentric to suspect that no two selves, Koi or Terran, should be so unharmoniously meshed, and that psychoses like schizophrenia were probably universal among sentient creatures.

Tiring of fireside psychology, she clambered across the clearing and up onto a jutting spur of rock. Through a break in the trees, she discovered the valley spread out beneath her. The distant colonial city sprawled in miniature, the high-rises along the lake, the incoherent jumble of the business district, the suburbs fanning out along the radial arms of freeway, reaching into the hills. A sullen yellow haze hung over it all, obscuring detail, and her bird's-eye view brought home at last how large the spread really was. Farther beyond the buildings were acres of clear-cutting and torn earth, the telltale lesions of terraforming. *That's what makes the colony so reminiscent of Terra. The great earthmovers are down there gobbling up the alien dirt and spitting it out again as a Terran look-alike.*

She sighed, not entirely sure why this should bother her. So many things once familiar now seemed strange and distant. She was sleeping well nights, no longer bothered by the hard dry ground or the blackness of the night. She had discovered the stars, the alien stars, and Arkoi's two little moons. Why hadn't Bill Clennan thought to mention that Arkoi had two moons? Was that another of those items that gave tourists the creeps?

She heard Ra'an's quiet footstep behind her. He followed her gaze toward the valley.

"You ought to point your camera at that," he commented sourly. "Terra has a glorious future planned for Arkoi."

Jude groaned softly as visions of the gray Terran megalopolis filled the remaining green below and crawled up the hills toward the Guardians.

"The idea does not appeal to you?" he challenged.

"You know, Ra'an, sometimes I can't figure out whose side you're on. No, it doesn't appeal to me." How to explain it to him, when she herself was amazed that the familiar urban topography of her home world no longer beckoned? "I guess I never thought about preserving land on Terra because there isn't any left. Oh, maybe a few thousand acres, scattered over the globe in parks, but not like this, not endless wilderness."

"All things have an end, Ms. Rowe."

"But it's so *vast*!" she exclaimed with a sweep of both arms that halted halfway as if quailing before such scale. "If only you could *see* Terra, you would understand. Like . . . umm, well, the hospital complex I was born in was the size of that whole city down there, and there are thousands like it, just hospitals. I was raised in a crèche—a government nursery; I was an unwanted child—with forty thousand other children who never saw the open sky except on a school trip now and then. No moon, no stars. We never had true darkness, or weather. Everything is inside, streets, stores, houses, everything, even some of the small parks, inside where the air is filtered and safe to breathe. There are some livable zones outside, for the rich and the bosses, but for most of us, it's the inside, all our lives. Can you blame the tourists for streaming to Arkoi? Even if it's only a week they can afford, once in their lives, it's a week outside."

"One week times fifteen billion Terrans," he added bitterly. "They crowd our land and litter and deface it and are not touched by it."

"Which tourists have done since time immemorial," she admitted. "You have to stay longer than a week to get up the courage to reach beyond the tourist routine into the real nature of a foreign place."

"And you, Ms. Rowe? Do you have that courage?"

She shook her head to his challenge. "Ra'an, hate if you must, but don't do it blindly. Hate those who stand on that beautiful lake shore and see only a rising bank balance, the select few making their fortunes exploiting the fact that for most Terrans, no matter how badly they treat it in their ignorance, Arkoi is the Promised Land. Even if they never see it, its existence gives them hope, and that, on Terra, is in slim supply."

The alien was crumbling a stick between his fingers. "Very eloquent, but, I'm afraid, appallingly short-sighted."

"I wouldn't expect you to understand compassion," she snapped, disgusted.

"Compassion?" he retorted. "Where is *their* compassion? What is the good of a Promised Land to those who only know how to destroy exactly that which you claim they value so highly? It's wasted on them!" His voice rose; the stick lay in shreds on the ground. "What about the Koi? Should their way of life be sacrificed to squeeze out some last feeble ounce of Terran hope? What good will hope do the Terrans when they have ruined this world as they have ruined their own?"

Jude faltered. "In ruining Terra, we should have learned our lesson." *At least some of us.* She had to believe that, that some lessons could be learned, or give up all belief in humanity . . . whatever that was. "Besides, there's so much room here, Ra'an, and so few of you."

"Ah, yes," he murmured, suddenly quiet. His face worked unreadably, his violet eyes fixed on her as if she herself were the danger. "And so many of you."

And Jude heard what his eyes were telling her. He might as well have said it out loud. For a moment, she held her breath. "There *are* Others," she whispered.

But Ra'an did not hear, following another thought. "I was a small child when you Terrans first arrived, a boy, impressionable. I listened then to such excuses. Do you think you are the first to offer them?"

"Ra'an, there are Others, aren't there?"

"We learned what comes of listening to Terrans, of giving that inch that grew into a valley and soon will encompass our entire world if the Terrans have their way!"

His words came sharp and hard, but Jude barely listened. "Where are they, Ra'an, the Others?"

"The early ones who came, the pioneers, the visionaries, we were patient with them, because they were so vibrant, because they carried their beliefs like torches, because life burned in them so fiercely. It was only later that we realized the grimmer realities that their brilliance hid from us, and by then the damage was done."

"Ra'an . . ."

"Now we do nothing but contain the disease, and we are dying . . . as they died."

Her insistent question froze in her mouth as a wave of grief enveloped her, Ra'an's grief, heartsick despair that drained the strength from her limbs.

"Dying of idealism," he whispered. "Dying of good intentions."

She knew she did not understand, but the tears came anyway. She wanted to offer comfort, support, anything, an instinctive reaching out to a creature in such pain, when suddenly inspiration cried out inside her head. Jude held herself very still. Images came, images of a man, tall and eager, a shock of pale hair, a smile reminiscent of . . . who? A heavy pack slung carelessly across his back. And then a name. It floated unbidden to her tongue. "Daniel . . ." she murmured.

The alien stiffened, the great violet eyes widening in anger, disbelief, some complex emotion she could not identify.

"Daniel Andreas," she repeated, amazed that her brain should play such tricks.

"Enough!" he hissed through gritted jaws. "Who told you about Daniel?"

Her face was blank, puzzled. "Nobody . . . I . . . the name . . . it just came into my head."

"You'd heard it before. Somewhere." Every syllable was a pleading growl of pain.

Jude shook her head fearfully, and Ra'an lifted his head to the shadowed mountains with a moan of anguish.

"What is it, Ra'an? What did I do?"

With a rush, he grabbed her arm, twisting, and threw her away from him. She stumbled backward against the rocks and fell. *Should I have lied to him? What could I have said?* She tried to scramble up, but he lunged after her.

"You have no right!" he cried. "Not you, not a Terran!"

Desperate, she turned to run. He caught her wrist and twisted again, hard. She went down among the jagged stones, gasping as he held her down. With her free hand, she fumbled at her waistband, where Clennan's little stunner was strapped behind her belt. She tore it loose, struggling to push herself away from him, but he saw the gun and swore harshly, a quick Terran oath, and knocked it from her hand, crushing her down against the rocks with his knee until she could do nothing but whimper.

"Should have left you out here days ago!" he raged. He caught up the stunner and leveled it at her, then suddenly let her go with a shove, threw the gun aside, and stood back. "There are fitter punishments," he snarled, breathing hard, compressing his fury into a gorgon stare through slitted purple eyes. The slits shut. His body went rigid with effort.

78

Jude screamed. Flame seared through her. Agony, hot and molten, burned into every fiber, every cell, boiled up through the marrow of her bones, up through her lungs, choking her screams. She collapsed and fell, into blackness.

CHAPTER 14

Clear morning light flowed past the plum blossoms outside the window onto a cool brick floor. Meron's tawny bare feet left little prints in the moisture as she padded about the room, replacing a cup or a book in its proper niche.

"You have turned this house inside out every day for nine days, Mitchell," she said. "Soon I will think you are brooding."

Verde slumped in a wicker chair, frowning reflexively at the pine-planked walls. "At some point I'll understand why he did it."

"We don't know that he has."

"Merry, Merry, benefit of the doubt is all very well and good, but . . . Ra'an vanishes, Clennan drives into the hills with the woman and comes back alone. Put two and two together. Clennan gave him a pass, he got through the border, and now he's taking a Terran through the Guardians."

Meron looked unhappy, her childish face crinkling up like an old man's. "He has wanted to go back for a long time."

"I know, I know, so do you all! But only Ra'an would go and do a thing like this!" Verde rubbed his eyes viciously. "Can he make it through the Wall, do you think?"

Meron's eyes were drawn to the doorway, where the madman James stood peering in but refusing to cross the threshold. "Even for a Koi, the Wall is perilous," she replied.

"But the Wall is weakening." Verde sighed, got up, opened and shut a cabinet. "He didn't take much if he intends to stay."

The Koi clicked her fingers along a row of crude wooden spoons. The shelves held stacked wooden bowls and crockery plates. "These are colony things. He will not need them."

"It must be odd for you, being colony-born, I mean, to know so much about a place you've never seen." He took her small

hands between his own huge ones. "Someday, Merry. Someday."
Her eyes glistened as she nodded. Verde turned away, moved.
He went to the bedroom door. The bed was neatly made, the
shelves piled with dark clothing. "I don't see Daniel's old
chessboard in its usual place. I guess Ra'an feels he needs that.
He was always better at chess than opri, anyway. Like Daniel.
One hell of a chess player, but he never did get the hang of
opri."

"They are no ways the same," said Meron, recovered. "Chess
is a game. Opri is a process."

"More like a philosophical discussion, I'd say."

"Perhaps. Ra'an was not good at opri because he kept wanting there to be a winner."

"Ah. Well. So do I. But not in games. In life." He ran a
finger across the black Terran-made wood stove dominating one
corner. It was clean. Its brass fittings shone. "Daniel once told
me this thing was over a hundred years old, and he'd always
dreamed of building a house around it. I guess James should
have the house now, with Ra'an gone."

Meron nodded toward the doorway. "I do not think he will
come in here, Mitchell. It is a . . . what is it? . . . a haunted
place for him."

"Umm." Verde paced about a bit. "You know, you should
have let Ra'an go a long time ago, let the Wall down just
long enough to send him through, before he was angry enough to
betray you like this."

Meron sat at the round wooden table, holding her hands in her
lap like a gift. "For many centuries we have labored to bring
ourselves away from what Ra'an has become in a short lifetime.
You see how easily the Balance is upset? To live a proper life,
the forces within us, our emotions, must be kept in Balance, but
Ra'an's anger, his hatred, is uncontrolled."

"He resents being shut out," offered Verde.

"But his own anger is the cause. There is great power in
Ra'an tel-Yron, but his hatred has strangled it by tipping the
Balance too far. To restore it, he must let some of that anger go.
But he will not. He hoards it. And so it builds and builds until
his mind can no longer contain it and it must leak out, causing
pain to all of us. It is uncomfortable for a Koi to be around
him."

"I didn't like it much either," said Verde dryly.

"Since we have worked our way up from the black era of the
towers, the Koi have come to take Balance for granted. But
consider Ra'an, and you learn its terrible fragility, not only

within a single mind, but among our people as a whole. Imagine us, each Koi mind, as the smooth and oiled parts of a great machine. That machine's steady workings are the Balance. Then understand the damage that an abrasive, unbalanced object such as Ra'an could do if it were dropped into the works. This is why we have kept him in the colony."

"But that's only made him worse, Merry."

The little Koi unfolded and refolded her hands. "I know. The Koi do not well understand the effects of isolation on the mind. I can't help thinking that if Daniel were still alive . . ."

Verde nodded, and both of them glanced at the door where the madman waited, listening, eyes to the ground. "A lot would be different if Daniel were still alive."

CHAPTER 15

Jude woke in pain with the night silence licking around her like water. She lay still, and the pain ebbed slightly. The fiery inexplicable assault from within had passed, leaving in its wake the deep ache of bruised nerve and muscle. Something underneath her pricked at her sore limbs. Slowly, she felt with her fingers and found the edge of a blanket. She tried to move, could barely raise her head to look around. A tiny campfire hissed gently a few feet away. She was alone.

She lay back with a moan, fighting through her dizziness and nausea to concentrate, to understand what had happened. Clarity would not come. Her wounded mind stumbled like a cripple when she tried to think. Around her and the meager coals, the night was an impenetrable void. It offered no answers, only its silence, her solitude and the little fire, hissing secretively to itself like an idiot. Dimly, she thought of Ra'an, out there somewhere in the darkness perhaps, watching, perhaps returning. Sick and despairing, she wept, and with her weeping came dreams and drifting and more dreams and dizziness, then more drifting. Much later, she dreamed that someone came with gentle hands and lifted her up to put a shining cup to her lips. The liquid ran down her throat, sweet and warming. She was laid down again and slept, dreamless at last.

A mule woke her next, in the daylight, wuffling at her cheek like a dog. Jude stared up at it and raised a finger to its velvet nose. It regarded her sympathetically, as if assessing her well-being, then moved off.

She sat up into a soft golden morning. The mist still clung to the trees like cotton wool. Her pain had vanished. She surveyed the clearing apprehensively. If only the sun could chase away the nightmares in her brain. The mules were gathered at the far end, heads together as if in conference. At the other end, a still figure sat hunched up on a rock, staring out over the valley.

Ra'an. Oh God. She flattened herself to the ground, but the alien turned and watched her for a while across the brittle grass, then rose and came toward her. Swiftly, she gathered herself to run, knowing it was useless. Nothing Bill Clennan had taught her had saved her last night. *Too late.* The alien was there. She recoiled, awaiting his attack.

None came. Instead, he threw something down in front of her. It bounced onto the blanket. The stunner.

"There were to be no weapons," he accused.

She could not collect herself enough to point out that it was he who had been the aggressor. "For protection," she murmured. "It's only a stunner."

"I know what it is," he spat in disgust. "Did you think I wouldn't know what else it is?"

"What else . . .?"

"Because I am Koi, do you think I'm an idiot?"

"No, Ra'an, I . . . what do you mean?"

He held up a small disc between thumb and forefinger. "This." Still she looked bewildered. A shade of doubt crossed his taut face. "Where did you get the stunner?"

"Bill Clennan gave it to me just before he dropped me off."

"And he didn't tell you of certain . . . improvements he'd made on it?"

Jude shook her head. "He just told me to hide it."

Ra'an let out a long breath. He held out his hand for the stunner, which she had picked up from the ground. "Give it to me."

She hesitated briefly, feeling its weight in her palm, so comforting. Then she surrendered it. He held it out where she could watch and pressed an innocuous stud at the base of the handle. The handle clicked and popped open. He fit the metal disc into the cavity. "It's a bug," he said nastily. "Didn't your wardmates teach you about bugs? Clennan's been listening to every word we've said."

Oddly, she felt betrayed. Pretending to do her a favor, Clennan had planted a bug on her.

"There hasn't been much for him to listen to," she said quietly. *Why did I ever think I could trust him?*

Ra'an glanced toward the mountains. "Enough, perhaps."

From the depths of her defeat, she wanted to scream, *damn the bug, you nearly killed me. Why? And how?* Instead, she said, "Will you believe that I knew nothing about this?"

"I don't know." He removed the disc from the gun and crushed it under his heel. Then he handed the stunner back to her and said with deadly irony, "Keep it if it makes you feel safer."

She thought of the very potent weapon he seemed to carry within himself. "I don't want it."

"All right." He pulled back his arm and sent the gun hurtling into the trees, then called one of the mules over. "Ride today," he ordered. "It will be easier."

But it was not easier. Riding is hard work for a novice, but it afforded her a welcome distraction. With great concentration on her part and greater patience on the part of the mule, she learned something of the horseman's art of grip and balance, clinging for her life as the agile creature trundled up the switchbacking route that Ra'an chose to take them up the rocky slopes. On ledges Jude would not have attempted on foot, the mule found hold for his tiny hooves, scrambling precariously as the shale crumbled beneath him.

The tree line was passed as abruptly as walking through a door. The terrain assumed a desolate, stubborn attitude, littered with weatherbeaten boulders that blocked their ascent. Every crevass was choked with bristly gorse that snagged in her pantlegs and clawed at the mule's shaggy coat as he pushed his way through. The wind quickened and grew cold. Jude wrapped herself in a blanket. Ra'an stalked ahead in moody silence.

At dusk, there were no trees for shelter, only a low hollow in the rock. The sun took all warmth with it when it set, and the mountains were a barren, storm-tossed ocean around them. Ra'an scraped together a fire out of dried moss and a few meager twigs. The mules stood close, heads inward, forming a windbreak. They didn't seem to mind that the gusts ruffled their long fur backward and whipped their tails into their eyes. Jude made them her anchor on that windswept mountain, her one unshakable reality, as the reality that had been her life floated away in gauzy layers. Up here, there were no names, no places, just infinite emptiness. Cold moonlight on the beaten granite, the wind that bit into her with icy teeth—these were sensations beyond human scale. But the mules were warm. They muttered among themselves like old men and munched their grain without panic. And they acknowledged her presence, in their animal way, and she loved them for it.

For the alien, she had not existed all that day. He was shut away in the mood that had occupied him since the morning, brooding deeper than his usual silence. Jude huddled in her blanket and fumbled with numb fingers at the camera in her lap. It stared at her like some foreign device, a plastic puzzle box that had once been as familiar as her own hands, a part of her identity. That old identity could find no place up here, and the purpose that had brought her had been so superficially imposed by Ramos and Clennan that she could not prevent its drifting away into the wind. Clumsily brushing and repacking a lens, she decided that her only purpose now could be survival.

But her survival depended upon Ra'an, not only on his knowledge of the wilderness, but on his willingness to help her survive.

She vowed to be more careful, more alert for the danger signs, even though each time his anger had turned on her, it had come without warning. She must learn the source of that anger, and avoid arousing it. But that required fitting the pieces of him together into a coherent picture, and each time she tried to do that, she failed. She thought of the Koi back in the colony, wishing she had met some of them, not understanding how a people made up of such as Ra'an could be kept so easily under the Colonial Authority's thumb.

Covertly, across the sputtering fire, she watched him. He was still eating, always slower than she. His shoulders sagged. He looked tired, older, very much as she felt. As he ate, she coveted every mouthful, still hungry but afraid to ask for more. She stowed the camera in its case and resigned herself to sleeping until breakfast. She brushed away the dry grass and dirt that the wind had blown over her sleeping bag, and pulled it closer to the fire.

Ra'an stirred, startling her. He pushed some more twigs into the tiny blaze. The gesture was fitful, like the shrugging of a burden from one arm to the other. "You know what they will think, at the other end of your little eavesdropper?" he murmured. "They will think I have murdered you."

"Probably," she answered faintly, thinking how close it had

84

come to that. "I'm not sure they'll care much, except for the effort they've wasted on me. They can find other photographers. It was you who were crucial to this operation."

"Did you really think they wanted you up here just to take pictures of the mountains? They were hoping I'd show you a way *over*."

His tone was flat and tired. It contained no threat.

Jude nodded. *What does it matter anymore if he knows?* "You must have suspected that."

"Yes. Because of my reputation as an outcast, they assumed I'd be easily bought."

"Then if it wasn't the money, why did you agree to bring me up here?"

"The pass."

She could barely hear him over the wind. "What?"

"The border pass. It was the only way I could get out of the colony."

"And what were you planning to do with me?" she pursued cautiously.

His face was tight with self-disgust. "Leave you out here somewhere."

"But you haven't, yet."

"And won't. Not now."

"Why?"

"I've enough guilt already," he replied obscurely.

"Where will you go now?"

"Home."

"Home?" she echoed blankly. "Back to the colony?"

"The colony is not home." He gestured toward the dark mountains to the north. "Home is Ruvala, where I was born. Yes, you guessed right. There *are* others, an entire population, outside of this ring of mountains that have only been called the Guardians since the Terrans came."

"Then there is a way over."

"Many. The actual route has never been the problem. The dangers are more than geographical."

"Yes. I had guessed that also."

"But I will find a way through. I have to get home, to see it again, before it's too late, before the Terrans gobble it up as they have the colony."

"Ra'an, they haven't gotten past the Guardians yet."

"We can't hold them back much longer. When the dam bursts, all Arkoi will be inundated with Terrans, and our way of life will perish in the flood." A bit of his spark returned, then

85

died. "I will not spend these last years suffocating in the colony. When the end comes, at least I'll be home."

"And me?"

"Do you want to go back to the colony?"

"No."

He seemed relieved. "I couldn't let you, anyway. If you told them what you know, it would only speed up the end. Believe me, Ruvala will be a great improvement on where you've been." He leaned forward to put the fire out.

"Wait, Ra'an." Jude dared to put a hand out in protest. "Please. If we're going to do this journey together, I need to understand a little better, about you, about this place."

He balked, flared briefly like the dying fire, then slumped back. "I don't know where to begin," he said bleakly.

She scraped together every last dreg of courage that his reasonable mood had inspired and ventured. "Why not begin with Daniel Andreas?"

To her surprise, he did not rear back in rage. He gave a soft, rueful laugh, and shook his head, and she knew that, for the time, the fight had gone out of him. "Daniel . . . he was a stubborn one, too." He smiled to himself, and Jude read gentleness in him for the first time. Shaking his head again, he looked up. "But that's not the place to begin."

He busied himself with the fire for a bit, buying time, then addressed the young flames that rose to light his troubled face. "There are certain things I must explain, if I can—I owe you that much for being able to face me after . . . well, it will not be easy for me, partly because I don't understand it all myself, mostly because what I do understand, I . . . haven't wanted to accept."

He dragged a hand across his lidded eyes. "Mea'ara! I'm so tired of it all. It was a reflex in the colony to hate you. You were Terran, a means to an end, I looked no further. Then you gave me further reason, reason to envy, which I repressed and denied until it was no longer deniable, and then, there you were, lying at my feet like a broken thing." His hand stopped and tightened on his temples. "Hatred was eating me alive in the colony, making a lethal weapon out of me." He dropped his hand and glared at her helplessly. "You must understand that. What did you do with your anger in the Wards? Didn't it twist in your gut when you lay down at night?"

She met his glare squarely. "In the Wards, they tranquilize you, Ra'an. They leave you nothing but indifference. I went dormant for six years."

In the silence, the icy wind screamed through the rocks. Then Ra'an remarked, more subdued, "You know, we have no camels here."

"Unh?"

His wide mouth angled into a half-smile that was more of an ironic grimace. "Daniel had an expression about the straw that broke the camel's back."

"Ah. Yes?"

"That was you. The straw." He tossed another twig onto the fire. "Have you ever," he continued reluctantly, "had reason to suspect you were telepathic?"

She shrugged lightly, figuring this was another obscure reference. "No. Why?"

Bitterness edged his words. "Are you always in the habit of picking names out of strangers' heads?"

"Names . . .?" She realized he was serious. *Wait. Telepathic?* "Oh, Lord . . . it can't be."

"Oh, yes it can be, here. If you'd never heard of Daniel Andreas before, didn't you wonder where his name came from?"

"Yes, but . . ."

"Where else but out of my head?" he growled.

"But how . . . me?" *Telepathic?*

"I wish I knew!" he answered fervently. "From that first encounter, I suspected something of this, but it was too . . . bitter a possibility, easier to deny than to face. But when you stole that name from me, I had no denials left. Only blind outrage." His voice dropped. "I did you more damage than I intended. I hope you'll believe that. I may be a lot of things, but I am not a murderer."

Jude's reality was growing shakier than ever. "But if it is telepathy, how can I now when I never could before?"

"You've probably never found yourself with another telepath before."

"Ahhh?" Another piece of the puzzle clicked into place.

"No," he cautioned. "Before I misrepresent myself further. I'm not, at least not completely. But I should be, and you . . . shouldn't." He stood and paced to the edge of the darkness, the wind whipping at his black canvas jacket. "I'm not saying this the way I meant to . . . it's not a subject I can be easily rational about, but I owe you some objectivity, if I can manage any." His hands worked through his long hair as if it were the source of his frustration. He began again, off into the cold night. "What would you say was the most basic skill you were taught as a

87

child? The one which you absolutely required to function normally in adult society?"

Jude pondered in silence, shivering by the fire.

"Language," he supplied impatiently. "Language is the basic social tool for a Terran, is it not? For the Koi, it is halm. Literally, it means 'the brain's tongue.' Very anatomical. You call it telepathy."

"A race of telepaths? That's incredible!"

"Is language incredible? Yes, I suppose it is, if you take the time to consider it deeply. What I mean to say is that there is nothing magical about halm, except at those highly sophisticated levels where language also approaches the mystical. In a way, halm is less mystical, as it is less fraught with ambiguity. Halm cannot lie, as language nearly always must, due to the inadequacy of words. You may think a wrong thing, but not intentionally, if you know what is correct. And like language, halm is a skill—you must learn to hear with the mind's ear what the mind's voice is saying."

"You can hear what I'm thinking?"

He gestured restively. "I told you, I haven't the skill. But even if I did, halm is not for eavesdropping." His tone was a reference to the bugging disc. "Only if you spoke to me, with your mind, would I hear you, if I could." His hands worked at his hair again. "Yet there are echoes," he said softly. "Indistinct, but . . . and I have been deaf for so long." He fell silent a moment, looking down, then said with strained indifference, "Why you, I don't understand. Halm normally requires a greater degree of empathy than I would expect you to have for . . . such as I."

Jude considered the implications of that statement. *Doesn't he know how beautiful he is?* She decided to remain clinical. "It's not words mostly, except for the name. It's not as if you were speaking to me. Emotions, like anger." The pain of his attack lingered sharply in her memory.

"The talent is unrefined in you, untuned to the subtleties. Or perhaps when you meet other Koi, you will find that it is my own blockage that gets in the way, as it does with them. Perhaps you have full halm capacities and don't even know it." He laughed mirthlessly. "You missed your schooling, too. What were you doing instead? I was too busy learning Terran from Daniel Andreas."

His irony was still obscure, and she didn't answer. After a pause, he came back to the fire. "I'll tell you the story, since there's no longer any reason not to, and if understanding brings

88

tolerance, as they say, it will be safer for both of us." He knelt by a pack and extricated a leather-bound flask from a hidden pocket. In the firelight, the cap shone richly of hand-wrought silver. On the case Jude could make out tooled letters, worn from years of handling: D.K.A.

"This," he murmured slyly, "is one of the things you Terrans do very well." He filled the cap and handed it over to her. She sipped gingerly, not quite trusting. It was brandy.

"Where did you get this?"

"In a store," he replied tartly. "We do have them in the Quarter, you know." His accent faded as he slid into skillful parody. "How else could we make our living ripping off the tourists?"

"I refuse to be goaded," she said, and smiled as the brandy warmed her throat. "Tell me your story."

He raised the flask to his lips and took a healthy swallow. His voice assumed a brittle tone, his eyes veiled: the mask of the raconteur. "So. One sunny day nearly thirty years ago, we all woke up and found aliens in the Menissa Basin. Yes, it has a name, a Koi name of its own. And this peculiar occurrence was the first prospect of major change in a world that had existed unchanged for hundreds of years.

"My mother and father, a biologist and our equivalent of a sociologist, respectively, were sent out from Ruvala to help deal with what has come to be called the Arrival. What Terran historical accounts refer to as 'an insignificant Native population' was actually a reconnaisance team of fifty-three, mixed in with the local community of some nine hundred who happened to be living in the basin already.

"They were committed to a five-year study period, during which the policy was to be friendly, passive, and above all uninformative, even misleading, until such a time as the aliens were judged to be responsible enough to be introduced to the rest of the population . . . which, according to the census of that year, numbered around another hundred million or so. But as you may have guessed, that time never arrived.

"I was four years old at the Arrival, too young to be left behind in Ruvala, so my parents carried me with them into exile."

"At least they cared enough to bother," Jude commented wistfully. "Mine just dumped me when I got in the way."

"Such is not our way, though life in Menissa after the Arrival could never be lived our way. If we make it to Ruvala, you will see for yourself how great the sacrifice really was.

"Schooling, for instance. My parents were kept very busy. It was an emergency situation." He stared thoughtfully at the flask in his hand. "I don't think they knew it could ever be too late for me, and if they did, I never would have listened."

"Too late for what?"

"I should have been in school with the local children of Menissa, but when you are a stubborn boy, the future holds no immediate reality. For me, the aliens were far more fascinating. You see, halm skill is traditionally developed during early adolescence, in the classroom, like any other academic discipline. What tradition doesn't tell you is that if you don't learn it then, you may never learn it."

"Why? If it's a skill, it should be learnable at any age."

Ra'an shifted, irritated by her interruptions. A brief unquestioned recitation could skate along the surface where it was less painful. "The brain learns certain skills in stages. It's the same with language. I have read of the phenomenon of wild children in ancient Terra."

"Not so ancient. We have them still, a new urban variety found in the underground service mazes. But it is not clear whether those children have no language because they didn't learn it at the right time or because of some brain damage. Besides, it's not the same. They can't communicate at all. When one is as articulate as you, Ra'an, telepathy is a luxury."

"Not in a telepathic society," he insisted. "Your society is built around the assumption that people can talk to each other. The deaf, the dumb, all those who can't, are disadvantaged and must exist outside of that society, one way or another. Koi society is constructed around halm, and the same principle holds true."

"But is the isolation as complete?"

Ra'an's jaw tightened. "Oh, yes. Do you think I am outcast by choice?"

"No, of course not. But it still seems that there must be some way of awakening a talent you were born with."

"We're all born with it, dammit, Terrans too, apparently!" He was becoming exasperated. "It takes teaching at the right time to develop it."

"I never had any teaching, but . . ." She found herself speaking of the incredible as if it were a reasonable reality.

"I've tried everything!" he snapped. "I am shut off from my own people, my own relatives perhaps! Halm is total communication, and I am denied it!"

90

Encouragement was only making him angrier. She changed her tactic. "Maybe they will be able to help you in Ruvala."

He ceased his ranting and collected himself with another swallow from the flask. "Yes. I do have hopes of that."

"Please," she soothed. "Go on."

He looked away as if he regretted beginning the conversation, rubbing his forehead in tired resignation. "Well. So there were all the Terran scientists going busily about their digging and scraping and analyzing, and there was I, racing around after them. They seemed so harmless to me then, and probably, if the scientists had been the only ones to come from Terra, there would be fewer problems even now. They wanted answers, yes, but not our world for their own, most of them. Still, my elders were wary around them, and disapproving of the amount of time I spent with them, which I did not understand then, since the Terrans mostly ignored me. Except for Dr. Andreas.

"Daniel had a son my age, you see. His colleagues thought he was crazy to bring a small child along on a scientific expedition, but Daniel had that boy collecting rocks before he could talk. There were no other Terran children for him to play with, and I was there, so we learned our Terran together—me, gangling and eager, hauling Daniel's specimen cases around, and James, always scrambling behind me to keep up with me."

"He was a geologist, Andreas?"

Ra'an nodded. "Like the others, a compulsive discoverer. But somehow, of all those who came and went in those early years, he seemed the least strange—alien—to us, perhaps because when he discovered our geology to be identical to his own, he did not slink home disappointed. He decided to discover us instead.

"When he moved out of the Terran base camp and into our village, his colleagues gave him up for lost. Even the anthropologists went home to their air-conditioned domes at night.

"The process of codiscovery was exciting for a while, but after the fourth year, relations began to disintegrate. The Terrans grew bored with Menissa. Their sights broadened. Uniforms were seen with increasing frequency about the camp, which didn't worry us until we found out what they signified. Many of the scientists gave up and went home. The developers moved in. The first explorers ventured into the mountains too poorly equipped and unused to true wilderness travel to get very far, fortunately for us. Machinery and building supplies were imported to construct what the Terrans considered to be proper buildings. Once they had all the dangers worked out of the transport process,

91

more Terrans poured through the corridor every day. We began to realize they intended to stay."

He sipped again from the flask, a delicate gesture of punctuation. "In the fall of the sixth year, a small delegation, my parents among them, were dispatched in secret to report home on what was decided to be a seriously worsening situation, bad enough to require them to present the evidence in person. They left me in Menissa, thinking they would return. They never did. Three weeks later, the Terrans sent out their first major expedition to explore the mountains commanded by Duncan Langdon. It disappeared without a trace."

"What happened?" Jude asked breathlessly.

"Based on the delegation's report, the decision had been made back home to apply a final defensive measure. From a secret location within the Quarter, a barrier of halm was raised around the entire colony, to imprison the Terrans without their knowing who or what was responsible."

"A barrier? Like a wall?"

"We call it that. Actually, it's an area, a zone of psychic disorientation, hallucinations, of . . ."

"Madness," she whispered.

"Yes. I'm told it can be a rather pleasant way to die."

"Is there such a thing? Where is this barrier?"

He nodded behind him, toward the mountains. "Out there. We'll reach it soon enough."

"You mean *we* have to go through it?"

He found some dark amusement in her stirrings of panic. "I told you the dangers were more than geological. If it's any comfort to you, knowing what the Wall is is half the battle."

"Out of the frying pan . . ." she muttered. "It's not true that Langdon's expedition vanished without a trace. I've read his journal, or pieces of it."

"Brought back by another expedition's mad survivors. I've read it also. I remember Langdon vaguely. He was a religious fanatic."

Jude told herself that it was only the cold that made her shiver so. She wrapped her blanket tighter. "It all seems a bit extreme."

He grunted harshly. "One sure way to deal with a contagion is to isolate it, or so we thought. It has not been easy for the Koi who have maintained the Wall day in and day out for twenty-three long years. It is mentally exhausting, and a barrier like that does not permit the passage of halm through it, so we in the colony have been cut off from the rest of our people since the moment it was raised."

92

"So you haven't seen or heard from your family since you were, ah, ten? That's worse than never having known them at all, like me. What did you do?"

Ra'an welcomed the digression from the subject of the Wall. "Daniel took me into the house he had built in the Koi village. He involved himself less and less with the Terran colonists and their burgeoning city. He became the father I had lost, and James the brother I had never had. It worked as a family unit for a while, the other Koi accepting his presence graciously if still warily. But as the years went by, he grew moody. He would keep me up late at night questioning me about where my parents had gone—it seemed he alone among the Terrans had noticed their absence, my fault perhaps. After he had exhausted himself and me and gone to bed, I would lie awake tortured by the secrets I kept from the man I loved more than anything else." He paused to raise the flask once more, then shook it gently, assessing how much remained. "Nine years we kept that up, loving and hating like any father and son, I suppose, but with one difference. He *knew* I was keeping something from him, and with all his great capacity for forgiveness, he could not forgive me that. He never told any Terran his suspicions. Some insight and his love for the Koi held his tongue. But it became a private preoccupation. His moods grew worse year by year until it made our life together impossible.

"My nineteenth birthday arrived. That is the age of majority for a Koi, and we celebrated, but it was more of an argument than a celebration. Daniel got drunk, I got drunker, in the course of which painful insanity, I broke down and told him everything I knew, which was precious little, my association with Terrans being rightly considered a security risk. But my childhood memories were enough."

He took the empty silver cup from Jude's frozen hands and capped the flask, turning it over in his hands and tracing the tooled initials absently. "He disappeared two days later. Left me a note about taking care of James. He'd left. Without me. Walked off alone into the mountains."

Jude shivered inside her blanket, unable to speak.

Tonelessly, he continued, as if by mere reflex. "Of course, they took James away from me. Sent him to relatives back in Terra, though his home was in the Quarter and he was old enough to decide for himself. They insisted. But he came back. Six years ago, in uniform. Came to visit me in the Quarter. It was an awkward reunion . . . full of silences. He told me he was going out the next day with the Kramer expedition. I tried to

93

dissuade him, knowing . . . but too much distance had grown between us. He blamed me for our . . . his father's disappearance.

"He wouldn't even stay in the Quarter that night. As he left me, he stood in the door of his father's house and swore to me that he'd find Daniel or hold me accountable." Ra'an ended his recitation, drained, with a face as old as the rocks beneath them. The night and its winds pressed in about them. The mules shuffled uneasily.

"I've read Kramer's journal, too," Jude whispered hoarsely. "James came back once more, didn't he?"

Ra'an nodded dully. "That journal was all he had with him. And now they turn him loose in the streets to scare the tourists."

"I have met him," she added after a while, not really sure he was still listening, so lost and far away did he look on his side of the fire. "In a restaurant. It was odd, really. He singled me out of a crowd and played at riddles with me. I liked him."

"Ah," he murmured.

"He said some very strange things . . . as if he could see into the future or something, as if he knew who I was, but he kept insisting it was who I *would* be."

"Ne'e carel atha, veruth de'ir na celeratha," Ra'an intoned.

"What?"

He sighed, staring into the dying flames. "There is a sect among the Koi, called the Diamo, who believe that the future is knowable—but their idea of how to decipher it is rather obscure. That is a favorite saying of theirs: 'The future foretold by the madman is the holiest.' " He shook his head. "James. I killed them both, you see."

"Not you," she said quickly, soothingly, wary of his somber mood. "Their dreams killed them. They were caught in the throes of a vision more compelling than reality. That's the stuff martyrs are made of. There's never any way you can stop them from destroying themselves as they charge out in search of their brave new worlds, despite all your reasoned advice."

Ra'an looked at her as if she had misunderstood his entire tale. "Ms. Rowe, the 'brave new world' that the Andreases sought is a real one. It's waiting, over these mountains, and I couldn't help them to it." He glowered into the fire, remembering. "I knew I had to get out of the colony the day they brought James down from the foothills."

"Why did it take so long?"

He shrugged. "Timing. The Terrans are not the only ones trapped in the colony, remember. The great border fence was installed soon after the fate of Kramer's party was learned.

Besides, I didn't try too hard at first. Neither Daniel nor his colleagues had prepared me for those who would come after them, and I had thought I could find a place among the Terrans. It took me a while to recognize that the new Terrans didn't care how well I spoke their language or how Terran my upbringing had been. To them I was a 'Native,' and thus feared and despised.

"My own kind were even worse, in a way. Lacking halm, I was treated like some kind of deranged child, whom they felt uncomfortable with but owed special care. I couldn't bear being the object of their infinite patience, knowing that through their sympathetic smiles, they were speaking among themselves in that secret language I would never know." He threw her a shielded look, half guilt, half defiance. "As you yourself have experienced, the one thing I could express was my growing anger. Or rather, the anger expressed itself, spilling over at the slightest provocation. Only by the most rigid discipline did I learn some control over it . . . some. Not enough. It was easier just to avoid those to whom my presence was painful . . . Do you really want to hear this?"

"Yes. If you don't mind."

He gave a tired, impatient sigh and his words came like the rattle of distant gunfire. "Fourteen years I lived alone in Daniel's house, the last six of them scheming for a way to escape. I watched helplessly as the city spread like a blight across the basin, hating the Terrans more each day but knowing they were my only way out. I performed the occasional secret favor, nothing that would compromise the Koi, but enough to win the trust of the Terran Alien Division. I was aiming at a border security rating, and then . . . you came along." He flicked her a cold, pained look. "Well, you got me the pass, I should be grateful for that. But understand my bitterness when the first being with whom I might be able to halmspeak turns out to be a Terran!"

Halmspeak. She grasped at the word as if it could explain the mystery. "Perhaps your Terran upbringing encourages it," she reflected quietly.

"Perhaps," he replied, his jaw setting stubbornly. "But at least understand the injustice of it."

Jude pursed her lips, a gentle tightening against his complaint. "Ra'an, it's going to be hard to be sympathetic if you insist on treating me as a lower form of life, but I do understand. I'm an outcast, too, remember. As for justice, you talk as if it were some sort of birthright. All I can say is that if you've *ever* known real justice, you're one up on me. Justice is another one of those martyr's dreams.''

''Very cynical,'' he reproved without a great deal of conviction, as if the passion behind his plea for justice were more artificial than he cared to admit. ''Why did they put you in the Wards?''

Jude walked right into his snare. ''I was involved with the underground. I got caught.''

He arched an eyebrow. ''A political dissident who doesn't believe in justice?''

''In the impossibility of ever obtaining any.''

''Yet you went to jail for it.''

Jude uncurled her stiff legs and stretched them in front of her. ''I don't think I had fully considered the risks until it was too late. I don't see myself as martyr material.''

The fire had died. She heard him move, a shadow lighter than the blackness, saw the pinpoints of coals scatter as he kicked them apart. ''There is a certain freedom in cynicism,'' said his voice pensively. ''A passivity that frees you from responsibility . . . and anger, once you've decided that neither will get you anywhere. Cynicism is a comfortable retreat, is it not, Ms. Rowe?''

She did not exactly want to agree with him, for his tone made it an accusation, but she was too tired to think out her own conflicts between her present limbo-like passivity and her one-time impulse toward social justice. ''Cynicism is survival,'' she said, trying not to sound defensive.

''Yes,'' he said heavily, and she could not tell if he spoke in acceptance or regret. His boots ground the coals into the rock, and the wind blew hot ash into her face.

''Go to sleep,'' he said flatly, ending the discussion.

CHAPTER 16

In a cobbled square near the Native Quarter, a play was in progress. Banks of floodlights held back the night. A crude stage had been lashed and pegged together out of rough-sawn planks, and hung with painted cloths and obscure symbols woven in rope and straw. Thin banners tied to saplings revealed their colors darkly in folds of purple, ocher, crimson. At the four corners of the platform, torches burned, dulled to an angry orange by the white glare of the lights.

To the soft syncopation of a drum, the players danced and chanted.

Tourists crowded around the scaffolding, gawking at the dancers, fingering the draperies, laughing and talking and waving programs at acquaintances spied across the square. The program supplied a title, "The Tale of Danical," and a plot, but the audience found greater amusement in their own interpretations, engaging in loud disputes between self-appointed experts defending their pronouncements on the significance of this gesture or that prop.

The players were masked. The tallest wore an authoritative wooden scowl, carved and polished like an ancient icon. The mask was topped with a tin helmet studded with spikes. As he danced, the Scowl wielded a staff much taller than he, counterbalancing its weight with deft movements of his body. At the tip of the staff was a red globe, with other tiny globes set around on circling rings, like a model of the atom or of a solar system. Another player danced with bowed legs and drooping back. His mask was a grotesque of weary subjection. The drummer's mask was featureless, a wooden disc with a round hole through which his teeth and tongue glistened as he sang.

The play was half over when Verde arrived. The square seethed with frantic comings and goings, some tourists still lingering to watch, most merely glancing at the performers and moving on. With Meron bobbing at his sleeve in her persona of a Terran ten-year-old, Verde wove his way across through the crowd, keeping a firm grip on her hand. He found a free space against the wall of a café that commanded a clear view of the whole square, and settled in to watch.

The Scowl in the spiked helmet brandished his staff with a roar, and the drooping man fell to his knees, quaking. From his cloak, which was painted with red leaves, wheat sheaves, and bright-green wave symbols, he pulled a basket of little straw dolls. The few who watched closely could see that each doll was dressed exactly like the dancer, who was now gingerly laying the dolls at the Scowl's armored feet. The Scowl grabbed up the dolls and, as he danced, began to construct an elaborate doll pyramid that rose into a tower made of doll bodies. More and more dolls came out of the cloak, which appeared to be made entirely of pockets. One by one, they enlarged the tower. The

Scowl's chanting fell into a kind of litany, menacing and low, building toward a crescendo, only to be drowned out by a sudden blare of jazz and singing from a sidestreet, and doors slamming amid the calls of revelers.

Verde's attention was split between the players and the armed uniforms milling through the crowd. He eyed the Scowl with some apprehension. "Hrin's performance gets more barbed every year," he commented to Meron. "If the censors had any idea . . ."

"And the trappings get more elaborate." She pointed to woven rope totems. "Those are new this year. He's worked on them for months. Hrin puts a lot of his energy into this charade."

"Art's a handy outlet for dissent on Terra," Verde commented. "At least it used to be. You've got to really veil it now to get it by the censors." He grunted, distracted. "The police are out in force tonight. This is no crowd the kid could lose himself in."

"Lacey knows you would look for him here," Meron answered. "He's probably hiding in the Quarter."

"Where in the Quarter could he hide that you wouldn't know about?"

Across the square, a repair robot tinkered with a communications service box, unconcerned as the mob jostled around it.

"That's the last of them." Verde nodded toward the robot as it retracted its tool arms and chugged away. He glanced at his watch. "Even better than I predicted. All fixed in twenty-five minutes, and nobody's the wiser." He sucked a knuckle speculatively. "Tourists do seem a little extra-hysterical tonight, though, don't you think?"

"A few of the hotels were without power until the emergency systems cut in. And there's always a lot of hysteria on Discovery Day."

"I'm sure Lacey is doing his best to spread rumors of sabotage by the Dark Powers." Verde's worried eyes met Meron's calm ones, and they turned to leave. As they passed the café door, a hand touched Verde's sleeve.

" 'Scuse me, friend." A man faced them, handsome, smiling. "Mitchell Verde, right?"

Verde frowned, as if jogging his memory. Meron eased around into his shadow.

"No, you don't know me," the man continued jovially. He was dressed in tourist white, pressed and spotless. "Guy in the café pointed you out. My name's Bill Clennan. I'm here on business for a while. Pete Tappas told me to look you up."

Verde forced a smile, drawing an arm around Meron's narrow

98

shoulders. A weak gambit, Clennan, he thought. What an idiot. "Tappas, the old devil! How is he?" Did he also tell you that we haven't spoken since I called him an unprincipled son of a bitch and a lot worse besides?

Clennan showed his perfect teeth again. "He's fine, fine. His old irascible self."

Verde reconsidered. Good for you, Clennan. Picked up the hedge in my voice right away. He attempted a more suitable casualness. "You here on Pete's business?"

"Nah. I'm just a bureaucrat these days, taking care of a few dry details." Once again the charming grin, below opaque brown eyes. "You're with Conservation, I hear. How 'bout a drink someplace quiet?" He waved a helpless hand at the deafening crowd.

Curiosity won over caution. Keeping his arm around the little Koi, Verde followed Clennan into the café, toward a back table where they wouldn't have to shout to be heard.

"Actually," corrected Verde, "I run the local office of the Veterans of Exploration. These days, Conservation and I don't see eye to eye on the application of policy, I'm afraid. Consider me the loyal opposition." Verde watched Clennan carefully, wondering what Intelligence was after him for this time.

But Clennan nodded, the very picture of sympathy. "That's always the problem when a bureau is run from Earthside," he agreed. He chose a table away from the others, and pulled out a chair, gesturing for Verde to sit. "Didn't know you had a son, Verde," he continued cheerfully as Meron squeezed between them. "You old enough to drink, pal?"

"This is Merry, and she's a girl. Daughter of a friend. Wanted to see the play, even if it is past her bedtime." Verde's eyes smiled at Meron.

"Yah." Clennan sat back, stretching luxuriously. "Quite a do going on out there."

"Discovery Day always draws a big crowd, and this *is* the thirtieth anniversary. The hotels are bedding people down in the dining rooms. Business is booming. Been watching the play?"

"Well, I caught a few minutes of it. Looked very intriguing."

The corners of Verde's mouth twitched. "Oh, it is. But don't worry if you've missed the beginning. It goes on for hours. Spans the entire history of a mythical empire. Something best absorbed in small doses, wouldn't you say?"

If Clennan caught the hint of sarcasm, he opted to remain unruffled. "Mythical empire, eh? Whose?"

"It's not clear. It's part of the Koi oral tradition, but like most

99

myths, Danical's origins are obscure. Legend says he built the towers, that he was a great ruler who grew corrupt with power. The play chronicles his rise, the long list of his misdeeds, and his eventual downfall. As I said, it goes on for hours, and every year it seems to have been added to somewhat.''

"What happens to Danical?" asked Meron innocently as she nudged Verde under the table.

"He bleeds his subjects dry and bankrupts his empire building an army to conquer the universe. He's destroyed in the end. It's a simple, moral tale.''

Clennan was signaling a waiter. "Sounds pretty violent coming from these quiet little Natives."

Verde gave Clennan's back a sharklike grin. "The Koi have a surprisingly violent history if you go back far enough. They are an ancient people.''

"Maybe that's why there are so few of them—killed each other off, eh?" Clennan's smile was affable, his eyes probing.

Verde's shoulders professed ignorance. "Maybe so. Now they get their violence off their chests once a year performing 'Danical.' " He knew he shouldn't be drawn into discussing the Koi with Clennan. He could say his reason was to gauge the extent of Clennan's knowledge, but in truth he simply could not resist making subtle fun of the Intelligence man, even if only Meron was aware of it.

"Ah," said Clennan as their drinks arrived through the crowd. "That reminds me, Verde. You might be able to help me out with a little advice. I gather you know the Natives as well as anyone, right?"

Here it comes, thought Verde. My own fault. Meron was building a tiny house out of toothpicks.

Clennan continued as if his card had been picked up. "I'm into a bit of busy work for one of the bureaus at the moment, and it seems they had a Native doing some kind of job for them, out beyond the border a ways, and they've lost contact with him. Wonder if you've heard anything about it?" He unpocketed a slip of paper. "His name's, ah . . . Ra'an. Know him?"

Verde nearly shut his eyes with relief. They've lost Ra'an. Whatever he's up to, he's run out on them. No defection after all. Beside him, he could sense Meron stilling, as she silently relayed the news to every Koi in the Quarter. And I thought Clennan was after me! Even so, Verde was conscious of eggshells beneath his feet. "Sure," he replied easily. "Everybody knows Ra'an. He's the local eccentric. Don't know much about him except that he keeps to himself. What was he doing up there?"

"Oh, some kind of survey work, nothing important—" Clennan broke off as the café was plunged into darkness.

"Not again," Verde hissed.

There was a moment of dead silence. No one moved. Then frightened wails echoed through the streets, and in the café, there were shouts and an avalanche of bodies rising in blindness. A chair was knocked over, then another and a table. Drinks smashed to the floor. Glass and ice crunched under scrambling feet. Verde could not see a thing. He grabbed Meron's hand as it brushed his knee and pulled her against a wall, working his way to where he knew the back door was.

Clennan shouted over the din, "Verde! Where are you? What about the kid?"

"I'm all right," said Meron steadily as the big man bumped into her and held on to her shoulder.

Verde's outstretched fingers found the door latch. He yanked it open, surveyed the blackened street. The floodlights in the square were dead. Spectral shadows raced by, yelling, under the dim red glow of an emergency light. More glass shattered, a window this time, then others. In the distance, sirens began to shriek.

"I think Lacey just lit the proverbial powder keg," Verde muttered to the little Koi. He sheltered her under one arm and ran toward the square. A mob blocked the way. Police strobes flashed images of panic as he pulled up sharply and flattened against the stucco, panting already. He had read the weather signs correctly. The manic celebrating had boiled over into riot. The security police waded in with clubs swinging.

"Holy shit! What's got into them?" Clennan drew up beside him. His white shirt glowed pink in the emergency lights. As the police pushed through the square, the mob veered and surged down the sidestreet.

"Montserrat's!" Verde shouted to Meron, and plunged in the other direction. He ran along the wall, hand outstretched to guide him through the darkness. The wall dipped into a doorway, and Verde stumbled over a body doubled up on the ground. A woman moaned in terror. He stooped to help her up, but she screeched and flailed her arms at him.

"No! No! Get away! Not me! Not me!" Her fists pounded at his face. The sirens wailed louder, and more bodies stampeded by as the mob began to close in around them. A fat man tripped,

101

knocking Clennan sideways against an iron railing. He pulled himself up and grabbed Verde's arm.

"Leave her, for God's sake!" he yelled, spitting blood. "Get us out of here!"

Verde dropped the screaming woman and ran, ahead of the mob, dodging shadows that sprang at them out of blackened alleys, running low and hard, fighting for balance on the wet, glass-littered pavement. His lungs ached. Meron ran behind him, encouraging. They rounded a corner, Clennan in the rear.

"This way!" Verde's sleeve tore as Meron grasped at it blindly. With a fistful of cloth, she swerved into a narrow passage. Verde twisted to follow, but stumbled again and felt his legs sag with terrifying finality. Clennan materialized out of the darkness, caught him, and dragged him to his feet.

"Too old for this," Verde mumbled.

"Easy, pal," said the Intelligence man hoarsely. "Where to?"

Verde pointed unsteadily to where the shadow of Meron danced up and down midway in the alley. She gestured desperately for them to hurry. Shouts sounded close behind them, over the burping fire of police stunners. Clennan swore, his free hand instinctively brushing his hip. He had come unarmed, not wishing to confront Verde with a weapon showing.

"Can you make it?" he asked the older man, keeping one arm tight across the frail back. Blood ran down his jaw from a wide gash across his left cheekbone.

Verde nodded weakly. "I have to."

They ducked down the alley, moving as fast as they could through the maze of crates and garbage. At the end they turned, ran two blocks after Meron's fleeing form, turned again. Halfway down another alley, the little Koi waited panting beside an opening in the wall. The two men reached her at a limping run and tumbled through the door. It closed seamlessly behind them. When Clennan glanced back, there was no hint of a door, just clean whitewashed stone. Ahead were dark empty streets lined with little shops, ghostly in the dim light of the double moons. The sirens and stunnerfire were shut away behind a great steel and stucco wall. Somehow, they were inside the Native Quarter.

Clennan peered around uneasily, supporting Verde as the exhausted older man fought to catch his breath. He shook his head briskly. He felt stupid, out of his element, suddenly vulnerable. And he cursed what he now saw as his own negligence. He had never been in the Quarter before and did not know his way around, or what to expect.

102

Up ahead, Meron was pounding at the door of a café. Flickering light leaked through a broken, shuttered window. Above, a sign swung gently in the hot night air. "Café Montserrat," it read, in an unassuming carved script.

The wooden door was opened and shut behind them. Blundering through smoke and candlelight, Clennan eased Verde into the nearest chair and leaned one bloodstained arm against a rough-hewn column. They were in a long low room flanked with high-backed booths, tables scattered comfortably in the center and a bar at the far end.

"More lanterns in the back room," he heard a woman call, a Terran voice. A stocky black man barred the door and turned to Verde in concern.

"Mitchell, you all right?" He grabbed a pitcher from another table and sloshed dark foaming liquid into a glass.

"Yeah, Damon," Verde wheezed, taking the glass gratefully. "Just not in shape anymore. Might see if you've got bandages around for Mr. Clennan here."

Damon's eyes narrowed as he took Clennan in. "Oh. Well. Sure." He grunted and went toward the back of the café, where he could be seen talking with several people, one of whom glanced Clennan's way.

Meron was talking softly, reassuringly, to someone scrunched up in one of the booths. Clennan saw long scrawny legs in patched gray pants and large hands gesturing wildly. He could not hear a word of the frantic whispered conversation.

Verde set the glass down with an air of decision. "Meron," he called, waving her to a seat beside him, his face set and grim. Meron came over.

"James was worried," she said.

"Put me in touch with Lute."

Meron looked up at Clennan, who was still clutching his column, confused, wary. Then she looked back at Verde, questioning.

"I know, I know." Verde nodded heavily. "I picked a bad time to fall." He leaned over and muttered under his breath, "We could have lost him; now we're stuck with him. There's no time. Get Lute for me."

Damon returned with an old first-aid kit, which he handed to Clennan. "Why don't you have a seat over there, Mr. Clennan," he insisted, indicating a table on the other side of the room. Clennan eyed him suspiciously but obeyed, feeling his way through unfamiliar waters.

"Anyone else get caught in this?" Verde asked as Meron settled herself beside him with eyes closed.

Damon nodded toward the back, where a stout blond woman was bandaging a limp, oddly dressed figure. A spiked helmet lay on the bar, crushed and bloodied. "Hrin says the mob tore the scaffolding right out from underneath them. Doesn't take much to set them off, does it?"

"Not these days. Damon, we've got to take a hand in this. That mob will come straight to the Quarter if they're not brought under control. And as long as Lacey is running around free . . ."

A telephone shrilled by the bar, and Damon went to answer it.

Meron spoke quietly at Verde's elbow. "Lute says Lacey is not in the Quarter."

"Tell him I fear for the Quarter, and that if we can't find Lacey, we must help the . . . somebody else to find him."

"But . . ." Meron's childish face registered several levels of shock and apprehension. "Lacey will never withstand questioning!" she whispered.

Verde put his face in his hands. "I know. But he's bound to be caught eventually, and the sooner he is, the less chance of this blowing up into a full-scale massacre."

"And the sooner he can be forced to reveal . . ." Meron's urgent whispering died in confusion. "Oh, what are we to do?"

Verde sighed raggedly. "Better talk it over. It's your decision, of course."

Meron relapsed into silence, her eyes closing again as she continued her conference with the old Koi sitting in his garden half-way across the Quarter.

Damon hurried over from the bar. "That was Mike, from the guard booth at the gate. The police have been searching the Quarter and they just found a cache of plastic explosives in a trash bin . . ." He stiffened, realizing he had been talking too loudly. Clennan had risen and was moving toward them. "Near Stahl House," Damon finished in an appalled murmur.

Verde groaned hopelessly. "Of all places! How could he?"

"Plastic explosive, eh? How quaint." Grasping for command of the situation, Clennan yanked back a chair and sat. "What are you up to, Verde?"

Verde's fingers did a nervous little dance. "Just trying to restore a little order," he answered more steadily than he felt.

"Just trying to help your Native pals hide the rest of their arsenal?" demanded the Intelligence man with the air of one who thinks he has it all figured out.

Verde's jaw set like a bulldog's. "We don't use that word around here, Clennan."

Clennan had expected a different reaction. "Word?"

" 'Native.' "

The room was suddenly very quiet. Bill Clennan looked around him, saw for the first time the dark face of the costumed player glaring at him through a veil of bandages, saw Meron's orange tunic showing inside her bright Terran jacket. He remembered where he was. Once again, his hand dropped to his weaponless hip. "You better tell me what's going on," he growled as Damon moved around behind him.

"We don't need to tell you anything!" Verde returned hotly.

Meron's eyes fluttered open. "Lute's heard about the explosives. He's calling a Gathering."

Verde nodded as Meron rose and went to the back to sit with Hrin and the other Koi by the bar. Relaxed and still, they sat as if waiting, listening for something in the distance.

Damon produced a bottle and glasses. He filled three of them to the top and drained his in a gulp. Verde followed suit. Clennan frowned, bewildered by the shift of mood in the room. His eyes darted back and forth from the Koi at the bar to the men he now realized were his captors. Verde shoved a glass in front of him.

"Have a drink, Clennan," he said mordantly. "This may take a while."

"*What* may take a while?" The drink looked very good to him right then. He dabbed at his bleeding cheek, which was beginning to ache.

"I'll tell you one thing," Verde continued, jabbing an angry finger at him. "That stuff they found in the Quarter wasn't put there by any of these good people, the people who have just taken you in and saved your goddamn ungrateful skin, *Mr.* Clennan. So you can take that back to your fucking bureau. And the next time Intelligence wants advice from me . . . oh, yeah, we know who you are . . . they can ask for it without any of your bullshit charades! Pete Tappas!" he spat. "That crap artist!"

Damon laid a restraining hand on his friend's shoulder.

"Okay, okay," Clennan backtracked still fumbling with the implications of "Natives" like little Meron running around masquerading as Terrans. "If you leveled with me now, it could save you some trouble with the authority."

Verde fumed. "I don't make deals, Clennan. I know they've been looking for something to pin on me for a long time, but riots in the streets are more their doing than mine. You don't hear me pushing the Dark Powers routine. That mess out there is just the sort of thing I've been working to prevent since I came here! As long as you guys and the Colonial Authority encourage

105

fear and hatred of the Koi, you're setting them up for genocide!'' He fell silent, turning his empty glass in his hands.

"You ought to take care of that cheek, Mr. Clennan," advised Damon impassively. He wet a bar rag with whiskey and passed it over.

"Jesus, Damon, let him bleed to death, for crissakes!" Verde's attention strayed toward the bar, where the Koi now sat with their heads bowed. He played with his glass and chewed his lip.

Bill Clennan watched him for a moment, then commenced bandaging his cheek with dazed deliberation. "Here I am, having a nice quiet drink in the middle of a riot," he grumbled, "and over there is a goddam seance going on. Nothing makes sense in this damn place." He tore off a strip of tape. "I never used to make mistakes like this."

"Don't worry," the black man offered. "It stops bothering you after you've been here long enough."

"The no sense or the mistakes? What's long enough?"

"That depends on the individual."

"Is that supposed to make it all clear to me?"

Damon chuckled, his big head bobbing a gentle negative. "I doubt if I could do that, Mr. Clennan. Clarity has a way of sneaking up on you here."

"Yeah? Well, I'm ready."

"Are you?" countered Damon slyly.

Behind them, the person who had been hidden in one of the booths emerged. Clennan had forgotten he was there. When his bare feet hit the floor and he pulled himself erect, Clennan realized it was one of the loonies, one he'd seen before. The loony came over to them and hunkered down between Clennan and the black proprietor, arms and elbows resting on the table. He reached one long thin arm out to diddle with his fingers in the water rings left by the glasses. He began to draw, filling the entire table with damp line fantasies, except for a circular area directly in front of Clennan. Damon and Verde had withdrawn into their own thoughts, waiting the decision of the Koi. Clennan's eyes were riveted to the tabletop. The dry empty spot in front of him was an invitation, it cried out to be filled, and he watched with dreamy fascination as the madman's hand swerved across the table toward him. The loony looked up at him briefly from his crouch beside Clennan's chair, as if to be sure he had Clennan's attention. Then he moved his hand to the center of the dry spot and began to draw. He drew letters, big curving script letters in a line of moisture on the scrubbed wooden surface. Clennan read the letters to himself, and then out loud.

"L-A-C-E-Y. Lacey. What's lacey?"

Verde's head swiveled, his expression very close to dread. He stared at Clennan, then at the madman's hand retracing the letters as they dried. "My God," he whispered.

At the end of the room, the Koi stirred. Meron walked solemnly through the candlelight to the table where the Terrans sat. She had never looked more like a small child as she stood before them, frightened, at a loss.

"Do what you must," she said.

But Verde, his eyes fixed on the letters reappearing on the tabletop, could only mutter hoarsely, "James has already done it for me. . . ."

"Lacey?" Clennan was repeating to himself. Suddenly the syllables clicked in his head and became a name, one he knew. "Lacey! That kid who hangs around with you, Verde. Look, this loony is writing his name on the table."

Verde winced and let out a despondent breath. "I see that." He looked to Meron and received her despairing nod. He turned back to Clennan, his eyes tired. "Lacey's the guy you're after, Clennan . . . Mark Lacey. Check Terran records of juvenile offenders, you'll find all you need. Lacey is your saboteur, and he'll keep at it until he's stopped. Get your men on it, Clennan. Find him before the whole colony blows up under us."

Bill Clennan held himself in check for a drawn-out second, wondering why he believed this information. It could as easily be a decoy to cover the real culprits' escape, but the tension in the room told him otherwise. The revelation of Lacey's name had cost these people something valuable.

A siren screamed by outside and the Intelligence man stood shakily. "If I need you, Verde, where can I find you?"

"Here or my office next door, if either of them is still standing."

Damon unbolted the door and pointed Clennan in the direction of the Quarter gate. After he had gone, the madman moved into the chair he had vacated, the anticipatory light in his clear gray eyes foiling the innocent expression he turned to the others at the table. Verde was studying him with a puzzled frown, but Meron's concern was elsewhere.

"Lute wants you to understand, Mitchell," she began soberly, "that the major reason for our decision is that we are having serious difficulties with the Wall. We cannot maintain it with any strength in the atmosphere of psychic chaos generated by this riot. A guardian cannot do a full shift without becoming exhausted."

Verde smoothed back her flax-blond hair, then eased an arm around her. "Time to do some planning," he said.

"How long have we got?" asked Damon, while beside him the madman began to chuckle softly to himself.

"I'd guess twelve hours, maybe only ten, before they find Lacey, if they really pour the heat on." Verde drummed his fingers, then ran them through his own hair in a gesture that ended with a frantic shrug. "Once they've got him, it'll take the interrogators another couple of hours to work their way through to anything critical—as far as they know now, he's just another terrorist. Once they come up with the information they haven't asked for, they'll be all over the Quarter like a pack of army ants. He doesn't know much, but he does know that the Wall exists and that there are Others out there. That's enough to blow the whole game right there." He shook his head and looked around at solemn faces. "Thirty years of secrets down the drain. We're all in for some heavy questioning."

Meron smiled bleakly. "Electronics and drugs are no match for halm, or our secrets would have been torn from us long ago, but . . ."

"Yes, I know. The Terrans among you are not so fortunate. Lacey knew that Stahl House was a focal point, but I don't think he ever learned what it conceals. So, Damon, it's the cellars for us, I'm afraid."

The black man roused himself, gazing around his café wistfully. "A price worth paying," he acquiesced. "I'll get Jeffries and the others on the phone."

"Nuuh, don't use the phone. Mine's tapped; yours probably is too. Meron can take care of getting in touch with everybody. We'd better see to the provisioning. This could be a long siege." He called back to the bar. "Hrin, can you make it home alone?"

The Koi in bandages waved his assent.

"That's it then. To the cellars." Verde took Meron's hand. "Keep an eye on James, will you? He couldn't stand it cooped up down there, and they'll never think to haul him in."

The madman had laid his head down on his arm and gone to sleep. Pale long hair spilled over his bony elbows. Meron regarded him with fond bemusement. "I'll do my best," she said, and her brief loving smile was like a flash of sun through gathering storm clouds.

CHAPTER 17

A chill mountain rain stung at their backs as they clambered along the bottom of a ravine. Water ran between the rocks beneath their feet and in trickles down the backs of their necks. Ahead, the ravine opened into a stony depression between two ridges, the one they must climb rising steeply in a vast barren pile cut across with crevasses like knife wounds gouging the mountainside. They picked their way across the bouldered flatland and rested in the shelter of an overhang. The alien nosed about restlessly, not searching so much as absorbing every detail, every stone or patch or lichen.

Jude wiped the rain from her face with the corner of her jacket. Her skin was raw from wind and sunburn, and now she was wishing for another layer of clothing to ward off the cold of the higher altitudes. Ra'an seemed comfortable at any temperature, used to the heat and uncomplaining in the cold, warmed perhaps by his burning drive to attain the other side of the mountains. In the five days since they had first passed the tree line, their route had taken them down into the forests and back up again. Now the snowfields loomed above them, shrouded in icy mist. Jude no longer questioned how, so ill prepared and ill equipped, they were going to make it over the Guardians. The alien led the way and she merely followed, and in this acceptance, a truce between them had been formed. His pace never slackened, and often he would pull ahead and be out of her sight for hours, leaving her to trust to the mules, who always seemed to know which path he'd taken through the tortuous landscape. And their patience with her slower pace was unflagging.

She straightened from relacing her boots and leaned against the cold rough rock. "Where did I ever get the idea that the expression 'natural order' indicated some sort of organized pattern? These mountains look like some titan just threw them in a heap and left."

Ra'an came in under the overhang, pushing his damp hair away from his face with both hands as if wiping away thoughts that were pressing on his mind. "Daniel once said the basin looked like the biggest and most recent impact crater he'd ever seen. I hope he got far enough to see it all from this vantage point, because that's exactly what it is."

"One of those things from the sky?"

He shook his head, half admiring, half grim. "Battle scar. From the ancient days, when the Koi played around with the big weapons as the Terrans do."

She glanced around apprehensively. "How long ago was that?"

"Don't worry. It's not hot. It never was. Even clean weapons can topple a civilization."

"Is that what happened?"

"Several times. Or so history tells us. Until finally the weapons were put aside."

Jude sighed. A history lesson would be interesting, but she did not relish another anti-Terran lecture. She chewed neutrally on a cold protein cake and changed the subject. "Ra'an, I know this will sound absurd, but you know how there are times when you're sure you see something out of the corner of your eye, but when you look, there's nothing there?"

"That," he said too quickly, "is an easily explained optical phenomenon, especially when you're tired."

"I know that, but it usually doesn't happen as consistently as it has been to me this morning. Are you sure there's no one living up here?"

"Yes. Ignore it. Just ignore it. I told you, you must control your imagination in the Guardians."

She found the extra sharpness in his tone suspect. "Is it happening to you, too?"

"No," he replied abruptly, then waved to the mules to follow and moved on up the slope.

They spent the afternoon toiling up the ridge. Toward evening, the rain became a downpour. Soaked to the skin, they found a shallow cave to cut the main force of the wind. Ra'an pounded metal spikes into the rock and stretched out a tarp to form a slanted roof. The sheltered area was very small and crowded with mule packs and sleeping bags. He dug out an ancient solid-fuel stove for the first time, to provide the only warmth they had felt all day, and to prepare a cramped meal. He moved about under the tarp with care, as one will when forced to share an intimate space with a stranger. Rain blew around the edges of the shelter and made the blue flame of the little burner hiss and spit. The alien ate quickly, unusual for him, sitting cross-legged

110

on his bedroll, the damp tarp inches above his head. Jude sipped her soup, coveting its warmth.

"Will you tell me more about halm?" she asked finally.

"Must I?" he said into his plate.

"Not if you don't want to, of course."

"I don't." He finished eating and turned off the stove, collecting tin pots and plates into a pile. Then he said, "Understand that for you, it is just information. For me, it is . . . somewhat more." He lay down and turned his back to her.

Jude's mouth tightened. "That's not quite fair, Ra'an," she said into the darkness. "You can't just tell me I'm telepathic and let it go at that. How am I ever going to understand? I mean, what if we can, I mean, you know . . ."

"If you're going to learn halm, I'm not the one to teach you. Too dangerous."

"But what if you tried halmspeaking when you're *not* angry?"

"No!" he snarled, and as his anger sizzled in the air, she understood its defensiveness. He didn't want to know if he could halmspeak her. The possibility was more than an outrage to his sense of proper justice; it was a personal threat, an encroachment on his carefully guarded privacy.

She leaned back against the wet rock wall. Under the meager shelter, he lay so close to her that she could hear his tight breathing over the drumming of the rain. She was sharply aware of his physical presence, an arm's length away, and realized that however vocal she had been about accepting, even insisting on, his humanity, the concept had remained intellectual until this moment. Now he lay next to her and she could not block the thought of him, remembering his lean body moving ahead of her in the rain, aware of his strength at rest, his breathing slowing into sleep, chilled under damp blankets, muscles perhaps aching as hers did. The night admitted no differences of color or culture. The alien was a man asleep.

Seeing him so, with such sudden clarity, she was moved. Vague maternal urges stirred, and other urges she had denied until now while forcing his hard beauty to a distance in her mind. Here, in the darkness, where her expression could not be read and rebuffed, she raised a hand above him in musing benediction. *Child of sorrow, do you dare to hope that all grief will be ended by the return to a childhood memory? That all would be well if only you could bring back a dead old man?*

He roused, and half turned toward her. "What?" he muttered sleepily.

Her mind retreated, stunned. "Nothing," she answered, and lay down in wonder.

Her groggy head and the faded essence of dreams told her she had slept badly. The rain had stopped and the morning sky was a luminous gray the color of the rock, giving the various impressions that either she was enclosed entirely within a sphere of rock, or the stony ground itself was cloudlike, insubstantial.

Ra'an was awake and had already packed and loaded everything but the little burner, which sat on a flat stone, warming the nutritious mush that passed for breakfast each morning.

As they started out, the sky was threatening, rolling up dark banks of cloud across the paler gray. But the weather held. By midday, they gained the crest of the ridge and stood panting to survey the desolation of rock that stretched before them as far as they could see. Long rugged ranges, gray and black and brown and white, with deep barren valleys between, banded by a smoky cloud layer that isolated the upper crags in visions of ruined fortresses floating in a misted lake of sky. Jude felt her strength draining away like water through a sieve.

"How long?" she asked faintly, gazing ahead.

"Forever, if we went that way." He pointed off left to a range that differed from others only in being somewhat closer. "That way."

"How do you know all this if you've never been up here? Is this the way you came as a child?"

"Hardly," he replied but would not elaborate further than to say, "Nature provides many effective compasses, and I do know where I want to get to. I've put together a sort of map over years of listening to this conversation and that."

"Look how that big cloud band cuts all the way across the mountains. That must be one hell of a snowstorm."

Whatever he was about to say, he thought better of it. He waited for the mules to catch up, then moved off down the rubbled slope.

Late afternoon led them around a high, weatherbeaten spur. Trudging along behind the mules, Jude saw Ra'an pull up sharply at the top of a low rise, and reach out a hand to steady himself against a boulder.

"What is it?" she called.

"Come and see for yourself."

She scrambled up to where he stood. On the other side of the spur, a narrow canyon dead-ended into the mountainside. Bits of grayish foliage clung to its scarred walls. Under the rush of wind in her ears, she heard the muffled chatter of water running through rock. Pockets of mist floated in the shelter of overhanging ledges, very still despite the wind howling in the upper reaches.

Dropping her eyes to the canyon floor, she saw what he was staring at. Traces of buildings, so broken-down that at first she did not pick them out from the natural rubble. Fragments of masonry walls scaled the canyon's steep sides, flanked with crumbling steps cut into the natural rock, ending at the canyon's mouth in the scars of an avalanche. Scattered about among the ruins were bits of metal objects, some rusted beyond recognition, some of more recent manufacture: a bent tent frame with shreds of yellow plastic still clinging like battered pennants, a tumbled-down windbreak built from the stones of more ancient buildings, a fireplace half-standing, washed clean of soot.

Slowly, Ra'an made his way down until he stood amid the debris. Jude followed closely, glancing about as if she expected voices to challenge them for trespassing. The wind screeched at the canyon mouth.

Ra'an stooped, picked up a rusted tin cup. Its handle fell away in his hand. He tossed it aside, and it landed with a soft crunch. He went from piece to piece, examining each with slow care, and moving on to the next. Over the wreckage of the fireplace, he grunted softly and dug among the stones, uncovering a flat case of still-lustrous metal. He tried the lock. It held. With tools from his pack, he battered the lock, then pried it open, working at the lid with a rusted length of steel pipe.

The folded papers inside crackled as he drew them out, hand-drawn maps, yellowed sheaves of figures, printed tables, and computer printouts. They had notes and measurements scribbled in their margins, and their seams gave as he unfolded them gingerly. There were two pencils, much worn down, a red and a blue; a compass; a brass metric scale; and a drawing pen caked with ink. Farther down, a faded photo of a child, a credit book with the name McAllister stenciled on the cover. Finally, a penciled duty roster, which Ra'an stared at for a long time. Jude peered around his arm and read the names columned under the duty headings:

Survey	Site Patrol	Com	Mess
Amato, D.	Kleinst, I.	Kramer, D.	Andreas, J.
Drucker, M.	Kreeger, L.	Segovia, C.	Yung, P.I.
LeFevre, P.	Trilling, R.		
McAllister, A.			
Peety, R.			

Kramer! Andreas! The lists continued, but Jude could read no further. She could see only sad eyes above a whimsical smile. *Ah, Poor James!* She turned away as Ra'an continued to gaze at the paper, then carefully refolded it and replaced it in the case, which he stowed away in a pocket of his pack. Then, his mouth set in a hard line, he began to scour the campsite in widening circles. Jude shadowed him silently, unwilling to be left sitting alone in the wind. They moved gradually outward toward the canyon walls, where they found two large piles of stones, and a third, smaller, farther on.

"The lucky ones," Ra'an remarked tightly over the stone piles. "There was still someone left to bury them." He moved on toward the boulder-choked head of the canyon, and the mist-drenched walls closed in around them. The gurgle of water echoed above their heads. For Jude, it was like walking eyes open into the airless corridor of old nightmares, timeless, silent but for the sound of water, running endlessly.

Ahead, Ra'an hesitated before the rising jumble of rocks. His fingers twitched and fisted around his belt. "Wait here," he ordered, though she thought he had forgotten she was there.

She watched him disappear over the rocks into the gorge, and was seized with terror the moment he was gone from view. Alone, her phantoms played their tricks at the corners of her vision. Looking up, she could see only the mist hanging leaden above her. Not for anything would she have looked behind her.

She waited frozen for a ten-minute eternity, until at last his dark head reappeared above the boulders. His face had death scrawled across it, but his shoulders sagged with something like relief. Whatever he had found, it was not the one he feared to find. Jude felt a rush of gratitude that she was no longer alone with her dread, and thought then that she had never seen anyone look so drawn and tired as this man who stood balanced on the rocks, gazing behind him. The awkwardness between them forbade her the offering of the sympathy she yearned to give, one human to another, yet she wished him comfort with all her heart, and relief from his loneliness and the suffering he laid upon himself, and he stopped as he climbed down through the rocks and turned to her a face softened with confusion and surprise. They regarded each other uneasily, the moment of touching shimmering between them, he amazed, embarrassed, she embarrassed and drifting in a complex current of emotion.

Then he frowned and set his face again, and came down to her, his eyes on the ground. He held his hand out, palm up. A thin gold circlet lay there, a woman's finger ring.

114

"This one was not so lucky," he said, and closed his hand around the ring with abrupt finality. Moving back down the canyon, he stopped by a length of masonry, pensively fingering the ancient smooth stones.

"What was this place?" asked Jude in a whisper. "I mean, *before* Kramer and . . ."

"Many things. A long-ago crossroads, a center of learning, what you might call a retreat, but more properly a confrontation. Most recently, a ruin and a place of ghosts, where Terrans learn answers to questions they never meant to ask." Then, with resignation and a long slow glance around him, he said, "I am glad that Daniel was spared this death at least."

"Spared?"

He raised the ring again between two fingers, turning it in the late cold light. "Far better to lie in some unmarked gully out there somewhere, anywhere, than to die in this place, alone yet not alone. And where a son can later come to find you . . . as I found this one."

CHAPTER 18

When at last they halted and Jude had fallen into numbed sleep, the dream she could not recall from nights before came stalking her in earnest.

It began as her colony dreams always had, sun-washed and pristine, but now less vivid than before, the music and gull-beast song dimmed as if with distance, the crystalline landscape obscured by a thickening mist that clung to her outstretched fingers like cobweb when she tried to brush it aside.

She turned and found the mist encircled her. She was trapped in a cylinder of cloying white, in silence as utter and suffocating as a layer of earth. She knew her eyes must struggle to pierce that fog, that her ears must listen as hard as they could in that silence that was like a fog, though her body ached with the effort of it and her blood roared at her temples. Over the storm noises of her body, she strained to hear, and there it was, far off, a voice calling, over the grinding approach of heavy machinery. It was not a random voice. It was almost remembered, soft and sane, and it called her name. She leaned toward it willingly, weak with terror as the background squeal of engines quickened. The voice approached and enveloped her like a lover promising salvation, and she surrendered to it, only to find herself wrenched about in sudden violence, forced to face the coming thunder of the machines. Bright lights flashed through the fog, searching, and out of the whiteness loomed the giant robot claw of a terraforming tractor. The voice reproved her, lectured. There was a lesson to be learned here. But she knew only her terror as a dozen razored spikes glittered overhead and the mist caught at her limbs, shackling her writhings until she could only watch and scream as the spikes sank inexorably toward her.

Then there was a slap across her face from nowhere and she bolted up. She was wound up in her sleeping bag, and the night hung dark and quiet. A shadow moved to her side as a match flared and faded into the soft glow of a lantern. Ra'an crouched beside it, watching her.

"Drink this. It will help," he said, holding out the silver top of his flask to her. She took it with hesitant shaking hands. The liquid smelled sweet and vaguely familiar. It was not the brandy she had expected.

"What is it?"

"Sedative. A home brew. Drink it. I'm not going to poison you."

Jude drank gratefully. Waking, a sense of threat enveloped her still, a compulsion to spill her dream out Cassandra-like, but the alien's cold, stern look prevented her.

"I'm sorry I woke you," she said inanely.

"I'm surprised it took this long," he answered obscurely. "You'll get a dose of this every night from now on. You need the sleep."

"You must think I'm a terrible coward."

Ra'an grunted softly. "The Guardians demand something other than courage from those passing through their gates. Those back there"—he gestured behind him—"were not lacking in courage."

"What, then?"

His voice was low, almost gentle. "Knowledge. Conviction that a thing is what you think it is, not what it appears to be."

"What if you have no idea what it is in the first place?"

He took the silver cap from her, rinsed it with water from his canteen, refilled it with brandy, and drank. "Believe the compass in your head. It will always tell you which way is up and down if you listen hard enough."

"Not so easy when the fear is yowling inside you."

"I know." He capped the flask. "But that, Ms. Rowe, is the essence of survival. Remember that when we get to the Wall."

The drug was working. Jude yawned. The cold night seemed soft and comforting. "Ra'an, I . . . ." She yawned again.

"What?"

"Uh . . . thanks." It was all she could express of her sudden urge to reach out and curl up against the security of him.

Distantly, Ra'an shrugged and snuffed the little lantern.

In the morning, Jude felt more alive than she had in many days, alive enough to wish vainly for a bath and a change of clothes. In the Wards, a certain perennial grubbiness had seemed in keeping with the environment, but out in this wind-purified wilderness, she found it increasingly offensive. Wetting her shirttail with a few precious drops from her canteen, she dabbed fretfully at her grime-streaked hands, glad that she could not see her face, then gave up and stretched. Ra'an was awake, wandering among the contents of the mule packs, spooning mush into his mouth and counting quietly to himself. She watched as he set the cup aside with an air of decision and stuffed one of the packs with the simple trail gear they had used all along, and loaded it onto the nearest mule. The remainder, all the winter and mountain gear, over half the food, and various other equipment that had provided her with an illusion of preparedness, he gathered into a pile, then laid the tarp over it, fastening the corners down with climbing pitons. As she saw her camera case disappear beneath the tarp, she realized he intended to leave all this behind.

She struggled up from her sleeping bag. "My cameras!"

Ra'an looked up and seemed to sigh. "Still holding on to that pretense? You haven't taken a picture in days."

Jude bridled. The cameras were her last link with her former self. "That doesn't mean I won't want to!"

He chuckled dismally to himself and pulled back the corner of the tarp. "Help yourself."

She temporized. The heavy camera pack did not look so tempting. "What about the rest of this stuff?"

"We won't need it, and we need the extra weight even less. Had to bring it this far so no one would find it."

"Why bring it at all?" *Maybe if I took just one? But what about film?*

He raised his eyes to the cloudbank lying thick along the upper ridges and pointed toward the peaks that towered beyond. "I

117

never said we were going *over* the mountains, but I had to make your friends think we were."

She realized that she could not leave her cameras behind yet. She hauled the pack out and strapped it to her back.

That day's long climb brought them to the edge of the clouds. Suppressing the echoes of her dream that the white mist wakened, Jude swallowed her capful of golden liquid and slept soundly.

At dawn, the mist formed a ceiling above their heads. Ra'an loaded their packs on the mules, then shook loose a coil of rope and knotted one end around his waist, measured out a pace or two, passed it around Jude's, then tied the mules together in a line behind. He moved about his preparations with a quick, nervous efficiency, a true hint to Jude that the hard part of the journey was now beginning.

When he had finished, he spoke to her sternly, and the mules gathered around with their ears cocked.

"We'll eat as we go. There'll be no stopping until we are through this. I don't know how long that will be, but we'll go without sleep if we have to." He pulled a small plastic packet ouf of a pocket. "These will help keep you awake. Now. Listen to me as you have never listened before. In there . . ." He paused and glanced over his shoulder at the mist as if it were something living, something resistant, like marsh water or a jungle. "I can't warn you specifically what you will find. That's why I haven't wasted my breath explaining things to you. It is possible that the explanation would be more frightening than the reality. What I do know is that you will witness the fabric of your reality being stretched to the breaking point, perhaps beyond. You must not fight it. Let it wash over you, forget about logic, accept anything. Reason won't help you in there."

Jude smiled wanly. "The compass in your head."

"Just so."

"Sounds like advice for getting through a bad trip," she joked nervously.

"If that helps you, use it. Above all, concentrate on where you're going. Know where your foot is going to land every time." He turned to face the mist.

"Ra'an . . . you haven't said it, but this is the Wall, isn't it?"

He nodded seriously. "This is the Wall."

They pushed into the mist. At first, Jude found it rather pleasant. It was warm and windless, as if they were indeed inside. And it was silvery. The mist laid a metallic luster on everything it touched, the round smooth stones, the sleeve of her jacket, the swaying length of Ra'an's long hair moving in front of her. More like a cocoon than a wall, she thought, as the mist closed around them and they walked into stillness like the surface of a lake at dawn, mirrored, waiting, where a scattered pebble set up a rattling in the bones.

Soon, Jude could not help it. Her dream floated back to her. She caught herself trying to listen for sounds that weren't there. And then, as she listened, there were sounds there. Not the machine noise she dreaded, but a muttered whisper, close behind her. Reflex turned her head, but behind, there was only the mist. The whispering stopped. She took a deep breath and resolved not to fall prey to a siren imagination. She fixed her eyes to the path and the slim rope that tied her to her one remaining reality, the tall alien who led her deeper into the mist.

The murmur came again, from her left, and again, a few paces farther, from her right. Jude ignored it. Or tried. After an hour of trying, an entire conversation raged around her, within range of hearing but too muffled to be understood. The tone was clear enough, however, and it was distinctly unpleasant, especially as the voices seemed familiar, as if all her worldly acquaintances had lined up on the other side of the mist to pass around insulting remarks about her.

Jude worked harder to ignore them. She thought about Terra, tried to remember it as home, to recall the good moments. Gray images of the Wards crowded her head. She called up Bill Clennan, tried to distract herself with visions of his grinning, handsome face, but could only see the traitorous stunner spinning through the air into the dark forest. She thought of Ra'an and could only remember his cold, violent anger. Only the darker side of her mind thrived in this mist. Thoughts flowed backward and stopped where she did not want them to, and the voices nagged like a cloud of insects, growing piercing, insistent, distinct enough for her to pick out phrases, whole sentences. *Listen.* Her heart was pounding. *Listen.* She focused her attention on the alien's straight back a rope's length ahead, seeking calm in the regularity of his stride. She gave up trying to blot out the voices, and instead absorbed their judgments as passively as she knew how.

There. That was her crèche mother's exasperated sigh. Another bad report. ". . . I don't think she cares if she has any friends . . ."

And that. A cutting laugh from the leader of her cadre in the underground. ". . . never could trust her with anything, you know, important. She's only in it for something to do . . ."

Another, unfamiliar. ". . . but then all photographers are voyeurs, don't you think? Living off other people's lives . . ."

". . . a good technician, yes, but she's got no vision . . ."

". . . I never miss an exhibit, darling, but of course we've seen all this before, now, haven't we . . ."

Jude's teeth clenched. There was painful truth in much of this. *Show yourselves, you self-proclaimed critics! Let me answer you!* Critics knew nothing of vision, at least no critic that she had ever known. *Gross injustice!* Seething with hurt and frustration, she began to mumble back at the voices, then thought, no, she would tell them off later. Just now she must watch where she walked, because the mist was trying to trip her up, and if she should miss so much as one step, if one tiny pebble should roll loose, like that one there, that little silvery . . .

A sharp tug at her waist jerked her forward. Dazed, she glanced around in panic. *What's that? . . . oh, the rope!* She rubbed her palm across the rough fibers of the knot to clear her head. She had come to a complete standstill, had been staring at the ground in front of her, her mind a blank.

"What's the matter?" Ra'an's sharp query hit her like a slap.

"Nothing," she lied. "Just stumbled." Chilled to the heart, she grasped at the canteen he held out to her, trying not to see him as forbidding as he loomed over her in the mist.

Later, he doled out a meal of dried fruit and protein cake. Jude called to the mule behind her to walk beside her as she ate. She fed him crumbs to feel his whiskered muzzle on her skin, and throwing an arm across his withers, she pored over a series of names for him before settling on one he seemed to approve of. She called him Job, in sympathy for his trials in the wilderness, and her own, and made him privy to her life story, hoping to drown out the voices' slanderous chatter with her own.

Much later, though her exhaustion told her that night was approaching, darkness did not come. Only a subtle thickening of the fog and a hollowness that made their footsteps ring. The air was humid and oppressive. They ate supper walking, and the mist grew denser until Ra'an was no more than a slightly darker shade of gray stalking ahead of her. Jude swallowed a stimulant tablet and prayed for strength.

Soon she could not see him at all, or the mules behind her, though she could hear their hooves clattering along the shale. The voices too had vanished. It was lonely walking in the mist with only hoof noises for company.

When her feet disappeared, and the fog was winding itself around her waist, the first true shrillings of terror edged up her spine. Another hundred paces, and she was totally blinded, sure that the ground beneath was growing suddenly treacherous, sure that chasms yawned on either side, perhaps in front, and if she stumbled . . . something like a cold hand brushed her cheek. She did stumble, arms flailing, grabbing for the rope.

Ahh!

She felt the mule Job go down behind her, her skin prickling at his wheezing grunt and the skitter of his hooves fighting for footing on smooth rock. She waited endless seconds for what she knew must come, and moaned helplessly as his weight, falling, dragged at the rope wrapped at her waist. She grasped it where it played out in front of her, felt it go slack in her hand. Her fingers touched frayed end. As she was hauled inexorably backward toward the edge of the precipice she knew awaited, her throat contracted around screams that would not be born. Dragged to her knees, she grappled at loose stones and screamed soundlessly until she had no breath left. Panic engulfed all reason, and her mind reached out blindly.

Ra'an! In the emptiness, a distant presence.

Ra'an! The flung-out tendrils of her panic grazed something solid. Eyeless, she clutched at it.

Ra'an! A vehement wordless negative shook off the contact.

Help me! She reached again, with the iron grip of the dying, and fastened herself around the hard knot of the alien's consciousness, clinging, screaming, pouring her entire failing self into her desperate plea for help. She forgot the fallen mule, and the pressure from the rope vanished unnoticed. The alien mind bucked and fought against her storming of his private battlements, this Terran invasion, gathering all his fear and hatred into a panic as unreasoning as her own. He lashed out in defense, driving his anger like an icicle into her mind. Stunned, crippled, she fell away. Her hold on him slipped. As she fell away, all balance fled. Up and down lost meaning in the void that rushed up to swallow her, as she twisted and tumbled until every direction was down, and she fell endlessly, keening like a damned soul.

Ra'an felt the rope go taut at his waist, and followed it back hand over hand to where she lay, face down, clutching at the stones and screaming.

"The rope!" she cried. "It's broken! It's broken!"

He snatched at the rope, held it up. "The rope is not broken! Look!" He forced her head around to look at the knots, still securely fastening them together. Her eyes stared sightlessly.

"The mule fell! I can't hold on!" She wept and moaned, grasping at the ground.

Ra'an shook her angrily. "Look! Listen to me! The mules are right here! There's no place to fall here!" There was a drumming in his head, like a desperate hammering at a locked gate. He shut it out and grabbed at her arms to pull her up. She resisted, clinging still to the ground with bloodied fingers, knees, feet, all awareness of him submerged in the flooding of her panic. She babbled at his feet, a mindless lump of flesh and terror, and as he stared helplessly, a vision of James Andreas hit him with a sudden rush that left him horror-stricken and trembling. Guilt rose like gall in his throat, bitter choking guilt, and pain that took his breath away. No! Not again! Not another death by my negligence!

She was innocent. She meant him no harm. Innocent but for being Terran and a woman. Innocent but for unintentional trespass on his guarded brain, whose hypocrisy was to claim longing for such a touch, then throw it off in violence. Solitude crushed in on him. His tight-stretched anger strained until it snapped like a lute string. His reflex hatred must be put aside, was put aside, was already an impostor. It had poisoned him for the touch of another mind, a mind now teetering at the abyss. Somehow he must pull it back, or lose his own in self-loathing. Not knowing how he was to do it, he gathered his brain and called to her.

Nothing. No reply. He called again, a random, ignorant searching. Still she tore at his hands and screamed.

Now guilt raged up again, and loneliness. Ra'an panicked, and in his panic, reached instinctively with all the power that had lain locked in his genes until desperation should cut it loose. He reached, and touched chaos, and knew he would lose her unless he could descend into the madness with her and pull her out.

Afraid, damp with effort, he reached again, farther, deeper, swaying dizzily as her confusion swept over him like nausea, pushed deeper, fighting his panic and the agony of vertigo, reached, and found her, touched a shred of conscious mind that lay crumpled at the back of her brain.

Jude. He reached, felt her stir under his touch.

Ahhhhh. . . .

The shred was pliant. Amazed, moved beyond understanding, he held it in his mind like a rag doll, savoring its presence, insensate as it was, as balm for his solitude. But what to do with it? It wanted only to sleep, to blot out the terror and chaos it fled from. He knew he could not let it sleep, yet feared to frighten it further. How had his mother soothed his fears before the day she had left him alone? With words, gentle words. So he talked to it, spoke parental nonsense to it as if it were a child, and it responded without knowing it spoke.

Jude's wracked body ceased struggling. One arm about her waist, Ra'an lifted her up. The mules gathered close, lending their support. They pushed on through the mist, the alien talking to the rag thing in his mind, sparing only as much of his concentration as was needed to lay one foot in front of the other, and to listen. The mules would hear it first, he was sure, so he trusted them to lead him onward. He learned a strength he did not know he had, keeping her with him in his mind, fighting off her confusion and his own, without pause to consider the astounding thing that was happening to him. Later, there would be time for that.

Eons further, when he thought he could not go on, the mules pricked up their ears. Ra'an listened harder, and heard it at last, a low pulsing beating its way to him through the void. Elated, he pushed on harder, staggered under his burden, half fell. The signal beckoned louder. He steadied himself, struggling ahead until the mists swirled and cleared. He faced a towering wall of mountain rock. With a gasp of triumph, he dragged the limp body to the wall and gave over a portion of his mind from her care to a search of the rock's pitted surface. There! His hand shook as he laid it in the palm-shaped hollow in the stone. He closed his eyes, weak with apprehension, and willed the wall to open. A cavity appeared. Crying to the mules, he sprang into it. They clattered in behind, and the opening vanished.

Ra'an collapsed against the smooth inner wall and clutched Jude's body in his arms. His dark hair fell over hers as he buried his head in her shoulder.

CHAPTER 19

———•◦•———

Jude stirred sleepily in her void, moved closer to wakening.

Ra'an?

Here.

I can't move. Can't see.

It's the drug.

So strange.

Yes.

There's movement, sighing. Where are we?

On the huruss, heading for Ruvala.

Ummm.

How do you feel?

Nothing. Only you.

. . . Yes.

What happened?

Later.

She tried to conceal her next thought, to hold back the impulse, but it was impossible to lie.

I love you.

I know.

Is it all right?

He didn't answer, and she thought the void that held her chilled a little. She asked again, dizzy with fatigue.

Is it all right?

An answer came as her consciousness retreated into sleep, to mingle indistinctly with the movement and the sighing.

. . . I can't . . . I don't know . . .

CHAPTER 20

It was soothing, the motion of the train, so she rocked with it for a long dreamy time before she forced her eyes to open.

She lay on her back. The air smelled of lemons and cinnamon. She gazed straight up. The ceiling was a gentle brown, padded in a criss-cross pattern with silver tufting buttons on the intersections. She rolled her head to one side. The wall was paneled in dark lustrous wood with a fine elaborate grain.

She moved, tentatively. There was the firm support of a mattress beneath her, a feather pillow, and smooth sheets. Draperies hung on three sides, enclosing her in geometrics of rich earth colors. She lay in a soft brown cocoon that swayed her gently back and forth.

The huruss. She knew where she was. He had told her that, during the dim time of her confusion.

The huruss bucked softly, reawakening her. She raised a slow arm and flexed her fingers, recalling how recently she had not been able to. Her hand was scratched and filthy, fingernails bloodied, torn away or hiding dark bruises beneath their scabs. Jude shuddered, let her hand fall back on the sheet, lay still, absorbing sensations of comfort.

She made a leisurely study of the wall alongside her. Its oblong panels were inlaid with intricate mercurial designs. She searched for pictures, for a logic in them, an image here or there among the polished swirling of umber, fawn, and ebony, but their logic defied her. Each panel was a celebration of hue and movement, gentle contrast, asymmetry, yet somehow they conveyed a distinct sense of place, a craftsman's memory of weather, landscape, light, time, distilled in abstract, a Rorschach for the senses.

Sudden curiosity roused her. She was no longer content to lie still. Her back and scalp itched. A brief exploration told her she still wore her muddied trail garb, though the boots had been shed somewhere. She rubbed her nose. Dried blood flaked away.

I would probably kill for a bath. She knew then that she was feeling better.

She raised herself on one elbow and felt among the curtains for an opening. *There*. She peered through, drew one aside. The brown cocoon was windowless, softly lit from an undiscernable source. The floor was carpeted in a thick woven mat the color of bitter chocolate. Her camera pack leaned in a dusty lump against her berth. At the other end of the car, another berth lay open. Ra'an sat near it at a table unfolded from the wall, with a battered chessboard set up in front of him. He had already found his bath, for he was clean-shaven and sleek, dressed in a rust-brown silky garment that wrapped around and tied at the waist like a Terran kimono. The brown was a deeper echo of his skin; the garment draped around him with easy familiarity. Stripped of the armor of his habitual Terran black, he looked relaxed, almost vulnerable.

Jude had no idea what she could possibly say to him.

But Ra'an glanced up, and gave her a long look over the chessboard, and said, "I expect you would like to wash."

She nodded, for once grateful for his cool manner.

"First door to your right. You'll find everything you need."

Jude roused herself stiffly and padded to the door he had indicated. She traced with a finger the lettering carved on it. Never before had she been faced with an alphabet that she couldn't read. These letters looked as if they had been invented for the sole purpose of being chiseled into gleaming surfaces with clean, efficient strokes. With a not unpleasant thrill she thought, *The true point of entry into an alien land is when you can no longer read the road signs*.

"Does this say 'Men' or 'Women'?" she asked lightly.

"It says 'Bath,' the only distinction you'll find here. Just learn to knock before entering."

"Like now?" Her eyes widened. *Why did I assume we were alone on this train?*

He shook his head soberly. "It's all yours," he said, and turned back to his chessmen. Jude opened the door.

The interior of the bath was a piece of jewelry, precious turquoise set in shining wood. The wood was dark, molded in smooth curves. The turquoise was porcelain, all the fixtures, the sink, the bath, the exotic streamlined toilet, all glazed in the vivid blue-green of a tropical pool, and traced with a spider web of deeper blue where the color had settled into fine cracks beneath the glaze. She found herself staring at the toilet. On second glance, it was remarkably conventional. She gave it an amused shrug. *I suppose there's no reason to expect it to be different. After all . . .*

The huge mirror above the sink she avoided until she had washed every part of her several times with the clear brown soap that smelled of citrus. Then she confronted the glass apprehensively. A clean but haggard face stared back at her, with eyes peering a trifle dazedly out of great dark hollows that showed even through her tan. She toweled her short hair vigorously, hoping to breathe some life into it, then brushed it back with a comb carved of something like ivory, though translucent and veined with gold. A pile of kimonos waited neatly on a shelf, of various colors and rich patterning. Ra'an had obviously chosen the severest of the lot for himself. Jude found one in sea green laced with muted silver and blue, and wrapped it around herself, sighing at the luxury of its silkiness against her abused skin. *Primitive . . . ?* With a hand on the polished wooden doorlatch, she reflected that this huruss was far more sophisticated and grand than anything she had ever traveled in back home, even when on an expense account. How far astray she had been led, all Terrans had been led, by these quiet subtle aliens. She shut the door behind her, drawing a hand along the fine paneling as she wandered down the car, gathering her nerve to face him.

Ra'an was still engrossed in his one-man chess game.

"I'm starved," she announced, because she was, and because food was a nice, neutral subject.

His eyes appraised her warily. "You look a lot better than you did a few hours ago."

"So do you. . . . Have we got any food left?"

"In the galley."

The huruss possessed a lovely, compact kitchen, outfitted in brushed aluminum, milky glass counters, and more of the lustrous wood. The equipment she couldn't make head or tail of, so she began rummaging through cabinets until she found utensils and a cold chest stuffed with vegetables. Chill fruity odors filled the kitchen, odors like colors, crisp greens, tangy yellows and oranges, musky purples. She lifted out a round waxen melon, and turned it wonderingly in her hands. Ra'an came into the kitchen behind her and took it from her, gazing intently at it as if he had never seen a melon before. He held it up, and she could see the light shimmering through its misted skin.

"It's a peri," he said thickly. "We grew these in Ruvala."

But Jude was too busy with other wonders to catch the emotion in his voice. "Look at this. And this!"

She made him name them all, pushing one into his hands and

127

grabbing it away to replace it with another almost before he could speak, oblivious to the bittersweet pain of his remembering, until the counter was littered with fruit and vegetables and he was demanding in cold exasperation, "Are you planning to eat them all?"

Jude laughed, unheeding. "How do they keep all this stuff so fresh?"

"By picking it yesterday."

"How do you know that?"

"The hurra are serviced each time one is summoned." His jaw was tightening with irritation.

"Summoned ?"

"Summoned. Called for. Did you think we sat in that cave and waited for the next regularly scheduled arrival?"

Her smile died, and she turned away to begin putting vegetables back in their drawers. "Ra'an, I don't remember a whole lot about that cave," she replied quietly.

He looked vaguely ashamed. "No. You wouldn't." He moved away from her, down the counter. "It's simple, really. If you know in advance, as most Koi do, that you have a long-distance trip to make, you place a reservation at your local station. In rare emergencies, such as ours, you put in a call to the central computer, and it finds the nearest available car, or cars, if you need more than one, has it serviced, and sends it out. When it arrives, you punch in your destination, and that's all there is to it."

"Computers. Magic kitchens. Fresh fruit. Wow."

"The huruss operates all over the planet. Used to run into Menissa, but they filled in the tunnel when the Terrans arrived. My parents' reconnaissance team were the last passengers.

"I'm beginning to see what you meant about life-style sacrifices on the part of the Koi exiled in the colony."

"You've barely scratched the surface, Ms. Rowe."

"Wow," she repeated. "Who can afford all this? I mean, all *this*, for two people and . . . where are the mules?"

"Our second car is a stable car."

"Must have cost a fortune!"

"Public transportation," he replied with a trace of smugness.

"Public? You mean, anyone can travel like this?"

"Any Koi. If they travel at all, which they don't very often." He reached for a small blue fruit and tossed it between his palms with studied casualness. "A telepathic society has less need of physical journeying." He put down the fruit. "For instance,

128

there's no such thing here as a freeway. There are local road systems, but they're kept to a minimum.''

"Ah. And what about air travel? Oh, I forgot . . ."

His smugness returned. "No, it's perfectly possible, if the Wall isn't screwing up your instruments. The Koi toyed with air travel in the past, but we abandoned it when a properly clean and quiet method eluded us. Besides, we outgrew the need.''

"Oh.'' If he felt like it, he would no doubt explain this further. She knew it all had to do with the painful subject of halm, so she didn't press him. Instead, she frowned at a bank of dials and buttons. "Any suggestions as to how this works?''

Ra'an looked it over dubiously, then said, "Try this.'' A spot on the counter glowed warmly.

"The stove!'' Jude crowed delightedly.

"Pure luck. I was really too young for cooking the last time I was in one of these. At home, my father wouldn't let me near the kitchen.'' He smiled crookedly. "He swore I had no sense of taste.''

"Well, even if you'd cooked up a storm as a four-year-old, these things might have changed a bit in thirty years.''

"Not really. It's Terran thinking that machinery must be constantly redesigned, even if the change produces no visible improvement in its performance. If a machine exists to do all your work for you, that is an obviously infinite line of development. Here, machines exist to aid in doing the work as efficiently and, more important, as pleasantly as possible.

"Now, kitchen equipment,'' he continued, patting the countertop as if it were a lab specimen, "has an easily obtainable efficiency apex. There's not much mystery about what you want it to do, and they got it doing that in the best way possible years ago. No need to change it. No need to buy a new stove every five years.''

Jude grinned. "May the gods of conspicuous consumption strike you dead.''

He passed over a light enameled pot. "Fill this. That's the water tap.''

She continued her exploration while he diced vegetables with deft quick strokes, as if to prove that he could be as neat and efficient as the kitchen.

"I can't find the meat anywhere,'' she said after a thorough search.

"There won't be any.''

"Ahh, right. Clennan told me . . . but wait, there was meat in our trail rations . . . ?''

129

"You're forgetting my upbringing. Daniel ate meat whenever he could afford it, and I did what he did."

She leaned against the counter, watching him thoughtfully. "I'll bet the Koi don't distill brandy, either . . . am I right?"

"You are," he answered, his face averted. "But it is possible to get quite drunk on Ruvalan wine, I am told."

"Ah, but I'll bet it takes longer." When he remained silent, she pursued, "You really are a kind of hybrid, aren't you, Ra'an? I mean, there's Koi and Terran, and you, somewhere in between."

Ra'an slammed the knife down on the counter. Jude backed off. "Hey. Wait. I only meant that coming home will involve a few life-style sacrifices on your part also. I hadn't seen it that way before."

His fingers thrummed the countertop, then relaxed. He picked up the knife again. "Nothing I can't do without," he muttered and scraped the vegetables into the pot.

I won't miss the meat, Jude mused, as they ate in silence. *It's not as if I got much of it back home, even before the Wards. And the soy substitutes will be no loss, especially if everything here tastes as good as this does.*

"The only problem with using the huruss," Ra'an commented suddenly, "is that I had to use my name to call the computer. It'll send the information along to Ruvala. They will be expecting me."

"Is that bad?"

He shrugged, uneasy. "Leaving the colony on the sly will be considered a kind of treason. Dereliction of duty, or whatever. Also, I fear . . ."

"What?"

"You've seen them. You called them the gull-beasts."

"They do exist! I knew it!"

He stared at his plate "I couldn't believe you'd actually seen them. That was one of the first hints that you . . . It takes halm to see the shanevoralin in flight."

"How did you know I saw them in flight?"

"The only place where they come to rest in the colony is a small walled garden in the Quarter, where you could never have been."

"Shanevoralin." Jude savored the word. "Why would you be afraid of a bird?"

"This is not some mere Terran bird, Ms. Rowe." Absently his hand stroked the leather casing of his flask, which he had

130

brought to the table with his meal. "It was not the full truth when I said that the colony was totally isolated from the Koi outside. The shanevoralin bring news back and forth, of a sort."

"Like a carrier pigeon? They used to have those on Terra."

"The shanē carry picture messages, in their brains. The name means 'wings of halm' in the coastal tongue. They are . . . how can I explain it . . . like blank recording discs. The images they carry are picked out of Koi minds, little flashes of halm transmission that are vivid enough to attract the creatures' attention, as fish will swim after a bright pebble rolling with the current.

"There are some who develop a special rapport with the shanē—old Luteverindorin in the Quarter, he is sea-bred, and the shanē love him. Often they will come when he calls them, but even he can't be sure where they'll fly next."

"And what makes them a threat to you?"

"An outcast in the Quarter, an angry misfit, is sure to excite the interest of the shanevoralin. They may have brought such news home to Ruvala."

"Come on—your family will be ecstatic to see you after all these years."

He fidgeted. "The return of the prodigal? I don't know. Misfits are considered dangerous to the health of the community, and community is very important to the Koi." He paused, then went on in a rush, "I haven't seen my parents in twenty-three years; I don't even know if they're alive. I haven't seen my home in thirty. I don't know what it's like to live as an adult in a normal Koi society. Maybe it's too late to learn. And then," he continued with effort, "I walk into all this bringing a . . . a Terran with me."

"Ah yes. The rat in the woodpile."

"What?"

"A kinder version of an ancient racial slur."

He was silent for a moment, pensive, then put his head in his hands. "And then there's the matter of halm."

"But it would seem," she reminded him quietly, "that you're not as deficient there as you thought."

"Perhaps not. We'll see soon enough." From across the table, she could see his thumbs pressing hard into his jaw. He shook his head slowly, as if giving something up. "Jude . . . I have to tell you . . . you know . . . the Wall, I could have made it easier for you, but I was hoping you wouldn't make it through."

"Without you, I wouldn't have."

"I know," he said dryly. "In the end, my conscience . . . ."

"Oh." She sat back. "Is that all. Well, that's all right."

131

He seemed surprised. "All right?"

"Yes." Her tone was cool, thoughtful. "I still think there's something that would do us both some good."

"What?"

A final moment of courage-gathering, and she rose from the table. She crossed to her berth, leaving a rustle of silken fabric on the floor behind her. "Come to bed."

He didn't move.

"If you didn't want it," she said from the bed, "it would be easy to say no."

"I don't understand why it's so easy for you to say yes, after what I just told you."

She smiled wistfully. "Who said it was easy? But I'd like to give it a try, if you don't mind."

He came and stood by the bed, hesitant. Then slowly he drew the sheet aside and sat down beside her. His eyes avoided hers, instead followed his own rust-colored hand as he slid it along the pale length of her body. She felt it tremble as it came to rest beneath the curve of her breast. A ragged breath escaped him.

She reached for the belt wrapping his waist, but he stayed her hand with an abruptness that sent a thrill of doubt through her.

What if he is different from other . . . from humans? What will I do?

As if he had heard her, he reached to loose the belt himself and shrugged his kimono to the floor.

"Do you see anything that frightens you?" he asked.

She brushed her fingers across the tight skin of his belly, felt the muscles quicken to her touch. "Nothing. Should I?"

He leaned, and kissed her tentatively, suspicious even of his own desire. Her mind sought his, touched, and shrank away from the chill of his refusal.

"No," he insisted. "Not that." He hovered over her, unable now to pull away. "Only this." He kissed her again and took her in his arms to cover her body with the cool smoothness of his own.

132

CHAPTER 21

Slouched in a pool of green light in his darkened office, Bill Clennan jabbed an accusing finger at the man on the vidphone.

"Come on, Murphy, do I have to get out there and do everything myself? Verde's flesh and blood. He can't have vanished. Get on it, man!" He slapped the disconnect button, then grabbed the plastic cup he'd been mangling during the conversation and lashed it against the wall.

Five days. Five fucking days. Three major blackouts. No water in half the city, the whole colony in an uproar, repair robots on the blink. Clennan pushed his chair back with a snarl of frustration. They must have built this damn matchstick city overnight.

Clennan had all his men out on the search for Lacey, along with the reinforcements Ramos had sent in from Terra. The kid remained at large. And now Mitchell Verde had disappeared.

Verde's file lay open on the desk, clean as a whistle. Clennan found such cleanliness suspicious. He was learning a co-practitioner's sort of respect for the old conservationist. Verde walked the line of legality very carefully. He took good care of the loonies, earned his meager pay. But were the loonies the only reason Verde stuck so hard to the Quarter? Clennan flipped off the fluorescent above his head and sat in the dark rubbing his eyes viciously. He wanted a long talk with Verde. He'd sent Murphy, the only man he could spare, to the Café daily. All very pleasant: Mr. Verde was just here, sure to be back later. The black proprietor was nowhere to be found either. Only Natives, smiling and helpful, even in the midst of the turmoil that was laying waste to the city.

"Natives." Clennan pondered the relationship between Verde and Koi. It was like finding a blank page in his file. If it didn't mean anything, why was it there?

The Natives. He hadn't given them much thought before, except as a potentially useful tool in his own enterprise. Now he realized his ignorance of them was a handicap. He flipped the light back on and scowled at his desk, at the rat's nest of printouts, search reports, equipment requisitions, piles of paper he hadn't even glanced at. Waste paper, all of it, and on top a pile of dispatches from Colonel Ramos, who was pouring on the pressure.

Clennan ordered bouillon from the kitchen computer, made a face at it when it appeared, pale and tepid in its slot, but picked it up wearily. Anything to kill the taste of stale coffee.

He worried the bandage on his cheekbone. The wound was beginning to itch, a healthy sign, but one more irritant that he didn't need. So this is it, he reflected in disgust. The big favor from Daddy Ramos. The job that was supposed to be a picnic, because I was a good boy and paid my dues. Some picnic. A grimy office that's hardly any bigger than all the other grimy offices, and the luck to be standing on the powder keg just when the fuse is being lit. If I had the sense to be as paranoid as everyone else around here, I'd think someone was setting me up. He flicked the piled dispatches with an angry finger. Julia, get off my goddamn back!

Container of pale soup in hand, he rose and wandered out of his cubicle and across the hall to the dispatch room, to listen restlessly to the radio reports coming in from the search teams. Nothing. Static. Creaks and whistles. A babble of voices networked all over the colony, coming up with a big zero. Clennan shook a dozing dispatcher awake.

"Pump in some caffeine, Jose." He scrutinized the big schematic map of the colony illuminating the wall above the desks. It was colored by sector, spotted with forty green numbers that crawled antlike across its face. He squinted at numbers, noted an aggregation of them in the waterfront area, and leaned over a dispatcher's shoulder.

"Seventeen, twenty-nine, thirty, and four. If they're not hot onto something, tell them to spread out. We can't afford the overlap."

Four desks down, an operator glanced up. "Mr. Clennan, we're getting a priority-A request from the colonial police. They want more of our men on riot control."

"Tell 'em to stuff it."

The operator caught his neighbor's eye and shrugged. "Yessir, Mr. Clennan."

Riots and looting are police problems, Clennan muttered to himself. They won't give me the authority, I ain't taking the responsibility. "If they'd declare martial law as I asked them to," he complained to nobody in particular. "But no, that's bad

134

for business." As if drunken mobs roaming the streets were good for business.

He sipped at his cold broth, letting his gaze slip down the wall to a second map hovering above an empty desk, darkened but for a single bright dot. The dot was stationary. It had not moved since the audio had cut out in a flurry of muffled shouts ten days ago, but the trace signal was still broadcasting, from somewhere up in those mountains, so he kept it alive, just in case. The darkness of the map chilled him, and the pregnant stillness of the red dot. His mouth twitched briefly. He'd scoured the transcripts, listened to tapes over and over, trying to piece together what had gone on up there in the Guardians. Screw that Alien Division and their bright ideas, he thought bitterly. Not my fault that this one went wrong.

The next desk over was completely shut down. The much-publicized penal expedition had foundered in mutiny while still within radio range. The mountains had swallowed up the escapees, but for the few who staggered half-crazed back to the colony, preferring a life in the Wards to another day Out There.

Those mountains, Clennan swore. Those goddam mountains!

Then there was a howl of radio static, and pandemonium broke out in the communications room.

"Hallelujah!" A whoop from radio desk seven. "On target! Roger, one-oh, keep him in your sights!"

Clennan loped down the line of desks, checked the map. "One-oh. Larsen. Okay. O-kay! Buena Vista sector. Four and nine are in the neighborhood. Send them in!" He leaned into the microphone. "One-oh, Central, stay with him. We're sending reinforcements."

"Central, one-oh, Roger. Off we go!" The man on the other end could barely contain his triumph.

Clennan calculated swiftly. Buena Vista. The most exclusive suburbs. The kid was hiding out in the scare parties in the bungalows. Good cover. This Lacey's no fool, as we should have guessed by now.

"Central, this is one-oh. We've got a lot of dressed-up civilians here who think we're part of the entertainment. Request permission to stun if necessary." The listening operator shot an inquiring glance at his boss.

"Go ahead!" Clennan shouted. "Whatever you have to do, just get in there and get that kid!"

Lacey was out cold when they dragged him in.

Search team 1-0 slapped one another on the back in exhausted pride.

"Had to hit him full power to bring him down. He'll be out awhile," team leader Larsen explained as Clennan surveyed the boy's slack face, sullen even in unconsciousness.

"Anything on him?" he asked, knowing the answer beforehand.

Larsen shook his head wearily. "Not even a match."

"Send him down to Sensory Dep. I've got some business to tend to in the Quarter. Don't start on him till I get back." He scrawled a signature. "How many civilians?"

"Oh, a dozen or so will wake up with headaches tomorrow, but I doubt there'll be any charges. They seemed to think it was a great way to end a party."

Clennan grunted, writing. "Scare party?"

"Yup. They were right in the middle of offering a sacrifice to appease the good old Dark Powers when we came charging in." The team leader chuckled with mirthless irony.

"What was the sacrifice this time?"

"Don't know. I was, ah . . . busy. You see it, Williams?" His aide smiled out of a soot-blackened face and gestured with both hands. "Very impressive. Something with diamonds. Almost took it with me."

Larsen rubbed his cheek with a grimy palm. "What happens to these 'sacrifices,' anyway?"

"Don't know, but I'd sure like to," Clennan replied. "I guess it's not really illegal, but I'll bet someone has been making his fortune at these parties while we've been busting our asses! Break your men, Larsen, but send someone down to the Transport Terminal to get a message to Colonel Ramos. Williams, you tell Dispatch to notify the Colonial Authority. Big publicity release, all media. Maybe it'll quiet the crowds a little to hear that the cause of all this hoopla is a real live human being."

Clennan strode toward the door, his brain changing gears. Now that Lacey was on ice, he'd track down Verde himself. Give Murphy a rest. He touched his bandaged cheek thoughtfully. Verde's right on one score: One of these days, we've got to do away with this Dark Powers bullshit. Superstition is not a reliable tool for civil control.

He winced as he stepped out into the street. So late in the day, it was still like walking into a steam room. Sweaty, musty heat. Clennan loosened his collar. It even smells like madness out here, he decided. The heat alone could drive you nuts.

He commandeered a cab and directed it to the Quarter. The shop-lined streets were a mess but quieting, as the rioters regrouped in the bars to slake the thirst of a long day's destruction. The few surviving maintenance robots puttered around sucking

136

up broken glass and litter. As he rode, Clennan reviewed his strange encounter at Montserrat's: There had been the blackout, the first riot, that weird seance thing, with Verde waiting as if he knew exactly what was going on, then the implication that some momentous decision had been made, enough to prompt Verde to rat on the kid Lacey, supposedly one of his confederates, even though it involved some other kind of risk to do so. Obviously, the kid knows something that Verde and the natives don't want to get out. What? When I question the kid, how will I know what to look for? A talk with Verde could give me a hint.

The orange sun ball fell behind the Guardians as the cab moved through the entertainment district. The driver slowed to a crawl to nudge through the crowd. The power was still out here. Without the usual blare of neon and floodlights, the streets were darkly unfamiliar. Doors and windows gaped. Signs hung at wounded angles. The fighting and looting had abated, leaving the area in a state of ambiguously cheerful anarchy. Torches made of chair legs and clothing soaked in alcohol were carried high amid sharp-pitched shouts. A group mentality had invaded the streets. No one was out alone. Raucous singing emerged through the flung-open doors of the candlelit bars. The cab was turned away at one corner by a police roadblock and made a six-block detour to get itself headed toward the Quarter again. Peering through a cracked window, Clennan told himself that he was just as glad he hadn't seen the outside of the Intelligence Complex in five days. The colony looked more than ever like Terra tonight. He yawned. The soup had made him sleepy, and he still tasted cold coffee.

The cab driver swore sharply, and Clennan was thrown forward as the car pulled up short with a screech of tires. A man had backed out into the street in front of them. Thin arms hung stiff at his sides, fingers splayed out in panic. From the sidewalk, a mass of people yelled at the man, taunting him. Pale hair whirled about his face as he whipped his head from side to side, eyes fixed wide on his tormentors. He began to back across the street.

"One of the loonies," supplied the cabbie over his shoulder. "Why don't they leave the poor jerk alone?"

The man backed himself up against the display window on the far side of the street. The crowd jeered and dug one another in the ribs with manic glee. Bottles were raised and passed, insults flowing freely with the liquor. Then, from the midst of them, an arm wheeled up. A bottle flew. The window behind the terrified madman shattered. Liquid and glass sprayed all over him. He fell to his knees with a howl, covering his head with his arms. The crowd cheered and began to dance across the street toward him.

Clennan snapped a tired order to the cabbie. "Radio the police and get moving. There's nothing we can do."

The cab nosed its way into the mob. A woman hoisted herself onto the hood and waved back at the cabbie's irate gesticulations. Grinning drunken faces fastened themselves to the windows, fists pounded at the roof. The cabbie gunned his engine.

But suddenly the faces were withdrawn. A gust of hysteria swept down the street. The clamor surged to a fevered pitch. Clennan glanced back to glimpse a small orange blur racing toward the stricken madman, to throw protective arms across his chest, to plead and push frantically at his assailants as they crushed in around him. Blond head, familiar. Clennan started. Wait! That's . . . Verde's little Native kid! His hand shot to the door handle. With a shout to the cabbie, he was out and running, not knowing quite why or what he planned to do single-handed against an angry mob. He beat his way in, grabbing arms and shoulders and flinging them aside until he spotted, between the thronging bodies, the madman cowering on the sidewalk and Meron rearing up above him to face the crowd. Clennan had almost reached her when a man in front of him cried out in desperate pain, staggered, and collapsed. Meron swayed and clenched her eyes shut, and another attacker screamed and doubled over in the middle of a lunge. The mob roared. Clennan shoved aside an arm that swung at him and felt his nerves go taut at the cracking of glass against the pavement. He looked, saw a hand raised, clutching the jagged neck of a bottle. The mob surged violently around him and roared again in unison as the hand ripped downward, then up and down again. The madman shrieked like a soul in hell. Clennan tore his stunner from his belt and fired point-blank ahead of him. Bodies stumbled and fell. A woman clawed at his face, her nails raking the bandage from his newly healing jaw. His free hand whipped out. He slashed it across her mouth. He found himself against the wall, leveling the stunner at the howling crowd, bawling at them to back off, as the squeal of sirens hit his ears.

The police stormed in with heavy stunners and sticks. The mob broke in all directions. Clennan flashed an ID, yelling for an ambulance, then lowered his gun and stared, frozen, at the fragile body sprawled on the concrete. Blood was matting already in the golden hair. As he stared, the madman crawled over,

138

to take the broken head in his lap. He bent over it, rocking and weeping. Dark ribbons dripped along his knee.

Clennan turned his back. He wiped his mouth and there was blood again, the taste of it on his tongue, mixing with cold stale coffee. The madman keened and keened.

An officer elbowed through the cordon to pull Clennan aside. "Got someone here who claims to be a relative, but . . ." He indicated a fair-haired woman in an orange tunic.

"Let her through," Clennan snarled breathlessly. "Where's that fucking ambulance?"

"On its way, sir. They're busy tonight."

The woman knelt beside the body, touched the bloodied hair just once, ever so gently, then turned to Clennan. "Let us take her home."

"Lady!" the officer broke in. "She's got to get to a hospital, and fast!" He shook open a blanket. "These people don't understand about hospitals, Mr. Clennan."

The Intelligence man shot out a restraining hand. "Let them go," he ordered. "It's too late anyway."

"There'll have to be an investigation, sir . . ."

"Let them go!" Clennan helped the madman to stand and lifted Meron into the cradle of his thin arms, then turned to the Koi woman. "If he's too weak, I'll carry her," he began, then wondered what had made him offer what he knew would be refused. The answer came to him too fast. Guilt.

But the woman regarded him without rancor. "No, thank you, Mr. Clennan. James can manage." They turned to go.

"What was this all about?" asked the officer blandly, recorder in hand.

Clennan stared past him at the retreating forms balancing their sad burden up the street. "Xenophobia," he muttered, and the word rang in his head as if newly minted.

The officer shrugged. "Oh, yeah?" he said and walked away mumbling into his recorder. An ambulance drew up. White-coated orderlies piled out to dump the injured inside, slam the doors, and speed off. The remaining crowd was herded down the street, grousing at the end to their excitement. Clennan thought he heard an occasional drunken laugh. There's no way I'm going hunting for Verde in the Quarter tonight, he mused numbly, as yellow streetlights flicked on along the pavement.

"You want a ride, Mr. Clennan?" The officer waited at the door of his cruiser. The cabbie had long fled, but Clennan shook his head. The officer nodded dubiously and drove off.

Bill Clennan stood alone on the glass-strewn street for a long moment, looking at the blood drying on his sleeve. Then, telling himself all the while that he was going soft, yes, for sure, he leaned against the wall and retched until he had barely strength to breath.

CHAPTER 22

The deep-cellars of the Native Quarter were the masterwork of thirty years in exile. Thirty years before, an ancient tunnel passed under the lakeside village of Menissa, the huruss route across the basin. Now that tunnel ended under the foothills of the Guardians, its continuation hastily filled in by the Koi to prevent discovery by the Terrans as they blasted into the rock to erect their high-rises. But under the Quarter, a section had been left open, and above it and below it, the Koi carved out the deep-cellars.

The upper levels, the least secure, were earthen-walled, shored with wooden beams carefully doctored to look older than they were. These were used as cellars might be expected to be used, for storage and curing. Sacks of potatoes and other root crops waited along the walls. The shelves were lined with ceramic crocks. The middle levels, which began the descent into the bedrock, were an empty and diffuse warren of dead-end passages, littered with the refuse of unfinished digging, meant to imply a task abandoned incomplete. Actually it was an intricate maze, a defense against intruders. If the signposts were known, a path could be found through the maze that led to the lower sanctuaries, where the Koi had burrowed out of solid rock a complex of halls and living quarters large enough to secure the entire population of the Quarter, twelve stories below the surface.

Here, beneath the weavers' cooperative known as Stahl House, was concealed the workroom of the true "Guardians" from which the Wall was generated.

The deep-cellars now also hid twelve Terrans, who received the news of Lacey's capture over the colony's public radio station with a mixture of relief and dread.

"At last!" Verde paced, terrierlike. For five days, he had haunted the radio, straying from it only to eat or grab a few hours of fitful sleep. Luteverindorin had been concerned about the radio, fearing detection of the cable, but Verde had pleaded for some direct link with the events outside, and his companions had been grateful as well, for he would have driven them crazy without something to keep him occupied.

"At last!" he repeated. Now he could move on to his next worry.

The two other men in the lantern-lit cavern exchanged glances. Ron Jeffries pushed his cabbie's hat back on his scarred forehead and stabbed a needle through the shirt he was repairing. "Bunch of morons. Five days, for crissakes. Shit, did I overestimate them."

"Or underestimated Lacey," put in Damon quietly, rising from his crouch by the radio. He maneuvered his bulk gracefully to a crate and picked up a notebook and pencil.

"Nah," said Jeffries. "Young Mark knows his stuff. I tried to tell you that. His old man and I worked demolition in the Army Engineers before I joined Intelligence. He was good, but the kind of guy to pass a skill on to his boy without thinking what the kid would do with it."

Verde moved around in the shadows restively. "Now we wait and see how much they pry out of him. Dammit, I want to get up there, get the feel of it. I can't do any good sealed in down here!"

"You can keep your mouth shut down here," returned the black man with uncharacteristic brusqueness. "Lissa said there's been some Intelligence guy in the café every day looking for you."

"Yeah. Murphy. Who the hell's Murphy?"

"Another moron," Jeffries supplied.

Verde grinned in spite of himself. "Ron, you're one hell of an advertisement for your old employer."

Jeffries nodded slyly and went on sewing.

"Is Clennan a moron?" Damon asked.

Jeffries considered. "Maybe half a moron. Nah, I don't know. More interested in getting ahead than in being a good eye, as I remember. I could name you more than one head Bill Clennan stepped on on his way up, but he's clever about it—you know, the glad hand, the big smile, and most of the jerks never notice the bootprints on their skulls."

Verde rubbed a palm against the chiseled rock wall as if trying

141

to will it away. "Lute said this morning that the Wall is down to half strength."

"They shortened the duty shifts again yesterday," added Damon. "Hrin came by while you were asleep, looking like death itself. He said fighting the interference from the rioting is draining even the strongest of them."

"With Lacey out of action, that should quiet down a little," said Verde without much hope.

"I wish I understood this halm stuff better," Jeffries mourned.

"If the Wall is like a radio signal," Damon explained simplistically, "the random psychic energy of the mob is like static jamming it."

"It's not just the rioting, it's the sheer numbers of Terrans in the colony now. Even standing still, they generate interference." Verde leaned against the rock with an explosive sigh of frustration. "Lacey, Lacey, if only you'd listened."

A wistful grin lit Jeffries' eyes. "Maybe, if we get lucky, and they don't find us or blow us up trying, maybe the Koi will evacuate us to the Interior. I'd like that." The lantern hanging by his head threw his weatherbeaten face into harsh relief. He looked like a wiry little gnome bent over a bit of mischief.

"No," Verde chastised. "We have to stay where we're needed."

"For what? You yourself said we weren't doing any good down here, and up there we'll all be marked men when Lacey gets through singing his song."

Verde's frail back straightened. "The Koi have been living in exile for thirty years."

"Not all of them." Jeffries' red beard framed a dreamy gnome-smile. "When I was a kid back on Terra, there was still a little preserve near Inverness that I went into a lot, just to wander. Oh, it was all rock and heather, land they just hadn't gotten around to building on yet, but I had this fantasy, you see, that one day, if I wandered long enough and far enough, I'd find a place that nobody else knew about. Something untouched. A stream, full of white stones and ripples, a little pool with grassy banks, dappled with the sun or bright in the full moon. Something like that. My place, you know? Where I could stay forever, safe, and no one would bother me." His grin broadened. "Such dreams I had as a kid!"

"Not an uncommon fantasy for a Terran kid," said Verde dryly, guarding his own sun-dappled inner visions.

"True. But someday," and Jeffries' eyes were serious over his grin, "I'll find that place, Out There."

"I hope you do, Ron," said Damon.

"That's running away." Verde's tone was hard.

"Ah, perhaps, but you were running, too, when you first came here. We all were. Where's the shame in running if there's no hope left where you are?"

"There's always . . . ." Verde broke off as the canvas at the entrance was drawn aside with a heavy rustle. "Lute! Sneaking up on us again!" He waved a relieved welcome. "They caught Lacey, did you hear?"

"Yes."

The strangeness in the old glassmaker's manner brought them up short, the unnatural stiffness of his ancient back, the pause as he waited for their attention. Damon rose uneasily. Jeffries laid his needle down.

Verde wet his lips. "What is it, Lute? What's happened?"

Lamplight flickered across Lute's silvered face, glimmered in the tears gathered in the corners of his eyes. He moved aside, holding back the door drape, and James Andreas stepped into the room. He carried in his arms a limp bundle wrapped in the sheer yellow linen woven by the Koi for one purpose only.

Verde's blood thinned to an icy trickle. He reached out a hand, let it fall. "Who is it?" He saw now, behind James, Lissa waiting, and behind her Hrin and many others of the Quarter, filling the twisting dark corridor as far as he could see. James bowed his head over the shrouded form in his arms.

"It's Meron," he whispered.

Verde turned pleadingly to the old man, begging a denial, but Lute nodded, and his tears began, gently, to wet the furrows in his cheeks. Damon murmured a prayer in his ancestral tongue. Verde was conscious only of the anger wrapping its claws around his heart.

"How?"

"The mob. She tried to rescue James. They killed her instead."

Jeffries bowed his head, while Damon wept unashamedly. Verde moved close and, in the silence of death that fell among them, folded back the linen around the head. The sight of her numbed him, the tawny still face, flaxen hair washed clean, the bloodless white-edged gashes across cheek and throat. He traced his thumb along the line of her jaw and drew the linen back in place, then raised his head to exchange a look of misery with the one who carried her, and found not misery or madness but cold hard sanity, staring with sudden authority out of the ravaged face of James Andreas. A dim primal reflex trembled in Verde's gut.

"James . . . ?"

143

The gray stare was unblinking. "Yes. I am here."

"My God." The trembling descended to his legs. He backed up a step, but Andreas' eyes held him like a vise.

"First we must mourn her," Andreas murmured, but Verde heard it as an order.

"Yes." He mastered his trembling with his grief. Remembering the broken child within the shroud, he put aside his awe, for there were last honors to be paid and farewells to be said before he could grapple with the miracle he saw now burning in the eyes of James Andreas.

"Damon," he said, his tongue like dust in his mouth. "Call the others."

Down the winding vaulted stairs the solemn procession moved, nearly three hundred strong, Andreas tall and stately in the lead, Hrin beside him raising high a torch that glistened on the silvered head moving in step behind them. Down, down, and through a natural cavern where their sandaled footsteps echoed with the dry rustle of the autumn wind and the torch flames lit the walls with winter amber. Koi and Terran, they crossed the floor in a long flickering line. Before the farthest wall, Hrin lowered his torch. Luteverindorin stepped forward to fit his palm into a hollow in the rock. The opening appeared. Quenching their torches one by one against the stone, the line passed through, Hrin waiting at the door like a solemn angry god until the last had gone. Then he followed, and the opening sealed itself behind him.

They walked through arching smooth-walled corridors pooled with the pale light of suspended globes. Faint breezes sighed along the polished stone. Verde walked and mourned a long dry mourning, but the icy claws still fisted around his heart, and at the back of his brain, he pondered the wonder of James Andreas.

They brought her down the long corridor and up the endless crooked stair to a windy cave where the lake waters rushed in through secret passages. They laid her on the stone bier of Menissa's ancestors, set on a ledge above the waves, and ringed the bier in silence. As they stood, a flock of gull-beasts swooped in on the wind, circled low about the gathering, and settled with a thunderous clapping of wings on rock shelves high above.

Luteverindorin approached the bier and laid a wrinkled webbed hand on the shrouded head. He unwrapped the linen until it lay in folds of soft yellow around the body, then, bending, kissed the forehead, and stood back, his arms raised in final salute.

"Dur manit ma!" he cried out.

"Ma degenit su," three hundred voices chorused.

144

Now may she return, Verde intoned silently.

The bier glowed orange-, yellow-, white-hot. There was a crack and flash and in one searing fireball, the body was consumed. Hot wind pulled at Verde's eyelids as he closed them against such awful finality.

When the bier cooled, there was ash, white and fine as the furred breasts of the gull-beasts. Luteverindorin unwound a strip of yellow cloth from his wrist and swept them carefully into an earthenware bowl. As he bore it around the horseshoe from Koi to Koi, each laid a finger to the ash and touched it to his tongue.

He came to Damon Montserrat, who touched the ash and crossed himself.

He came to Mitchell Verde, whose hand shook as he raised it to his lips.

He came to James Andreas. Andreas touched the ash, and his fingers to his tongue, then cupped his hands around the old man's on the bowl. Old Koi, young Terran, they gazed deeply into each other's eyes. Verde watched with sudden stabbing intuition. Halmtalk!

And Lute nodded, his own solemnity touched with a certain awe. Andreas took the yellow cloth and bound it around his pale forehead. Then he grasped the bowl in both hands, stepped to the edge of the ledge.

"Dur manit, ma degenit su!" he cried, and flung the bowl into the tumult of water below. The strip of yellow whipped about his head like a banner. The shanevoralin rose as one from their perches and wheeled, screaming, above his upraised arms.

CHAPTER 23

The huruss cannoned smoothly down its bedrock tunnel, but Jude tossed in her berth and moaned, then jerked awake, sweating and shaken, when Ra'an touched on the light above her head.

His dark faced frowned. "Nightmares? Still?"

She shivered. "This one had real people in it. James, your

. . . James Andreas, and that man who takes care of him, in a huge cave with a lot of Koi.''

"But you've never seen any other Koi."

"I knew who they were, as you do in dreams."

His frown deepened. "What were they doing?"

Ouside the small pool of light around her berth, the car was shadowed, earth-brown and mysterious. Jude gathered the bed quilt around her knees, grateful for his questioning, for the compulsion to fell him her dream was this time too strong to resist. "There was a carved stone bier and a little shrouded corpse, a child or like a child, with hair so blond it shone like silver through the shroud. The . . . James stood beside her, then turned his head and . . . looked at me, as if I were there, then there was a great burst of flame and I heard the gulls . . ."

Ra'an lowered himself to the edge of the berth. "He *looked* at you?"

Jude nodded and shivered again. "As if he wanted to make sure I was watching."

His long fingers tied speculative knots in the silken fringe of the quilt. "This is a traditional Koi funeral rite that you have dreamed, a ritual you could have no knowledge of. Your other dreams, were they like this?"

"Not so . . . real, so complete, as if I were there. The others were like watching from a distance."

"I attributed the dreams to the influence of the Wall, but we're free of that now." He fell silent, staring at the carpeted floor, then spoke again, wrapping himself in a cool didacticism. "One of the properties of halm is that the shock of a traumatic event befalling one portion of the population is instantaneously transmitted to the rest . . . or so they tell me. As a still-unpracticed telepath, your mind is most receptive during sleep. Thus it is possible to assume that you dreamed the truth, as it was happening. Describe it to me again."

As neutrally as she knew how, Jude said, "Ra'an, I could show it to you."

"No."

"As you wish." She began slowly, resurrecting her dream in meticulous detail from out of the obscuring gauzes her brain had already laid over the painful memory. Talking, building the picture in her mind, she saw again the circle of mourners, the swooping gulls. *Perhaps I can just send it to him, like a videgram. It can kind of play in his brain without violating privacy, be there before he knows any better.*

Ra'an listened to her careful words describe the taut profile of

James Andreas bending over, lowering the yellow shrouded bundle to the bier, while internally Jude focused the image and thought hard of sailing it at him like a glider. *Is this how they do it?*

". . . and the old man pulled aside the yellow cloth, and Andreas turned and—" Ra'an jerked away sharply and she knew the image had found its mark.

"Meron!" he gasped. He was too stunned to object to her trespassing. He rose and paced the length of the car. "And James, he seemed so . . ." Gripped by a sudden invasion of thought, he shot a hand out to the wall for support and shook his head in denial. His mouth worked soundlessly, just the barest escape of breath, then he mumbled, "Ah, James . . ."

"Different!" Jude breathed. "Why did he seem so different?"

Ra'an turned away, brushing the back of his hand across his eyes in his characteristic gesture of distress.

"Ra'an?"

"It's nothing. I . . . just had this . . ." Again, the hand across the eyes. "I don't know. For a moment there, I felt as if he were looking through you, at *me*. I . . . no wonder you wanted to show it to me." Further realization brought bitterness seeping back into his voice. "You're not supposed to be able to do that, sneak up on me like that. What kind of telepath *are* you?"

Jude tried to meet his glare, could not, and looked away with an earnest apologetic shrug. "A Terran telepath?"

Only hours later, she was shouldering her camera pack to join Ra'an where he waited alert and silent by the huruss door. She had no idea what time of day it was, or night, and remembered how it was only prison routine that had told her in the Wards. She fussed at her freshly laundered trail clothes, sorry to see Ra'an tight in his Terran black again.

Ruvala. Home of angels? She was about to find out. A worm of doubt worked at her anticipation. *What if they will not have me?*

The huruss broke its flight in a long gliding hiss. Jude braced her knees against a jolt that never came. She was unaware of the moment when motion ceased, just that a wakeful hush had settled over them. The huruss had stopped. Ra'an's silence radiated a steady pulse of anxiety that pounded against her eroding confidence. But she held herself still. There was nowhere to run, and what could her doubts and waiting be compared to those of the returning exile beside her?

The door sighed open.

First reflex was terror, and stumbling backward, hands raised as if against a blinding light. Sound and light. A concussion of birdsong, a firestorm of sun and shadow, dazzling pinwheel color, odor, taste, coolness and heat, an assault, an anarchy of sensation, rushing, laughing, wooing, engulfing until touch was all that remembered reality and she reached out blindly for the solid anchor that might slow her tumble into the maelstrom. Her fingers found wood and cool metal, and she relaxed, trusting the lessons learned at the Wall. She let the torrent surge around and through her until she floated upward without panic and rode it like a streamborn leaf.

With the easing of her heartbeat, the chaos receded. Out of sensual riot, fragments coalesced, perception was reordered, not into normalcy but close enough to sanity for a mere human to grasp.

The landscape breathed. It would not admit to a steady here and now, but like a proud beast exhibited its inexorable slow fluxing for all to see. Eons ago, at the window of a high-rise hotel room, Jude had resisted this rhythm, fearing that loss of self that humans label insanity. Now that rejection itself seemed insane. Why resist, if acceptance brought divine visions in the very particles of light? There was magic in the sparkle of water against the forest greens, magic in the flow of wind and pinesap, of warmth across the cheek, in the arching of the back and the stretching of arms and hands and fingers, magic and gentle ecstasy.

A bird sang close by. Jude sighed from every bone and nerve, woke from her reverie and stood unaided, calm.

"Welcome home, Ra'an," she said to the alien beside her.

"Even so . . ." he murmured.

For a long while, they remained at the doorway, staring, absorbing, regaining their balance.

Ruvala Station.

"What do you see?" she asked at last, for it was not immediately obvious.

The Koi in him understood, though he began haltingly. "More beauty than even a biased memory could conjure, yet it's only . . . here, a wooden platform, weathered, footworn."

"I see parts of it that are newly laid, there, so fresh the sap's still beading on the boards."

"Some benches there, with low backs."

"And others over here?"

"A peaked roof above, and carved support posts twisted with vines and purple flowers."

148

"Do you see a hint of frost on the leaves?"

"And wait . . . a bird?" He squinted upward, unsure.

"Yes!" Jude laughed delightedly. "Singing us a welcome."

Ra'an ventured a careful step onto the platform. "He seems to be the only one," he observed, perhaps with relief.

They agreed that the station was deserted, despite Jude's conviction that there had been voices to be heard a moment ago. By the sun, it was late afternoon in Ruvala, warm and fragrant, deep summer. The station sat in a clearing, not wide but very green. A stream fell in a rainbowed arc to the grass from a semicircle of cliff. Nearby, the dark hole of the huruss tunnel pierced the rock.

The rock was rock, steady as it had been for centuries, the tunnel only slightly less ancient than the rock. But the stream was another matter.

"It wavers," Jude pointed out. "As if it weren't quite sure where it was meant to run."

"Time and change," Ra'an supplied.

"Time . . . the tower! My first day in Arkoi!" She explained her double vision from the monorail. "Image overlaid on image, echoes, like this!"

He nodded. "I remember this stream from when I was a child, but it's changed course a bit since then, so what I see is both of them, what it was then and what it is now."

As he said it, a shiver pricked her skin. An echo of Andreas, who had insisted he saw not her but what she was to be. "Ra'an, I have no past here, so what am I seeing?"

"Describe it to me."

"There are many streams, coexisting, but one of them doesn't shimmer like the rest and that's the real one, the now. Somehow I can tell that."

His mouth pursed thoughtfully. "All of its pasts, with no memory of your own to take focus from the rest? Perhaps. As you spend time here, you'll find your brain learns how to sort it all out, to let the present come through strongest."

"Thank heaven. Right now I'm not sure I'd know where to step. The few flashes I had like this in the colony terrified me. I thought I was going nuts." She let out a long shuddering breath. "Is this what Langdon, what they all tried so hard to capture on film?"

"No doubt. The Wall now dampens this phenomenon in the colony, but Langdon went out before the Wall had built to full strength."

Jude sighed again, and admitted defeat. "Ah, Ra'an, no won-

149

der you sneered at my cameras. I might as well junk them here and now. No mechanical device is going to capture this! I mean, it's *behind* our eyes, really, isn't it?''

He shrugged. "I don't understand it myself. But they say wherever there is halm, this phenomenon persists."

"It's glorious, isn't it? Like hearing all the harmonies in a piece of music simultaneously. Color so vibrant, light as if it were alive!" She stretched rapturously. *Who needs cameras!* "And those trees . . . !"

"Yes. The trees." Ra'an had seen them and was smiling a smile at last unmarred by bitterness. "The trees *are* Ruvala," he said softly.

Beyond the stream, the trees began. They rose like the piers of a cathedral, soaring from bases as broad as houses into a green infinity. There was nothing wavering about the trees. They glowed with ancient life, their image clear and sure.

"Past or present make no difference to the trees," Ra'an remarked, and Jude nodded. His cryptic statements were beginning to make sense to her.

She left her camera pack lying on the platform and followed a faint path through the sweet-smelling grass. Crossing "stream present" on warm flat stones, she approached the first tree joyously. Up close she lost all sense of the whole. The tree was a spread of massive trunk whose rugged bark called out for a loving caress. Where the base split into arching roots, age and weather had hollowed out caverns higher than her head. Inside it was dark and smelled of earth. Green and golden light flickered through the vaulted openings and dropped stained-glass patterns on the dirt floor. Jude laid an ear against the inside wall, and the tree sang to her, in the most profound of basso groans that vibrated in slow, swaying chords from its taproot mining the bedrock up through every cell to where the wind plucked at its highest branches. It sang of age and storm and fire and the myriad tiny lives passing like seconds beneath its canopy, and Jude's listening was like a sleep.

And then another voice came singing through the forest.

Jude woke, and peered out from her woody cavern. A creature approached, gliding through the tall fern undergrowth with the wary grace of a fawn, a form in motion the colors of the forest, a dark head passing through haloes of sunlight. Smaller dappled creatures leaped along at its side.

One of Arkoi's angels, at last? She watched it from her hiding place, nervous, elated. It stopped a few paces away, listening, a very young and human-looking angel with black hair flowing

150

around bright eyes, which it focused directly on the tree with a puzzled expression. Jude shrank against the inside trunk, then thought, *But wait, I'm not afraid,* and stepped slowly forth. The young angel did not seem startled, only vastly curious. It looked her over as if confirming to itself that she was real, then with a look of comprehension, a beatific smile spread across its face. It warbled at her, incoherent music, and she smiled back, understanding nothing but its tone of amazed discovery. The companion creatures squeaked and bounded in circles around them.

Ra'an's voice rang out from the station. The angel turned eagerly, straining to see through the tree trunks, as if Jude were seeing it for the first time, it became human, male, a dark-haired adolescent full of bright impatience who gestured for her to follow as he jogged off toward the clearing, surrounded by his leaping retinue.

At the platform, Ra'an was unloading the mules. He looked up at the little group trotting across the grass, and waited unmoving as the young stranger came to stand directly before him like a mirror image. Watching them face each other, Jude was amazed that the resemblance had not struck her immediately, the same long lean body, the blue-black hair, the russet skin. Doubled, their beauty dazzled her.

Ra'an said nothing, made no gesture of greeting. He stared at the boy, waiting, a dark contained presence against the child's mobile warmth. So alike, yet not alike at all.

Jude wanted to break through this tension, to urge Ra'an to speak, to give a little just for once, but sensed the monumental effort going on inside him.

Oh God, let him hear. But the stranger's smile showed only eager deference.

Ra'an's shoulders sagged. His eyes shut, a terse flick, then opened in a face set hard against despair. The boy's youthful patience broke. He warbled more of his gay music, and it was language this time.

"Comea, malin," he said to Ra'an, with a bow so slight it might have been a shifting of his weight, or a reaction to standing still for such long minutes.

"Comea," Ra'an replied slowly, hoarsely.

The stranger ducked his head with a bashful grin. "Lo mana malin dai," he offered. "Elgri."

"Malin . . .?" Ra'an looked completely dumbfounded.

The boy nodded.

"What's he saying?" Jude demanded.

151

After a moment, Ra'an replied, "He said: 'Welcome, I am your brother Elgri'. . . . I never had a real brother."

Elgri was unperturbed by Ra'an's doubting frown. "Elgri tel-Yron Nari," he continued.

"Nari means 'the youngest of his parents,' " Ra'an supplied.

Jude took a step backward. "Ra'an, how can you doubt him? Look at the two of you! Surely not all Koi could be as much alike!" She held out an impulsive hand to Elgri. "My name is Judith . . . oh." She stopped, flustered. *Do the Koi shake hands*? But Elgri had attempted in a split second to figure out her intention. He took her hand but did not shake it, and they regarded each other awkwardly for a moment, then burst into simultaneous giggles like old school chums.

Ra'an watched them laughing together. "Tho manit Gemai'an," he broke in stiffly. In his mouth, the language was not music. "Terran," he translated, to make sure his barb hit both targets.

Elgri sobered, measured Ra'an briefly, glanced back at Jude. Then his grin blossomed again, and his shoulders heaved with an insouciant shrug as he let forth a stream of chatter so voluble that even Ra'an eased his guard a little and shook his head, more a tremor than a negative. "He says . . . he says you laugh too much to be a *real* Terran. What other kind of Terran does he think there is? And he also says that I am too much like my . . . our mother, to be as bad as they say I am."

"They?"

"The shanevoralin, I have no doubt."

Elgri caught the word. "Shanevoralin m'e anahir peo," he remarked with a gesture of youthful dismissal.

Ra'an looked at him oddly, asked a question. Elgri laughed and shrugged again.

"He says," Ra'an translated slowly, "that the shanevoralin don't tell the truth anymore. That they come from the colony filled with images that can't be true." His tone sharpened. "What, does he think they make it up, the shanē who have no thoughts of their own?"

"Ra'an, be patient. Perhaps he's too young to understand about the colony."

"No Koi in the colony can tell the shanē what to record, or where to deliver it. It's totally arbitrary. How can he think the shanē would *lie*?" He rubbed a fist against his jaw, staring at Elgri fixedly.

Elgri looked uncomfortable, and warbled off another paragraph of melody. Even to Jude, it was obvious that he was changing the subject.

152

Grudgingly, Ra'an translated. "He greets me from my parents. My father, Kirial, has been called to Council in the Ring, but my mother awaits me. He says he is thirteen, born after my parents returned from Menissa, and that . . ." Ra'an continued with difficulty. "He is sorry that he and I cannot mindspeak as brothers should, but he is still learning his halm."

Either the boy has an instinct for the generous lie, Jude decided, *or Ra'an should not give up hope.* Now she watched as Elgri reached inside the marvelous garment that wrapped his slim torso like supple bark, all layers and drapes and hidden pockets. Beneath a flap of green at his hip was a flash of red, like a bird's bright underwing, and his hand brought out a small wrapping of leather. He picked it open delicately to reveal a pile of amber crystals that glittered moistly in the sun. Ra'an caught his breath and without hesitation took one and held it up to the light. Elgri sang a brief phrase of encouragement.

"What is it?" Jude asked.

"A Terran might call it honey." Ra'an turned the crystal in his fingers, then put it to his lips with the reverence of a communicant.

"I thought honey was liquid. It's a black-market item on Terra, you know. There's pollution in it, but people pay lots for it anyway." *God. I'm just babbling.* She shut up and took a small chunk when Elgri offered. She tasted it gingerly. Nectar and ambrosia. From the musty depths, the phrase came swimming up. The crystal tasted as she imagined a field of wild flowers would smell. She held its sweetness on her tongue, reluctant to let it dissolve too quickly.

Ra'an picked up a large one and held it on his palm like a solitaire diamond, remembering. "Daniel brought some books back from Terra once. The bindings were stiff and cracked, the pages fragile. At night, we would leaf through them carefully and he would tell stories of Terra and point out pictures of plants and animals now extinct. I often think he was hoping I would say, 'Oh yes, we have those here,' but I was only twelve or so at the time and had not told him of Ruvala and the others.

"But once, I found a picture that did look familiar. 'Those are hummingbirds,' he said, waiting for me to explain why this drawing of tiny extinct Terran birds should rivet me so. I never told him. . . .

"We have such birds here, you see. Long ago the Koi taught them to gather the flower nectar that they live on so it could be collected and processed like this." He studied the sugar jewel on his palm soberly. "Many households in Ruvala have a flock of

153

lai, as the birds are called, that have been with them through many generations."

"But how do you teach a bird to do such a thing?"

"Halm." Abruptly, he shoved the crystal in his pocket. "It has many uses, you see."

"The gulls and now the . . . the lai? Are all of Arkoi's animals halm-gifted?"

"With varying degrees of sophistication, yes. You can't transmit rational thought where the brain is not developed enough, of course, but emotions, intentions, desires, images, yes, enough for some degree of communication."

Jude glanced at the mules, peacefully cropping the grasses of the clearing. "No wonder the Koi are vegetarians."

"Yes."

"It's the Wall that drives the animals out of the colony, isn't it?"

Ra'an nodded. "Except Terran animals without halm, and those like the mules with enough brain to cope with the Wall as the Koi can. And the shanevoralin, who, being creatures of halm, thrive on all its aspects."

Now Elgri was tiring of all this incomprehensible conversing, and fidgeted from one foot to the other. The little forest animals caught his mood and began their leaping and squealing again. Ra'an took a long look around the clearing. He nudged Jude's camera pack with a booted foot. "Still carrying these around?"

She reached for the strap. She could not yet leave this part of her to languish in an alien clearing, though the cameras felt like dead weight as she hefted the pack.

Ra'an shouldered his own pack. "Well," he announced, "I guess it's time to face my mother."

They followed Elgri into the great woods, the mules behind and the forest creatures gamboling up ahead in ecstatic escort. Jude saw many paths shimmering in the freckled light, but the one that Elgri led them along was solid and pine-soft beneath their feet, the way for most recent comings and goings. The air was mossy and cool, pocketed with warmth and the tang of evergreen. A fugue of birdsong caroled their passing, and every so often, Elgri would sing out, a string of notes without words, and from a nearby branch or thicket would come a signal of bright feathers and a chirruped answer.

Elgri's cheerful acceptance of his arrival had hardly eased Ra'an's mood. Jude tried distracting him with chatter.

"Too bad your father is away. What's the Council in the Ring?"

"The Ring is where the council meets," he replied halfheartedly. "The Council is a governing body of sorts, actually the hub of the halm web that ties the scattered populations together, at least that's what I gather. In the colony, the Ring is not spoken of out loud unless one is very sure a Terran is not around to hear, and that limited my knowledge also."

"I thought you said your father was like a sociologist? Some kind of government consulting work, then?"

Ra'an gave his short laugh. "Put away your ideas of bureaucrats and civil servants. Every adult Koi serves in Council, for some months at a time, on a rotating basis."

Jude considered this. "Sounds unmanageable. How do they maintain any consistent policy or authority?"

"I don't think you have yet managed to grasp the real significance of a society of telepaths," he retorted, annoyed. "Halm is a technique, yes, and it has specific uses. It is also, however, a way of life. Think how different your life would have been on Terra without electronic communications."

"Slower. Less complicated. I'm not sure that would be so bad."

"Communication is the only weapon against ignorance," he insisted pompously.

"Only if what you communicate means something."

"With halm," he went on, oblivious, "you have the possibility of the simultaneous melding of every Koi mind. Cultural and geographical barriers mean nothing anymore. No need for elections or party politics. A single will can be forged in an instant, yet no individual go unheard."

"The ultimate democracy," Jude said with more than a hint of skepticism, for her lessons in democracy had convinced her that it was not possible, not in the real world, where people could only agree to disagree. "I'm still surprised that anything gets done. Who administers this will of the people, and what assures that he or she will abide by it?"

"Administering is done on the local level, completely decentralized, one of the advantages of maintaining a low level of population growth. When they needed something done in the Quarter, they all got together and it got done."

"But the Quarter is one isolated community with a strong common interest. What if community interests come into conflict with each other?"

"The interest of the whole is the interest of the comunity!" His tone grew so sharp that Elgri threw a worried glance over his shoulder. "With halm, all such differences can be resolved! Did

155

you think it was a toy, a mere convenience? That all I am shut away from is the luxury of a private conversation? If that's as deep as your understanding goes, you don't deserve the gift!''

He can't help it, that this bitterness consumes him like a cancer. Can you ask an amputee to be grateful for the rest of his body? Can you ask him not to be preoccupied with his handicap to the exclusion of all else? "I'm trying to learn to deserve it, Ra'an," she answered quietly. "Perhaps I must fully develop it before it can be fully comprehended.''

He left her with a sound of disgust and moved ahead to walk alone.

He expected a miracle. Perhaps he still does. Like a pilgrim approaching the shrine for a cure. Like Langdon, like Daniel Andreas, looking for angels. Like Ramos and Clennan, even. All searching for their private angels. *And me? I am finding miracles I never asked for.*

They came out of the groaning pines into orderly fields checkerboarding the rolling hills of Ruvala, neat squares of yellow hay and red-silked corn, divided by lush green hedge rows. Far ahead, a mule-drawn wagon trundled down a dusty gravel road, balancing a tall stack of hay bales. The heady pungence of cut grass thickened the air. The distant hills were blue with evergreens.

The road led over a rise beyond which lay another stand of trees, basking in the open fields. It was a massive dome of leaves thirty, forty meters tall, curving in a smooth hemisphere down to the waving grass. As they neared, Jude saw that the branches left a space just higher than a tall man's head, all around the bottom of the dome.

As they passed under the canopy of branches, Elgri stopped to turn an expectant eye on his stranger-brother. Ra'an stood like a man in a trance. Jude looked around in wonder.

The house was the trees and the trees were the house. It was impossible to tell where one began and the other ended. Several thick trunks formed a ring under the center of the dome. Around each trunk curled a stair shaped either from the living tree or by the ultimate in subtle artistry. Woody vines spiraled up to form handrails, following the steps around to where they opened onto wide low-slung branches, then up again to the next branch, and up and up until the leaves obscured them. Each branch supported a collage of slatted blinds and glass and panels of woven reed that refused to differentiate inside from outside, but Jude sensed that these were the living quarters and that she would find that

156

there was an inside when she got into one. She counted these areas, at least two dozen, with a few that shimmered insubstantially, ghosts from the past. The house was more populous once, she decided, and just then felt a featherweight tingle inside her head. A halm touch. Not like Ra'an's hard unpracticed presence, but polite, like a soft knock, a request for entry. Uncertain how to answer it, Jude turned around, searching. At the foot of a staircase stood a woman, graying but strong, who was holding out a hand in welcome to the tall grim stranger who could only be her son.

CHAPTER 24

A hollow-eyed Bill Clennan shoved through the swinging doors of the Interrogation Wing, trailing startled aides and hurling orders like so much garbage. The latest dispatches from Ramos were crumpled in his fist. Stalking into the control room, he settled himself at the console with a curt nod to the technician in the next seat. In front of him was an opaque glass panel, a microphone, and a keyboard. The technician's fingers twitched, the booth lights dimmed, and on the other side of the glass, hard whiteness flooded the isolation chamber.

Mark Lacey, naked and bruised, lay strapped into a metal recliner. Biotelemetry leads were taped to skull, chest, and groin. IV tubes ran to each arm. As the lights came on, his eyes snapped open, rolled wildly, and clenched against the glare.

"You could have cleaned him up a little," Clennan muttered. "How long's he been awake?"

"Forty-five minutes, and terrified the whole time." The technician indicated the vital-signs monitor, where the heart line was running like a scared rabbit.

"All the better for us. Maybe this won't take too long." Staring through the glass at the boy, for a moment Clennan could not will his voice to ask for audio. The cruel wires pinning the genital area transfixed him. His own groin tightened in sympathy. He had watched these procedures back on Terra, but had never been forced by rank into the lead seat before. Beneath the technician's ready fingers spread two rows of luminous keys, whose labels proclaimed the intimate little agonies and delights that he, Bill Clennan, could invoke to persuade Mark Lacey to, as they still said in the locker room, spill his guts. An unfortunate turn of phrase, Clennan decided. No scars would remain from this surgery, except in the various pleasure and pain centers of Lacey's being. Again in the locker room, it was said that this method had been used to debrief the returned expeditionaries, when verbal interrogation had failed to produce what Intelligence considered to be proper information. Clennan rubbed at the bloodstains on his sleeve. He had not had time to change. Had that poor loony been put through this? James? Had the Native woman called him James? That would be James Andreas, then. Momentarily, the face of Mark Lacey became the keening, bloodied face of James Andreas, strapped to a metal chair. Clennan realized he was having another failure of nerve and worried about his career. He checked his watch. It was 10:00 P.M.

"You," he growled to the aide waiting at his back. "Get me some coffee and whatever you can find that passes for food around here." He signaled the technician. "Audio when you're ready. Let's start slow." He leaned over the mike and made his voice as paternal as he knew how. "Okay, son. Just relax. We've just got a few questions to ask you."

Thirty minutes later, having found out nothing more than they knew already from the kid's record, Clennan asked for an increased drug dose. Invisible persuasion crept through the tubes into Lacey's veins.

Clennan eyed the luminous keys. "Disorient him."

Nodding, the tech touched a key. Immediately, Lacey's hands groped at the arms of the recliner. A moan, of fear more than pain, broke from him.

"A few straight answers will make the world right again," urged Clennan into the mike.

By 11:00 P.M., they had Lacey's admission that he was responsible for all the sabotage, no great surprise to anyone present, but a relief, as it meant the search teams could get some sleep. Lacey explained in vivid detail, as if once forced he enjoyed bragging about it, how and where he had stolen the explosive, how he had put it to use, his entire strategy and his motive: to scare away enough of the tourist business to collapse the colony's economy. Why? Arkoi did not belong to the Terrans. Clennan thought this smacked of Mitchell Verde, but though he used the technician's every nasty suggestion, hurting the boy to the point of incoherence, he could not get him to implicate anyone else in his plot, not the Natives, and not Verde, the one name Clennan was hoping to hear.

They took a break, and Clennan sent a tape of the first session by hand messenger across the Transport Corridor to Ramos, who waited on Terra for a blow-by-blow. He almost wished Ramos were present. The boss would enjoy this process a lot more than he was.

Back at the console, he took a long swallow of cold coffee and settled in to find out what he really wanted to know.

"Now. I want to try another tack. I think he's weak enough by now. What can you do there to make him feel angry and real paranoid?"

The tech hesitated, then went to work. Lacey's battered face rewarded his efforts with furtive scowls. When he saw the mouth draw tight and harden, Clennan said, "Now, Mark, how come your good friends are letting you take the rap?"

Lacey growled. "Don't have any friends."

"What about Verde? You worked for him for free—you must have admired him."

The next was lost in a jumble of rage. Then: "Verde. Always playing God."

"Is that so? Not very nice. How does he play God?"

More jumble. "Stahl House." Low giggles.

Clennan turned to his aide. "Check the map."

The aide studied and shrugged. "Nothing."

Clennan dredged his memory. "Did you look in the Quarter?"

"Nothing on this map."

"Get in someone from the Alien Division."

"They don't work at night, Mr. Clennan. It's two o'clock in the morning."

"Then fuckin' well wake one of them up!" Clennan sent the aide scuttling. He returned his attention to the boy. "Tell me about Stahl House, Mark."

"They could kill us if they wanted to."

"What's that? I don't quite get that, Mark."

"They could, you know."

Clennan leaned over the technician. "What're you feeding him? I want him coherent." To Lacey he said, "They?"

Lacey laughed, deep and on the edge.

Clennan frowned, "Throw in a little bravado," he whispered to his right. "Make him feel important." The tech's fingers busied themselves.

159

"Are they friends of yours?" Clennan insinuated into the mike.

"Sure!" the boy replied loudly. "What'd you think, I'd go around blowing up the world for nothing?"

"You were doing it for them?"

"They need help."

"Why do they need your help if they can kill us themselves?"

"Ehh," Lacy sneered. "They don't like killing much."

"All right. But how would they kill us if they decided they wanted to?"

"With their minds. They can do anything with their minds."

In the booth, the technician caught Clennan's eye and twirled one finger at the side of his head.

"Regress him," Clennan said quickly. The tech shook his head, but reached for a lighted dial.

"Uh, Mark, I have some friends like that. Do we have the same friends, do you think?"

This time the laugh was a sly hoot. "Guess."

"Give me a hint."

"No."

"Do you have a *lot* of friends? Before you said you didn't have any."

"More than *you* could count! C'mon, you're not guessing."

"You have to give me at least one hint. Like, who would they kill if they wanted to?"

"Well, not me. You. All of you."

"All of me?"

"Terrans, stupid. All the Terrans!"

Clennan clicked off the mike and sat back. Oh brother, Ramos is going to eat this up! "They" can only mean the Natives. Lots of them, eh? He leaned forward.

"Mark, how well can *you* count?"

In a mere twenty minutes, Bill Clennan's wheedling and gamesmanship informed him that Ramos' dream had come true: There were Others out there beyond those infernal mountains. Lacey hadn't exactly said so, and in his present state, he had no real grasp on numbers. The technician thought the whole line of questioning was a preposterous waste of time, especially at that hour, but Bill Clennan *knew*.

"Do a little Skinner on him," he said. "I'm going to send this tape off to Big Julie. Get him reward-conditioned—we'll see how that works."

*   *   *

It didn't. Somehow Lacey had pulled a little of his remaining self together and was a paradigm of evasion. Clennan gave up and went back to anger/paranoia at much increased levels.

Into the mike he snarled, "Those Native friends of yours ain't worth shit!"

Lacey's whole body jerked in rage. "Oh, *yeah*?"

Six in the morning. Clennan was back in his office cubicle. The session had ended when Lacey fainted for the third time. Clennan couldn't stomach it any more, not without some sleep, at least. Six days straight he'd been running on uppers and naps.

The full report had been sent out to Terra. While he waited for a reply and new orders from Ramos, he drank more coffee, popped a few pills, and replayed the tapes.

That there were other Koi beyond the mountains, he was sure. That the loss of the expeditions could be laid to the Koi, he was also sure, but not of how. The how was where understanding clouded. The kid had babbled about mind weapons. Telepathy, for God's sake, and some kind of psychic wall. How to approach such nonsense? Was it code of some sort? The half-awake straggler dragged in from the Alien Division had been so little help with the concrete information Lacey had provided that Clennan hesitated to approach him with this. Besides, Ramos would want it kept quiet for now.

The Jewel will love this, he assured himself, and in the midst of stuporous fatigue, permitted himself some optimism. When I get some sleep, this'll all make sense. I can count on a promotion. I can start looking for that boat I've been meaning to buy. Everything's finally falling into place. Once the Natives know we know, they'll have to cooperate. I'll get this place quieted down and it'll be a real nice place to live. Yup, Julie's going to owe me for this.

He clicked off the tape relay, dropped his head to his desk, and fell asleep.

CHAPTER 25

"We are the cleansing flame!" James Andreas leaped up on the bier and paused to let the echoes of his voice chase around the cavern, commentary on the shocked silence of his audience. The yellow linen still bound his forehead. He stretched his pale thin arms in exultation. "We have been passive long enough! While we suffer in Menissa, the Others dream in ignorance! How many deaths such as this will it take to waken them? We cannot wait to find out! The cry must be raised, the armies gathered!" Andreas let the murmurs surge around him. Along the surrounding ledges the gull-beasts stirred to his rhetoric, and his huge emaciated shadow seemed to crucify itself upon the rock wall as he once more raised his arms, incandescent with his vision.

From a darkened corner, Mitchel Verde watched in disbelief. "Mernon woud not have wanted her death to be the cause of such as this. James' timing is brilliant, of course. Hit them right after the funeral."

"Our Wall made him what he is," mourned Luteverindorin. "He is our own weapon turned against us."

"Six years of abuse from Terran tourists haven't helped much either," Damon reminded him gently.

"We must reason with him," urged the old Koi.

"Reason? What makes you think he's any more open to reason now than he was before? The shock has articulated his insanity, not cured it."

"Mitchell, we must try."

"Lute, Lute." Verde laid a comforting hand on his friend's knee. "Let him rave. It'll pass. Surely you don't think anyone here will support this lunacy he's proposing?"

"Look around you. Look in faces for what I can hear with my mind. Look at the eyes of the young, whose only knowledge of the Interior and the Others is a romanticized memory, those who were not consulted when their exile was decided. Look at the eyes of Hrin."

162

Verde looked, picked out Hrin across the multitude of listeners. The tall young Koi was poised tensely against a wall, long years of resentment expressing themselves in the rapt attention he gave to the madman's exhortations. Looking closer, Verde found many whom he had known, considered friends, now listening with willing faces.

"You remember I told you of the Diamo and their prophecy that saviors are due among us. They also believe that insanity is a truer vision." Lute turned his gaze across the gathering. "Hrin has only heard of these beliefs through his elders, yet he preaches them now and has won followers, especially of late."

"But . . . ."

"Madmen are sacred to the Diamo. Yes, Mitchell, even among the Koi there are occasional madmen."

Verde was unaccepting. "Lute, these are our friends, people we know and respect. They're polite, they listen, but they are not going to throw away the most basic tenet of Koi society to run after a madman! Will they forsake the ideal of Balance because some young lunatic tells them they deserve justice?"

"Not justice, my friend. Vengeance. Don't you hear it? That's what young James is preaching!" Lute stood as tall as his small stature would permit. "Sit down and listen, Mitchell, for this is important. There is a belief that you must forsake, now, if you are to help us. For as long as you have known us, we of the Quarter have been a closely knit, highly motivated community, and we have managed to perform well so far. But we are fallible, too. All men are fallible, Terran or Koi!"

"I know that, Lute . . ."

"I don't think you do, or you would understand that James Andreas will find a following. He will call vengeance by another name, as the Diamo say that only through Imbalance can the righteousness of Balance assert itself. Or perhaps he will be bold enough to call it what it is, but hear me, he will find his following. Our task will be to keep it to a minimum, as best we can."

"Gods," Verde breathed.

Across the cavern, Andreas jumped from the bier and began to move among his listeners. "We will leave this infested city! We owe it nothing! We will find ourselves a purer battleground! Our passage through the mountains will strengthen us! We will awaken the Others and our army will be forged!"

Shaken, Verde reconsidered and wracked his brain for the proper argument to counter Andreas' emotional manipulations. Andreas circled, exhorting with broad sweeps of his arms. With

163

his unerring gift for finding the crisis in every moment, he chose a path that would lead him eventually to Hrin. Verde rose stiffly to his feet and stepped out of the shadow to intercept him.

"James." He had done some rabble-rousing himself and knew how to make himself heard without seeming to shout. He cast himself as the voice of wisdom, the patient father confessor. "A holy war, James? Has your poor mad brain been nursing apocalyptic visions all these years?"

Andreas eyed his old protector with compassion and tolerance. "Ah, Mitchell. You rebuke me, when you of all people should understand the necessity of what I do."

"I? Why me? My holy wars have never been fought with violence."

"And they have always failed. Do you fear for your life, Mitchell? But you've already given all you have for the Koi. Why withhold this final sacrifice?"

"I fear for the lives of the hundred million Koi you would send weaponless against the Terran war machine! Yes, the Koi outnumber the Terrans in the colony, but there's a whole world of Terrans on the other side of the Transport Corridor, and the Koi are not a fighting people, James. You who presume to speak for them must recognize that!"

A sly smile spread across Andreas' haggard face. He stepped back and spread his hands in a show of innocence, addressing the crowd at large. "Weaponless? The Koi are not weaponless. Every people are a fighting people when their existence is finally at stake, and the Koi possess a weapon far deadlier than any yet conceived by Terrans! Deadly enough to level each and every Terran with a single blow!"

The silence in the cavern awaited the madman's revelation. But Andreas seemed to drift off momentarily, and the silence became discomfort, the anguish of anticipation. When Verde shifted and cleared his throat to break the silence, Andreas raised his head and interrupted him with a growling whisper.

"Halm."

Verde recoiled. "What?"

Luteverindorin spoke up, his words charged with subtle outrage. "Since when is halm a means for killing?"

Andreas faced him evenly. "I know of the ancient past as well as you, since it was from your mind that I learned of it."

"Then you should also have learned that only by the forbidding of such practices have we climbed up from the wreckage of those ancient days!"

164

Verde's head swiveled back and forth. "Lute, what is he saying—that halm can *kill*?"

The old Koi lowered his eyes.

"Can and will!" Andreas hissed.

"How dare you!" Verde exploded, though Luteverindorin reached to restrain him. "How dare you suggest such a thing! Since when do you speak for the Koi!"

The madman turned visionary did not hesitate, though a fleeting sadness haunted his clear gray eyes. "For this while, I must," he replied gently, as if explaining a punishment beforehand to an errant child. "Only a Terran may bring to Terrans this terrible destruction. The Koi must not bear the guilt."

"It is a lost skill," Lute admonished. "You will find no one who knows how to do this thing."

Andreas' smile managed to be both saintly and knowing. "It is not in the skill, my honored teacher, but in the intention. The readiness, as the poet says, is all." He paused, and the smile vanished like a snuffed flame as he advanced on them step by step. "*I* can do this thing. *Have* done this thing. *Will* do this thing."

Lute's body trembled, with rage or pain, Verde could not tell, but he stepped between them quickly. "James, there are other solutions. We could give them an ultimatum. By now, Lacey has probably told them everything he knows, and they'd believe a threat. We could force a total evacuation."

Andreas raised a mocking eyebrow. "Lacey will give no more information," he stated. Lute watched him with dawning horror.

"James, James," Verde insisted. "Anything is better than massacring five million innocent tourists!"

"Innocent?" Andreas countered, beginning to move again, to circle. "Innocent? Would they spare the Koi if the choice were theirs?" He whipped the yellow linen from his head and held it aloft to the gathering. "Did they spare our Meron, those innocent tourists?" He wrapped the linen around one wrist so that it waved in echo to his movement. "Evacuate them? They wouldn't leave. They couldn't leave. They are Terra's occupying army, whether they know it or not. Those who sent them here will put weapons in their hands when the time comes, and that time will be soon. I have *seen* it!" He laid both hands across his eyes. Verde could not repress the image of an actor playing a tragic role. "I have seen it here!" cried James Andreas. "And I know that our answer to the Terrans must be a weapon of our own!" He bent and snatched up an unlit torch from the floor. He raised it above his head, a blinded beacon.

"Who will light it for me?" he called, and the listeners fell back before the blatant symbolism of his dare. Again he began the circuit of the cavern, moving in ever-widening circles, wooing his audience, taunting, mesmerizing, stalking their support like a starved predator.

"Mitchell," Lute whispered faintly. "I worry for young Lacey."

"I've lost him," Verde murmured, one hand trailing out after the defiant madman.

"*This* is my vision!" Andreas cried out. "See it! On the white shoreline we will gather! Who will light the torch to carry us there? Our minds shall number in the millions! Come, light the flame!" He stretched his arm and his whole body upward until the blackened torch towered above them. "Our deepest energies will combine in a lightning bolt of halm!" The torch hissed and seemed to flare. All eyes were riveted to it. "We will raise a righteous flame of halm to scour our land of the invaders!" The torch swooped downward as he wrenched it in a terrible arc, and the air was full of fire. The shanevoralin rose screaming from their perches. The listening Koi gasped as one.

"His halm is very strong," Lute rasped at Verde's ear. "Do you see the flames dancing around him? Such power alone could draw the people to him!"

Verde could not see the halm fire, but he sensed the surge of power through the cavern, felt the lust for vengeance erupt within his own brain. "No. *No!*" he howled into the clamor.

"Now! Come with me now! Light the flame!" Andreas circled faster, white hair, white skin, radiant heat in the form of a man, dead-black torch held out in a sphere of fire. From out of the moaning crowd stepped Hrin. The gull-beasts shrieked. Andreas stopped, held up a hand for silence. With the other he held the torch out in offering. The two faced each other, Andreas aflame, Hrin dark with conflict. Unable to move, Verde watched the balance slipping as Hrin felt blindly in a pocket, his eyes fixed on the madman, and brought out a Terran pocket lighter. Verde squinted against the garish plastic glare. The lighter seemed to glow with its own rabid fire on the Koi's ruddy palm, and as Hrin readied the lighter to strike, Verde saw in him a reflection of Ra'an and understood how much more than Terran lives was at stake, that the frail and precious goal of Balance, integral to all that was best and special in the Koi nature, had found its ultimate denial in the person of James Andreas.

Hrin lifted his burning lighter to the torch. The flame caught and rose. Still Andreas held it out, his gray eyes mirroring the blaze. "Will you come, brother? While the Terrans hatch their

166

plots above, we will open a way through the tunnels of your ancestors. Will you carry the fire?"

"The torch is yours to carry," Hrin challenged doubtfully.

Andreas tossed his head with a luminous smile. "Ah, but I have no need of it. My vision lights my way."

Hrin raised a hand to the torch. Andreas kept his hold. "Come! Carry it for me!" He removed his hand. The torch shivered with the agony of Hrin's indecision.

"N'e carel atha, veruth de'ir na celeratha," Andreas quoted softly as a lover's caress.

Hrin's arm snapped up. "To the tunnels!" The torch blazed above his head in affirmation. Of the three hundred Koi who filled the cavern, half joined their voices in a single shout.

Andreas whirled and leaped to the cavern entrance. Verde felt the shock of one final halmic exhortation pass through his body, and Andreas was gone, running down the passageway on bare, silent feet, sure and fleet and ravenous.

Hrin hesitated but a moment, then charged after him. Others followed, and when movement ceased and the only sound was of feet slapping along distant rock, little more than a hundred remained. The shanevoralin had vanished.

"Through the huruss tunnels?" Verde demanded. "He can't make it through that way, can he? Without food or water?"

"Or fresh air," added Damon. "Who knows? We won't know unless he does make it, and then . . ."

"And then . . ." Verde looked around weakly at faces as stunned as his own. He returned the grasp of comfort from Damon's strong hand and let out a groaning sigh. "Lute, correct me if I'm wrong, but this halm weapon of James' will not be selective, will it? When he says he's going to kill all Terrans, he means *all* Terrans, ourselves included?"

Slowly, sadly, the old Koi nodded.

CHAPTER 26

A rough hand shook Clennan awake. Julio Ramos stood over him, his bulk decked out in full uniform so that the tiny cubicle seemed full of polished brass and creased trousers. A small army of subalterns waited in the corridor, eyes and ears averted. Clennan staggered to his feet, brushing hair out of his eyes.

Ramos was literally rubbing his hands with excitement. "Had to come, Billy, had to be in on this myself! This is the big one, boy!"

"I'm . . . ah . . . glad you're pleased, sir. Glad to be working with you, sir, I mean, directly."

"Well, you'll just carry on with your little investigation. You're doing a fine job, Billy, fine job." His eyes narrowed as he jostled around restlessly in the cramped space. He automatically lifted papers from the littered desk and put them down again. "I'm here to oversee the mobilization."

"Mobilization?" Clennan echoed groggily, not sure he had heard right.

"Going to restore some order in this town," Ramos asserted. "Start throwing tourists in jail if we have to."

"I tried to persuade them to declare martial law," Clennan began.

"So we'll be bringing in troops and equipment." An aide came to the door with a clipboard full of papers. Ramos glanced through them and nodded. The aide scurried away. "I'm planning a full-scale assault this time, no more of these pansy expeditions. No halfway measures, you know?"

Clennan decided he wasn't awake yet. "Assault on what?"

"Out There, Billy, Out There!" Ramos pushed through his entourage at the door and bore down the corridor toward the dispatch room. Clennan struggled after him, pausing only to douse his face at the water cooler.

"This room'll be big enough," declared Ramos, peering into Dispatch. He moved in and took immediate possession. He shoved a pile of tapes and coffee cups to one end of a long table, sent a few loungers scuttling back to their desks, and patted the cleared surface. "I'll want detailed maps of the Native Quarter and a list of any Terrans with connections there. I want to know their comings and goings, business dealings, private lives, etc."

"We have most of that information, sir," said Clennan. "But at this moment . . ."

"Then while the colony police are quieting things down, my men will round up the Natives for one-on-one questioning." He answered Clennan's look of dismay with a wave. "Now, I know we've tried that before, but this time we know what we're looking for. Won't hurt to try. Leave no stone unturned."

Clennan pointed along the wall. "The maps are in alphabetical order according to sector."

Ramos pounded the table with his palm. "Here, Billy, here. In front of my eyes."

"Right." Clennan yanked open a file drawer with a little too much pique, then caught himself. He unfolded a sheath of maps in front of his chief and stood back, waiting.

"Ah. Thanks. And we'll *keep* those Natives in detention this time," Ramos said.

"Isn't the Quarter detention enough, sir?"

"Bill." Ramos looked disappointed. "You heard what that kid said. This goddamn Wall or whatever it is is operated from somewhere inside the Quarter!" He flattened a sweaty hand against an opened map. "We've got to tear it apart stone by stone."

"So you believe what the kid said about this telepathic stuff. How do you explain it?"

Ramos shrugged. "No stone unturned, Billy. When you've got a lot of weird things happening, sometimes it takes something weird to explain them. I've been trying to tell that to the upstairs boys for ages. This'll show 'em!" Ramos grew serious. "I knew those Native bastards were protecting something! Once we find that Wall mechanism, it's over the mountains, full force. Arkoi will be ours in six months!"

Clennan's head was spinning. Armed assault against an invisible barrier? Could Ramos accept such a paradox calmly? "Right. Then, I guess I'll get back down to Interrogation and drag some more details out of the kid."

Ramos shook his head, easing his weight into a chair. "Forgot to tell you. The kid managed to do himself in this morning."

"*Killed* himself?"

"Don't worry, Billy. Not your fault. Long hours like this, people got to sleep some time."

"Wait a minute. That kid killed himself? *How?* He was in isolation, drugged, plugged in, strapped down, totally monitored . . ."

Ramos took out his handkerchief and blew his nose. "Its not exactly clear. The medicom tapes show a sharp pulse rise around eight A.M., then his EEG went completely nuts. Twenty seconds later, his heart stopped beating, brain death soon after. Unbelievably fast, the whole thing."

"Who was on duty?"

"He was getting himself some coffee. When he came back, it was too late."

Clennan checked his watch desperately. "It's nine-thirty! Why didn't anybody wake me?"

"They were still falling over themselves trying to figure out what happened when I arrived." He favored Clennan with an avuncular wink. "Told them to let you sleep in a little. Don't worry. We'll get the information we need." He turned his attention to the map pinned under his palm. "Now, what about this fellow Verde?"

What indeed? Clennan realized he was sweating, though the air conditioning was on full blast. For a man who does not believe in premonition, it is an awful moment when he first feels it stirring. Puzzle pieces. Lacey dead, instantly, mysteriously. Just hours after he had made claims of murderous abilities on the part of the Natives. Then Verde's Native kid, more fuel for his premonition in the just-recalled image of her, eyes clenched shut, attackers dropping around her without being touched. Then there was Verde's own disappearance. Coincidence? Clennan's gut told him no. If Ramos was willing to believe in telepathic barriers . . .

Got to track down Verde, he decided, giving in to obsession because it was the only possible lead he could see. Verde knows. Verde is the key.

CHAPTER 27

Evening bathed Ruvala in a honeyed lavender darkness. Under the great leaf dome, the reunited family gathered for dinner on a wooden platform set within the central ring of trees. Jude decided to play the tourist, as an excuse for doing a lot of obvious listening and looking. The homecoming had not proceeded as she had expected, and she had nothing but her powers of observation and deduction to explain what was going on.

The diners sat on woven mats and cushions embroidered with bright calligraphy at a low round table broad enough for twenty. Clusters of small luminous globes hung from the upper branches like glowing fruit. Outside the circle of light, runways of polished inlay radiated off to smaller platforms of varying heights, gathering here a shadowed mass of cabinetry and shelves full of richly bound books, there a plush rug set about with more cushions and squat tables bearing painted vases of flowers or bowls of fruit. Beyond, the thick trunks with their stairways leading upward into the leaves.

In being introduced to the family, Jude had learned that Yron was not the surname she had supposed, but the name of the wondrous tree dwelling itself. Thus, all who lived beneath its branches were tel-Yron, no matter what their lineage.

Gathered around the table, beside Ra'an and herself, was his mother, Rya, who had taken Jude in hand with delicate courtesy as the only family member who shared a language with her, guiding her through the afternoon until the family convened from the fields for dinner, asking few questions, showing off the house, all the while using Jude as a barrier between herself and her stranger son, inhibiting conversation beyond the level of small talk.

Next to Rya sat her sister, Dal, younger than Rya, shorter and rounder, with blue-black hair untouched by the silver that streaked Rya's thick dark braid. Beyond sat Elgri, now feeding berries to a large blue-and-yellow bird perched on his shoulder, and beside him wriggled Dal's twin children, a nine-year-old boy and girl,

171

who regarded Jude with frank but cheerful curiosity every time she said something in her outlandish language. The larger part of their attention was lavished on their grizzled, energetic grandfather, Gire'en, as he explained in detail some mysterious process that Jude could not quite catch, though she enjoyed his attempts to clarify with spoons and piles of crackers laid in patterns on the tablecloth. Completing the circle was the twins' father, Tekhon, a stocky blond man who Jude learned was from the vast grasslands to the south. He had met Dal at a market fair one year and came to live at Yron soon thereafter. The twins were ruddy-skinned, like their mother, but had inherited their father's flaxen hair, so that Jude, who could not void the comparison from her mind, thought that this was what angels would look like if they ever got sunburned.

Finally, stationed at strategic corners of the platform, were three shaggy wolfish creatures, resting their giant heads on four-toed paws and casting hopeful glances on bowls of food passed from diner to diner.

The meal, which had been spectacular, was nearly over. There had been huge bowls of wheat cooked with spices and mint, little flaky pies filled with egg and cheese, stuffed vegetables and broiled fruit to be eaten with thin crusted brown bread, more fruit and hard crackers, and a sweet-sour cheese that was eaten with a spoon. Now occupying the center of the table was a flat blue dish heaped with crystallized nectar. Laying aside the emptied rind of a peri melon, Jude concluded that Rya had laid out a feast to celebrate her son's return, for she could not imagine such plenty inhabiting an everyday table.

Yet it had been strangely unlike a celebration. Like Rya, the family had welcomed the travelers warmly but without occasion, as if they had merely wandered in for supper from next door. The adults asked politely after their particular friends who had gone to live in the colony all those years before, but they had not, they said, known these people well, and though their interest seemed genuine, it was without urgency. Even the giggling curiosity of the children was focused on how funny the strangers were rather than on exploring the oddity of whatever place they might have come from. The twins did not seem to know what the colony was.

Jude felt out of phase. It was not just the language barrier or her own conflicting reactions to this place that played such havoc with her perceptual mechanisms, even to the point of leaving her slightly nauseous. Food and darkness had eased the nausea somewhat, as the table, the food, the people sitting around it, were definitely here and now, unmuddied by any shimmering echoes from the past. Jude was grateful to be able to enjoy her meal.

As for the language, the closest thing to a conversation in an incomprehensible tongue that she had ever experienced was when she had once, back in school, tried to eat lunch with a clique of math students. Here she had Rya on one side and Ra'an on the other, translating when they remembered. She managed to understand most of the dinner chatter, enough to know that, clever and brilliant as it might be, it was merely that: chatter. Keyed up from their arrival and Ra'an's expectations of a confrontation, Jude was at a loss as to how to interpret this overtly casual reception of two runaways from the supposedly dreaded Terran colony. *Don't they care where we've been? Don't they mind what I am?*

There was one clue. After Rya's first gentle probing, Jude had felt no further attempts to mindspeak her, and she could tell from the degree of Ra'an's withdrawal that he had not managed the halm contact he waited for. Jude was not about to violate some unknown protocol by trying to halmspeak herself, but she did sense, underneath the symphonic swelling of talk and laughter, a continual murmuring, a silent conversation of which she was picking up only the static, the adults perhaps, halmspeaking among themselves. Whatever it was, it was giving her a violent headache to replace the receding nausea.

Beside her, Ra'an fought his own inner battles. Jude wondered if his bewilderment and growing anger was as apparent to the others as they were to her. His attempts to steer the conversation toward a serious consideration of the problems in the colony were met with bland attention and an artful change of subject. No mention was made of Ra'an's exclusion from the halmtalk. *Is this to spare him pain, or is it merely that it's awkward to admit that you're talking behind someone's back?*

As she listened carefully for further clues, she realized that she had not heard anyone interrupt all evening, that there were no overlapping private conversations, but a unified flow of talk in which everyone took part. Even Rya's translations to her were worked into the whole, and though the flow was rapid and organic, there was never any confusion about who held the floor at any given moment. As she sat back and analyzed it, even when the meaning eluded her, the structure was awesome. A musical comparison was not out of place. This was a kind of performance she was witnessing, a dinnertime concert complete with theme and variations, soloists and improvisations. They

173

were so skilled at it that they could include a Terran who could not even read the music. As well as one of their own who hadn't played in years and didn't seem to be sure that he wanted to.

Now Elgri embarked on a long recitation that Rya explained involved a neighbor and her dairy herd. Jude noted how the boy's back straightened as he began, and now she understood that the slight quaver in his voice probably meant a touch of stagefright, that he had taken center without being quite sure that his material would work. The neighbor and her animals, it seemed, were having a dispute over milking hours. Elgri took one part, then the other, and from the glee his performance evoked among the twins, it was clear that imitations were his strong point. As the story ended amid general laughter and applause, Elgri sat back flushed and grinning with an I-made-it look in his eyes. Only then did Rya turn to Jude to elaborate.

"The, ah, the cows . . ." She searched her rusty Terran vocabulary between giggles. Her command of the language made quantum leaps with each hour spent renewing it in conversation. "Always they come home to milk when it is dark. Now in the summer, the night comes later, but then it is Seyanna's dinner hour when they come, and the cows say the milk is not right if they come home earlier, and this happens every summer, and well, you see . . ." Rya threw up her hands in helpless merriment.

Jude joined dutifully in the laughter, though she could see why the farmer would not find this funny. Ra'an smiled thinly and refilled his mug with the hot yeasty drink that Tekhon had brought at the end of the meal. His fingers played impatient rhythms on the leaping ceramic fish that served as a handle, but as the conversation turned, he did make a wan effort to discuss the year's projected harvest with his uncle-in-law. Tekhon's conversational music was unembellished and logically structured, to suit his subject matter or perhaps his own nature.

At last Rya rose, collecting an armful of dishes. The children did likewise, while Dal and the elderly Gire'en sipped their drink comfortably and continued talking. Jude reached to gather their plates along with her own, and they looked up surprised, laughing. The static in Jude's head buzzed a trifle louder.

"They will bring them when they are finished," Rya said gently. "Come. I will show you the kitchens."

There were three kitchens, and except in size, for they were enormous, they were to Jude's eye exact replicas of the little galley on the huruss. The appliances bore no brand label or extraneous decoration, yet the rooms were in no way impersonal. Rya showed her how to load the big dishwashers while Ra'an

174

trailed along moodily, reacquainting himself by poking into cabinets and cold chests.

"Rya," Jude asked experimentally, "would I find exactly the same kitchen anywhere in Arkoi?"

Rya seemed puzzled. "The same kitchen? No, ah, a kitchen is designed to the needs of the house."

"Well, I mean the equipment."

"Ah, yes. That is the same, ah, standard."

"All from one factory? A monopoly?"

"No, there are assembly centers in every region."

"But they don't put their name on the pieces they build?"

"Or compete with each other in price," Ra'an put in.

Rya's smile was blank. "They put a number on each so that they know how many they have built. Also it is for repairs."

Jude pounced. "So they do break down!"

Rya searched for the subtext in this inquiry. "Nothing is perfect, of course. You have to take care of things, and then they last a long time." She looked around the room as if seeking out an example. "This kitchen is the new one, added when I first brought Kirial home. It has behaved very well."

"That would make it around thirty-five years old," supplied Ra'an smugly.

"But how do the factories make a living?" Jude objected.

Rya struggled to recall that particular Terran idiom.

"I mean, they must have calls for about one stove a year!" Jude elaborated.

Rya took this literally. "There are about two hundred assembly centers, so each one serves around a hundred thousand households. If all equipment were replaced on a conservative cycle of one hundred years, each center would still have one thousand kitchens to assemble every year, so you see that they are kept very busy."

"That's busy?"

Ra'an chuckled mordantly as he watched Jude struggle with memories of robot assembly lines cranking out a thousand stoves a day.

"There's always a waiting list for new appliances back home," she said. "You're lucky if a stove lasts two years, never mind thirty-five." She tried a new tack. "But don't they get bored, building the same stove year after year?"

Rya looked her over with mild surprise. "I raise the same crops year after year and it does not bore me."

"But you have your work. I mean, Ra'an told me you were a biologist."

"Whatever I do is my work. The builders of stoves have other work as well. The assembly centers do research, in metallurgy perhaps, or microelectronics. As my time is divided between the laboratory and the fields, so theirs is, between the lab and the workbench." Rya laughed. She had finally caught on to the lesson she was teaching. "Ah, you are a Terran after all, my dear. Come. I will show you the rest."

All the mechanical requirements of the household were neatly concealed below ground level: the kitchens, pantries, laundry, water supply, and heaters, an array of luxurious baths that were again reminiscent of the huruss but palatial in size. There was a large collection and distribution plant for the power gathered from solar and wind devices mounted at the top of the tree dome. The layout of rooms and corridors was a bit baroque, owing to the need to avoid the trees' root network, but many entrances from above ground provided quick access to any area.

Rya's extensive laboratory wing with its attached infirmary showed an impressive but homey practicality, so that Jude didn't really think it incongruous to find a gleaming lab in a household that ostensibly lived off the land. The infirmary was Dal's kingdom, which she ruled, as Rya did her lab, in the evenings, on rainy days, outside the growing season, or whenever an emergency arose.

As they climbed back upstairs, Rya laid a motherly arm around Jude's waist. "It is only a house, after all. Someday you will see Quaire'en. Now that is truly a marvel."

"Quaire'en." Ra'an's murmur was like a sigh.

"Quaire'en is the great seaside city," Rya continued. "A city of glass built into the sea cliffs! It's like living inside a crystal. When I first went there as a little girl, I thought I was dreaming!"

A city of glass. Jude's balance wavered briefly. *I did dream of such a city,* she thought, but held her tongue.

"Lute was from Quaire'en," Ra'an commented darkly.

Rya's habitual smile deepened. "Yes. Does he still sing the sad sea songs? He had quite a voice in our younger days. Ah, so many friends, so long ago."

"That's all the colony means to you, isn't it?" growled her son. "Memories. You don't really care what's going on there now. Well, I can understand that. Life is very pleasant here; why should you trouble yourselves?"

Jude wished she could protect this lovely smiling woman from what she knew was about to happen.

"That must be why you tell Elgri that the shanevoralin are lying?" Ra'an pursued, building up steam.

"Oh, the shanē." Rya dismissed them with a gay wave, just as Elgri had done. "Unbalanced creatures. They thrive on crisis, and neglect the profounder truth of the everyday. Ra'an, I know the shanē do not lie, but by their very nature, they do distort the picture. The exiles weathered many crises when I was one of them. They will weather many more. We have not forgotten. We think of Menissa often and wish them strength in our Gatherings. Come," she said to Jude cheerfully as if the subject were closed, "let me introduce you to the lai. They love to hear compliments on their handiwork."

"Rya!" Ra'an blocked her path. "What if I, who have just come from the colony, tell you that the shanevoralin do not exaggerate? What if I tell you that crisis *is* the everyday, that the situation is worse than you could ever imagine? Will you believe me? Or am I just another unbalanced voice to be humored and ignored lest I disturb your precious complacency?"

Rya's smile did not weaken, and Jude thought her either very brave or very foolish. "How serious my son has become," she teased him girlishly. "Your first night home in nearly . . . what is it, Ra'an, can it be thirty years? And you will only give us frowns and gloom? You have not even told me how Daniel is."

In the silence that followed, Jude felt ice creeping through her veins, even as the warm night licked about them.

"Daniel is dead, Rya."

At last the smile faded. "Ah. I am sorry."

"He died trying to find you," Ra'an continued tightly. "After spending nine years trying to be the parents who had deserted me."

Tears glistened in Rya's eyes. "There are times when one must sacrifice to fill a greater need," she replied simply.

"And it's easy enough to replace one son with another."

For the first time, Jude witnessed Ra'an's compulsive bitterness lash out at someone other than herself, and she wondered what she could possibly find to admire in this angry, ungenerous creature. "Ra'an, that's unnecessary," she said.

"Is it?" he retorted. "You don't think she should see what I have become, what life in the Terran colony has done to her eldest son? How can they help me if they don't know what I've come from?" He turned away and took a controlling breath, aware of his own angry energy charging the night air. Rya's hands floated upward in a reflexive warding gesture.

"Ra'an," she pleaded gently, "we are not so callous as you think, but what can we do? If we break the isolation of the colony, the security of the Wall is compromised. Those who went into exile understood this. They were all volunteers.''

"*I* was not a volunteer! And the safety of the Wall is already compromised! It grows weaker every day. Do you think the Terrans meekly accept their imprisonment in Menissa? Live this precious idyll of yours, Rya, savor every calm and perfect day in Ruvala, for believe me, those days are numbered!'' He bore down on his mother mercilessly. "There are over five million Terrans in the colony now. And more each day.''

Rya's eyes widened in shock but also in pain.

"Surprised? Well, think how surprised you'll be when they come boiling over those mountains and find you ignorant, unprepared, without a strategy to resist them! In fact, there's no point in resisting the irresistible, is there? Perhaps you all secretly realize that. Is that why you hide out here in Ruvala, ignoring the warnings of the shanē and telling yourselves pretty stories about the brave and dedicated exiles? *Is that why, Mother?*''

Cringing, Rya cried out in an anguish Jude recognized.

"Ra'an, stop it!'' she shouted, pulling the older woman to her protectively, even as her own brain burned with his invading fury.

As always, when recognized, the anger vanished. Rya tottered in Jude's arms. Ra'an groaned, flicked Jude a desperate glance, and fled without a word.

Jude helped Rya to a sitting area and a soft cushion. Rya sat a moment, recovering, blotting her tears with the long sleeve of her robe. "I will call a House Gathering tomorrow,'' she said finally with a sigh of acceptance. "But he must not bring such anger into a Gathering.''

Jude's tongue brushed her lips nervously. "If you are saying what I think you are, he can't, ah, join in your Gathering, Rya. That anger you felt, he has no control over it.''

"Cannot join, or *will* not?'' A hint of stubbornness appeared in Rya's voice, and Jude knew that Ra'an was not entirely a Terran product.

"*Can* not. I . . . he thought you knew. His . . . halm is blocked somehow.''

Rya's fist pounded her knee. "This uncontrolled anger only an adolescent would be excused for! I felt no blockage but the blockage he himself creates!'' She quietened, then grew sad. "So. There at least the shanē spoke true.''

"Rya, he sees himself as some sort of defective. He really believes in that blockage. He's very unhappy, your son.''

"I see that.'' Rya collected herself and rose. "Then you will

178

both come to the Gathering and *speak* to us of all this, and we will try to understand. Come upstairs, Judith, my dear, and I will show you your room.''

Jude followed Rya up three rounds of stairs out onto a walk-way running atop a huge branch. A few paces through a tunnel of leaves and without passing through a door of any kind, they were in a cozy apartment. There was no ceiling, only the leaves rustling overhead. The floor was a series of small planked sections stepped up and down to suit the contour of the tree branch. Walls were sliding glass panels that could be moved about to enclose as much or as little of the space as the climate or the user demanded. Now, in the summer night, most of the panels were stacked in one area, forming a corner in which nestled the bed. Roll-up reed blinds provided privacy while allowing free passage of air. Cotton rope matting covered the planking, one step up to the low wide bed, a step down to a sitting area furnished with a hooked rug of muted lavenders, and big burgundy cushions. Two more steps down led to a tiny basin and toilet area, and hidden all about where most convenient were little shelves and cabinets for clothing.

Rya rearranged a glass vase of wild flowers on a shelf above the bed. ''This is one of our guest houses, impersonal but . . .''

''It's lovely, Rya, and so are you, and your family, to take a stranger in so gracefully, a . . .'' She swallowed her last word too late.

''A Terran?'' Rya shook her head. ''What has my son been telling you about us? I had always hoped for the time when I could receive my Terran friends in my own home, when everything is worked out and the Wall can come down.''

Jude's back drooped. ''Don't look for it in the near future. Your son is often driven to extremes by bitterness and hatred of the Terrans, but what he says is true. There are Terrans who suspect your existence out here. I was sent by them, in fact, to find you, to discover a way over the mountains as many others have tried and failed.''

''The madmen in the streets . . . the shanē have shown us some of that also.''

''Yes. But Ra'an and I made it through. Is that because he is Koi, or because the Wall *is* weakening?''

''I don't know,'' answered Rya thoughtfully. ''There are strange murmurings on the halmweb. We get reports . . .''

''Of what?''

Rya interrupted her reverie with a laugh. ''Oh, it's nothing.

179

There is a kind of superstitious sensibility in vogue in certain quarters. Like the weather, it will pass.' '

Jude glanced around the suite and up at the ceiling of leaves. "Rya, all this loveliness, it really is in danger."

"Not tonight, I hope," she replied, fine lines crinkling her ruddy face. "There, there, child. I'm not laughing at you. It's just that I am tired. We will speak of it tomorrow. Let me see now . . . Dal promised she would hunt up some clothing. Here." She opened a virtually invisible closet and rustled around, selecting a simple white shift with a velvet yoke. She held it up against Jude's body. "Will this do for the night?"

Jude nodded, while wondering fleetingly if she would ever again choose from a closet hung with her *own* clothing. "It's wonderful, Rya, that your Terran is so fluent after all these years."

"Kirial and I practice now and then," she replied, pleased.

"Then truly you have not forgotten the colony."

Rya sighed, and Jude heard subtle resignation. "No, we have not. We speak Terran as a . . . what is it . . . a parlor game, but secretly we understand that one day we will need it either to protect ourselves or to take part in some new Arkoi." She went to turn down the tapestry bed cover. "Do you need anything else?"

"Would there be something like an aspirin around?"

"Aspirin. Ah, yes. I mean, no. We do have painkillers for serious injury, but . . . you do not need that." Rya came close and looked at Jude intently. "Your head hurts you."

"Is it that obvious?"

Rya smiled knowingly. "Come sit with me awhile." She nestled cross-legged among the cushions in the sitting area and patted the rug beside her. As Jude joined her, Rya took her hand and began gently to massage her fingers.

"It was you who explained to me why Ra'an could not sit in on the Gathering. You must understand, then, the source of your headache."

"Well, sort of."

"Halm is a gift that one must learn to use, but even before that, one must learn to accept that it is there at all. Even Koi children who grow up with adults to whom it is second nature often find acceptance the most difficult hurdle of all."

"I guess I accept it intellectually."

"That is not enough. Part of you is listening very hard while the other part is refusing to hear. It is this conflict that creates the

180

headache." Rya's strong fingers worked at Jude's wrist, and the pain in her head lessened. "Accept the gift. Choose to listen."

"I will try." *Ra'an was surprised, Rya, but you're not.* "Did you know other Terrans with halm potential when you were in the Colony?"

"Several. Of course, we could not tell them, or help them to develop it, without endangering our security. Daniel Andreas was one, and I recall thinking that his son had very strong potential."

Jude felt a sudden chill. "James?"

"Yes, that was his name."

"James is one of the lunatics in the streets now."

Rya's fine eyes, the same violet as her son's, narrowed in sympathy. "Ah. He lost them both, then."

"He?"

"Ra'an." Rya shifted her massagings to Jude's thumb joint. "How did you become aware of your halm?"

"Ra'an. For some reason, halm contact is possible between us, in a crippled sort of way, at moments of extreme . . . well, usually when he's angry."

"Interesting. Then you should be able to help him with his blockage. There is great power there. I felt it."

"He won't really let me." She caught Rya's nod. "That's because it's me, a Terran. He would welcome a Koi who could help."

"Perhaps Anaharimel. She is a great teacher in Quaire'en."

"Tell him of her! Regaining his halm is all that matters to him."

"Is it?" Rya looked pensive. "Well, perhaps it is now. When it was time for him to learn it, all those years ago, he was not so eager. It meant being Koi to him, and he only wanted to be Terran. But perhaps Anaharimel."

She said it without rancor, and Jude found her eyes filling with tears at the complex structure of rejection and loss represented by Rya tel-Yron and her stranger-son. She looked down at Rya's long-fingered hands, so like Ra'an's, kneading her palm. "You know, Rya . . . I never had a mother either."

The older woman stopped, moved. She took both Jude's hands and patted them. "Is the pain better now?"

"It's gone."

"Then get to bed now." She rose and went about turning out all the glow-globes but one over the bed. "Sleep well, Judith," she said and was gone.

Alone for the first time in many weeks, Jude got up and

wandered about the little tree suite touching, exploring. She washed and undressed, then slipped the white shift over her head. The fit was far from perfect, but the smooth fabric was soothing against her skin. Unready yet to sleep, she returned to the cushions, digging her toes into the thick loops of the rug, burrowing into this padded comfort like a small animal. She smelled the sweet wind blowing in off the hay fields, and stared out into the leafy darkness at birds sleeping in the branches.

She thought of Terra—home no longer—a foreign country in her mind, like the Wards, like the colony. She thought of Bill Clennan and what he would give to know what she knew now. What he would do with that knowledge made her shiver, even more so when she admitted that two short months ago she would not have cared. What an extraordinary distance she had come since then.

"You should be asleep." Ra'an stood in the entry, his face hidden in shadow.

She threw him a disgusted look and turned back to her study of the leaves. "You should be ashamed of yourself."

"Ummmh." He came in and nosed around the room as she had done. He was wearing only a pair of loose-fitting dark pants. Jude tried not to look at him. *If he's trying to be provocative*, she thought, *he's certainly succeeding*. At his thigh, lounging in the blousy folds of his pantleg, one hand grasped the amber neck of a wine bottle.

"They do care, you know. You did sort of fall out of the sky, after all," she said to his naked back as he silently examined a small clay animal he had found on a corner shelf. "Give them time to get adjusted to you *and* the bad news you bring."

"I'd rather not talk about it right now," he growled.

Her patience was thinning. "Do you want to talk about how much wine you've got left in that bottle?"

"Very little. Can't you tell? Oh, and you were right. It does take longer."

"Rya is calling the household to a Gathering tomorrow, so we can tell them about the colony. Doesn't that indicate some commitment to action?"

"So I should go, to be shamed by my own family?"

"They need to hear what you have to say, Ra'an. I'm going."

"Fine. You go." He raised the bottle to his lips and drank with eyes closed.

"All right, how about this? Do you know of a teacher of halm called Anaharimel?"

"How would I know of such things?"

"She lives in Quaire'en," Jude pursued doggedly. "Rya says we should go see her."

"You and my mother certainly have a lot to say to each other." He leaned against a bit of wall, gazing outward into the dark. "What does it all matter, anyway?"

"Give it time, Ra'an! See it as a different confrontation from the one you'd prepared for anyway."

"Jude, please. Don't try so hard." Tired cracks had appeared in the armor of his anger.

"You expected angels like everyone else."

"What?"

"You expected miracles to blossom the minute you got here. Welcome to paradise, here's your halm, here's the solution to the world's problems, step right up!"

"I did not!" he flared. "But I did expect fertile ground, at least!"

"Ra'an, you've got it, if you'll only take the time to look for it!"

He snapped his arm back to send the clay animal smashing into the corner, then caught himself. With utmost care, he placed it back on the shelf. "I didn't come up here to argue." He picked up a little ceramic bowl full of scented petals, scattered its contents on the floor, and sloshed wine into it. "Here," he said, offering it to her.

Jude pulled herself up from her cushions and came to take it from him. She looked at him over the edge of the bowl as she sipped. "Are you waiting for me to seduce you again? Is that it?"

A pale hint of amusement touched the corners of his mouth. "No, I thought I could take care of that myself this time."

She drained the little bowl and set it down, then leaned her cheek against his chest. "Every time I touch you," she murmured, "I expect sparks to fly up."

The hand not holding the bottle slid around her waist to draw her tight against him.

CHAPTER 28

Drowning again in dream.

An incadescent figure fled through lightless vaults trailing an aura of fire.

Such awesome power.

Hold him back. He must not come.

Now he stops, thin arms stretched wide in welcome.

Who stands before him, who bars the way?

The beach spreads wide around them, a glitter in the distance.

This is not welcome. Ah, no! She cannot move.

Help the one who bars the way!

The black sea closes over. The water is her terror and she must breathe it in.

But wait. Light in the midnight ocean. Gentle pressure. Voices pulling toward the surface.

Listen. Do not struggle.

Help him! Help the one who bars the way!

Do not struggle. Wake.

She woke, sweating, lying spread-eagled on her back as if pinned to the bed. It was dark, and the only sound was the rustle of leaves and the breathing of the man beside her. But in her head, the voices still attended her.

Have you come back to us? Rya hovers solicitously.

She hears Dal smile encouragement.

How odd, to lie in bed with voices in your head. She labors to clear a thought, to ask them: *Is it Ra'an who bars the way?*

Gire'en sooths. Tomorrow we will speak of it.

But he comes! The white beach! The cliffs of glass!

Tekhon's solid presence is like an arm to lean on.

Sleep now.

Sleep. You are safe with us.

Sleep.

The voices were gone. The nightmare paralysis was gone. Jude stirred in her tangle of quilt and nestled closer to the

184

sleeping man, resisting the compulsion to wake him that remained after the dream had fled. But as she touched him, he turned over and took her in his arms.

"Cold," he murmured, groggy with sleep and reawakening desire.

"The dreams again." She shivered.

His hand caressed the inside of her thigh.

"Ra'an, listen to me." The compulsion was too great.

He heard the tremor in her voice and came finally awake. "I'm listening."

"I think . . . I'm convinced you're in some kind of terrible danger."

He reached over her head to touch on the light. "What?"

Her hands fluttered. "Now I'm embarrassed because it sounds so silly, but I *had* to tell you."

He studied her seriously. "Another dream. Tell me."

She told him the dream, hoping he would scoff and dismiss it, but when she had finished, he lay back, silent for a moment, still as death, then a long hissing breath escaped him. "Maybe it's me he's after."

"Ra'an, what's going on? Why do my dreams make more sense to you than they do to me?"

"Perhaps because they are intended for me." He sat up, hunched over crossed legs, pondering this revelation. "What if your dreams are not, as we thought, the result of random halm impulses? What if somebody has been sending you exactly what he wants me to hear? Or know. Or fear."

"Who? It would have to be a Koi, right?"

"You of all people should know better than that." His fingers twitched the bed cover back and forth. "I think it's James Andreas."

"But why?"

"Suppose he has some rational . . . well, maybe not, but some purpose in mind for me. He can't reach me directly. We have no halm connection, he and I. So he uses you as a conduit. By planting suggestions in the form of dreams in your head, he seeks to direct my actions along some predetermined path."

"In the dream you were trying to stop him from doing something."

"Yes. I wonder what."

"The implication was that he was prepared to kill you if you got in his way."

"No. The implication is more than that. Otherwise he wouldn't be trying to tell me ahead of time. He *wants* me to be there, wherever it is, so that he *can* kill me.''

"Ra'an, this is crazy. Why?'' ·

"For Daniel's sake? Revenge?''

"Look, if he wanted to avenge Daniel, he could have killed you back in the colony.''

Ra'an shook his head impatiently. He had fastened onto the vengeance theory. "His mind was too scattered then. Some extraordinary thing has happened to snap him into focus. That's what I saw when you showed me your dream on the huruss. This new focus. It's like light burning through a lens. Lethal.''

Jude was suddenly galvanized. "But he's coming here! In the dream, the beach, the cliffs of glass! He was there!''

Ra'an'a eyes narrowed. "Quaire'en. It can only be. If he's headed there, we don't go to Quaire'en.''

"But Anaharimel . . . the halm school - . . .!''

"Ah, yes. A pretty trap my brother lays for me. If this teacher is the only one to give me back that which I lack, how can I not go to Quaire'en?'' His jaw hardened as he answered his own question. "So be it. I will not. I will not go to Quaire'en. I will not take his bait. I will not live out this destiny he plans for me. I am sick to death of being manipulated, used by Terrans. Daniel is dead. The past is dead. I want only to be left alone, here in Ruvala. I have lived half my life already without halm. I will live the other half the same.'' His fist clenched defensively, as if to assure himself that he believed his own words. He turned off the light and lay down, his desire forgotten. "If you dream again, tell me nothing about it.''

And what about me? Jude wanted to ask him, but did not.

CHAPTER 29

Warm fragrant air and freckles of sunlight filtered through the leaf canopy. Beside Jude, the bed was empty. From the heat smells, she knew it must be midmorning already.

She washed hurriedly and rummaged through the closet for some clothing, any clothing but the same trail clothes she had

186

been living in for three weeks. She tried on a loose-fitting shirt colored like an iridescent shell, but decided she was unable to make a spectacle of herself. A pair of baggy trousers made her thin body look like a stick above the waist. A robe-like garment with half-sleeves seemed too formal, and she was not used to skirts. After she had emptied the little closet onto the bed, she hung everything up again and pulled on her own worn shirt and pants. They were clean this time, after all, and they did feel comfortable.

Fleetingly, it bothered her that the Koi clothing, although it had fit her body perfectly well, had not felt comfortable on her. Was this some hint of an inability to assimilate? *Is that what I want?* she wondered. *To assimilate? To become Koi, or half Koi, as Ra'an is half Terran? He certainly isn't very happy that way.*

Then she thought, *Gods, give it time, you just got here. Find something to do, make yourself useful, but give it time.*

She trotted across the branch walkway and down the circular stairs. The dining platform was deserted but for several bright-green birds pecking at crumbs on the tabletop and one of the wolf dogs alseep in a corner. Jude nodded to herself. The true sign of being a guest is arriving at table long after breakfast is over. She stood listening. The great tree house felt completely empty. Not even the murmur of halm static in her head. They must all be out in the fields. But wait. Having made a conscious adjustment in her brain to listen for halmtalk, she now felt a gentle nudge, like a greeting without words. Across the platform, the giant dog creature raised itself up from its nap and ambled over to her. Jude had been introduced to three of them, and was unsure which one this was, but she touched its shaggy head in welcome. What had Rya called them? The gria. They reminded her of the mules who had shared her journey, so she could not help but like them immediately. As she stroked the gria absently, thinking of her mule friends, an image formed in her head of herself blissfully asleep, followed by a sense of inquiry. She glanced around, startled, but the beast nuzzled her hand patiently, and she remembered what Ra'an had told her about the animals in Ruvala. She knelt down to look it in the eye.

She thought a question. *Where is everybody?* The animal blinked at her in placid incomprehension. Jude scolded herself. *Don't think in words and expect a beast without language to understand!* She tried again, laboriously working up an image of Rya, then each of the others in the family, ending with a question. Immediately the gria wagged its massive tail, and

187

visions of the hay fields streamed into Jude's head, of Tekhon and Dal loading heavy bales on a wagon while Elgri adjusted the harness on a mule, of Gire'en and the twins gathering eggs from long rows of nests, finally of Rya singing as a flock of minute birds whirled around her head. No sign of Ra'an. Jude formed Ra'an's image again, but the gria lowered its head and seemed to shrug. Jude ruffled its ears by way of apology.

"Of course you can't know where he is," she said aloud, "unless he has the halm to tell you." She was beginning to get an inkling of what Ra'an had been missing.

She fumbled for a way to ask the gria to take her to Rya, finally picturing herself and Rya together. Obligingly, it shook itself and led her off through the tree trunks to the outer edge of the dome, where they found the older woman fussing among the blossoms of a flowering hedge. All around her hovered the little birds, the lai, no doubt, and very much like hummingbirds they were, long needle beaks set in a blur of beating wings.

Rya smiled a welcome, and static hummed in Jude's head. She tried vainly to make sense of it, then looked at Rya helplessly.

"I'm sorry. I can't . . ."

Rya laughed. "You must stop thinking so hard! I merely wondered if Theis had offered you anything to eat."

"Theis?"

Rya indicated the gria. "Otherwise she seems to have taken care of you."

"Ah. Yes. She's been wonderful."

"She has been interested in Terrans ever since I explained to her that her cousin, the dog, is the one animal the Terrans have learned to live with." Her eyes sparkled, softening the reproof. "Come. Meet the lai. Then you will eat." She held her palm out and four of the winged blurs settled on it, peering at Jude with bright eyes. Then Rya shooed them away gently and parted the leaves of the bush she had been working on. Fastened on the branch were several thin glass tubes. Leaning closer to look, Jude saw each contained an amount of clear liquid. Rya loosed one from its housing and emptied it into a bottle she carried strapped to her belt.

"Proper cooking crystallizes it," she explained. "I make mine in my lab because I can keep an eye on it while I work, but of course that is not necessary. Did you sleep well after your nightmare?"

"Yes. When will you call the Gathering, Rya?"

"After dinner is the usual time."

"I see. Do you have any idea where Ra'an is?"

188

"He went out early with Tekhon and Elgri. The bales are lying in the fields and there are reports of rain heading our way."

Jude digested the idea of Ra'an doing fieldwork. "I'm surprised you're not more mechanized here. I mean, you do have the technology."

"Yes, but we are a small household. We do not need it. Where hands and backs can do the labor, why take their work away from them?"

"All right. Then there must be something you can give me to do."

Without even a moment's polite equivocation, Rya replied, "There is always work that needs doing." She put her tubes aside and led Jude out into the warm sun to a luxuriant stretch of dark greenery. Along one edge were stacks of rush baskets. Rya caught one up and passed it to her.

"The ripe ones are deep purple," she said, hitching up her skirt and wading into the rows to show Jude where the berries lay hidden under broad blue-green leaves.

"How many should I pick?" Jude asked with widening eyes.

"As many as you can!" Rya returned gaily. "What we don't eat right away, we trade or preserve. There's never any waste. If you get tired before dinnertime, take the baskets to the kitchen. I'll have Theis bring you something to eat." She gave Jude a maternal pat and returned to her own labors.

Before dinner? It's barely lunch. Jude's heart sank as she gazed over the sea of berry bushes. She had the distinct impression from Rya that what looked to her like a potentially vast effort was a task normally left to small children and the elderly. She lowered herself to one knee, careful not to crush any stray vines, and began to fill her first basket.

Three hours later, she sat back on her heels, two brimming baskets sitting at the end of the row. The task was not hard as she had feared. The ripe berries were easy to distinguish and practically fell off the vine into her hand. As she worked, the hot clear sun baked the last ounce of tension from her journey-worn muscles. She felt completely relaxed for the first time in years.

She nibbled at the vegetable pastry that Theis had delivered in a small cloth sack. Above her head arced a sky so blue it hurt to look at it. A golden haze clung to the fields and tree-dotted hills like a blessing. The fine shimmer that still warped her vision wrapped distant objects in an aura of magic. The midday stillness was so profound that Jude fancied she could hear the young vine

189

shoots pressing up through the rich loam between her toes, so profound that it brought tears of recognition to her eyes. Poor Langdon's journal had not been the ravings of a lunatic, but an earnest attempt at accurate description. The mistake had been to assume he was talking about religion, when what he was trying to record was a firsthand view of paradise, or something surely close to it.

It was hard for her to worry in such blissful surroundings, hard to remember the grimness of the colony, hard to believe that one could be threatened by dreams and distant madmen.

She bent back to her berries in contentment.

The cool shadow of Yron fell long across the berry fields when Jude stood up clutching a final basket. Her back ached and her knees were sore, but she was pleased with her afternoon's labor. She could look forward to a wash and dinner and feel she deserved it. She lugged the basket to the end of the row and set it down beside the others. Five full baskets. She stood back, admiring the burgundy glisten of the mounded fruit, then pondered the problem of transporting five overflowing baskets in one trip to the kitchens. Her legs tingled, weakened. *Still not in shape.* As she bent to sit down, a wave of dizziness struck her. *Too much sun?* She straightened, swaying, and looked up. A sheer wall of rock towered over her, not as in a vision but as if it were there before her, so real that she could see chill light glimmering on each needle of the pine scrub clinging to the ledges. The sky glowered gray. The rock was dark and slicked with rain.

Now what's happening to me? She dropped to her knees and touched soft grass and fertile earth. She looked again.

At the foot of the scarp, a dark hole gaped, like a . . . *Ruvala Station? No. Too barren and cold. But yes* . . . She could see a single broad rail curving through the boulders. She waited, knew she must wait and watch, expecting the sudden blur of the huruss to emerge from the tunnel mouth. Instead, the blackness expanded, drawing her inward until it filled her entire field of vision. A pinpoint of light bobbed at the center of the void. It grew, nearing without a sound.

Jude buried both hands in the grass which her touch insisted was there, and hung on for dear life. *This waiting is unendurable!*

And then he was there, stepping into sunlight.

The rain. What happened to the rain?

He stood in silhouette against the dark rock. Behind him a raised hand brandished a torch whose flame paled against the brilliance of the man ahead. Others followed from the tunnel, a crowd, a flock that gathered around him as he lifted his arms in benediction.

He comes! He comes!

She felt him perilously close and knew the madman was among them.

The dizziness struck again. She reeled and was back in the green berry fields. Alarm bells clanged in her brain. Come! Come! shrilled the alarm. Her body twitched with the impulse to run. *He comes! He comes!* her brain echoed, confused. Her head swiveled in panic. Across the fields, she could see Tekhon and Dal and the others heading in from all directions. *A halm alarm?* She broke and ran for the house.

The family met in commotion on the dining platform. The adults immediately settled themselves on the cushions surrounding the great table. The twins and Elgri hung back, curling around the three gria, who crouched with ears alert.

As Jude stumbled up breathlessly, the Koi turned expectant eyes on her. "Sit with us," Rya insisted. "Such a signal has not come for many years."

"Did you see him?" Jude gasped. The alarm still beat its rhythm in her head.

Rya frowned. "See him? Who?" The halm signal ceased. "Tell us later," Rya said. "Come listen." She turned to her son. "Ra'an?"

From the stair post where he had been leaning distantly, Ra'an gave an awkward shrug intended to remind them of the pointlessness of including him, but he slouched over and pulled up a cushion next to his grandfather.

The circle quieted. Jude concentrated on tuning her brain to what she imagined might be maximum receptivity. Nothing happened. She stole a glance around the table. Except for Ra'an, who was watching her darkly, the others sat relaxed, eyes closed. Waiting? Jude eyed Rya's hand resting lightly on the table beside her. Would physical contact complete the circuit?

But Rya murmured, "You must learn to listen."

Jude listened.

And the message was rolling through her mind like a flash flood, so fast and complex she could grasp only snatches. Images, no words, a sequence of action: a rocky scarp in the mountains, squat towers of masonry, a silent crowd in a courtyard, a pale-haired man in . . . Andreas!

Her recognition ricochets around the table.

Tekhon finds her first. Who is it?

Her lips struggle soundlessly, for it is Ra'an she must warn and she is floating in the halmweb and cannot verbalize.

Ra'an!

Tekhon is insistent. *Who is this man we see?*

The one who comes. James Andreas.

She feels Rya's gasp, and the circle is flooded with a memory of a towheaded child slowly turning a huge rock crystal in fascinated hands.

Ra'an! Jude fixes his position across the table and sends the image of Andreas bolting toward him. Touching his mind is like walking through darkness. He limits her access, resists her presence, but the image captures his interest.

What do they hear of James?

She tries to draw him into the circle.

He resists. *No. I cannot.*

Come, try, it will be easy now.

No. Tell me the news of James.

You could hear it yourself!

No.

She must be his bridge to the circle.

Where is James?

She cannot name the mountain towers, but Tekhon is near and knows it well.

The retreat of the Diamo. A Terran has found his own way through the Guardians.

She passes this along, and feels Ra'an shudder. His mind goes racing away along several potential futures that all begin with James Andreas and the Diamo.

There is more. The man in rags addresses the crowd. His passion touches their upturned faces with fire. Jude cannot catch the words. *Tekhon? Rya?*

A suspended moment, then a current of horror stirring the circle. Dal breaks contact abruptly.

Jude cannot grasp it. *What? What?*

Ra'an is demanding to know.

I cannot find them in the web.

Then they have barriered themselves.

Wait. One last fleeting image: the long white beach and the cliffs of glass. *Quaire'en.* The circle disintegrates.

Jude sat stunned on her cushion. Why were they looking at her with such fearful compassion?

Ra'an leaned forward impatiently. "James and . . .? What else?"

192

Jude looked at Tekhon helplessly, forgetting that they did not share a language.

"Rya?" Ra'an pursued harshly.

Rya chose her words very cautiously, as if she were laying eggs in a basket. "James . . . when you told me he was mad, Judith, I did not imagine . . . he preaches his mission to the Diamo. They are hailing him as a savior."

"Mission? Savior?" Ra'an zeroed in where she had chosen to be vague.

"He claims to be raising an army, to . . ." Rya faltered. "To drive the Terrans from Arkoi."

Ra'an grunted. "Fine idea, but it'll never work. A Koi army wouldn't stand a chance against the Terran military. This must be some subterfuge of his. He knows better than to send out an army of Koi."

Tekhon interjected a hard comment, and Rya implored. "How can we speak of such a thing?"

Tekhon would not be put off. He turned to Jude and painstakingly, she deciphered his transmission. She sat numbly when they were done. "Wow," she breathed. "Is that possible?"

"What?" Ra'an demanded.

Jude wrapped her arms around her chest. "It seems that what James has in mind is not expulsion but murder . . . every last Terran in Arkoi with one blow."

Ra'an scoffed. "How the hell does he plan to do that?"

Jude could barely form the word. "Halm."

His dark face froze. He shot her a look of remembered guilt, having special knowledge of halm's potential as a weapon. He rose from his cushion and moved off to sit alone in one of the upper reading areas.

Jude turned to Rya. "What are you going to do to stop him?"

Rya studied the fine grain on the table. "He can only be stopped if the population wills it."

"If? You mean he might find enough support to . . .?"

"He has timed his coming well. I told you that superstition was in vogue, and the Diamo are right at the center of it. The population nurses a secret impatience with the Terran situation. To many, passive resistance is no longer the panacea it once was. They miss their friends in the colony. They are tired of waiting. They want it resolved."

"Is impatience sufficient motive for mass murder?" Jude thought her voice sounded shrill.

Rya touched her hand lightly, an attempt at comfort where there was little she could offer. "Of course not, but who knows

193

what other phantoms James Andreas will raise in our collective mind? He may rouse us until we no longer question his choice of weapon." She nodded, considering the possibilities as she spoke of them. "Where Balance has been the norm, his Imbalance might infect unwary minds, might spread like a fever." Her voice faded to a whisper, and she spoke of it to herself. "We must be on our guard."

Tekhon also, and the others, seemed lost in thought.

"I can't believe it," Jude said loudly.

Rya blinked and returned. "The message says he leads his followers toward Quaire'en. No doubt he plans to put the issue before the Council. A Terran has never brought a question to the Ring before, and the Council would be within its rights to refuse to hear him. But if his halm is as strong as the message suggests . . . yes, he may find support even among the Council members themselves."

"And?"

Rya continued doggedly. "If he has enough support, the Council will be required to call a World Gathering to debate the issue. And if the Gathering decides in his favor . . ." Rya's look was eloquent.

Jude recognized this retreat into rational discussion for the defense that it was. "But this could actually happen? He could do it?"

Rya's long-fingered hands, so like her son's, worked ineffectual circles on the tabletop. "It has been many hundreds of years, but yes, halm was once used to kill. The history is taught in school as a warning, in eyewitness accounts that have been passed down from teacher to teacher." Her hands stilled. "So vivid. I remember I was so horrified after that lesson that I could not bring myself to use my halm for many days." She stopped, cleared her throat. "Forgive me. I am not used to so much talking."

Jude hoped it was more than a tickle catching at the Koi woman's throat. "Won't the other Koi share this remembered horror?"

"Many will, yes, but others will fear the Terran horror more."

"The Terran *horror*?"

Rya answered softly. "This seems extreme to you, I know, but you have no memory of Arkoi as it was before the Terrans came. It is easy to remember it as much more glorious than it really was, and so hate the Terrans for taking that treasure away." She stirred and took Jude's hand again. "But, child, there is hope for you. The best defense against halm is halm

194

itself. Your halm may save you, if it comes to that. You need only learn to control it."

"Hope for me?" Jude repeated dully. She had not thought far enough to personalize this insane threat. Suddenly Rya's distress seemed superficial, disabled by premature resignation. "But there must be something that can be done! Don't you *want* to stop Andreas?"

Rya looked shocked. "Of course. If the Gathering is called, I will do my best to speak out against him."

"What about before that? Before the last minute?"

"What would you suggest?"

Jude flailed inwardly. The only deterrents she was familiar with were execution or the Wards. *Don't the Koi have jails?* "I don't know. Isn't there some legal recourse? What do you do if someone does something harmful to your society?"

Jude was sure that Rya flicked a glance in the direction of her son. "Harmful to whose society?"

"Anyone. People. Lives. I was thrown in jail for a lot less than he's advocating!"

"If a majority of our population agree with James Andreas, it would be wrong to stop him, would it not?"

"But . . ."

"Judith, please. Be calm. Perhaps it is only the Diamo who have received this outrage favorably. They are extremists. The general population is not so volatile. They're not likely to desert their fields and go running off after a Terran madman. I will contact Kirial tonight in Quaire'en. We will see what the reaction has been in the Ring." She stood up, ending the discussion with a smile. "It would be helpful if you could bring the berry baskets to the kitchen when you have time." She helped Gire'en to rise, then hurried off to organize the dinner.

Jude climbed to where Ra'an sat staring at the floor and settled on a cushion beside him.

For a long time, he didn't move. His hands kneaded the edge of a pillow as if it were resisting his control. Finally he said, "Could that be what I am supposed to stop him from doing?"

Jude tried to read through the mask of conflict on his face. "Why should a Koi who hates Terra try to stop a Terran from killing Terrans?"

His laugh was more bitter than usual. "I am Koi, yes, by birth. But I am also the Terran that Daniel brought me up to be. Apparently James understands that better than I did. I had to come home to Ruvala to see it . . . not that I had any desire to learn such a lesson, to know for certain that I don't fit in here any more than I did in the colony."

"Time, Ra'an, give it time."

"You keep saying that as if we had any, either of us. James will not leave me in peace now. You and your damn dreams."

Not my fault! Jude shrank into her cushion. "I didn't know . . ."

He made a dismissive gesture. "If you hadn't come along, he would have found some other way. You couldn't have known you'd fit right into some lunatic's idea whose time had come. Only James knew that."

"Then you believe he can read the future?" Jude was too numb to muster true incredulity.

Ra'an cocked his head in a qualified negative. His tone was remote, as if debating an interesting philosophical dilemma. "What is prescience, really? Predictions based on present knowledge. It's taking an educated guess. James always, like his father, had an extraordinary brain, missed nothing, remembered everything. And so, when madness encouraged leaps of insight that a so-called sane mind would reject, James became a brilliant guesser and at some point or another began translating his guessing into action. He must have started planning when you arrived. He obviously knew another Terran with halm when he saw one. It was all falling into place for him." Ra'an lay back against his cushion, hands behind his head. He stared up into the shadowed leaves.

"And now, he's betting that I cannot reject Daniel's legacy forever; that, although I am Koi, I will not be able simply to stand aside and watch him butcher five million Terrans, no matter how much I may think I despise them. He is betting that because I loved Daniel, I will step in and try to stop him."

"Ra'an, it's so inconceivable. The lives of millions resting on the blood feud of two men?"

"No, to give James his due, avenging Daniel is probably a convenient by-product of his greater mission. I am sure he genuinely believes this is the only way to save Arkoi, and there's no question that that is where his loyalties lie."

"But what could *you* do to stop him? Your mother didn't seem to think there was anything that could be done, until the Gathering."

"Well, as the Koi see it, there isn't anything. I would have to use Terran methods, running around the countryside like a politician, rallying support against him. Then, of course, there's always assassination." He lowered his head. "But I can't do that. I cannot murder my brother."

196

"Yeah, well, your 'brother' may be about to murder you and me as well."

Ra'an's perception of her danger seemed to have been delayed. He studied her seriously for a moment, then shook his head. "Clever, clever James. But I won't take this bait, either. Don't ask me to be drawn into this for your sake."

What?

For a moment, she couldn't breath. "No . . . ah. No." She tried to pump resolution into her voice, to pretend that she would not have expected otherwise, but the easy coolness of his refusal was like a knife in the heart. "Rya says my halm will probably save me anyway, if I work to develop it. I think I should go to Quaire'en tomorrow."

His head moved slightly. "So soon?"

She stood up, a bravado gesture. "Why not? Why not be where the danger is? I can work with Anaharimel and watch James Andreas bear down upon the city. It'll be very exciting." She could not help it. Accusation crept in at the end. "Besides, there's nothing for me here, is there?" She stalked across the platform, then stopped and turned back. "I don't blame you for rejecting the role James intends for you, but I hope you'll be kinder to your mother now on the subject of complacency!"

Stung, he raised himself from the cushion. "The Terrans are not my responsibility!" he growled.

"Saving lives should be everyone's responsibility!"

He turned on his side. "Very noble. Tell that to a Terran."

"I *am* a Terran!" She stood very still, concentration directed inward, as if she had suddenly forgotten he was there. *I am a Terran.* Considering this, she walked slowly toward the staircase.

CHAPTER 30

———•◦•———◦•———

Jude passed the night alone and unsleeping. Early in the morning, she heard someone come down the walkway toward her room, hesitate, then turn around and walk away. It took all her strength to keep from running after.

Just before dawn, she fell asleep, and instantly the madman

197

was with her, or she with him, on his progress through the greening foothills below the mountain retreat of the Diamo. There was a stone-and-thatch village by a rushing stream. A mill, lying deserted at noon, its front door open to the sun. A child toddled out of the crowds lining the cart track. Without breaking stride, he stopped and swung it to his thin shoulder. The crowd cooed and cheered. Caught as she was within the iron grip of the dream, she resisted, wishing for the halm power to call out to the admiring throng, *He knows just what to do to win you, can't you see? He's studied you so carefully and so long.*

But a voice in her dream answered, *What does it matter, if I bring them what they want? See how they flock to me?*

Over his head, the shanevoralin, his familiars, wheeled and screamed in ecstasy.

She woke. It was daylight. She roused herself and went downstairs to search out Rya. The dream had made up her mind.

She found Rya in the underground lab, absorbed in her computer. Jude pulled over a stool, watched for a while, but finally could not wait.

"Will you help me get to Quaire'en, Rya? To study with Anaharimel?"

Rya looked up from her keyboard. It had no keys but a pattern of light trapped within a grid. "The dreams?"

Jude nodded. "They won't leave me . . . *he* won't leave me alone."

"The halm school is protected. Halm cannot get in or out. In that silence, Ana can teach you the proper barriers. When do you want to go?"

"As soon as possible. Today?"

Rya's hands played across the grid, stopped, started, then pulled away. She set the computer to run the program and sat back in her chair. "So that's it." She reached into a drawer and pulled out a cloth-wrapped bundle. "When he left this morning, Ra'an asked me to give this to you."

"Left?" Jude tried not to sound too surprised.

"He said he was going into the upper forests for a week or so. To get reacquainted, he said. You did not discuss this?"

"He wants to be alone, is more like it," Jude replied. She cradled the packet in her lap but did not open it.

"I had thought perhaps that there was more between you than that," Rya ventured with some delicacy.

Jude shrugged more casually than she felt. "His original homecoming plan did not include bringing a Terran along—I just sort of happened. He'll have an easier time learning to live as a

Koi again without me around to remind him of his life in the colony.''

Rya's dark eyebrows arched slightly, then settled into resignation. ''I hoped that the shanē were wrong about my son. I want to believe that he wishes to regain his halm and live as a Koi. But if that were so, he would go to Quaire'en with you.''

''He can't go to Quaire'en!'' Jude blurted.

''Of course he can.'' Rya frowned as if discussing a recalcitrant child.

How could you understand? Do I even understand? Jude only nodded, accepting. *He must not come to Quaire'en!*

''I can arrange for an evening huruss. That will get to Quaire'en at midday tomorrow. I will let Anaharimel know to expect you. Take Theis if you like. She has been to Quaire'en and you will be in need of company.''

''Thank you. You've been so kind, Rya.'' She said it flatly, but Rya leaned forward and took both her hands in her own, favoring her with a long searching look that offered no admonitions or advice, merely support. Impulsively, Jude leaned over and kissed her cheek.

Rya smiled. ''We'll hope to be hearing from you soon on the halmweb.''

Jude stood, clutching her bundle. ''Did you speak to Kirial last night?''

Rya's smile flattened. ''Yes. The news was ill. Already Quaire'en is a divided city, even before the madman's arrival. Some fear him, others await his coming. The Council is deciding whether to hear his case.''

''In my dream, the people followed him wherever he went, as if he could touch each individual and know what promise will bind them to him.''

''Halm can have that power,'' said Rya. ''But some will still refuse to pay the price he requires. We must put our faith in that.''

''Umm.'' Jude had little faith left. *Out of the frying pan . . . At least in the colony, there was no one trying to kill me.* ''Well, I'll be in Quaire'en when Andreas arrives. That should be interesting.''

She left Rya with her computer and climbed back up to her room. She laid the bundle on the bed and unfolded it. Inside was the leather-cased flask and a note: ''Work hard on your halm, and when you see James, give him this and tell him I refuse his challenge. Would you have me ask of you, stay here and die for my sake?''

199

It was not signed. *What makes him so sure I will get anywhere near James Andreas?* Jude picked up the flask, traced the tooled initials. She had vowed not to be sentimental, but could not help wondering if she would ever see Ra'an again. Anger rose up in her against the man whose initials now blurred before her eyes. How different would things be if Daniel Andreas had not been so obdurate as to walk off into the mountains alone?

Brusquely, she rewrapped flask and note and tossed them into the bottom of her knapsack. She took her cameras down from a shelf, stared at them for a while, then bundled them up in a shirt. That package she would leave for Ra'an. She would keep her part of their original bargain.

As she went downstairs to find work until the evening, she vowed she would have a great deal to say to James Andreas when she saw him again.

CHAPTER 31

In the early dawn the whitewashed walls of the Quarter were damp and cool. Verde eased himself through an anonymous doorway and stood listening. It was several hours too early for the few brave tourist shoppers or the roving gangs of looters still prowling the city. Verde pulled a shapeless cap low over his forehead. His old shirt and pants, an obvious mark of identity, had been discarded for the dull-orange regulation tunic. He had never tried passing for Koi before and hoped that many years of close observation would serve in lieu of practice.

From the shadow of the doorway, Ron Jeffries called to him in hushed tones. "Four hours, Mitch. Then we send out the dogs. Should be me going out there. I used to get paid to sneak around."

Verde smiled tightly. "Told you you should have learned the language. You stay put whether I come back or not."

"I should have tied you up down there. What're you going to learn out here that the Koi can't tell us?"

Verde returned a heedless wave and started down the narrow

200

street, reining his usual hurried gait to the sedate pace more suited to an elderly Koi out walking in the early light.

He crisscrossed the Quarter for an hour, meeting no one, not even Koi, though he expected they would be stirring soon. Nearing his office, he spotted two members of the colonial police, not among those normally assigned to the Quarter, lounging against the outside wall of Montserrat's. The café's mullioned front window had been smashed again, and bits of broken chairs were strewn about on the pavement. The door to his office lay invitingly open, but he could see scatterings of paper breaking up the darkness of the floor inside, and he was willing to bet that a mere molecule sent across the threshold would set off alarms in every guardhouse in the colony, not to mention the one at Clennan's bedside.

Verde took the long way around the square, noting that the booth by the front gate was manned by several men he had never seen before, wearing Terran army insignia. He whistled soundlessly. The army. The Colonial Authority must have called in reinforcements to deal with the rioting. He stole a glance through the steel grating. It was quiet outside. The guards smoked casually, but the street was littered with cans and bottles and charred debris. Farther down, smoke rose from the sodden remains of a shop. For once, Verde's feelings about the thick wall and locked gate were unambivalent. The outer city was undoubtedly in worse shape than the Quarter.

He was headed for Luteverindorin's house when it occurred to him to wonder how much Clennan and his boys knew about his normal patterns of movement, and therefore which Koi they would have under surveillance, if they were smart enough to think that far. He decided merely to scout that end of town and return to the cellars while his luck held. He chose a circuitous route along one side of the big central square, but halfway down the line of buildings, the street he was aiming for was suddenly choked with armed men marching in rank. Verde fought the instinct to shrink into the nearest doorway. There was no hope that his orange tunic would be missed against the stark white walls, perhaps the rationale behind the choice of orange in the first place. He kept his head low and his steps calm, but his nerves tautened until he thought he must break and run. The soldiers marched right by him with little more than a glance in his direction. Verde congratulated himself on the success of his disguise. He slipped down the street they had come from, nearly breaking into a trot until he heard shuffling ahead. He padded cautiously to the next corner and found the street again crowded with soldiers, a large detachment leaning about polishing their stunners without talking.

Now Verde was getting worried. He plodded across the intersection in plain view, not breathing until he was out of their sight. Then he stood for a moment calculating how long it would take him to reach any one of the hidden entries to the cellars, first at a disguised walk, then at a dead run. Seven minutes at a walk to the nearest. He headed in that direction, cursing the impatience that had brought him out of his hiding place.

A mere block from his goal, a burst of radio chatter sounded in the next street, followed by the sharp clack of weapons being raised to ready. Seconds later, the Quarter erupted with soldiers.

Verde's heart started up madly, and he knew he must calm himself for his health's sake. He assumed the soldiers were searching for him, and spent some thought on what to do if he did get caught, but gave it up with a laugh, knowing suicide was the only answer. And here he was worrying about his heart. His escape route blocked, he put his faith in his disguise and sat down in a doorway pretending to doze.

But the soldiers were not searching. They had divided into groups of three and were going from house to house, banging on doors, bursting in and rousting out the occupants, driving them into the middle of the cobblestone street. Barefoot children, old women in their nightclothes, half-dressed, pulling scant clothing over their nakedness, the Koi went so calmly that the soldiers grew suspicious and shouted their orders, shoving them into line, driving them up the street. If there is violence, Verde noted, it will not be the Koi who started it. The bedraggled mob neared his doorway. He was glad that those with any reckless streak in them had already followed James Andreas into the tunnels. He sank his head farther into his shoulders, despising the necessity to remain quiet in the face of such an outrage. But he was powerless, like the Koi, and a wanted man, it seemed. The best he could hope for was that the soldiers would drag him along with the rest.

The soldiers spotted him. One stalked over and grabbed him by the arm. "Get in line, gramps," he ordered, shoving Verde toward the others. His companion broke down the door Verde had vacated with the butt of his rifle, a heavy-duty weapon that Verde could not recall having seen in the colony before.

Gentle hands supported him as he was pushed into the line of prisoners. They returned his desperate glances with murmured

202

Koi greetings, an assurance that his secret would be safe with them. He felt secure that even his imperfect Koi would sound fluent enough to the soldiers and asked those near him if they knew where they were being taken.

No one had overheard anything, but when they reached the great square, long lines of trucks from the vegetable farms awaited them. Verde was aghast. They're rounding up the entire population of the Quarter, he realized. He caught a glimpse of Luteverindorin stumbling as he was hauled into a truck on the other side of the square, then he too was being prodded toward the back of a truck and had to fight to keep from falling himself. They were packed in body to body until no one could move. The younger Koi squeezed tightly together to leave room for the old people to breathe. The loading doors were slammed shut and a metal bar slid into place. Verde closed his eyes and tried to ignore the beads of sweat running down his face. He could not free an arm to wipe it away. The truck started up with a crushing jolt that was only the first taste of the next hour's agony.

When they finally jarred to a halt, the doors were yanked open and the bruised and shaken occupants were blinded with a flood of hot sunlight. They were herded out onto a hard-baked dust field enclosed by an impressive electric fence, no trees, no shelter, only some dry grass surviving in scattered clumps, and not a sign of water. Just the sun and the dust and truckload after truckload of suffering Koi being penned up like animals.

Verde searched through the crowd until he found Lute. The old man was dazed and coughing. Verde took his arm and led him out of the thick of the dust. He eased Lute onto the ground, then dropped beside him, panting.

"What is in their minds now, I wonder?" wheezed Lute when he had breath enough to speak.

"That son of a bitch Clennan is behind this, I'll bet." Verde surveyed the corral with a growl of impotent rage. "No water, no shelter. Do they want us to die out here?"

"It would save them ammunition," Lute commented.

The old man's dry smile brought Verde up short, defusing his anger. "Right, Lute. If I learn to think like you, I'll live longer. Concentrate on positive actions. First thing we've got to do is organize a group of Terran speakers to demand some water. I'd do it, but I've got to lie low."

Lute continued to smile through the dust, like the sun setting in chiaroscuro. "Ah, Mitchell," he said fondly. "Were you to find yourself by some great error in that Terran hell your legends

203

tell of, you would be firing off letters of protest for better conditions to old Scrooge himself.''

"Old Scratch, that is, "Verde corrected, moved to gruffness by such indefatigable good humor. "You sit tight for a while. I'll go see what I can do.''

It was not until twilight that water was finally hauled into the detention camp. It came in metal barrels labeled with army stenciling, and it was hot from sitting all day in the broiling sun. A crate of plastic cups was dumped alongside, plus a truckload of cracking tarps and a bundle of bent aluminum poles. Verde looked it over in dismay. There was not enough of anything. For the night, they spread the tarps out on the dirt, too exhausted after a day in the sun to worry about how they would protect themselves from it on the morrow.

In the half-dusk, searchlights snapped on at the four corners of the compound. Verde squinted into the glare. There was a commotion at the gate as a line of shiny green jeeps pulled up to disgorge more brass than Verde had seen since his last Armed Forces Day on Terra. A burly man in dress uniform led the parade among the trucks and crates. Verde crouched in the dirt and watched him walk the perimeter with a gaggle of officers. The searchlights escorted them like celebrities. A bodyguard of infantry marched ahead and behind, kicking up a cloud of dust that blew across the yard into Verde's watchful eyes.

He searched for Bill Clennan's square-shouldered profile among the group, figuring the Intelligence man to be always on hand to show visiting dignitaries around personally. But the burly, balding officer was doing that, as if he owned the place. He talked and gestured, his voice raised above the others'.

The army. Verde chewed his sunburned lip. So much army around all of a sudden. He noted that the officer ignored the prisoners entirely.

After dark, the food arrived, a tasteless soup in half-barrels and trays of meat hash. Verde was starved enough to eat it but had to refuse like the others, on the chance that some alert soldier might notice a lone meat eater. It could have been soy hash, growled the old conservationist to himself. This is either Clennan's idea of an insult or he's learned less since he's been here than I thought humanly possible. Even the most insulated of the colonial bureaucrats had figured out that the Koi were vegetarian.

204

But one of the guards patrolling the food line noticed that the hash was left untouched. He strolled over to another guard and jerked his thumb toward the greasy trays. "Not good enough for them." He nudged his companion in the ribs. "Good enough for us last night, wasn't it?" The companion laughed, put his hand to his stomach, and moved off.

So they're feeding meat to this army, Verde mused. He tried to kill his hunger with soup, then stretched out in the dirt near Lute, who had mercifully fallen asleep as the sun set. Sunburned and weak, Verde was at a loss for ideas. The maintenance of the Wall had been shifted to the detention camp for the night, to allow those who had been in the cellars at the time of the roundup to get some rest. At dawn, they would have to take over again. Such exacting work could not be done in noise and dust and heat.

What to do? In the morning, Lute was going to try once more to contact the fickle shanevoralin. They had not been seen since James Andreas had vanished into the huruss tunnels. The glassmaker thought he could persuade them to carry a warning into the Interior. But what could the Others do to aid the colony without exposing themselves? Perhaps they already had their hands full with James Andreas. Perhaps they were in fact flocking to his vengeful banner. Who could tell what went on beyond the mountains?

Verde floundered in doubt. Could it be, he ventured to ask himself, that James had the right solution? The only possible solution? He let his swollen eyelids droop. He had to believe that tomorrow he would know what to do.

CHAPTER 32

On the rail to Quaire'en, the huruss rocked, raising ghostlike memories of Jude's first ride.

Was it only three nights ago? She toyed with the memory, replayed it into fantasy. *I should have followed him into the forests. We could make love on the pine needles.*

A smile intruded, dazzling under wide gray eyes as clear as spring ice.

The crowd roared in silent approval. Halm shouts. The great brick courtyard overflowed with men and women intent on the dazzling smile.

DAMN YOU, JAMES ANDREAS!

The halm shouts echoed his name in praise.

At her feet, the gria stirred in her sleep and whimpered.

CHAPTER 33

The once luxuriant lawn of the Transport Terminal lay beaten into dust under the boots of incoming troops. Heavy machinery had cut deep tracks, turning up the sod like a plow. Bill Clennan stood hands on hips beside the elderly jeep he had commandeered for the day. Though he had parked in the green shade of a huge spruce, the merciless heat wrapped itself around him, making it difficult to move except in slow motion. He watched a new shipment of arms being loaded out of the corridor, crate after crate of recent-issue laser rifles to replace the regulation stunners. On Ramos' order, killing weapons were being brought into the colony for the first time. He saw the plastic-shrouded bulk of a mobile laser cannon, first in a grinding line of two, six, a dozen of them. And all about, a slow-moving swarm of men, working as if their own limbs weighed as much as the loads they were struggling with. Nothing but troops and weaponry was incoming these days. In order to wrest power from the Colonial Authority, Ramos had immediately declared martial law, and closed the incoming corridor to tourist traffic.

The outgoing corridor was besieged by long lines of frightened tourists with their baggage and their children, fleeing the continuing waves of violence that not even Ramos and his strong-arms could stem completely. Mountains of vegetables rotted in the sun, awaiting a slack moment when there might be room for their transport. There was shouting and coughing and babies crying, but dominating the chaos was the ominous chug of the laser cannons pulling away from the terminal.

Clennan had no official reason to be out at the corridor. Some curiosity he could only label as morbid, given his present state of mind, had drawn him away from the endless and pointless hours with the Natives in the Interrogation Wing. So far, from the hundred or so who had been strapped down, drugged, probed, and manipulated, nothing new had been learned. His attempts to prove Koi guilt in the death of Lacey had aroused a far greater horror in his prisoners than he himself felt, as if the cause of death was evident to them, though they denied this, and more threatening than the loss of one Terran delinquent would indicate. Questioning the Natives was the most frustrating job Clennan had ever been faced with, yet their calm strength impressed him. He was mystified by their uncanny ability to evade the persuasions of his drugs and wires. Even as he raged at them from behind his glass panel, he began to admire this strength, and at last, when their suffering began to work at his own rising guilt, to subtly encourage it. As each fruitless session ended, he would tell himself that Ramos would never get anything out of the Natives, and he would know that the certain sense of pleasure this gave him was perverse, yet there it was.

And so he had left the shelter of the air-conditioned Intelligence Complex and driven out to witness the militarization of Arkoi firsthand. He had to understand why a course of action that would have stirred his ambition and his most patriotic urges a month ago now filled him with dim dread. It was as if the influx of men and laser weapons were a personal threat, one he could not yet articulate, beyond recognizing that their arrival trespassed on territory that without his being aware of it had grown precious to him.

He was unused to self-analysis and thus unskilled, but observing others for hints of an answer, he noticed that vague unrest permeated that part of his staff which had lived in the colony the longest. When one of them was on duty in the interrogation booth, he displayed a lack of enthusiasm equal to Clennan's own. Then there was little trouble enforcing humane procedures during the questioning. There were other signs: pointed graffiti in the lavatories; rude cartoons on the staff notice boards, with a focal character redrawn as a paunchy military officer; petty arguments between the old staff and Ramos' reinforcements; sudden dead silences in a room when Ramos or one of his aides appeared. It was also known that the roundup and detention of the Koi had practically caused mutiny among the colonial police normally assigned to the Quarter, public enough that Ramos had seen fit to make an example of the most outspoken by transferring them to the work details at the corridor.

From his patch of shade, Clennan could see two of them lugging a big metal container toward a waiting truck. Their tanned bodies stood out among the pale, sweat-drenched backs of the new recruits, bringing a satisfied smile to Clennan's lips. Those two would not be victims of the epidemic of heat prostration and major sunburn that was crippling Ramos' precious citified army.

And then, as he did at least ten times a day, Clennan thought about Mitchell Verde. He had given up hope of finding him, though he still had a few men detailed to the search, to satsify Ramos mostly, men whose personal loyalty he could count on. He did not want Ramos to get to Verde first. In fact, he was not sure he wanted Ramos to get to Verde at all.

He knew he was preoccupied, that he had allowed Verde to become a fixation, tinged, it was becoming clear, with envy, because Verde *knew*. He was a part of Arkoi, could come and go and disappear into it at will, assimilated, inducted into its mysteries. Verde was the reason Clennan listened hard during the interrogations, Verde was the reason that a pile of old teaching tapes of the Koi language now crowded Clennan's desktop, along with several dusty casettes from the Museum of Cultural Anthropology. Verde was no longer his quarry but his quest.

The door of the incoming corridor hissed shut. Clennan checked his watch automatically. The next shipment was due in thirty minutes. Shipments every thirty minutes, twenty hours a day.

Clennan decided he had had enough. Was it the heat or his troubled thoughts that had his stomach churning as he eased himself back into the ancient jeep?

As he turned into his cluttered office, a hand grabbed his elbow. It was one of the interrogation technicians, pink-faced, still a boy. Clennan guessed he'd been crying.

"What's up, kid?"

"We lost one, Bill," the boy blurted. "Ramos is down there and we lost one."

"Lost what?" he asked, although instantly, he knew.

The tech leaned against the smudged wall, eyes wide. "He's a devil. He enjoys it!"

Clennan gripped the boy's shoulders gently. "What happened?"

"This poor lady . . . he just kept yelling, 'This is the one, I'll break this one!' And when she didn't scream or anything, it made him madder."

208

"And?"

"Well, she died, Bill." The tech gazed at him uncomprehendingly. "It wasn't anything I did, it was just like she'd had it and turned herself off." He shook his close-cropped head. "So then Ramos gets up and slaps me on the back. 'Good job, son,' he says." The boy broke. " 'Good job,' " he sobbed. "Like it was me who killed her."

Clennan held the boy to his chest, soothing him with awkward pats. "There's always a first time for this, kid," he lied, for he had never lost a subject under interrogation. "You'll get used to it. It wasn't your fault." That is, he'd never lost a subject until Lacey. What the hell was Ramos *doing* down there?"

When the tech had control of himself, Clennan sent him to quarters. He ducked into his office, sat down at his desk, and stared at the wall. He should check in with Ramos. He should report back for duty. Duty? He could barely move. Ramos is killing people in my interrogation room. *My* room.

He lashed out at the air with a fist. I go down there, I'll yell at him, I know I will, and that'll be the end for me. Sent home in disgrace. He got up and stood by his open doorway as if there were bars across it. Distance—I need some distance.

And so he avoided his superior, avoided the interrogation room, which he envisioned as blood-spattered, though he knew better. He took a back elevator down and climbed into the old jeep. He drove around aimlessly for a while, then headed for the detention camp. He had a sudden impulse to check up on the constant reports coming out of his interrogation sessions that conditions at the camp were intolerable.

As he approached the steel enclosure, the stench hit him from a distance. He left the jeep at the gate and walked in. What he saw appalled him. Children and old people lay panting in the dirt under crude tarpaulin shelters. The tarps had been erected in close-set rows to maximize the amount of shade, but there were not enough to provide shelter for all. For most, there was only an edge of shadow, enough to protect their heads while their bodies must remain exposed to the blistering sun. For many others, there was no shade at all and they sat out in the open in collapsed heaps, or under little tents made from their own clothing. One corner of the corral had been isolated as a latrine. A cruel breeze blew across the camp, bringing odors of urine and sunbaked waste to mix with the acrid scent of unwashed sweating bodies.

The silence unnerved Clennan as he paced along the crowded rows. He heard no moans, no complaints, not even a child crying, though he saw several asleep under the shelters. There was hardly any movement at all, an occasional arm being lifted in lethargic adjustment, a head turning hopelessly in his direction as he passed. A few lone figures moved from shade to shade with cups of water, speaking soft encouragement.

Clennan realized he was scowling. He located the water barrels, knocked each one. Two were empty, the third nearly so. He took a plastic cup from a neat stack on top of a barrel and put it to the spigot for a test mouthful. It was hot and foul, and he spat it into the dust. He threw the cup down, then impulse made him retrieve it to replace upon the stack. That the Koi would maintain neatness in the face of such adversity further encouraged the shock of righteous outrage that set Clennan's jaw and sent him stalking toward the gate, demanding to see the officer in charge.

He was shown to one of the temporary domes set up to house the guards. When he found himself in the chill of airconditioning, the lingering poison of the water brought acid to his tongue. The scrub-faced officer was sure his career was over by the time Clennan finished with him.

Trucks were dispatched for fresh water, for additional shelter, for portable toilets and showers. Men were sent to strip the unoccupied barracks recently built to accommodate incoming troops. Cots, towels, soap, camp stoves, utensils, everything was to be brought to the detention camp. Clennan called out a civilian medical unit, placed an order for the vegetable shipments lying untouched at the Transport Terminal to be brought in immediately, ordered milk and bread and eggs, and finally called in a dozen men from his own staff to make sure his orders were carried out. He was gratified when the man on the other end of the line volunteered immediately.

He would have some explaining to do when Ramos found out. He did not really have the proper authority. The camp was not in his jurisdiction. But he no longer cared.

He reentered the camp and went about offering assurances that help was on the way, first in Terran, then in whatever broken Koi he could muster. The dazed skepticism that met his promises was like salt in his wounds, but he could not blame them for their lack of faith. I have always been the enemy, he thought, why should they think any different now?

He stared back toward the gate, the buoying energy of his rage deflated into depression. A face upraised, then quickly averted caught his eye. Of the several Koi moving around beneath the largest spread of tarp with water and wet rags, one looked familiar. As the Intelligence man approached, the Koi worked
_y to the farther end of the canopy and bent over a prostrate

woman, his back carefully turned in Clennan's direction. His face was hidden by a shapeless hat, but something in the angular tension of his shoulders or the big sunburned hands on a little man's body brought Clennan to full alert. He skirted rapidly around the outside of the shelter and grabbed the man's free arm. The man froze, careful not to spill the water he was holding to the old woman's lips.

Clennan's sweat-dampened fingers left streaks like claw marks on the man's dust-caked forearm. Ashamed, he let go but hovered over him, half wary, half amazed. "Verde!" he said hoarsely. "My God, Verde, I can't believe it!"

The conservationist flicked him a cold glance. "Not in uniform, Clennan? Not showing off your medals like everyone else?"

Clennan hardly heard. "You have no idea what I've been through trying to find you."

"I can see that for myself." Verde waited until the old woman had drunk her fill, then straightened and turned on Clennan the sort of look normally reserved for maggots eating the dead. "We helped you out, and this is what we get?" He spat, with a sharp gesture around the camp.

Clennan's face went slack. "Now hold on a minute! I'm not responsible for this mess!"

Verde's red-rimmed eyes echoed the Koi's weary disbelief. "I'm not buying the good-guy act, Clennan. You're just another murderer to me." He offered both wrists, one hand still gripping the grimy cup. "Do you haul me away now or do I get to finish what I was doing?"

Clennan stepped back. They know about the dead one already? "I don't know if I'm taking you at all," he muttered. "Look, Verde, I feel as bad about this as you do."

Verde's laugh was hard. "Sure."

"I'm trying to help, damm it!" Clennan was disconcerted by the desperation in his own voice. "I just spent an hour risking my job to make things a little more bearable around here!"

"We don't need your kind of help," Verde snarled.

"We need the help of anyone who sincerely offers it," a reproving voice corrected. Luteverindorin limped in out of the sun, supporting himself with a broken tent pole. He faced Clennan squarely. "So this is our inquisitor."

"Executioner," Verde revised.

Clennan's eyes took the old Koi in: the webbed fingers, the silvered skin. His stare was tinged with wonder.

"What help can you offer us, Mr. Clennan?" The glassmaker asked.

Verde murmured a warning.

"I've done everything I could on the spur of the moment," Clennan began. He thought he detected a smile in the old Koi's unblinking gaze.

"Can you stop the questioning?" Verde demanded. "Can you stop the murder of innocent people?"

Lute held up a gossamered hand. "I think Mr. Clennan means well enough, Mitchell."

Clennan's face softened. Absurdly, the Koi reminded him of his father. "Yes, sir, I do." He was riveted, like a small boy before a famous man.

Verde watched, checking his rage. When Lute put on the mask of power, few could resist.

"The question is," Lute continued, "how *much* does he mean well." Now he leaned his chin on his two hands grasping the top of his stick. "The thing we need most of all, Mr. Clennan, is to be free of this place, not necessarily all of us, but *some* of us."

Clennan shifted his weight, said nothing.

"You see, Mitchell?" Lute crowed softly. "He's thinking it over." He reached with thin webbed fingers for Clennan's arm. "If you will help me to walk a little, my boy, we will find a place to talk."

CHAPTER 34

The arrival in Quaire'en was a kind of homecoming. Before Jude's incredulous eyes spread the crystalline city that had haunted so much of her sleep since she had arrived on Arkoi. She saw it and understood how Ra'an could believe in James Andreas' power to know the future.

Quaire'en was both familiar and strange, shadowed by remembered nightmare but freshened by recognition and discovery. There was that same salt tang in the breeze, the same patient sighing of the waves, the sea-tinged light shifting through tiers of glass, and up above, the shanevoralin in flocks of hundreds, crying into an azure sky.

The halm buzz inside her head, subliminal in Ruvala, now

seemed nearly audible, an indication of the rich concentration of halm voices around her. Jude thought of the Wall, of the voices that had pursued her there. These were more mellow voices, companionable, but she would need to learn to turn them on and off, as she had learned to do with the softer buzz in Ruvala.

Anaharimel will teach me that, as she will teach me to be free of James Andreas!

The clear sun of Quaire'en filled her with anticipatory joy. The city's beauty enchanted her. She took immediate possession and wanted to be nowhere else.

A city of halm! Anaharimel, teach me to be part of this!

She could not wait to get to the school. She could not wait to learn. Even so, she dawdled in the huruss station with Theis at her side, pondering her next step. This was more than an abstract problem, for five meters beyond her feet, the stone ledge under the huruss track gave out into a transparent sheet without visible support. A vault of similar transparency arched overhead. To either side and beneath, the city tumbled down the cliffs into the sea.

Jude walked to the edge of the stone and looked down, unsure whether this glimmering floor was real or a time-past ghost. She looked into a prism, fractured images receding in a vertiginous plummet through layer after transparent layer to blue-green infinity. In the depths, color stirred, like pebbles at the bottom of a stream, the Koi walking among the tiers of the city, lives being lived, goods being traded, plant life swaying in the cool updrafts, water flowing, motion, sparkle, secret glimmers in the thousand facets of the jewel that was Quaire'en.

Jude slid a foot out on the polished surface. Then she heard the click-click of nails on the glass as Theis trotted happily out and stopped in the middle, as if suspended in midair. Jude ventured another step. She floated breathlessly above the city. On the tier below, several Koi passed under her, carrying baskets of fruit.

Theis led her to the top of a ramp that descended through the floor. They had a view of the entire city, cascading down the cliff in a fountain of glass, mile after mile of glittering rooftops and towers shaped like natural crystals, a hymn to geometry falling in cadence to the waves. In the distance, the cliffs curved sharply and dropped into the sea to break the surface farther out in white crags like a sand castle caught by the tide. It was too far to see clearly, but perhaps there were buildings there.

Theis nuzzled her with benign impatience. They moved on to

213

the level below, traversing an arcade of shops. Through the glass walls of any one shop, many could be seen, receding like an infinite reflection of diverse wares, of shoes and cookware and glass shelves stacked with bottles, of the shopkeeper and the shoppers, a multiple exposure of commerce. Quaire'en was like an artist's solid expression of the phenomenon of endless pasts visible in the present. *Intentional or subconscious?* Jude wondered. She did not know the Koi well enough yet to answer that.

The street, if anything one can see through can be called a street, bustled without pushing or noise. There were some dark-haired Koi, like the Ruvalans, and many more who reminded her of the plainsman Tekhon, solid and tawny, supporting enormous loads. Most, however, were unlike the Koi she knew. They were the locals, the sea-bred folk, with skin like the silvered side of a fish and silken hair so fine it seemed to float away from their faces like mermaid hair. As Jude made her way among them, they nodded with pleasant curiosity. She would feel the tickle of halm reaching for her untuned ears. Receiving no reply, their opalescent eyes would go to Theis and explanations would be exchanged. Then the Koi would smile perhaps a little distantly and pass on, leaving Jude unenlightened about how they felt at finding a Terran in their midst. The only clue was a subtle thickening in the halm buzz. *Ah, very sly of you, Rya, to assign me Theis as a guardian without admitting that my reception in Quaire' en might be less casual without her, with news of James Andreas so fresh in the city's halm web.*

The pair descended two more levels through the markets and came to where the street ended in a crystal lattice railing that ran around the four sides of a vast galleried court. Tall feathery trees rose up from the edge of a deep pool cut from the natural rock several levels below. The top of the court was open to the sky high above, so that a well of glass was formed, into which fell sunlight and air and little birds spiraling down to roost in the trees.

Walking around the gallery, they found several stalls selling prepared foods. Hungry, Jude lingered by a counter stacked with steaming pastries. Rya had provided her with a kind of currency, little packets of the lai crystals, to be used in trade. She discovered that one packet provided for a more than adequate lunch for both the gria and herself.

By midafternoon, they had descended deep into the city. The light took on a greenish tinge, the air was cool and moist. The streets were no longer laid out in orderly patterns but twisted around spurs of naked rock emerging through the glass floor.

214

The rock was incorporated into complex structures of both clear and translucent material, some boldly geometric in design, others with a logic less easily perceived at first glance. Patches of white sand and broken shells opaqued the floor here and there. Tall reeds grew in colored pots, and overhead hung forests of fern.

Jude worried that she was trespassing, for these were obviously dwellings. But no one challenged her. A small silver child darted by to vanish behind a facade that had before seemed perfectly transparent. Like the tree house in Ruvala, these homes were less a barrier against the outside than they were a refinement of space chosen for domestic use. Thus privacy was obtained without blatant shows of isolationism.

Farther along, open canals appeared, where the waves surged in along the glass walls. The sea bottom was clearly visible through the floor. Jude saw a turtle the size of an armchair glide across the sand, nosing through a garden of seaweed.

They came to a sort of intersection. Between two honeycomb dwellings was a space and a great roaring of water. Here the cliff face was exposed for a hundred meters, soaring toward a vaulted ceiling where a jagged cave spouted a torrent of water that dropped in a sparkling rush past bridges spanning the opening and into a foaming pool at the bottom. Groups of Koi sat around the pool, basking in the spray, content that their clothing was as wet as the rocks they sat on. Jude noticed several intense discussions in progress, and a glance or two in her direction as they passed. The halm buzz fairly roared. Even in this perfect city, tension walked the streets.

Opposite the waterfall, a tunnel led still farther downward. Theis entered confidently. As if walking into an aquarium, they entered a long glass tube that ran along the sea bottom. The sunlight filtered through the shifting water was green and uncertain. Schools of fish careened among the eel grass on the other side of the glass, and beyond glided the gray shadows of the bigger fish. They met no one in the tunnel, heard nothing but their own footsteps and the faint echoes from the city behind them. After ten minutes of walking, the tube began to rise, then ended in a sand-floored cavern. Theis trotted to the center and sat. Jude shrank back at the entrance. The cavern was lit only by the eerie glow from the tunnel.

"What now?" she asked aloud, peering into the dark recesses where she could hear water dripping. Her mind pictured dank pools slithering with threatening inhabitants, but she knew exactly why her imagination had strayed so suddenly. Sea caves reminded her of James Andreas.

"I'm not ready!" she cried out. Theis leaped to her feet in alarm, looking this way and that.

A pale shaft of light sliced across the cave from an archway that had appeared in the far wall. A young girl stood silhouetted, beckoning. The gria's head wagged. She crossed the damp sand into the light and waited beside the young girl until Jude collected herself and followed. As she passed beneath the arch into a long stair hall, the solid wall reformed behind her. Jude started, gasped. Her hands shot to her ears.

Deaf! I can't hear!

But she could hear. She could hear the distant surf reverberating through the rock and the cry of gulls echoing down the stairwell. It was a halm silence that filled her head. Not since she had entered Arkoi had she known so utter a silence, which meant she had never been truly apart from the halmweb until now. The silence was both a relief and a desperate isolation.

If this is the silence that Ra'an lives with daily, no wonder . . .

The young girl waited patiently at the foot of the stairs, smiling as if she understood Jude's confusion. Jude gripped the stiff hair on the gria's back for support and moved down the hall in a daze. The girl led them up the stone steps, a long spiral that mounted toward a brilliance of light.

They came out onto a white-columned portico overlooking the sea. Across a narrow strait of rough water, the city ascended the cliffs like a living jewel. At its feet, a white arc of beach stretched into invisibility. Jude made a moan that sounded like pain, and the girl turned and reflexively took her arm.

The white beach! He comes!

Jude stared at the beach, waiting for him to be there yammering in her head, sure that if he could predict this city and this beach, he could ferret her out in her place of refuge. But the silence held. She allowed herself to breathe again and looked down at her hands gripping the balustrade. The knuckles were white. She relaxed and allowed herself to be drawn away along the portico.

The sun was very bright and warm and the sea smells were filled with the piquancy of driftwood and seaweed drying on the rocks. The halm school was built on an island, or rather into an island. The portico itself was a wide shelf hewn out of bedrock, enhanced with a neat masonry of columns and balconies. Its architectural solidity was both comforting and confining, especially after the unrestricting structures of Ruvala and the city of Quaire'en. The stone was smooth-edged and pitted, giving even under its sparkling coat of whitewash the impression of great antiquity. Even the stone floor was whitewashed, and the girl in her white robe ahead of them was mostly visible for her dark hair and the shadow she cast as she moved along the white wall.

Ahead, the portico widened into a terrace shaded by a tiled roof. Twisted trees grew up through the rock. In a reed chair, an old woman sat propped up with cushions, conversing gaily with a group of young Koi who fluttered around her like butterflies. She looked up as Jude approached, and the children ceased their chatter to settle around her feet expectantly. Jude's guide joined her classmates on the floor, leaving Jude to feel minutely observed as she waited in her brown Terran trail clothes, knapsack slung over one shoulder.

The old woman raised a hand. When she spoke, it was in Koi, but the meaning rang clearly in Jude's head.

—Please sit down with us, Judith.

Jude sat. When Theis went to the old woman's chair and leaned against her knee with something close to reverence, Jude knew this was Anaharimel.

Like the walls and floor, Anaharimel was all white. Her white hair was pulled back in a soft bun. Her skin had the pale shimmer of the sea-bred. Her face was such as is called ageless, for though age had left its mark in a network of tiny wrinkles, it had been kind enough to leave unsunken cheeks, fine teeth, and the surprise of bright eyes that were seawater green.

Without introduction, Anaharimel began to tell a story. She spoke in Koi, the coastal tongue, Jude guessed, for its accents were unfamiliar to her. Again Jude understood every word. The story was a simple one, about fish and a great storm at sea. It bore no moral lesson nor particular information, but the children listened intently. When Anaharimel had finished, the turn passed to the silver-haired little boy sitting closest to her. His short tale was also told in the coastal tongue, but this time, Jude did not understand a word. Not even an image appeared in her head to help her along. She listened all the same, absorbing the watery undulations of a language that seemed to be made up of words as endless as the sea itself. Often it was difficult to say where one word ended and another began, so smoothly did the syllables roll into one another.

The next student, an older blond girl, began her story in an entirely different tongue, and this time Jude wasn't the only listener straining for understanding. The youngest sea-bred children had apparently not yet learned any of the regional tongues but their own. Jude began to see the method in this seemingly

217

random passing of time. If a story was in an unknown language, a listener must rely on halm for understanding. And as halm brought the meaning through, so would it teach the language. But what if a listener's halm was not developed enough?

She decided to concentrate very hard on her listening, but as in Ruvala, her head began to ache, so she went back to listening to sounds only. The blond girl was not gifted as a storyteller. She droned on and on until her voice mingled in Jude's ears with the plashing of the waves up and down on the rocks below, music that lulled with the warm sea breeze until her eyelids were heavy . . . a phrase entered her mind, gently like the smallest wave, and then another . . . words! Jude came awake, groped hungrily for the words as they once more dissolved into static. For a while all she could hear was the noise of her own despair.

—Remember that listening is the opposite of concentrating.

Jude glanced up, but the old woman sat back with eyes closed, head tilted against the cushions as if she had dozed off.

If I could blank my mind . . . For the first time, the possibility that she might not be able to acquire this skill in time to save herself from James Andreas eroded the confidence that had propelled her to Quaire'en.

I will think of nothing, she vowed.

But self-consciousness is a stubborn reflex, and Jude spent the rest of the afternoon failing to subdue it.

When the sun sank low enough to evade the roof, the terrace was flooded with late heat, and Anaharimel ended the session. As she rose from her chair, her step was quick and firm, and her body straight. There was no formal dismissal, but no lingering either.

—Wash up for dinner!

She went off down the portico with a swish of her long robe.

Jude's dark-haired guide stayed behind to lead her to an upper gallery lined with doors along one wall and open to the sea on the other. The girl stopped before the last door, gestured inside kindly, then continued on her way.

Jude entered a square whitewashed room. Thick wooden beams supported a lowish ceiling. The beams were smooth and dark against the white plaster. The floor was tiled in deep sea blue with a simple border the color of the sky. The furnishings were spare: a wooden bed with a firm, even pad, a sturdy table, shelves and hooks, a chair, a simple but complete bath. The water in the tap was sweet and chill. Jude noted a blue ceramic bowl on the table by the bed. She filled it at the sink and set it down for Theis, who emptied it gratefully.

Returning to the door, Jude gazed out over the green water. She could not see the beach from her room, only the broad horizon broken by the rocky island as it curled around to enclose a little bay. She had never known a place of such perfect beauty, a place where simply being there could make her happy. If she could learn enough halm to survive the coming cataclysm, she would find work that needed doing in Quaire'en. She knew the city would accept her. She had indeed come home.

Overhead, the sun flirted through the early-evening clouds. Once again, the landscape was working on her, as it had in Ruvala, soothing her, draining away the panic she had brought with her. Yet she knew that she had only to walk the few steps to the balustrade and lean out over the water to steal a glimpse of the white beach. That would bring the terror of her dreams skidding back to her.

Stay away, James Andreas! Give me time!

CHAPTER 35

———◆━━◆━━◆———

The latrines were the only area of the detention camp that offered any privacy from patrolling guards. The three men stood with their backs to the breeze, Clennan a little apart from the others and talking very fast.

". . . Next thing he wakes me and tells me the kid is dead." He spread his hands helplessly. "Suicide, he said, but I don't buy it."

"I wouldn't be surprised, after what you put him through."

Clennan showed his teeth uncomfortably. "I don't blame you for thinking the worst, Verde, but listen, I got a kid back at headquarters crying his eyes out because he thinks he killed that woman this morning. We don't kill in interrogation, at least not the way I do things. You may not agree with our methods, but I tell you we're not that damn clumsy!" He paused, touched the stunner at his hip. "Ramos does things different. I don't issue killing weapons like his soldiers carry, I left Lacey healthy, I swear." He was surprised that it mattered that Verde believe him. "I don't know, maybe Ramos did him in, don't ask me why. I just know there's no way he could have killed himself."

Lute drew little figures in the dust with the point of his impromptu cane. "You believe the Koi are responsible for this, don't you, Mr. Clennan?"

Clennan's face twitched slightly, then he nodded. "Something the kid himself said, I don't know . . ." His mind was overflowing with possibilities his mouth did not want to admit.

"If you think that, why do you come with an offer of help?"

Clennan made a show of gesturing around the camp. "Nobody should be subjected to conditions like this . . ." Once again, his voice trailed off. Then, with exasperation, he said, "This is going to sound real phony, but I don't really know why I'm here."

Lute smiled. "I think I do."

Verde grunted dubiously.

The old Koi fiddled with his stick a little more, then slid his next sentence out like a foot testing ice. "The Koi did not do this killing, but we must take responsibility for the one who did."

Verde's look said the old man was making a mistake. Clennan's abject slump didn't alter, but his body stilled.

"You know who killed Lacey?"

"Yes," Lute replied firmly.

A slight murmur of dissent from Verde caused the Koi to sign him to patience.

And Clennan's next question was not who. He asked, "How?"

Lute relaxed his purposeful stance with a small smile of satisfaction. He adjusted his webbed hands on his cane and tilted his brimmed hat farther against the sun. "And that question is why you are here, William. Come, it will be easier for you when you admit to yourself what it is you really want to know."

Clennan seemed to collapse a little further. The old man had skillfully led him to the brink of his dilemma. He was beginning to see it as a yawning chasm, with the Koi standing safely on the opposite side, forcing him by some personal magic to look down as the rock that had been his value structure slowly crumbled beneath his feet. But strangest and most frightening: with each fragment that fell into the abyss, the far side drew closer, offering an escape that was increasingly more plausible and inviting. "Aren't you afraid of what I will do with what you tell me?"

"No," replied Lute with angelic confidence, and Verde winced, privately praying that the gambit would work. He was beginning to take the possibility of Clennan seriously. Could Clennan's help tip the balance in favor of the Koi?

Clennan turned away from the old man's smile. The Koi had reached across the chasm with an offer of trust, and it shook him that he could hear such an offer and believe it. It was even more shattering that he could believe it and not be able to bring himself to manipulate it toward his own ends. Suspect impulses crowded in, morality, responsibility, a desire to protect . . . what? This world? *His* world? He paced away, as if removing himself from Luteverindorin would clear the fog in his brain. "I don't want to know anything," he declared finally. "Just tell me what I can do to help."

"Help what?" The old glassmaker persisted softly.

"Help this. Help you!" Clennan waved into the dust-choked heat. Verde was amazed to see the Intelligence man trembling as if with cold.

Lute was merciless. "Do you want to help the Koi or your conscience, William?"

"Couldn't that be one and the same thing?" asked Clennan tightly. The chasm was closing.

"Guilt is not belief, William. Guilt can be resolved by a deed or two. The penitent can go on about his way, self-forgiven. You felt guilty for what you saw here, and you made your gesture. If that is enough, be off. Your guilt we do not need, but *yourself*, well, that is another matter."

"I wouldn't trust me if I were you." Clennan looked cornered.

"Goddammit, man!" Verde burst out. "He's offering you your humanity!"

"No, Mitchell, humanity we all have, for better or for worse. Let us say that I am asking William to change sides out of enlightened self-interest. But to do that, he must truly believe that his interests and ours coincide."

Clennan shuddered, then threw his head back with eyes closed and whispered, "I do."

Verde shot Lute a look of bewildered admiration, for he could hear the conviction in Clennan's declaration and knew what it cost him.

"Understand my position," said the Intelligence man faintly. "It's not the job. I've already risked that willingly. It's just that . . . I mean, how do you learn to live in a world where the impossible is suddenly possible?"

Lute chuckled. "Change your definition of impossible."

The old man's clear laugh melted the last of Clennan's resistance. The hot sun beat down on them and the hard-packed dirt glared, but the old Koi seemed to glow from within. Clennan felt opaque, deadened, beside him. He kicked at a stone imbedded in the dust. "I envy you," he murmured to Verde. "I envy your conviction." He paced away, and his arm slammed down as if throwing away something hateful. "I'm tired of fucking politics! I mean, on Terra, you don't have much choice. Survival, you know? Politics is the only game in that town. But here . . ."

"Here it's not much better," Verde commented.

"We could *make* it better!" declared Clennan impulsively.

Lute smiled quietly to himself, listening.

"You know," Clennan continued rapidly. "I'm not the only one, either. Most of my staff would back me if it meant they could have a life here."

Verde chewed his lip. "I hear a deal being offered. But that's all right, because I'll bet a lot of the Quarter guards would feel the same way." He turned a little circle, energy returning. "Lute, maybe we need to consider a new kind of coalition. We need all the allies we can get." He glanced across the yard to the sprawling mini-city of barracks domes. "Is it the army that's ruining your picnic here, Clennan?"

Clennan gave a snort, edged with anger. "It's my own damn boss. Colonel Ramos, chief of WorldFed Intelligence. He's bringing the army in."

"The Jewel? In person?"

Clennan nodded soberly. "And listen, you ought to know . . . well, a lot came out in that kid Lacey's interrogation . . . about the Others, beyond the mountains?"

"I knew it," Verde groaned.

"It was exactly what Ramos wanted to hear, exactly. Now he's planning a full-scale military assault over the Guardians, after he uncovers the source of the . . . uh . . ." He could not say it. To say it was to believe it.

"The Wall," supplied Lute blandly.

"His troops are in the Quarter now, tearing it apart, as the colonel put it, stone by stone." Clennan looked at Lute seriously. "Will they find anything?"

"I doubt it," Lute replied, but now the heat and his fatigue were showing on him. He leaned more heavily on his cane. "But he has unwittingly obtained his desire by removing us from the Quarter. Those who were maintaining the Wall at the time of our arrest will soon be too drained to continue, even with our nighttime relief. The Wall will collapse.''

Clennan thought this over, his arms crossed and hugged protectively to his chest. ''But he won't know that. He still expects to find some big machine, something concrete to destroy, and I'll bet he keeps looking until he finds it. That could buy us time.'' It amazed him how easily, after all, the decision was made, how with the making of plans, the line was crossed. ''How long until the . . . the Wall collapses?''

''Hard to say,'' Verde answered cautiously, still weighing Clennan's intent.

The image of a collapsing wall sent a dizzy freedom coursing through Bill Clennan's body. It hit him like a drug. ''We've got to disarm him,'' he stated.

Verde scoffed. ''Now how are we going to do that?''

''You said yourself you've got more allies than you thought.'' Clennan almost had the answer. His brain raced. Keep talking, Verde. The answer is coming. ''You got anyone who can handle explosives?''

Verde shook his head in dismay rather than denial. ''Here we go again. We all saw how much good it did Lacey. What's the use? If we blow up the arsenals, Ramos'll just bring in more .''

Clennan's lungs constricted as the inevitable galloped toward him and swung him up into its saddle. ''Verde!'' he rattled. ''Verde, tell me!'' He grabbed the older man's arm. ''How much would it bother you to never see Terra again?''

Verde shrugged off the hold. ''I never intended to.''

''No, listen! What if you couldn't? *Ever*.'' Clennan felt Lute straighten beside him. The old Koi understood. Support was there, as if an aged but steady hand reached out to help him across his chasm of dilemma. Armed with his answer, Clennan jumped. ''We have to destroy the corridor!''

The conservationist opened his mouth in protest, but nothing came out.

''I know you don't like it, Verde, but don't you see, it's the only long-term solution there is. We've got to break the link completely.''

Verde's eyes narrowed. ''My God,'' he breathed, then his frown broke into a rueful joyous grin. ''Well, I'll . . . why didn't I think of that?''

''You mean you'd back it?''

''Cuts the problem off at the source.'' Verde nodded, shedding ten years as hope became his friend again. ''The corridor is the colony's lifeline. Sever that and it would be forced to learn

223

other ways to survive, Koi ways. Unsupplied, the colony could be converted."

"Won't exactly be nonviolent," Clennan advised.

"A quick gesture now will mean fewer deaths later. Fewer Koi deaths." Verde was working hard to convince himself. "What do you think, Lute?"

The glassmaker's reply was sad but assured. "We have experimented with patience. We have been generous with our world. Now I believe it is time to take it back."

Clennan whooped with laughter and release. "We can do it, too!" The rush of exhilaration set him dancing. "I have a car at the gate. I'll call a guard, get you two escorted out like I was hauling you in for questioning!" He clapped Verde on the shoulder, his clownish exuberance returned in force. He loped a few paces toward the gate, then stopped dead. "No. Christ. Wait a minute." He came back, fidgeting, as his trained caution won out over runaway excitement. "After the fuss I created this afternoon, I'm as visible as a checkered flag around here. Give me a day to set it up. No, wait . . . can't afford to waste that kind of time. Damn!"

Verde's grin withered. "Ramos is that close to ready?"

"Oh, Julie's very eager. But that's all right. We'll beat him to it." Clennan shoved his hair out of his eyes. "The unofficial channels work faster than the bureaucratic ones you're used to tangling with. Don't forget, I've got computer access and a top-level security clearance." He chortled like a schoolboy. "For as long as I can keep 'em fooled . . .!" He turned to Lute. "Now let me get this straight. This telepathy thing means you can talk to anyone, anywhere, right?"

"Any Koi, anywhere in the colony."

"Oh." Clennan glanced at Verde.

"It's not a gift that many Terrans have," Verde explained with a terseness that masked his own pain and regret.

Clennan rethought quickly. "Okay. Well, I can get you both out of here, but you, sir"—he turned apologetically to Lute— "will have to see your way to spending a few days in the holding tank at headquarters. It's no paradise, but it's cool and cleaner than this dump. And you'd be where I could get to you without raising Julie's suspicions. As for you, Verde, I can fix an exchange with one of my men. With all these imported troops running around, one more new face in uniform won't be noticed."

"A uniform isn't going to hide me from the colonial police," said Verde.

Clennan shrugged easily. "So we'll avoid them until the time comes for you to recruit their support."

Verde exchanged looks with Luteverindorin. "There's one more major variable you should know about . . ."

But Clennan was up and moving toward the gate. He flashed them a reckless smile over his shoulder. "Tell me later!"

CHAPTER 36

Round pebbles cemented into wide shallow steps cut a white-washed swathe into the darker rock. The stair switchbacked down to a stony beach where the waves cascaded against the great ranks of dolmens wading at the foot of the cliff. With Theis close at her side, Jude made her way down the path to join the students gathering in answer to their teacher's silent summons. It was still very early. Jude shivered as she passed through the tall shadows of the dolmens, and found a rock in the sun to settle on.

Anaharimel awaited them, clothed in white, bathed in white dawn sunlight, seated against a white rock. Whichever of her favorite spots she chose to hold class in each day, she was always there before everyone else. Jude pictured her each morning wandering the island while the school was at breakfast, a stark white wraith, agile as a girl, taking in the weather, the color of the day, the bite of the wind, in order to determine the most receptive location at that particular time for the teaching of halm. The choice made, the halm call went out, breakfast was cleared, and the day began.

As the last stragglers scurried down the path and found seats, Jude watched the little floating stones bob at the water's edge, wondering idly what kind of stones there could be that would float, thinking that Ra'an would know, because Daniel Andreas, the geologist would have taught him that. In fact, Ra'an would have delivered an entire lecture on the subject of the floating stones. Thinking that, she didn't want to look at the stones anymore, and determinedly pulled her concentration back to the class.

Increasingly, though the choice was never hers, Jude found

herself sitting somewhat apart from the other students. The island's halm barrier could not keep the news out, for the school was not closed to tradesmen or visitors. Each passing day brought more reports of the disrupting passage of James Andreas through the countryside, Jude became an unwitting focal point for the fears and confusion fermenting within the student body.

There were exceptions. The youngest, the little silver boy, had taken a fancy to Theis and accepted Jude as the gria did. Her other almost-friend was her dark-haired guide of her first day at the school, a Ruvalan girl named Pe'eva, who made touchingly awkward efforts to include Jude in the simple social activities between classes. They shared no verbal language. Jude's attempts to mindspeak a child whose halm was as undeveloped as her own were often discouraging, but just as often amusing, for Pe'eva concealed a determined gaiety beneath her solemn child's face. She was more than willing to struggle with the barriers of age and culture for the sake of communication. They could hardly be called confidantes, but Jude felt a tie with Pe'eva and could isolate her halm presence with growing ease, picking it out of the island's population of halm presences that had a few days ago been incoherent static to her. The other presence that had been clear from the first day was that of Anaharimel. Jude only wished that she could halmspeak Anaharimel as smoothly as her teacher could halmspeak her. The communication was still jerky and difficult. But each day, there was progress.

Today, Pe'eva had not been at breakfast and Jude could not sense her anywhere. Haltingly, she framed a query to Anaharimel, working in images where she could not form halm words.

(Image of Pe'eva) *Where?* (Expression of concern)

—Pe'eva? Her family needed her at home for the harvest.

(Surprise) (Image of Pe'eva saying goodbye to Jude) (Regret)

—She asked me to bid you goodbye and say that she will see you again.

Jude made an extra effort, for she had not spoken to Anaharimel of her isolation, though she was sure the old sage had noticed.

(Image of Pe'eva) *Family* (Expression of disapproval) (Image of Pe'eva and Jude laughing together)

—Yes, they did not approve.

There was a pause, and Jude could feel Anaharimel searching her reserves of tact.

—The pilgrim mobs swept through Ruvala yesterday with their message of destruction. Pe'eva was not required to go home. She went because she felt she could be a voice in her homeland against What-is-to-come.

226

(Image of Pe'eva) *But . . . a child!*

The emotion of her reaction pushed Jude's message through.

—Not so much a child that she will willingly be made a murderer.

Jude buried a lonely hand in Theis' shaggy coat to offset the chill that threatened at the mention of "What-is-to-come." She hated the avoidance implicit in that euphemism and suspected that Ra'an had some cause to accuse the Koi of being reluctant to face issues directly. They seemed to do it not out of complacency as he assumed, but as one will when he has heard something so horrible that he doesn't know how to deal with it. Still, Pe'eva had chosen to act, and in her friend's bravery, Jude could find comfort.

Anaharimel raised her eyes to the rest of the class as her halm voice slipped from private to public mode in the ritualized class opener.

—Who will offer a story to enlarge our experience? Judith?

Jude had expected this. Anaharimel had her own ways of dealing with issues. Days passed at the school and learning progressed, and Jude had sworn to be ready when the moment came that she was first asked to recite. But her assessment of what was appropriate changed with each day.

What story should I tell??

The other students retold traditional Koi tales or incidents of local history, or often a personal experience would be humbly offered. Jude decided against the latter, though she ached to share with these children who shrank from her something of her life, to tell them of her time in the Wards, to express her love for their world, to win their sympathy, perhaps, to make herself more in their eyes than that-Terran-in-the-school.

She rubbed the rough warm stone for comfort. She had never given much thought to the use of myth as parable or fantasy as lesson, but the image of Pe'eva bearing home to Ruvala her idealistic convictions stirred up a certain guilt that Jude had been ignoring.

Here I isolate myself in an island monastery to acquire the skills for my own salvation . . . what might I be doing to save the other five million also threatened by James Andreas?

If I tell them of my life on Terra, it will only make the Terran "horror" loom larger. It's Andreas they must learn to question, and the horror he demands of them in return.

Jude stood, and haltingly, conjuring out of the white stones at her feet a vision of the long white beach where What-is-to-come would occur, she began tell the myth of the man called Hitler.

227

CHAPTER 37

———◆·◆·◆———

Within hours after his return from the detention camp, Bill Clennan jotted two Koi names on the check-in list for the holding tank. As two old Koi shuffled into the cell, the man on duty noted the time and added his signature without question.

"Colonel's back," he advised Clennan. "he's been yelling all over the complex for you."

"I'll just bet he has." Clennan shared a fraternal wink. "Look, Spiros, when you get off duty for the day, look for me in my office?"

"Sure thing, Bill."

Clennan made sure that Ramos had been away from headquarters all day before he went down to report. He knocked, then pushed the door open briskly, clutching a pile of folders.

"Tried all afternoon to catch up with you, sir."

Ramos was moving around slowly, pale under his peeling sunburn. "I was out at the corridor."

"Ah." Clennan was properly regretful. "Must have just missed you out there this morning. You look, ah, like you could use a little rest, boss."

Ramos regarded him owlishly. "I'm fine. A little crotchety maybe, but I hear I'm not the only one. . . . So you blew off a little steam this afternoon, eh?"

Clennan put his prop to use, slapping the folders down on the long table. "Well, look at these damn reports! How can I get anything out of these Natives if they come to me half dead from heat and starvation?"

"It's hot out there all right," Ramos growled. "But I don't need you losing it like a greenhorn. We got more important things to deal with than whether the natives are tucked in comfy." He sniffed, shrugged, and pushed a few papers around un necessarily. "Be easier on the men next time, Billy. "Did you get anything out of those two you just brought back?"

Like a hawk, thought Clennan, stepping more carefully. "Tossed

228

them into holding for the night. I'll get to them first thing in the morning. It's hard to tell them apart, but I'm pretty sure I saw these two hanging around Verde's office in the Quarter. Thought they might give us a lead on him.''

"Fine, Billy fine.'' Ramos sat back with a nod that pretended to be approval.

Clennan lurked by the door. What if I ask him why that prisoner died this morning? "They find anything in the Quarter yet?"

"Not so far.'' The Intelligence chief scowled into his paperwork. "I figure to give it another three, four days, then go ahead with the operation. We're ready enough, and the men are restless. This heat . . .'' He scrawled a signature distractedly. "That Wall thing can't be strong enough to stop a whole army.''

Three or four days! Clennan swallowed covertly. "I'm sure you're right, boss,'' he said as he quickly shut the door behind him.

For the rest of the evening, he haunted the Intelligence Complex, drawing certain men aside, testing, probing, feeling them out. Sentiment against Ramos was running even higher than he had suspected. By early morning, he had over a dozen he could count on, and that dozen assured him of two dozen others who could be expected to come over when the action began. Out of a staff of several hundred, it did not sound like great odds, but it was a strong beginning.

He selected one of the most trusted to make the switch with Verde, while the man named Spiros went to work in place of the late-night duty officer, who had been taken mysteriously ill.

Verde came out of the tank, furtively shrugging the army fatigues into place and yawning.

Clennan chuckled as he felt the plot thickening around him. He was beginning to enjoy himself. "Not the best fit in the world, but it'll do. Let's go, soldier.''

The old jeep rattled through the predawn city, avoiding scattered pockets of police and diehard looters. Verde directed Clennan around the back of the Quarter, away from the glaring lights that illuminated the searching and dismantling progress going on inside the walls. They left the jeep in an alley and slipped in by one of the many secret entrances. From there, Verde was deliberately circuitous, as only the Koi could have taught him to be. If Clennan was intending a doublecross, he'd never be able to retrace the route by which Verde finally brought him to the deep-cellars.

They tramped for nearly an hour through the downward maze, then turned into a final slanting passage, far below the Quarter. Faint light shone behind a canvas flap at the other end. Verde's pace quickened.

"Damon! Ron!" He shoved aside the flap. "By God, do I have a surprise for you!"

Sleeping men scrambled to their feet with groggy exclamations.

"Mitch! What the . . .!"

"Thank God. We thought . . ." Damon's dark bulk loomed in the lamplight as he reached to turn up the flame.

"How'd you get . . .?"

"Where . . .?"

Ron Jeffries' sharp growl broke through the hubbub. "What's *he* doing here?"

Verde took a light grip on Clennan's elbow. In the hush that followed, he could not completely repress a foxy smirk. "Bill, I believe you know Ron Jeffries. He'll be the demolition man you were asking for."

Not knowing what else to do, Clennan stuck out a tentative hand. "Hullo, Ron. Been a long time . . ."

"You bet it has." Jeffries looked him up and down gleefully, ignoring the hand. "So the catcher finally got caught." He peered up the passage for Verde's reinforcements, then remembered that Verde never carried a weapon.

"I know, Ron," Verde said, "You're wondering just how I managed this."

"Well, uh . . ."

"I told you I had a surprise. Mr. Clennan here has jumped the line."

"What?" The others echoed Jeffries' incredulous roar.

Verde gave a nod and a shrug and Clennan looked cautiously sheepish, like the good kid being rushed by the gang he has secretly wanted to join.

Damon merely said, "Wow."

But Jeffries' shoulders hunched up like a bull about to charge. "He told you that and you *believed* him? Mitch, what's wrong with you?" He grabbed for Clennan's arm to spin him against the wall, but Clennan ducked aside and in the same movement wrapped an elbow around Jeffries' throat, while the other arm knocked away the stunner that appeared in Jeffries' hand.

"Ease off, Jeffries!" he snarled. "You're too old for this . . .

230

oh, Christ.'' He pushed Jeffries away disgustedly. ''Old reflexes,'' he apologized to Verde, as the little man stepped between them.

''Lute says he's on the level, Ron.''

Jeffries growled a small obscenity, picked his cabbie's hat off the floor, and clamped it on his head.

''Convince me,'' he said.

CHAPTER 38

In Quaire'en, the lamps burned late one night. Jude wandered the dark island with Theis. Like the city, she could not sleep. She paced the upper reaches where the wind thrashed the scrub in sullen fitfulness, but she was drawn repeatedly to the rocky shore facing restive Quaire'en.

Finally she forsook her wandering and climbed down among the rocks to a water-smoothed slab of marble. It was wet with spray but still warm from the day. Jude settled on it and urged the gria close to her. A seawall had been here once, in a past beyond memory. Time and the sea storms had left it a jumble of foreign stone, in daylight impossibly white among the darker indigenous rocks, at night eerily responsive to each minute quantum of light that strayed its way. Under a full moon, or especially two, the marble glowed like the surf that wreathed it in phosphorescence.

The tide, too, was high and wild. The diamond reflections of the city lights chased from wave to wave. Jude huddled with Theis and smelled seaweed and brine and the damp wind, looking away from the city into the night shadow farther down the shore.

Thus it happened as she had known it would, that one night she would be staring into darkness and there would come the spark of a torch in the distance, then another, and another, the lights of a hundred thousand torches, maybe more, and she would know that ahead of them walked the one who needed no torch, for the blaze of his halmfire outshone all living flame.

Jude stirred on her marble slab. The water licked at her bare feet. Four abreast, the far torches stretched in a line that seemed to have no end. The wind rustled like the sound of their progress through the dry coastal grasses and down the switchback road to the sand.

And then the wind stilled. There was no sound but that of wavelets rinsing the rocks. The white beach reflected a chain of firelight that approached the city, then stopped and gathered itself into a circle like an animal settling for the night.

She could no longer hope for him to stay away. *And so he comes without fanfare. But then he needs none, now.*

Jude sent Theis into Quaire'en to bring back a firsthand report.

CHAPTER 39

In the deep-cellars, Ron Jeffries splashed water on his face and relapsed into silence.

Verde stretched and looked at his watch. "Noon," he commented with mild surprise. Jeffries had grilled Clennan for several hours and was still only grudgingly satisfied. The rest of the cellar occupants had trailed off at various points during the cross-examination, to finish their disturbed sleep, except for Damon Montserrat, who came in from the kitchen area to hand around mugs of steaming soup.

Clennan had stood his trial resignedly, as if he really couldn't blame anyone for doubting him because he wasn't quite sure he believed himself. Now he sipped at his soup and savored a new word he had just learned.

"Halm." He liked its mysterious roll on his tongue. "I don't remember . . . no, I don't suppose that would appear in the official language tapes." Wonderingly, he shook his head. "That's what killed Lacey?"

Jeffries rolled a cigarette, still lying in wait to prove Clennan a liar. "That's what could kill us all."

"Andreas. I was there the night the mob attacked him." Clennan eyed Verde sympathetically. "She tried so hard to protect him. I think she used it on the crowd, now that I have a name for it."

"Meron?" Verde frowned. "She was never taught . . ."

"Remember, Mitch," Jeffries broke in, "James said it's all in the intention."

"She didn't kill anybody, though," Clennan added.

"She probably didn't intend to."

"The question now is," Verde pursued, steering away from the painful subject of Meron's death, "whether to sneak enough Koi out of detention to provide relief at the Wall, or to let it collapse, so that direct halm contact can be made with the Interior. Otherwise, we'll never know if James made it through or how he's being received out there. We'll just have to sit and wait for his bomb to fall."

"Unless we drop ours first," suggested Clennan bluntly. "At least Ramos is a certain threat, and an immediate one."

"What does Lute say?" Damon asked.

"Lute says we must assume that James has made it through," Verde replied. "If we really think we can destroy the corridor, then of course he will let the Wall go. The voices of the Koi in the colony will be needed to speak against James and his fanatics."

Clennan drained his soup and set the mug down thoughtfully. "If the Wall prevents halm exchange between here and there, could the Wall keep Andreas out? I mean, protect the colony from him?"

"Several months ago, maybe. Now, no, not with all this Terran interference and the loss of those who left with James. The halm force he plans to amass would cut through it like butter. He knew that when he conceived this insanity."

There was a silence, then Jeffries slouched over and pulled up a crate beside Clennan. "So. When do we do it?"

Clennan laughed softly. There was an eager unbelieving edge to his laugh. "You know, the one thing you guys haven't asked me is *why*."

"Why what?" Jeffries demanded.

"Why I'm here, doing this, with you."

The three exchanged glances. "We knew *why*, Clennan," Jeffries explained, "we just needed to know *if*."

"We all know why, Bill," said Damon gently. "It just took you a little longer than the rest of us to come around."

"So I ask again," Jeffries repeated. "When do we do it?"

Clennan took a deep breath. "Day after tomorrow is the soonest I can figure. Sometime in the early morning, when the corridor's closed down for the twenty-four-hour maintenance check." He turned to Jeffries. "You're demolition?"

"Looks that way."

"Right, then. What kind, how much, and how many men?"

CHAPTER 40

In the streets of Quaire'en, he was called the Destroyer, but the name was not spoken aloud.

The halm school waited in vain that day for Anaharimel's call to class. In the morning, Jude paced along the colonnade facing the city. The pilgrim encampment spread down the beach in a cloak of rippling color. Now that it was no longer empty, Jude could look on the beach calmly. The visions that Andreas had fed her dreams with stopped at the beach. Only one prophecy was still to be accounted for, and thus far, there was no sign that Ra'an would appear from Ruvala's hills to play the role he claimed Andreas had laid out for him.

And what does he intend for me?

Theis returned in the afternoon brimming with vivid images: Andreas preaching at the water's edge, backing into the waves as his passion took hold of him; the gathering throng, rapt in his spell; the shanevoralin flocking to the incandescent power of his halm so that the city children raced down to the beach to see the sky fill with wings.

In the evening, before dinner, Anaharimel called the students to her at last. Jude was the first to arrive in the wind-tossed scrub grove at the peak of the island, Theis at her heels. Anaharimel sat erect in a shifting pool of sunlight, beneath a twisted pine. The students gathered but did not cluster closely around their teacher as was their habit, held now at a distance by the unaccustomed stiffness in her carriage.

—This is the news, my children. The Destroyer has arrived in our city. This morning he called to the Council and so great was his power that they could not deny him. The Council left the Ring and came themselves down to the beach to hear his case.

234

Jude shifted her weight but her feet were not asleep. The prickling in her limbs was fear.

Anaharimel spread both hands, an eloquent gesture from one who rarely allowed her body to speak when her mind could do it for her.

—The Council will decide if the Destroyer's case is valid enough for a Gathering to be called. It is my opinion that they will decide in favor, and that the Destroyer will demand that the Gathering be immediate. Therefore, my students, you must consider your choices. They are three: to lend your young halm strength, untested as it is, to the Destroyer's cause, or to speak out against him in the Gathering, or, lastly, to remain neutral.

James Andreas will not suffer neutrality willingly, Jude warned impulsively.

Anaharimel's halm voice grew stern.

—We will not debate the issue here. We must go from this grove prepared to make the personal choice that each will carry into the Gathering. Think over it carefully, my students. Consider every subtlety and ramification.

How can they? mourned Jude privately. *They're only children . . .*

—Those who choose neutrality had best remain here at the school, within the safety of the halm barrier. That is all. Choose well, that the Balance may be restored.

The class sat quietly for a moment, as the wind rattled the pines, then they rose to trickle off singly and in groups. Jude remained seated on her hump of dry grass. The teacher's pale eyes turned toward her.

—You are not satisfied, child.

Do you support the Destroyer, Ana?

Shock.

—I child? Never!

Then why did you say nothing against him? Your students would listen if you said that what Andreas cries out for is wrong.

—We do not need borrowed convictions. We need understanding, so that the choice is a true and Balanced one for each person who makes it.

But isn't that cowardice? Shouldn't one speak aloud for one's beliefs?

—As James Andreas does?

Jude sat back, stunned. Was that the real choice, after all? Between a morality shaped by majority rule, and one determined by whoever shouts the loudest? *Is there no finer, purer alternative?*

235

She remembered her debate with Ra'an across the mountain campfire. *Does justice exist? Is it attainable?*

Anaharimel offered no more. The late light tinted her with amber, as if she were carved from white marble. Jude thought she looked very ancient and proud, and sat in silence with her until the sun dipped into the water, hoping to absorb some of her teacher's calm.

If I hide on this island, I might be safe. He might never know I am here. Is there reason to do otherwise? Terra gave me nothing but pain . . . why should I risk myself in return?

Why?

And what of Ra'an? Will he need me if he should come?

Ah, the white beach.

Will he come?

CHAPTER 41

Back in his quarters in the Intelligence Complex, Bill Clennan shaved and changed his clothes hurriedly. He must make an effort to appear as awake as he felt inside, for if Ramos suspected he had been up all night, he'd want to read the reports from the interrogations that could be the only proper cause of a lack of sleep. Even the old reputation for late-night partying couldn't serve as a cover this time, with every bar in the city shut down. He glanced around the room, finally admitting to himself how much he despised its demented blandness. He threw his dirty clothes on the floor in a gesture of defiance and ignored the light switch as he left.

He took the elevator down to his office. He had fiddled the duty roster the day before, so that the technician scheduled into the interrogation booth was one whose loyalty he could count on. Another of his men would relieve him in the lead seat when the time came.

After a jovial tour through the Interrogation Wing, joking with the men, giving obscene excuses for his lateness, making his presence felt, Clennan checked in at the booth and began going through the motions of a day's routine questioning. An hour later, his replacement arrived and took over quietly. Clennan slipped back to his office, where the boyish technician, a creative programmer, awaited him. After the boy's experience with Ramos, Clennan had no trouble converting him to the cause. Together, they began to arrange for some sudden and unorthodox appropriations, whose source and destination would remain conveniently foxed up in the computer's circuitry for several days at least.

If they remained on schedule, that would be more than enough time. Later, Clennan returned to Interrogation to go through the day's reports and to pay a visit to the prisoners in the holding tank.

All the while, Clennan worked with a concentration that defied his lack of sleep and astounded those of his men who knew him well. The snappishness and haunted look of the past few weeks had vanished. The old good-timer manner was back, enlivened with an almost tangible electricity of purpose. His men fed on his energy and worked the harder for it.

Clennan felt like a runner getting his second wind. He had made mistakes, or he had blamed himself when circumstances had conspired against him. His self-esteem had bottomed out, but now he understood why, and he felt good again, potent. If Ramos caught up with him now, there would be no explaining away his machinations of the past twenty-four hours, not this time. But the risks were worth the runner's heady exhilaration, and so Bill Clennan ran, with eyes only for the road ahead.

CHAPTER 42

Twisting in her sheets, Jude cried aloud.

She is in the restaurant with the checkered floor. The young madman with the sane gray eyes sits across the table, smiling as if she alone could understand his pleading.

Where is my brother? He asks it so sadly that she aches to give him the answer he requires.

But no! I mustn't!

My brother, where is he?

No! I do not know!

The madman bows his head until his pale hair brushes the tabletop.

Help me, he pleads. *Only you can help me . . .*

Theis rose from her station by the open door and went over to nuzzle her friend awake. The twin moons hung over the dark water and the beach glittered with a galaxy of cookfires. Jude dressed and went out with the gria to lose her dream in the island's quiet night.

—You are a fine student, Judith.

Thank you, Ana.

—Had you been raised Koi, you might have been a teacher.

(Image of embarrassment)

—I've no need to flatter, child. I say this that you will appreciate your gift and use it wisely.

Yes, Ana. But the dreams . . . I thought I was safe from them, but he pursues me even here.

—The Destroyer?

Yes.

—You know that the Council has agreed to call a Gathering?

Yes.

—And still you ask leave to go see him, though it would expose your presence to him for sure?

I know him, Ana, from the . . . (Image of the colony) *Perhaps if I could talk to him before the Gathering . . .*

—He's deep in his madness, child. You will never dissuade him. But I understand that you must try, for your own sake, though it puts you in danger. But consider this: I judge that you are skilled enough to take part in the Gathering. Though the school barriers could not hide you, you can surely be hidden in the halmweb. This will save your life if the decision goes against the Terrans, but only if your heart does not betray you when the moment comes to strike. To remain safely hidden, you must lend your halm to whichever way the decision goes.

I understand, Ana. Perhaps the Destroyer will convince me, and I will not need to be hidden any longer.

—Perhaps. But hear me, do not try to halmspeak him, whatever the temptation, lest he draw you into his madness with him. Such is the power of a madman's halm. He may convert you against your will. When you make your decision, make it with Balance as your guide.

I will not halmspeak him, Ana.

—Or allow him to halmspeak you. I assure you he will try.

I will use the barriers as you have taught me.

—Dear child, do you not fear this encounter?

It is not Andreas that I fear, but what he would have us do. I fear the decision of the Gathering. Andreas alone will not harm me, not yet. Besides, there is a message I must deliver to him.

—Very well, then, child.. Go to him if you must.

Thank you, Ana.

CHAPTER 43

A day later, as dusk settled over the colonial city, a dented truck marked with the logo of the Colonial Maintenance Section parked out of the way of the unloading activities at the Transport Corridor. Banks of night lights cast premature shadows across the crowds of tourists still awaiting passage home. Tired, subdued, they gathered in clumps, clinging to their baggage, casting haunted eyes at the cordon of armed men that confined them to a small corner of the grounds.

The truck pulled into the shadow of the evergreens. Ron Jeffries leaned his arms and chin on the steering wheel and stared at the stucco building housing the corridor entry. Beside him, Verde chewed on a twig and watched the tourists.

"Look at them, Ron. They're terrified. The irony of all this is that Lacey probably *could* have scared the tourists away, with a little of the right kind of help from us."

Jeffries' eyes counted guards, weapons, paces from the target to proper cover. "Mitch, the tourists are not the problem."

"I know, I know. But you can see the irony. Poor kid. He's dead and here we are doing what he was trying to do all along."

Jeffries was unmoved. "Word is there've been no maintenance stops for two days. Ramos is working both corridors around the clock, more incoming than outgoing." He shifted slightly and braced a finger on the wheel as if sighting a gun. "If I place the charges to impact inward, and blow them right after a departure, we'll keep civilian losses to a minimum. I don't feel bad about the uniforms, but I'd rather not take too many of these good people out just 'cause they're trying to get home. Still, we're going to lose some, Mitch, no way we're not.''

"Yes,'' replied Verde pensively. "One for every Koi murdered during interrogation.'' An errant beam from a searchlight reflected off a moving tractor and brushed his face. His eyes fluttered shut with weary resignation. "You know, when Clennan first sprang this idea on me, I was seized with the most unholy joy. I knew it was the answer, the way out. It was like a shot of adrenaline. I was so sure I didn't stop to consider the consequences. I wonder if that's how all wars begin.''

"Mitch, for the love of . . . Look, with luck, this'll stop the war, not start it.''

"But it's fire with fire,'' Verde insisted. "All my life, I've believed there was a better way. By God, I've used every dirty bureaucratic and legalistic weapon known to man, but never once have I raised my hand in violence. But step by step, I've been forced into retreat, waving my signs and writing my letters, until here I am with my goddam back against the proverbial wall. *Now* when Clennan comes along and puts a bomb in my hand, I shout hallelujah! Pass the matches!'' Verde's taut little body hunched against the plastic seat, a posture as eloquent as a cry of pain. "How am I any saner than James Andreas?''

"Fighting back is better than dying,'' Jeffries offered with utter conviction.

"But where do you draw the line? How do you know when death is *really* the only other possibility?''

"You know.''

Verde's shoulders quivered like a fever victim's. "You and Clennan make it sound so simple. You guys take violence for granted.''

Jeffries did not disagree.

"Do you think I'm a coward, Ron?''

Jeffries chuckled his denial. "Shit, man, you've gone up against some heavies I'd never have tackled—big business, government, you know. Courage ain't determined by your choice of weapons. It's being willing to stick your neck out, and you've done more than your share of that.''

"But my weapons weren't working. Who would have led us along this route if Clennan hadn't suddenly discovered his conscience?''

Jeffries' hand worked at his gnome's beard. "Well, now, I'm still holding out for the possibility that Clennan sees this as a way to set up his own power base here in Arkoi. Mostly I think he's pissed at Ramos for horning in on what he sees as his territory. Since we need him for now, we make our thieves' alliance, but I'm sure keeping an eye on him when the dust settles.

"On the other hand, if you choose to believe he's sincere, it would seem you had a lot to do with bringing him over to us. The doers do, but the talkers set the climate, and change don't occur without the help of both."

"Help. Help comes from the damnedest places."

"Don't it though." They fell silent for a moment, watching the night shift gather at the incoming corridor to receive the next shipment.

"You know, we're still going to have our hands full with everyone who's trapped on this side when the corridor goes," said Verde. "What about Ramos? Maybe we can subvert his army, but I can't see ever winning him over."

Jeffries looked at him with fond incredulity. "We get rid of him, what else? All right, nothing that isn't necessary, I promise. Hell, once we destroy his arsenal, he can declare himself emperor of the colony for all I care. I ain't going to stick around here. If that lunatic Andreas don't manage to strike me dead, I'm heading for the Interior pronto."

"Somebody's going to have to stay behind to take the colony in hand, to integrate it into the rest of Arkoi. A Terran city in a Koi world? It won't be easy. And we don't know for sure that the corridor can be permanently destroyed. If we do it, and then, in time, Terra manages to restore the link, she'll come after us with every weapon she can muster."

Jeffries slid the old truck unto gear, hoping it wouldn't complain too noisily. "I swear, Mitch, you never wait for one problem to get solved before you worry the next one to distraction! Come on, old man, we only got two hours before we make the explosives pickup, and all four weapons hangars to check out beforehand."

CHAPTER 44

————••———————••————

Jude dawdled along the beach, letting the waves cool her feet
In the empty stretch between the city and the encampment, she
felt alone and powerless, not even able to recall what mad
impulse had brought her out into the hot sun to reason with a
madman.

Did I tell myself I was not afraid?

The smoke from cookfires rushed downwind to rasp at her
nostrils, but there was little noise. As she approached the first
ranks of the encampment, she found the converts eating a quiet
midday meal. In the shade of row after row of gaily colored open
tents and canopies, they sat in pensive groups without conversation
too deep in contemplation of the next day's Gathering to notice
as Jude passed among them in her white student's robe. *Like an
army,* she thought, then caught herself. This *was* an army, armed
with an invisible weapon of inconceivable power, waiting in the
still heat of noon upon the call of their leader.

And there the leader stood, alone by the waterline, gazing into
the foam at his feet. He was dressed in the same patched gray
uniform he had worn those weeks ago at their first meeting
though it was now a ragged ruin. He was as she remembered
him, perhaps a little taller, thinner, almost translucent. It was
extraordinary that he could remain so pale under the burning
Arkoi sun.

The Destroyer.

She walked toward him, feeling oddly maternal, but pulled up
short as a lean black-haired figure crossed her path, headed for
the water's edge to bring food to Andreas. But of course it was
not Ra'an, merely one who resembled him. She breathed again
and continued on. She came up behind Andreas as he was
distractedly refusing to eat despite the dark Koi's murmured
encouragements.

"James?" Her voice betrayed her with a tremor.

He turned with a wistful smile, as if she were the exact

242

person he expected to see. His luminous gray eyes took her in with a welcome she had not anticipated. "At last," he said.

The Koi at his side was not so delighted, but his protective gesture drew a rippling laugh from the madman and a restraining hand on his arm.

"Ah, Hrin," soothed Andreas. "We are old friends. She means me no harm. Cannot two Terrans stroll along the beach together on such a lovely day as this?" Hrin grumbled and stalked back toward the tents.

Andreas took a few casual steps through the wavelets, looking very pleased with himself. "Did I not tell you we would meet again?"

She was conscious that her head came only to his shoulder and that he walked with his head politely bowed to catch her words, his fine pale hair framing his face like a hood.

"You did," she replied. "But I never thought . . ."

"Ah, yes. And how are you doing with Anaharimel?" He laughed again as she looked up astounded. "No, I won't play mystical games with you, not with the final moment so close. All of Quaire'en knows there is a Terran learning halm with Anaharimel. It had to be you. Are you having success?"

Jude recalled her teacher's warning. "Some. It is hard."

"Your potential was strong, I remember."

Ra'an was right. You knew even then. "Progress is slow."

He frowned, then let pass whatever worry had touched him. "Be thankful that your learning has been gentle," he remarked, stopping to admire a gull-beast as it circled out over the water, banking against the wind. "Mine was not so. You never knew Meron, did you? You would have liked Meron."

"Meron?"

"The mob murdered her. I carried her to her funeral." He touched a shred of yellow linen bound to his wrist.

The funeral. The bier. Jude remembered, but didn't know what to say. Instead she decided to test Ra'an's theory of prescience. "Why did you say 'At last' when you saw me? Did you know I would be here, I mean, before you heard there was a Terran at the halm school?"

"It seemed likely."

"Likely? Based on what?"

"Factors." He waved his hand in the air puckishly. "Things, people, forces." He widened his eyes and made a mocking gesture of fruition. "Comings together."

So. Ra'an was right again. They do know each other well,

243

these two. Jude crossed her arms with a hint of defiance. "I don't think you are as mad as they say you are, James Andreas."

"I am brilliant, yes, and mad. A duality I cannot seem to remedy."

She thought he was teasing, and it outraged her that he should be so gay at a moment like this.

"This is a dreadful thing you are doing, mad or not."

"Yes, it is dreadful," he said reasonably.

"Then *why*, for God's sake?"

"Because I am mad," he replied with equal reason. And then determination settled into his drawn cheeks, pulling his mouth into a bloodless line. "Mad enough to know what must be done and to be willing to go through with it."

"Who says it must be done? There's got to be another way to protect Arkoi than murdering all the Terrans."

"There is no other way. I say this because I am Terran and know what the Terrans would do here in Arkoi, and so do you and I know that we cannot allow it, and so do you." He swept the horizon with his arm, then turned to include the white cliff and the city. "Do you not look at all this and say, 'This is my home, this is where I want to be'?"

Jude was amazed that tears pricked her eyes. She stared at the sand and murmured, "Yes. I do."

"So does every other Terran who sets foot on this soil. Without ever getting beyond the Guardians to see the real splendor of this world, they want to possess it. This cannot be. Will not be."

"But the Koi . . ."

"The Koi do not understand. They are schooled in inaction and must be led to protect themselves. Their solutions are stale, they will not admit that their world has been inalterably changed by the coming of the Terrans. Arkoi can never be again the way it was before, just by wishing and waiting for it. New methods, new thinking, must prevail. The Koi would debate and discuss until the Terrans ran their laser cannons up this beach to melt Quaire'en into the sea! Woman, be glad for my madness!" He gestured now at the sprawling encampment. "If it seems that only a madman spouting fire and mysticism can force them into action, then I will be that catalyst! Out of my imbalance, let a new Balance be born!" He smiled, pleased with his final epigram. "As the Diamo would say."

"Balance?" Jude swallowed. She felt her own balance teetering. His motives were impeccable, totally rational. Only his method proved him insane. "James, all you're teaching here is go-old-fashioned Terran hatred and violence. Do you think that can be unlearned once the Terrans are dead?"

"Its shadow will linger as a warning, and out of this crisis, a new consciousness will grow, new leadership will step forward to prepare Arkoi for the threat that will never really disappear. Terra will always be there, just a dimension or two away at the other end of the corridor, waiting to move in again as soon as the Koi let their guard down."

The corridor. Now that should be the real target. "There must be another way," she repeated dully.

"There isn't. The Koi need to be galvanized or they will not survive." His gaze followed another gull as it swooped down to skim across the waves. "How is my brother?"

"Your bro—?" *Speaking of hatred and violence??* "I, uh, don't know."

Andreas looked her over, gray eyes skeptical, then shrugged philosophically. "I expect I will see him soon enough. Tomorrow is the day."

Jude wet her lips. "I don't think you will, James. He doesn't care what happens to Terran or Koi. He just wants to be left alone. Ra'an may be your one miscalculation." She reached inside the sleeve of her student's robe. "When I left Ruvala, he asked me to give you this."

She handed him the wrapped bundle. He took it gingerly as if it might burn and lifted back the folds. Silver flashed in the sun and the madman's body shuddered as he revealed his father's flask. His thin hand closed around it, and she thought he would weep.

"He told me to tell you that he refuses the challenge."

Andreas stroked the incised initials with his thumb.

"He will not come, James."

"Yes." Andreas nodded, unheeding, tracing the letters. "Yes, he will come. He must come." He clasped the flask to his chest, and with a deliberate finger, pointed to a huge sea-bleached log stranded by the tide. The encampment made a wide circle around it. "He will come. We will meet, you there, here myself, and there"—he pointed up the beach away from the city—"my brother Ra'an. Then the dynamic will be complete. My work will be done."

He turned to look at her. It was not so much the absolute conviction in his voice that made her shiver, more its undertone of anticipated anguish. It left her wordless, struggling under his searching, pleading stare. The hot sun beat down on her, and she wondered why she was having trouble breathing. She felt as if an enormous weight were pressing in on her from all sides. She forced her lungs to open and realized the pressure was in her head. It was he, Andreas, probing, demanding entry with such peremptory power that it required all the strength of her halm just to maintain a barrier against him, normally a mere process of deciding not to listen.

Suddenly the pressure ceased, and Andreas continued as if nothing had occurred, though he seemed oddly satisfied. "You see, as I am the only Terran who can think like a Koi, my brother Ra'an is the only Koi who can think like a Terran. He alone fully comprehends that hatred and violence are basic to Terran nature."

"And not to the Koi? Sounds simplistic, James."

"The Terrans don't understand Balance. The Koi misunderstand Imbalance. Ra'an understands both, Balance and Imbalance. Only he can lead a safe path through the dual world. Ra'an is the future, the amalgam."

Jude found his reasoning obscure. "And you would kill him for that?"

"I?" The gray eyes blinked. "I?" For once she had startled him. "Does he think that? He cannot think that." Then he laughed in that gentle, tragic way that seemed to her so sane. "No, I will not kill my brother. It is he who will kill me . . . and you must help him to it."

What did he mean, Ana?

—Calm, child, calm. Why do you continue to expect reason from a madman?

We must not be fooled. He is more than just mad, Ana. Things he said in . . . (Image of the colony) *have come true.*

—He said something once, and later you allowed it to explain things you did not understand, but that would have happened anyway. He seeks to involve you, to tie you to him by convincing you that the future he sees is the only possible one. This is the way of the Diamo, beneath all their magical trappings. If all can be made to believe that there are no options, an intended future can be forced to come about. Yet as long as even one individual preserves her belief in free will, the future can be predicted, but never known.

But what possible need can he have of me?

—Perhaps he thinks you will bring Ra'an to him.

He is mistaken to assume I could do that.

—Nor would you do it. Come, child, think not of what the

Destroyer wishes you to do, but of what you yourself want to do. They may be the same thing, but then again, they may not.

Ana, I am frightened. Now I am frightened. It is possible that I will die tomorrow.

—Child, it is always possible that one may die tomorrow.

CHAPTER 45

Bill Clennan spent the final day distracting his boss while his men went about their frenzied preparations. By the time Ramos signed out and to go to dinner, he was exhausted by the overflow of paper and personnel that had flowed through his office from Interrogation. He did not invite Clennan to have dinner with him.

Later that evening, a radio operator in the Intelligence Complex waved to his buddies who were heading out to the newly opened officers' club, saying he had paperwork to catch up on.

At 9:30 P.M., a minor argument in one of the colonial police barracks spread to the others before Colonel Ramos, woken out of an early sweating sleep, could call several units of his military away from their normal duties to quiet the fighting. The chief of police was nowhere to be found.

Simultaneous unrest was reported in the detention camp. Guards complained of nausea and hallucinations, and the extra soldiers who were sent in from guarding the Transport Corridor fell victim to the same sudden infection. A network power loss disabled the electric fence temporarily. Several of the Koi prisoners were reported escaped and could not be found in the darkness.

At 12:15 in the early morning, a dented truck pulled up at the Transport Corridor and three men in Colonial Maintenance uniforms went quietly about their business, as the reduced work force unloaded the midnight shipment. Boxes were taken from the back of the truck and stacked outside the corridor entryway. Several of the loaders, transfers from the colonial police, did not return from their latrine breaks.

From the holding tank in the Intelligence Complex, Luteverindorin held conference with an exhausted Koi in the deep-cellars, who had left the circle struggling to maintain the Wall to receive instructions from the surface.

At each of four weapons-storage hangars, a maintenance relief crew showed their passes to the remaining guards and drove their trucks through the gates and up to the hangar doors.

As the colonial radio station closed down for the night, the janitors locked themselves in and barricaded the doors. They spread a hand-drawn diagram on a table and began to move furniture around.

Closeted once again with his young computer expert, Bill Clennan glared at his watch as if it were the enemy, and bummed the first cigarette he had had in years.

In Quaire'en, the white beach glowed pink with the early fire of the sun.

CHAPTER 46

The tide was early-morning low, the white sand spreading like a desert. Perched on the driftwood log as if it were a straight-backed chair, Jude watched her shadow shrink while the sun rose over the water, paling as it climbed, bleaching its own blood-pink from the landscape until even the sea was white and still. Jude had not chosen to sit on the log. When the first stirrings of dawn had drawn her down to the beach, she had tried to settle inconspicuously into the sand. But Andreas would not allow it. With stares and pouting, with insinuations that it would be merely petty to refuse him, he compelled her to the log, where she waited in exposed isolation, either prisoner or evidence in Andreas' courtroom, or perhaps both. At her feet lay Theis, muzzle on paws, making uneasy animal noises.

Andreas stood once more by the water's edge, continuing his silent conversation with the wavelets lacing his bare feet. A few paces away, Hrin squatted, a dark shape against the damp sand, his concentration absolute in the direction of the city. From there would come the members of the Council.

In a wide semicircle, the pilgrim Koi were gathering around their leader by the thousands, in a silence full of motion. The first ranks had formed early from the encampment, row after row had waited cross-legged in the sand for many hours already. Behind them, more rows filled in from a long line spiraling down the cliffs from the city and from surrounding towns and villages.

There was no hostility, no visible sign of the debate that had raged through the countryside for so many weeks. It was not possible to tell from the faces who favored Andreas and who did not. Most visible was their patience, full of the knowledge that no matter how long and painfully the decision was debated in the Gathering, in the end it must be by the very nature of the process, unanimous and unalterable.

Now Andreas looked up from the water, turning his gaze down the beach away from the city, stretching upward slightly for a clear view across the thousands of heads to where the beach ran to the south, empty and flat.

Jude echoed his movement apprehensively. Heat mirages rippled the distance. The white beach stretched as it had in her dreams. Was someone moving out there, coming this way?

Don't let him come. Please, don't let him come.

A sound like wind in dry wheat drew her attention back. Andreas did not move, but Hrin rose from his crouch on the sand as twelve Koi entered the semicircle in a solemn group. Hrin's broad back dipped in unconscious reverence as he went to meet them.

The Council, six men and six women of mixed ages and racial stock, wore no robes of office. As a group they were a symbol of ultimate authority; as individuals they held no power. Today each looked as if he or she wished this crisis had arisen when someone else was serving as part of the Council. They looked shaken, perhaps confused by the burden the madman had thrust upon them.

Hrin led them to the center of the semicircle, and they lowered themselves quietly to the sand but for one, a graying Ruvalan whom Jude guessed to be Kirial. She searched the father for a hint of the son but found nothing more than the physical resemblance tempered by age. Kirial stood forward a little, tall, less lean than his son. Only then did Andreas turn from his scrutiny of the far-off empty beach. The two approached each other, each wearing the same half-smile of recognition, and when they met, embraced lightly, sadly, then stepped apart.

"Well, James," said Kirial. His Terran was accented but fluent. "We will begin, then."

Andreas' eyes flicked down the length of the beach, then upward. "Wait a while yet, until the sun is higher."

Kirial was an elegant if not prepossessing figure, as he tilted his head quizzically, he seemed to be studying the madman from a great distance. "So. Even you would postpone the final moment," he observed softly.

Andreas' denial was arch. "When that moment nears, I will let you know it."

"Now *is* the moment, James." Kirial's dry light voice stayed neutral as it dropped to a near whisper. "What you have set in motion, not even you could hope to control. You may have a few moments, no longer. The Gathering is ready."

"The breadth of my control may surprise you, Kirial. The Gathering may be ready, but I am not. Therefore we will wait."

The Ruvalan's gaze was steady. "Well, since we must wait, you will not mind then if I ask you a question."

"The Council has asked its questions of me already."

"The Council does not ask this, I ask it."

Andreas hesitated imperceptibly, then shrugged. "Do so then, if I may ask one in return."

Kirial nodded graciously, then shed his neutrality like a glove thrown down to the challenge. "If Daniel were alive, would you still preach this horror?"

Andreas gave a hollow laugh. "That question has no answer, Kirial, you know that. You ask it only to hurt me, and I am beyond that."

"I ask it to know if there were Terrans alive whom you love as you did Daniel, would you sacrifice them to your vengeance?"

"You are my enemy afterall, Kirial, for you assume that there is no one that I love." The madman's thin shoulders drooped. "I am sorry that you misunderstand me so completely."

Kirial turned away curtly, but Andreas laid a hand on his robed arm. "My question to you, Kirial. Where is my brother? Are you keeping him from me?"

"Your brother?"

"Your son."

"Ah." Kirial shook off the hand coolly. "I would have thought to find him your chief henchman, as eager as you to spill Terran blood."

"This is not an answer."

"We don't know where he is, James. What Ra'an has in his mind you would know better than I."

"So I thought," Andreas murmured, almost to himself, turning for another glance down the long beach. His attention drew inward, as if Kirial had ceased to exist. The Ruvalan moved off,

250

his face grim. He stood alone in the sun momentarily, then made his way across the sand toward Jude.

"Judith," he said gently as he came up to her. He held out his hand Terran-style.

Jude rose to meet him and took the hand, grateful for the support implicit in his firm grip. *I must ask him now.* She wished she felt as confident as her formality made her sound. "Kirial, with my teacher Anaharimel as my sponsor, I request permission of the Council to join in the Gathering."

Over Kirial's shoulder, she saw Andreas slowly swivel to stare at her. *He doesn't like this. He doesn't want me getting lost in the halm web. He wants me where he can get at me. Why?* But it encouraged her to have caught him by surprise again. If Andreas meant her harm, then joining the Gathering seemed to be the right move. But she did not know for sure that he meant her harm. She watched him, using Kirial as a shield between them. He seemed about to protest but had himself invalidated his best excuse. He could not disqualify her from the Gathering for being Terran without disqualifying himself. As he stared at her, all remnants of whimsy, all the erratic gentleness that she had found to like in him, drained away, as if he had died while she watched, yet remained erect and staring, a rag-draped skeleton.

Jude knew both fear and the anguish of loss. "James," she whispered.

Unnoticing, Kirial smiled. "All halm is welcome in a Gathering, especially when it is supported by determination and courageous opinion."

Determined? Courageous? Ah, Kirial, I will only disappoint you.

But she kept to herself her intentions to use the Gathering as a refuge rather than a pulpit. Kirial leaned and lightly kissed her forehead, then straightened.

"We will begin," he announced, and crossed the sand to resume his place with the Council.

Andreas lowered himself to the ground, sitting stiffly, his back to the multitude. His eyes strayed for a final time toward the southern beach.

Jude's eyes followed his. Beyond the ranks of waiting Koi faces, the beach was empty.

The Gathering began.

Bill Clennan shoved back his chair and faced his computer whiz. "I guess that'll have to do us. One-ten. I'll get to the radio

251

station by one thirty-five . . . cutting it close, but . . ." He rose, stretching. "How long until the central computer notices your off-limits pattern?"

The tech brushed at his hair, though it was too short to fall anywhere near his eyes. The gesture was Clennan's. "Forty-five seconds to put the pattern together, another fifteen to broadcast a systems alert." He patted the keyboard as if it were a show dog. "This terminal will stay on line for another minute or so before Central discovers its address."

"The station terminal will go down with the alert?"

The tech took a drag on a dying cigarette, nodding. "But you can still broadcast as long as the power lasts. Central can't get to that, not after what I did yesterday."

"Right. So you'll wait till the last possible second to plug us into the transport network. Now, don't panic, kid, 'cause if you go too early, they'll have us for sure. The Jewel's never far from a terminal."

The boy exhaled ruefully. "Oh, he'll be the first to know, all right."

Clennan paced a little. He toyed with the zipper at his throat. He wished for darker clothing to blend with the night, but he had purposely worn his usual to avoid arousing suspicion. "On present corridor schedule, there's a one forty-five departure. Plug in at one forty-four fifteen. If the com network reports they're on schedule, link up with me at the station. I'll broadcast the go five seconds after the departure."

"Not much leeway, Bill."

Clennan shot him a dark grin from the door. He gestured at a heavy file cabinet. "Lock the door behind me and drag that in front. Then sit tight until we tell you it's okay to show your face." He took a last look around the little room. "See you in the next world, buddy. Let's just hope it's ours!"

With Kirial's call, silence descended over the white beach. The shanevoralin ceased their crying to circle on muted wings.

Jude readied herself to enter the Gathering.

It is like the ocean, Anaharimel had said. *You know how to swim, don't you?*

Jude eased herself into that ocean cautiously. The impact of a hundred million minds all present on one wavelength was profound in ways not even Anaharimel could have prepared her for. In observing the thousands crowding the beach, she had allowed herself to forget that the rest of the population who were not present in body would be still vitally present in the halmweb.

The ocean was warm and alive. Where she expected a chaos of voices, she discovered that a hundred million thoughts were not so disparate. Thoughts formed currents, some major, some minor. They flowed in and out of each other smoothly, testing each other's strength and temperature without conflict. She was aware of personalities surfacing and fading and surfacing again. It *was* like swimming, like swimming in an endless crowd, pausing now and then to touch and exchange a nugget of life with an open-faced stranger. Like a novice swimmer, Jude was awkward, roiling the ocean around her with her earnest thrashings until she learned confidence from the buoyancy of other minds. With confidence came control and soon she was floating free, learning that she must make her own separate current, for in this ocean she was unique. Like a land animal who has acquired gills, she would always carry the memory of the time when the water was not her home.

But running with the tides, Jude knew she was saved. There were depths in this ocean to hide her from the gray threat of Andreas that glided sharklike through the web. As his presence asserted itself, she stilled and settled to the shadowed bottom. The Gathering had been called to make a decision, and this required a formal presentation of the sides. As James Andreas began to argue his case, Jude discovered why Anaharimel had warned about the halm of madmen.

His aura dominated the web. She was mistaken to have ever thought him sane. His thoughts were not currents, they were riptides. Their whirlpool undertow was treacherous. His halmspeech came not in words but images. Words would have confined him within human limitations, and he wished to work his lunatic magic on a mythic scale. He began placidly, indulging in the heightened lyricism of a nineteenth-century landscapist, lulling the listening web with the poetry of mountains and forested valleys, painting a sentimental portrait of grassy fields along the shore of a sparkling lake. It was Menissa as he had known it in his youth, as yet unaltered by the Terran presence. Then black clouds loomed above the mountains and Andreas reared back and slammed in with nightmares to trample his pure paradise in a tumult of destruction. Jude heard her own cry of despair echoed throughout the web. Like a demonic holographer, Andreas surrounded them with a descent into hell. Machinery squealed, sirens keened, pumps and furnaces roared. The stench of traffic

253

and industry invaded the web, and when every mind was reeling, he heaped on still more, waste and garbage, blood and rotting flesh, fevered horror strobing into a hundred million brains, a writhing desperate heartbeat of horrors the color of fire and smoke. It was Terra he showed them, his own delirious version of Terra, whose pale men and women, as bloated as insect larvae, streamed shoulder to shoulder down endless urban canyons under skies sodden with poison. It was a vision of riot and rape, of the knife ripping the gut, of the flesh charred by laser fire, the madman's own horsemen of the Apocalypse howling across a land that in his vision became Arkoi; where mountains were gobbled up by mines, forests were leveled, and rivers grew sluggish with chemical infection. A hundred million Koi minds swayed with nausea, unresisting as Andreas drew them into himself and held them captive while through his eyes the Terran mob stalked them down the burning streets. Glass shattered at their ears, and helpless, they watched the flash of orange tunic and the upraised bottle slashing down, saw the livid splatter of blood on the blond head of a dying Koi.

He released them, spat them out to drift in isolation, withdrawn in numbness and dread from the halm contact that could have solaced them. Currents washed aimlessly against each other. The ocean stilled.

Overhead, the sun beat down on the beach and shanevoralin wheeled and screamed anew.

But within Jude a rebellious voice was rising. She fought it but could not silence it, even for her own safety. As if an old friend considered lost, even dead, had shown up unannounced, she was surprised to meet it here on this alien beach, to recognize it as her own. It was the voice that had long ago guided her down a dark and dusty air duct with a camera strapped to her belly, the same voice that had stirred under Ra'an's accusation of cynicism, stirred but not wakened, waiting for the proper time.

The time is now, the voice in her insisted. *Now, while Ra'an hides out in Ruvala's forests, abdicating responsibility. Now, when some voice, any voice, must be raised against a Terran tyranny as pernicious as any in the colony. Now is not the time to hide.*

And so Jude's voice rang out in the web against the tyranny of James Andreas.

Destroyer! What you would do is no better than the horror you show us!

Suddenly she was no longer invisible on the ocean bottom.

254

She was in the center of an arena, alone. Her challenge echoed against sheer sunlight walls, matching the roar of the beast-that-was-Andreas as it charged out of the black tunnel in pursuit.

Soft halm voices urged Jude to run, hide, seek the safety of the stands where she could lose herself among the crowds.

Detroyer! Extermination is Terran practice! Genocide is Terran history! Do you bring this bloodlust to the Koi so they can become like Terrans? Is this your mission, Andreas? So that when you are done, the Koi will do with Arkoi what the Terrans would have done anyway?

Her halm voice quivered. It was ragged and shrill. She could not articulate in this new language the passion that fired her recklessness.

James . . . can this truly be your mission?

The beast circled, mute and drooling. There was no longer a doubt that it meant her harm. Jude turned to face it, because not facing it, she feared it more.

Revenge is not justice, Andreas!

She circled as it circled, avoiding but unable to flee.

Help me, I cannot do this alone!

She looked to the throng, gathered at a safe distance.

Will no one stand with me?

Her resolution crumbled. She called out unheeding.

RA'AN!

The beast faltered as if reined by an invisible leash, but pulled itself free with a snarl. Jude edged backward, retreating before its charge.

I can't! I'm not strong enough!

And then, she was no longer alone.

—Far stronger than you know, child.

The clear resonance of Anaharimel sang beside her.

—There are yet a few, James Andreas, to whom Balance is more precious than vengeance!

And Rya was there, and Dal and the girl Pe'eva. Kirial added his voice, and solid Tekhon, and their defiance grew stronger with numbers, drawing others, strangers, who gained courage from their example. Their fused compassion was magnetic. Opinion reversed its flow to surge toward them in grateful retreat from the heat-sickness of the madman's harangue.

The beast-that-was-Andreas answered with a petulant shriek of rage. He called Hrin to him, and those who had followed him through the mountains. He summoned the Diamo. Like a barbarian general, he rallied his faithful in phalanx around him. His call to arms thundered through the web.

255

—LISTEN! OUR POWER RISES LIKE THE WAVE! THERE SHALL BE NO RETREAT INTO PITY. THE TIME TO STRIKE IS NOW!

Hrin echoed the cry, then others, in deafening fusillade.

Protests from the Council members coalesced into a single voice of outrage.

—The Gathering has not decided! No action will be taken without a consensus!

—I AM YOUR CONSENSUS! I AM THE DESTROYER AND THE MOMENT IS MINE!

Abandoning all protocol and with it the fiction that he would abide by the decision of the Gathering even if it went against him, Andreas launched a systematic purge of the web, clearing all resistance to him. His ferocious hatred was a weapon deadlier than a laser. Centuries of peace had left the Koi unskilled in mental combat. They had no means to fend off the agony of his attack other than to raise the protective halm barriers that also cut them off from each other. Andreas met with no counterassault. None could stand against him. One by one, Jude's allies were driven from the web, Rya, Kirial, Tekhon, all the others, hammered into submission and flight. The web contracted around her with each loss, the Destroyer's battle cry ringing in her ears. Andreas burned brighter as his forces swelled. They fed off his searing energy and gathered their own weapons of hatred to strike out at the Terrans across the mountains. Jude was in the arena again, with only Anaharimel beside her and the mad throng screaming for her head. The beast charged, out of control, and Anaharimel raised her defiance before it like a sword. In her calm was a suicidal determination. The beast faltered in its charge, a voice cried out.

—No! You will be needed!

Jude heard and knew that inside the ravening monster, the soul of James Andreas was still alive.

Anaharimel rejected his mercy.

—Not in the world that you would create!

—Halm teacher, he will need you!

—He?

—Stand aside. Alone, you have not the strength to stop me.

The beast edged closer, dancing in frustration.

What is he doing? Who will need her? Jude had an image of gnashing teeth, the beast momentarily leashed as Andreas sweated through a flash of lucidity.

James, who will need her?

—Ra'an will need her!

The mood of sacrifice was contagious. Jude thrust herself in front of her teacher's shield.

Protect yourself, Ana.

—But I do, child, that part of me that matters. I've no wish to be left alive when this horror of his is done, knowing that I did nothing to stop it.

But, Ana, you do not understand . . .

—Do you, child?

The beast lunged against its restraint. Andreas' buried voice was choked with effort.

—I knew it would come to this, halm teacher. You will be silenced without harm and thank me later.

With a final massive exertion, Andreas hauled back on the beast that was himself and gasped out a halm signal. The henchman prepared in hiding at the school slid forth to overpower the old woman as she sat in her chair on the whitewashed terrace. A drug smothered her into unconsciousness, and as surely as if she had died, Anaharimel's strong presence vanished from the web. The madman's moment of reason slipped away exhausted. Released, the beast grabbed control and shook itself angrily.

Jude stood alone before it, hopelessly vulnerable. She felt herself go calm with rage, and found that in that calm a new and heady power. Her halm voice no longer shrilled. Fear paled to a petty emotion beside the outrage building inside her. With her mind still meshed within the web, she grew aware of her body, standing, planting its feet in the sand. Considerations of strength or weakness, courage or fear, were pushed aside. As if fitting herself into the niche where she was always meant to be, she thrilled to the purity of unambiguous alignment. She understood at last what had really brought her to the beach. It was not to hide in the web. She could have done that within the physical safety of the halm school. It was not to speak out for the Terrans just because she also was Terran. She might weep for the murder of five million, even share the burden of guilt, but would not risk her life merely for the sake of theirs. What fired her, finally, was the sheer injustice of the situation: that the will of the one, or even the few, would be imposed on the many, without a chance for the many to offer up their own arguments. Under the pressure of the Destroyer's attack, the core of her value structure exerted itself. She knew at last what her cause was.

Fueled by outrage, she abandoned caution. She screamed at the beast, moving closer, taunting, as if eager for the end.

I will not be ruled against my will! Strike me down for that if you must!

The beast roared, tossed its head. Its spittle lashed her face.

Strike, you bastard, you nothingness, you negation! What are you waiting for?

But the beast did not strike. It charged and knocked her aside as if she were straw and stormed off on a new rampage through the web. It circled and circled, whipping its troops into a frenzy of bloodlust. Their voices broke overhead like thunder. The Destroyer gathered their strength to forge his weapon. Yet through the rising chaos beat a faint echo.

—There is still time for him, time yet for him to come, still time . . .

Jude heard it, the dying whisper of James Andreas, heard his pain and what it cost him to continue to broadcast his last desperate hope through the beast's cry to genocide. *Is it possible?* she wondered dizzily. *Could he be right after all? Could Ra'an somehow be the solution?*

And the beast still circled, winding the spring tighter, tighter building the pressure toward an orgasm of violence, priming its troops for the slaughter of millions.

"James!"

The call was dreamy with distance. Jude was not sure she had heard it at all.

"James!"

It neared, a panting cry. It settled through the submerged layers of the Gathering's awareness like a pebble sinking through water. The beast halted in mid-spiral with an answering roar of triumph.

Jude struggled within the turbulence of the web. She reached for her physical senses, remembered where her feet were, and dug them hard into the reality of burning sand. She slitted open her eyes to the glare of the noon sun. Andreas had risen and stood staring to the south.

A form distilled out of the heat mirage. A dark apparition raced toward them along the wet sand at the water's edge. Long black hair whipped in the wind.

Ra'an.

Jude's halmvoice rose in instinctive warning. *RA'AN!* He did not answer.

RA'AN!

The sagging of the madman's shoulders was unmistakably relief. With strength born of new hope, James Andreas grabbed control of his destroyer beast and brought it to a halt while the web seethed in passion and confusion.

258

Shivering in the hot sun, the madman waited for his brother to come to him.

Clennan knocked at the upstairs entrance to the radio station. He glanced down the grimy hallway and called out softly, "Liberator!" He was rewarded with the sound of heavy objects being dragged aside behind the door. A crack opened to reveal Damon Montserrat aiming a huge stunner. When Damon saw Luteverindorin at Clennan's shoulder, he threw the door wide.

Clennan hurried in. "One thirty-eight. I'm late. More of Ramos' damn roadblocks." He inspected the temporary command headquarters that he had never laid eyes on until that moment. The janitors had done their work. The layout was exactly as planned, totally familiar. Clennan strode straight to the little computer terminal, scanned the monitor array. Hand-printed labels read: NETWORK. CORRIDOR. AUX. He studied the maps pinned to the wall above the screens. So far, no surprises.

He counted chairs, ushered Lute to the one nearest the head seat at the console. Verde came in from the broadcast studio with a sheet of paper. Clennan read through the scribbles and crossings, nodding.

"A great spiel, Mitch . . . and you claim you're no good at public relations! Start broadcasting as soon as the explosions die down, all frequencies, and keep it up until you drop." He passed the paper back. "The tourists'll panic anyway, those left behind, but it might calm them some to know what's going on." He offered Verde a knowing look. "No more Dark Powers stuff, eh?"

Verde called up a meager grin and retreated into the studio. Damon replaced the desks and tape racks across the front door and followed.

Clennan seated himself at the console, flexing his hands like a concert artist. The terminal hummed comfortingly. Less comfortingly, the chronometer flicked seconds away with clicks that punctuated the silence with hammer blows. Clennan hunched, willed his shoulders to relax. "Review battle stations, Lute."

Lute activated the colony halmweb. The Koi assigned to each demolition or assault team relayed back their position and readiness. Clennan eyed the maps. He pointed to the central monitor. "When the kid plugs me in, it'll show up on this screen. You give the signal to the cellars, them let me know when the Wall is down."

The glassmaker smiled his assent. He looked undersized, out

of place against the plastic-and-metal chairback. He did not look nervous.

Clennan smiled back. The old Koi's presence was steadying. With his hands at forced rest to either side of the keyboard, Clennan watched the center screen, waiting for it to spring to life.

Ra'an reached the outer edge of the multitude. Barely slowing, he shoved his way through roughly. The crowd bent around him like wheat before a wind. Damp and breathless, he pushed into the open in the precise spot on the sand that Andreas had predicted for him. Jude groaned aloud.

Andreas trembled. His eyes devoured Ra'an with unholy welcome. "At last," he murmured. "We are complete."

Ra'an brushed sweat from his eyes, a nervous straining gesture. He looked haunted, worn, leaner and taller than Jude remembered. He had resumed his Terran clothing. The black pants and black shirt cut a knife-edge silhouette against the hot white sand and the paler garments of the Gathering.

A Koi alien among Koi. Jude ached for him, for herself. *He's accepted the challenge. James did not misjudge him afterall.* But she was no longer sure she understood the role James intended him to play. With Ra'an's coming, the focus shifted radically. Jude conserved her newfound strength and waited.

Andreas let a kind of smile light his face. "I knew you would come."

Breathing hard, Ra'an nodded. His opening gambit was dry mockery. "In answer to your summons."

"For our father's sake," Andreas urged.

Ra'an squinted, a fine twitching around his eyes, against the sun and the whiteness of the madman's face. His chest heaved in a brusque sigh, acceptance of the melodrama inevitable in such a confrontation. "For our father's sake," he echoed ritualistically. He made it sound like a concession, like playing along with a child's game, and as he spoke, he moved in closer. "But mostly for yours." His voice softened. "James. Leave this. Come home with me."

Andreas dipped his pale head, a coltlike shying. Tiny tremors shot through his thighs, up his back. His fingers pointed stiffly toward the sand. "Home, brother?" he asked, as if amazed. "To Terra? To Daniel's house in the Quarter? We have no home, you and I."

Ra'an advanced another cautious step, soothing, new dampness beading his skin. "Then we will make one."

The madman's spasms quickened. "Yes!" he hissed. "You will make it. Not for me, but for all the others. For that I brought you here."

Ra'an hesitated, shook his head. "I came on my own, James."

"You came because I summoned you!"

A final step brought them face to face. "I came because you need me." Ra'an reached, lightly touched the madman's shoulder as if brushing an insect. "Accept that, James, and know it means more than any futures you may intend to bring about."

"*They* need you!" Andreas cried, and stepped back to sweep an arm across the arc of waiting thousands. But the gesture was wild, and he fought to restrain his body from following its furious spiral. His gray eyes went wide with effort. He hugged his thin chest as if holding himself together and whispered, barely audible, "Brother, I am finished . . . nearly finished here . . . now it's up to you, from here on."

"What's up to me?" Ra'an frowned, then matched the whisper, pleading. "James, wait. This vision of revenge is your madness. Leave it. You can, right now, while you listen to me. Leave it behind and come with me. Let Arkoi determine its own future, as we will determine ours, together."

Andreas backed from the proffered hand, his eyes glaring. "Don't pretend you don't understand!"

Frustrated, Ra'an roared back, "I don't understand!"

Andreas' body jerked like a broken machine. "Then I must make it clearer," he snarled, the glaze hardening into a white glare. He fixed Ra'an with a taunting grin. "Come join our Gathering, brother, and you will learn what I have planned for you!"

Ra'an stiffened as if slapped. The rebuff was a cutting anguish, and he doused his pain with an instinctive surge of anger that radiated from him like waves on a lake. The throng murmured. Across the sand, Jude winced and readied her defenses. But Ra'an mastered himself. For a moment, he was an utterly neutral presence, suspended in time, and all gathered there on the beach were suspended with him, for the next move could only be his. He looked away, out over the azure water. Jude thought he sighed like a man preparing to take a matter in hand though it meant meeting death head-on. At last he turned and met the madman's glare. "You will take no further part in this Gathering, James."

The glare grew eager, hungry. "You cannot stop me. My mind is not yours to control . . . any longer."

Ra'an's moment of decision-making had rendered him stoical.

"It never was, James, no more than you allowed it to be, no more than mine was Daniel's to control, which I did allow, even encouraged. I've accepted that, James, do you hear me? It was not Daniel's fault, not the father's fault, if the son was too devoted. I can't blame Daniel because living as his son isolated me from my own heritage, from the halm-gift he had no idea he was keeping from me. I can't blame the Terrans either, I can't even blame myself. Not anymore." He paused, looked down, said hoarsely. "Events happen, we allow them to happen, not understanding their consequence. Later, we must accept them, or destroy ourselves in bitterness."

He looked up again and around the gathering, a flick of amazement at his own rush to confession in a public arena. His eyes skated past Jude blindly and returned to Andreas, intent, demanding. "I have forgiven Daniel, now that I have realized how much of my love for him had soured into resentment. You must forgive him also, James, and then you will lose heart for this massacre of Terrans, as I have." He offered his hand to the madman once more. "James. Please. Will you walk away down this beach with me and let the Koi decide for themselves how much blood they will spill?"

"No." Andreas tossed his head once, then again and again, until his fine white hair whipped about his face. "It's too late for that now, no, too late! What is set in motion must be completed!"

Ra'an's tongue moved across his lower lip as if finding the words distasteful before he said them. "I will try to prevent this, James." His voice slowed with deadly purpose. "I am not so harmless as you think."

Andreas jeered, but above the snarl, pride flickered briefly in his eyes. "*I know* what you are, brother," he urged softly. "Come, show me."

"I was always the stronger, James, do you remember that?"

The madman's body danced puppetlike. He turned to the throng and spread his arms wide. "The Koi without halm threatens me!" he cried tauntingly. He whirled back to Ra'an. "What will you do, brother? Break my arm? Pin me to the sand? Come, brother, we deal in greater powers here! Show me yours!"

Jude had a sudden insight. *He's goading him. He wants him to attack.*

Ra'an waited, impassive.

Do it! she called to him, but felt no reception, no reply. Andreas was behind her suddenly, looking down at her as she sat frozen on her driftwood log. His knees grazed her rigid back.

"You understand," he murmured, touching her hair with infinite gentleness. "We do what must be done to preserve the future." He raised both hands, and she could feel them hovering on either side of her neck like a chill breeze. She was lost in his tall shadow, mesmerized by the sure knowledge that at the other end of this moment of stillness lay death and destruction. Her eyes met Ra'an's briefly, tried to hold, but he pulled away.

Ra'an! You cannot prevent my involvement in this! James decided that for us, long ago!

"Well, brother?" chided Andreas. "I am waiting. Have you come all this way to do nothing? I will, we all will think you a coward. . . . Come, show me how you will stop me!" He laid his fingers against Jude's skin, so lightly that she felt no pressure, only their deathly cold. Fingertips caressed, searched out the vein, the nerve points.

The halm stillness was shattered. Raw power exploded through the web. Jude's brain rocked, recoiled, as the Destroyer raised his battle cry once more. The pent-up fervor of his forces boiled around him as he gathered them in readiness to strike.

But Ra'an still waited, unaware, watching Andreas, who seemed to stand before him calmly. hands resting on Jude's shoulders.

Jude started, tried to stand. Andreas held her down with iron strength. *He cannot hear the call! It will be done before he can lift a finger!*

—He will hear if you help him.

She opened her mouth, but his hand locked around her jaw. She struggled, wrenched her head aside, for an instant broke free.

"RA'AN!" she screamed. "RA . . .!"

The madman's hands circled her throat and tightened.

The center screen glowed green. Data rolled across, transport schedules, arrivals, departures. Desperately, Clennan scanned the figures, locked in on the item he'd been searching for: departure pending, 1:45 .

"That's it," he breathed.

The chronometer read 1:44:48.

"Do it, Lute." Clennan's fingers worked the keys and waited. 1:44:52.

Lute sent out the halm signal to the cellars.

The corridor monitor flickered. READY, it read.

"Good man, Jeffries," Clennan muttered. He watched the departure layout like a hawk.

1:44:59. The center screen blanked and began to rebuild the schedule information. Clennan sucked his cheek.

1:45. Outgoing: on-schedule departure.

Clennan nodded and looked to Lute for the signal.

Jude did not struggle. Her role was clear to her at last. As the pressure on her throat twisted into pain and her lungs ached for air, she reached out with her mind to hammer a warning into Ra'an's unyielding brain. She circled. She beat at the walls he hid behind. It was like beating bare fists against a rock. Her brain hurt. Her body was in agony.

He won't . . . I can't . . .! She feared that she would die before she could get through to him.

Do it yourself! she pleaded with Andreas. *I cannot!*

—You can, he replied, even as his grip tightened. You must. You are my only link. Would I put you through this if I could do it myself?"

Her lungs were empty. Her body spasmed. She could not hold it limp against its struggle for life. The pain blinded her and yet she did not pass out and so the pain went on and on and she could not scream. Through a halo of blood haze, she could see Ra'an watching her death throes as if paralyzed with horror and indecision. The roar of the Destroyer's army mixed with the roaring of her pulse in her ears. She thought of Anaharimel's calm in the face of death and subdued her panic for a final summing of all she knew by instinct and all she had learned during her days in Arkoi. She focused her halmvoice, fine-tuned it, for it was growing weak. She reached securely, without forced demand. She found him, touched him, wrapped her halmpresence around him. Her power was not in brute strength like the Destroyer's but in breadth, in resilience, and finally, in persistence. She overwhelmed him with her need, and as she had when she was dying once before, he opened his mind to her and listened.

She relayed to him the lethal passion spiraling through the web in answer to the Destroyer's call. She showed him the Gathering swiveling its sights toward the colony, preparing for genocide. She felt his shock, the sudden surge of his outrage. Now there was no hesitation left in him. He reached for her instinctively and hung on as if hauling himself out of a blind pit. His voice in her head sounded like her own.

Find him for me . . . be my eyes and ears to the web . . . find him, isolate him. You must aim the weapon for me.

The madman's hands crushed into her throat. She no longer

felt the pain, only a great weakness and a fading of the light. Dizzily she sought Andreas in the web, followed the searing trail marked by the Destroyer beast on the rampage, found and focused on it as it whirled to devour its pursuer. She locked in on it with her last seconds of consciousness.

Ra'an! Now!

Ra'an struck with such awesome power that the beast reared back with a scream. Andreas' body staggered. His hands flung themselves violently from Jude's throat as if her skin was fire. The beast's mad shriek of pain in the web was echoed along the beach as Andreas doubled over and fell to his knees. Aides, rushing to defend their leader, searched the web frantically for the source of the attack. The beast screeched and lashed out blindly in its rage and pain. Its own supporters retreated from its charge. Its troops milled in confusion. Ra'an was invisible in the web, tied to it by a link which became also invisible as Jude, gasping for new breath, recalled the lesson of the ocean and obscured herself in the chaos. She lined herself up so that Ra'an could strike again.

—WAIT!

—LISTEN!

The Gathering held its breath. Even the Destroyer beast froze mid-yowl and raised its muzzle to sniff out this new threat. Andreas raised his head from the sand, eyes wide with wonder and pain. Above, the shanevoralin flew loops and cartwheels in the air.

—WAIT! A faint new voice reached for their attention, many voices, growing stronger with each repeat of their message.

—LISTEN!

Those whom the Destroyer had driven from the web rejoined it cautiously.

—What . . .?

—Who . . .?

Andreas rolled in anguish on the sand.

—The Wall is down!

—THE WALL IS DOWN!

The beast screeched its frustration and denial as its troops slipped away from its control. The army raised to strike across the mountains sank back, distracted by the miracle.

—The Wall is down!

Long-lost friends and relatives flooded the web. They wasted no time on explanations or greetings but called for immediate attention.

1:45:05.

Clennan swallowed hard and leaned into the keyboard, he typed "GO LIBERATOR!"

Poised millimeters above three red buttons, Ron Jeffries' fingers dropped like stones.

The world shuddered. Every living thing in Arkoi felt the blow, as if the very air of the planet were being sucked away. Just as suddenly, the world was whole again, and the colony yielded up its predawn lassitude to chaos.

Split seconds after the corridor devoured itself in a flash of light and gouts of dirty flame and smoke, the armories followed.

From the deep-cellars and from hiding places in the city streets, on the run from the panicked Terran army, giddy with fear and joy, the exiles relayed a moment-by-moment account to the Gathering on the beach in Quaire'en: laser fire lighting up the still-dark streets, shadows running, swerving into alleys and doorways, barracks domes erupting into orange bursts of flame, and other images, quieter ones, that brought a wondering hope to the Gathering as it saw the eager glee of six colonial police officers accepting the surrender of a unit of confused Terran army recruits, or the renewed fire of determination in the eyes of Mitchell Verde as he sat by a microphone with Luteverindorin to broadcast his repeated message of peace.

It's over, thought Jude. *It's over and the Koi are guiltless.*

But Andreas rose, swaying. The beast was wounded but still on the loose. Its hunger for destruction was unsated, though its army had evaporated and its remaining loyalists lay cowed by the sudden reversal. It cast about for a target, saw Jude, and charged, roaring for blood. But Ra'an was alert, watching through her, and struck first.

The beast vanished from the web.

Andreas crumpled by the water's edge. Ra'an leaped after him and went down on his knees beside him. He pulled the ragged body into his arms.

"It's over, James," he soothed. "It's over. No more armies, no more violence. The Terrans took care of it themselves."

Andreas shivered feverishly. "Not over. So much work left to do. All those in the colony . . ."

Ra'an tried to quiet him. He smoothed matted hair back from the translucent brow and settled him more comfortably in his arms.

But the madman would not be silenced. "You must finish it, continue it, only you can do the task I meant for you alone . . .

ah, brother, understand that it could only be done this way. Do not hate me for the burden I've laid upon you, only you can do it . . ."

Ra'an raised his head to Jude. *Help me. Help me to save him.*

Jude touched her fingers to her bruised neck. *How?*

As I did at the Wall, for you. But I can't do it alone. You are the bridge.

Jude hesitated. *Anaharimel warns of the contagion of halm madness.*

I saved you at the Wall! Would you refuse James that chance? Would you refuse me the chance to try?

She rose from the driftwood log, stumbled weakly across the sand to kneel beside them. Andreas fixed her with wide gray eyes and smiled a ghost of whimsical smile.

"Halm student," he croaked. "Ana's and mine. You did so well."

Jude tried to smile but could not conjure one. "James," she whispered. She touched his bony wrist, and suddenly his smile fled and he wrenched himself around in Ra'an's arms and flailed out at her. "Terran!" he screamed.

Ra'an held him tight. His eyes implored. *Help me. There are two of us and he is weak. Please . . .*

She could not refuse him, seeing his brother love so nakedly exposed.

Come, then.

Andreas did not fight their entry. His power was spent. The beast lay insensate, though still breathing. His mind was like a leprous sore. It churned with hate and fear, feeding on its own sickness. Out of love for one man and compassion for another, Jude led the descent into hell, downward through layers of chaos, searching out some center where the soul might still live. She learned that fear smelled like death rot and hatred like burning flesh. Her stomach turned. She trembled, weakening, but Ra'an was beside her, urging and desperate. They staggered through a fog with a darkness ahead of them that pulsed and shuddered. To a Koi it might have appeared to be a void at the focus of the madman's being, but these two recognized its Terran machinery. This was the dark engine driving his insanity. It was guilt, that fed on the pitiless energy of his halmgift, and bred like a ravenous parasite until it consumed the mind that nourished it.

Ra'an pressed her onward urgently, into the grinding shadow of the Destroyer-machine, and there at the very core, they found a clear flame burning: James Andreas, son to Daniel, brother to the Koi, not enough of a man left to ever be whole again, giving up the last of its energies to search with the desperation of the dying for a way to shut the engine down.

Now that tiny flame cried out in its agony for Ra'an to do what it could not.

Ra'an recoiled from what it asked. He argued with it, prodded it, pleaded with it, surrounded it with love to urge it back to life and health. He sang to it, of their past together, of the father they had shared. He wove promises for the future. But the flame knew only pain, had only strength to gasp for one final mercy.

Jude, the matrix and observer, wept, as she held in her mind the agony of the man who had planned his own destruction and the grief of the man who must carry it out.

And he must. She knew it before he did. The flame might die, slowly and in inutterable pain, but the madness could rage on unchecked as long as the body lived. The body must be silenced, the engine smashed. The not-so-madman's purpose had been served. All around them, on the beach and in the halmweb, the reunited Koi rejoiced in a new appreciation of wholeness. The Balance that passivity and avoidance had allowed to slip righted itself once more.

Do it, she urged him. *Your grief is a lesser cost than will be demanded of us all if you fail him now. Forgive him for understanding better than you what must be done.*

The tiny flame flickered. Andreas stirred, the body reviving as the mad engine's pulse quickened. Deep in the madman's mind, the rising riptides of insanity swirled around them. In desperation, the flame leaped and sputtered. Blindly, Ra'an reached, cupped the hands of his mind around it, held it, though its dying fire seared his palms, until it went out. Then he turned to Jude that she might hold him steady as he called up all the power within him and laid the engine to waste.

Andreas went limp in Ra'an's arms. His jaw sagged as a final breath escaped. The sick hell that had been his consciousness sizzled and faded. The survivors were left alone. Instinctively they withdrew from each other, for the anguish of two was too much for each to bear.

Jude bowed her head and gave in to her grief.

Ra'an did not weep. Only his hand moved, distractedly, to brush the sand from the pale dead face.

Then he gathered the body to him and rose, staggering, settled the weight, and walked off down the beach alone.

CHAPTER 47

———••◆◆◆••———

Verde was still broadcasting when they dragged Ramos up to the station headquarters. He'd thrown on his dress tunic decked out with its ribbons and medals, over bare feet and pajama bottoms. Clennan winced at the handcuffs. Old habits of service stirred. He won't even do me the honor of being surprised to see me.

"Unlock him," he said to the men.

"Keep him locked," ordered Jeffries behind him.

Clennan shrugged, nodded. "At least get him a chair."

Ramos sat. The four colonial police officers arrayed themselves in watchful positions. One offered Clennan a compact hand laser.

"He had this under his pillow. Burned two of us before we took him down."

The cliché was somehow touching. Clennan had no desire to gloat. He had expected Ramos to rage in captivity, but he just sat there, neither meek nor defeated, just silently sitting.

He knows, thought Clennan. He won't look at me.

"He knows," murmured Jeffries.

The studio door slammed. "Damon's relieving me," called Verde as he came into the room. "If I have to read that announcement one more time . . ." He stopped when he saw Ramos. "Oh. What's this?"

"Behold the archfiend," Jeffries cackled.

"The man," said Clennan slowly, "who taught me everything I used to know."

Verde kept a wide berth. "What do we do with him now that we have him?"

Clennan shrugged, not able to be the one to say it.

"Answer's in your hand, Bill," Jeffries said flatly.

Verde spotted the pistol. "Now wait a minute . . ."

"I said nothing that wasn't necessary, Mitch."

Clennan said nothing. He stared at Ramos as if looking for some other answer, perhaps to an entirely different question.

269

"We can't just execute the man, Ron," Verde protested. "It's wrong. This is a brand-new world we're creating. Do you want it to be born in violence!"

"All birth is violent, Mitch. What'd you think's going on out there in the streets right now?" He circled Ramos and aimed his words at the back of the big man's head. "If we leave this guy alive, we ain't got a snowball's chance of getting off to a clean start. He'd dog us and fight us and sell us out every step of the way." He came around and faced Ramos from the front. "Wouldn't you, Julie?"

Ramos met Jeffries' glare, pursed his bruised lips, and nodded stolidly.

Jeffries grinned. "Attaboy."

Clennan stirred. "Ron." He passed Jeffries the laser. "He's yours. Mitch and I are going out for a little walk." As he passed Ramos, he reached to grip the beribboned shoulder gently. "Look at it this way, boss. Your whole life has been a preparation for a moment like this."

He guided Verde out the door and shut it quietly behind him.

CHAPTER 48

Jude hung back in the shade, behind the little crowd of Koi waiting in Quaire'en station as the huruss from Menissa glided to a halt. It carried the delegation from the colony. The only fanfare for their arrival was a cooling salt-spiced breeze whispering out of cloudless azure. Two weeks after the destruction of the Transport Corridor, the leaders of the takeover in the colonial city had entrenched themselves sufficiently to be able to look to the future and the problems of integrating a Terran city into a world of Koi.

First to appear as the doors slid open were a number of returning exiles. Since greetings and recent histories had already been exchanged over the halmweb, reunions with family and friends were warm and casual, but the last to emerge was a silver-faced old Koi who hesitated at the door to greet his home city with shimmering eyes. Yet he was not so lost in the emotion of his homecoming as to forget the several Terrans gathered at his side. The delegation stepped cautiously onto the station's transparent floor and gazed about in wonder. As the rest of the population listened in on the halmweb, Luteverindorin introduced the Terrans to the members of the current Council, who were acting as the official welcoming committee.

Jude memorized names and faces dutifully. She would have preferred to remain in retreat at the halmschool, soothed by its anonymous seclusion. She did not feel quite put back together yet since the shattering events of the Gathering. But the Council had asked for her help, and she felt a great debt to these people who welcomed her so easily and gave her a home. Anaharimel had agreed that some useful work would be a healthy distraction for her, so there she was. She would serve as translator for the Terrans in the delegation, as both a linguistic and cultural intermediary. The delegation numbered twelve, to match the number sitting at Council in the Ring. Among them were six Terrans: a tall young black woman who supported an older woman on her arm, a gnomish man with a red beard, a saintly-looking black whose name she caught as Montserrat, and behind him, a vaguely familiar face confirmed as Mitchell Verde, still looking as harried as she remembered him. For the man beside him, she needed no introduction. Bill Clennan, trim and eager, blinked away his sun-blindness and stared with open curiosity at the city of Quaire'en.

"Fanfuckintastic!" she distinctly heard him mutter, and Verde chuckled his agreement.

Crisis makes strange bedfellows. She tried to match the Clennan she had known with the Verde she had heard so much about. She would have thought them oil and water, irreconcilables, but there was no mistaking their obvious camaraderie as they stood side by side in the sun, Verde wearing as satisfied a look as ever a chronic worrier could, and Bill Clennan positively euphoric.

Well, Quaire'en will do that to you . . . or is it the prospect of a new life?

She wanted to choose the moment for her reunion with Clennan, but as the crowd jostled her into the open sun, he spotted her. There was an exchange of uncertainty, then he grinned ruefully and dragged Verde with him as he strode across the platform to envelop her in an unexpected bear hug. He held her away at arm's length, beaming, then fell momentarily inarticulate. "Well, girl . . ." was all he could manage.

271

Jude saw slight awkwardness in his handsome face but no remorse. *He probably figures that since we're both here alive, things worked out after he stranded me in the forest and that's all that matters. Maybe he's right.* And she thought then that she would like to know exactly what had come over Bill Clennan to make him turn on his bosses, but was not sure she wanted to get close enough to him to find out.

Verde sized her up more soberly, extending a large hand. "Ms. Rowe. I hear we have a good deal to thank you for."

Jude's head dipped unconsciously. *How much does he know?*

"If I'd known I was sending a telepath . . .!" Clennan jogged her shoulder in jovial pride.

"If I'd known . . ." she replied sternly, then smiled. His euphoria was catching, and she hadn't done a lot of smiling over the last two weeks.

Verde was immune to euphoria. He frowned slightly as he glanced around the station. "I expected Ra'an would be here."

Jude's smile died. "Didn't they tell you? He hasn't been seen since he left the Gathering." She felt her voice thickening and hastily cleared her throat. "Reports on the halmweb place him somewhere in the Ruvalan mountains."

"Alive and well?"

"Alive. Not very well, I imagine," she replied delicately.

Verde sucked his teeth, nodding. "He took the body with him?"

"Yes."

"For burial." Verde was brusque, and she saw that James' death had hurt him too. She reminded herself that this man, a stranger, had known both Ra'an and James for a long time, longer than she had. "That's just like Ra'an," he continued tightly. "James probably would have preferred a Koi funeral. Cleaner. More final. But to Ra'an it would seem only fit for both Andreases to lie in the same soil. More or less." Verde looked away, at the gulls and the green water. "James. Our poor lost soul. He said he would be Arkoi's savior, but I wonder if he had any idea . . ."

"Oh, he knew," Jude assured him quickly. "At least part of him did, the part he could still control. He used his madness as a tool until it overtook him, but even that he planned for, by assuring that the one who was stronger than he was would be there at the crucial moment."

"I don't understand."

"Neither do I. Well, *why*, yes, but *how* . . ."

272

Verde turned back, searching her face. "Will you tell me about it sometime, how it all happened?"

"I will. Sometime. When it's clear in my head. If you will tell me about Daniel Andreas."

"Daniel?" Verde sighed heavily. "Yes. I guess there's understanding to be found there, isn't there?"

"Look at that water!" Clennan exclaimed suddenly, to break the melancholy that had settled over them. "Mitch, this city's everything Lute said it'd be! Can't blame him for coming home, but we're sure going to miss him back there."

"With the Menissa huruss tunnel open again, the colony is not so far away anymore," Jude reminded him, grateful for the change of subject. "How long will you be in Quaire'en?"

He rubbed his palms briskly. "As long as it takes to get things squared away with the Council, no longer. It's not exactly a peaceful city back there. We've still got pockets of resistance to clear out. Fortunately for us, most of the rich and powerful hightailed it back to Terra when Lacey started his Dark Powers routine. But Mitch and I have our hands full in the colony, uh, I mean, Menissa."

Verde shook his head. "No, it's the colony now, Bill, for always. A reminder to all of us of the way things would have been but for James Andreas."

"And could be again, Mr. Verde," Jude added. "Terra will eventually discover a way to reconstruct the corridor. James didn't expect he could offer a final salvation. His gift was time, a chance for the Koi to ready themselves properly for the threat that's always waiting there, as he put it, just a dimension away."

Clennan's eyes hardened over his smile. "Don't worry, girl. When that time comes, we'll be ready."

CHAPTER 49

The tiled floor of her room was cool relief from the afternoon heat. She savored its dampness against her bare thighs as she sat with Theis, pampering her with a vigorous brushing. It was a pointless exercise, for the gria's shaggy coat had a mind of its own that did not easily accept the disciplines of grooming. But Jude's time alone needed filling with mindlessly absorbing tasks, to distract her from the brooding that had consumed her since the death of James Andreas.

She knew she must resist the treacherous luxury of guilt. She had seen guilt drive one man to bitter hatred and another to insanity. Yet the taste of guilt was fresh in her mouth. She had helped to kill a man.

She set the brush down and shook her hand. She had been gripping the handle until her fingers ached. She had helped to kill a man. Not just stood by, but taken part. Without her brain to serve as the link, Ra'an's lethal power would have remained locked inside him. She had unlocked it willingly, accepted murder as a necessity, to save him, to save herself, to prevent a greater massacre. It made sense. She could have made no other choice. And it was the choice that the victim himself had determined. But more than the murder, it was her easy acceptance of it that disturbed her, as if acceptance of murder was a given rite of passage into a more real world where professed ideas must be at last translated into action. Compared to this, her long-ago foray into espionage paled to an adolescent tantrum against boredom. Where would this new adulthood lead her? When one has accepted that it may be necessary to kill a man, what further violence might be approved by the same reasoning? Just when she thought she had found her morality, the very possibility of morality was being called into question.

She took up the brush and set to work on the thick knots in the gria's tail. Anaharimel would say that morality was a matter

274

of Balance. The Koi concept of Balance was attractive, but Jude still found its practical workings obscure. She absorbed what she could from her teacher and the other students, but so far it offered little balm to her conscience. The one thought that gave her comfort was the assurance that if she had not been there, James Andreas would have found another way to accomplish his purpose. In truth, James Andreas was responsible for his own death.

A knock at the door startled her. She could not remember having shut it. She looked up to find Ra'an standing in the opening, leaning against the frame. He was haggard, long unshaven. His dark clothes were grayed with dust. He moved across the room like a sleepwalker without waiting for her greeting and sat heavily on her bed.

"A martyr," he muttered. "He had to make a goddam martyr of himself."

Jude held herself still, hiding her relief and joy while she assayed his mood. She willed her hands to continue brushing calmly. "At least it worked," she said neutrally, as if she had seen him just yesterday. "That's more than most martyrs can say for their efforts."

"It worked," he echoed sadly and lay back on the pillow and closed his eyes.

"It was the only way," she offered, knowing that there was no possible solace for the loss he felt.

"He *made* it the only way. There could have been others, before . . ."

She brushed a while, then said, "The Council were wondering if you'd come back. They seem to understand that they'll be needing your help."

"They certainly will." He made a sound that was both a yawn and a profound sigh. "If they knew me as well as James, they wouldn't have wondered. What have you been telling them?"

"I told them to give you time," she lied. She'd had little hope for his reappearance.

"You're lying, but that's all right. I haven't given you much reason to have faith in me."

"On the contrary. You resist people's belief in you, but you come through at the last moment. That's what James knew that the rest of them didn't."

He stirred, ran a grimy hand across his mouth. "And you?"

There would be time for that later. For now, she merely said, "I suspended judgment."

"Very wise," he said dryly and yawned again. He rested his hand palm up across his eyes. "James left me with a lot of work to do."

Jude ceased brushing. "Funny. That's just about what Bill Clennan said. Another guy who came through at the last moment."

"Stupid bastard," Ra'an growled softly. "If he'd blown up the corridor a day earlier, James wouldn't have had to die."

She laid her brush down carefully. "You don't really believe that, I hope. Even James knew his disease was terminal. Had it been otherwise, perhaps not even he would have had the courage to use it as he did."

"Which was . . .?"

"To force you to be born." She rose to her knees as the elegance of James Andreas' strategy urged her toward eloquence. "He called you the amalgam, the first of the new breed that will become the norm in the new Arkoi, the Koi-Terran amalgam. The new world needs a new leader to suit its changed nature, it needs you, but would you be here now if James hadn't used his death to shake you from your cocoon? Would you have discovered the phenomenal halm power that you possess? Or would you still be walled up in Ruvala wasting your energies in hate like some bitter old man?"

Ra'an coughed gently, tiredly. "And this is what you've been telling the Council?"

"Of course!" she exclaimed.

His chuckle was a dry rustling in his chest. "James thought of everything. He even programmed an apostle to prepare the way for me."

Stung, Jude fell silent. She toyed with the stiff bristles of the brush. Then she said softly, "You are Arkoi's future, Ra'an. James gave his life to make that possible, knowing you would not be born without his help. Don't let his gift be wasted."

Ra'an turned his head on the pillow. "Ah. Not an apostle. A conscience."

Jude set her jaw against disappointment. *Why did I think he'd be different, softer? Well, so be it. This will be his strength, this stubbornness. He will need it to make them see the path they must follow.* "The Council is meeting in the Ring tonight," she said.

"Tonight? No. I'm not ready to be born, not yet . . . just want to sleep."

"They would want you to be there."

"Tomorrow," he insisted. "I need to be here tonight." His

276

hand slipped back from his closed eyes. "After all, you are the amalgam too," he murmured as he relaxed into sleep. "Or hadn't you thought of that?"

Oh yes, I have. I have indeed.

Jude continued brushing Theis until her coat shone.

M. BRADLEY KELLOGG was born in Cambridge, Massachusetts. She currently lives in New York City and designs scenery for the theater. A RUMOR OF ANGELS is her first novel.

SIGNET Science Fiction You'll Enjoy

SIGNET Science Fiction You'll Enjoy